PLAYERS ... OR PAWNS?

DAVID LLEWELLYN—one of the best intelligence agents in the business, he thought he had seen it all. But nothing had prepared him for the brutal challenge that awaited him in the Middle East.

SERGEI BRASTOV—the Soviets' man in Babylon. A brilliant chessmaster, he moved his pawns with unerring skill, supplying the Iraqis with whatever it took to crush the Israelis ... and spawn a nuclear war.

DANIELLA ZADIK—special assistant to the Prime Minister in Jerusalem, she was as beautiful as she was bright and efficient. Was she the perfect lover and confidante for Llewellyn? Or a Mossad agent assigned to spy on him?

MARTIN SINGER—Llewellyn's former associate, now employed by the American embassy in Israel, he was both outspoken and enigmatic. Was he, in fact, a dedicated idealist ... or a cold-blooded murderer and double-agent?

Caught in the savage grip of a potential nuclear war, they held the fate of the world in their hands. A staggering destiny forged in the heat of a single, blistering confrontation....

AMBUSH AT OSIRAK

AMBUSH AT OSIRAK

a novel by
HERBERT CROWDER

VILLAGE PAPERBACK EXCHANGE
950 STARKWEATHER
PLYMOUTH, MI 48170
75¢ WITH TRADE 459-8550

JOVE BOOKS, NEW YORK

ACKNOWLEDGMENTS

To my son George, who took the first steps with me into fiction writing.

To my sister Barbara, who first suggested that I try my hand at a thriller.

To Marjorie Miller, in whose Westwood workshop this book evolved under her skilled eye.

To the workshop gang for their assistance, with special thanks to Janis Laden Shiffman for her many contributions.

To my wife, Valarie, for her constant encouragement and for never doubting that I could do it

AMBUSH AT OSIRAK

A Jove Book / published by arrangement with
Presidio Press

PRINTING HISTORY
Presidio edition published 1988
Jove edition / February 1989

ISBN: 0-515-09932-5

Jove Books are published by The Berkley Publishing Group,
200 Madison Avenue, New York, New York 10016.
The name "JOVE" and the "J" logo
are trademarks belonging to Jove Publications, Inc.

PROLOGUE

The sun set early on the city by the Tigris. In the distance the venerable city lay suspended in the afterglow, reluctant to yield to the darkness that would bring with it the penetrating chill of the desert night. Across the intervening void swam the plaintive notes of the *azan*, the timeless call of the muezzin to the evening prayer.

The man in the khaki camouflage suit lying prone in the thick marsh grass felt a shiver run up his spine. Not from the coolness of the impending night, he knew, nor from the precarious nature of the mission that brought him to this forbidden spot. The azan often had this effect on him—some quality in the throaty vibrato with its flavor of the Orient, mysterious yet somehow familiar, cousin to the voice of the cantor and sung in the same melancholy key. It spoke to him of two great Semitic peoples with common origins and backgrounds, with destinies inextricably linked. Two peoples now divided by different religions and allegiances, sworn enemies in a desperate struggle that threatened the very existence of one.

For here, on the plain of Osirak, in the very shadow of ancient Babylon, where the Israelites once refused to bow down to the abomination of the golden ram idol erected by Nebuchadnezzar, another kind of abomination stood newly erected. Destroyed once, like the golden idol, by the fiery sword of Jehovah, with a little help from Israeli jets carrying 2,000-pound bombs. But since rebuilt, looming intact and ominous now, filling him with a deep sense of foreboding. The nuclear plant of Osirak. Atomic weapons arsenal for the forces of Islam in their sworn campaign to purge Israel from the face of the earth.

Osirak. With his knowledge of Egyptian mythology, the irony in the name did not escape him. Osiris, god of the Nile. Slain by his evil brother and relegated to the netherworld, the Judge of the Dead. There would indeed be countless dead to judge if the force

1

of the atom were ever unleashed by genocidal Arab fanatics against the sons and daughters of Israel.

It should be safe to move closer now. Under the cover of the gathering dusk he edged forward, moving on his knees and elbows in a commando crawl, the indispensable Nikon with its powerful telephoto lens and ultrasensitive film held in both hands extended ahead of him. Hard evidence. He knew that that was the only thing the Israeli high command would accept. They were not likely to take the word of a civilian spy, especially when it contradicted the findings of Aman, their own military intelligence agency. But there was no question in his own mind. The sightings he had already made from farther away, through the telephoto lens, had revealed something very different from the ZSU-23 antiaircraft artillery emplacement reported in the Aman advisories. Beneath the camouflage net suspended above the site to protect it from the prying eyes of spy satellites and reconnaissance planes, he had discerned a large tracked vehicle supporting a single radar dish and a vertical, boxlike structure rising three or four meters above the vehicle. The shadow from the encroaching net had obscured much of the detail at so great a distance. But one detail stood out in stark silhouette—the stiletto tips of missiles protruding from the top of the rectangular enclosure.

A new SAM installation! But which missile could it be? It was nothing like the sprawling SA-6, with its two distinctive radars and three-rail launchers, all on separate vehicles. It resembled no weapon system he had ever seen before, not even in pictures from the extensive Israeli Central Intelligence files that included Soviet weapons.

The conclusion was inescapable, reinforced by the elaborate effort of the Iraqis to conceal its existence. With the help of its Soviet "big brother," Iraq was girding the resurrected nuclear facility with batteries of some newly developed surface-to-air missile. Not with ineffectual artillery emplacements, or with more of the obsolescent SA-6 missiles, so easily countered and destroyed in the Lebanon campaign. But with SAM-X, the quick-reaction, lightning-fast Soviet weapon rumored to be in the late stages of development. And in the imminent re-strike of the nuclear plant by Israeli fighter-bombers, knowledge of the fact could spell the difference between success and disastrous failure.

Clever camouflage might fool long-range reconnaissance sensors from above. But there was no fooling a camera up close. The top of the rise ahead would bring him to an ideal vantage point, where the outline of the new missile installation would be framed against the still-bright western sky. Another dozen meters and—

Directly ahead, a staccato buzzing noise broke the stillness of the twilit landscape as the man in the camouflage suit froze. He recognized the sound—the Doppler audio from a radar personnel detector, a manpack device used by the infantry to detect the movements of hostile foot soldiers in the dark. He was also aware that the devices were notoriously prone to false alarms and would trigger on the motion of small animals—dogs, cats, rabbits, even birds. Slowly and noiselessly he rolled to his left, over and over until he reached the cover of a thick clump of reeds and rushes. He lay there, panting softly, struggling to get his breathing back to normal. They would come looking. Hopefully they wouldn't be too thorough.

He didn't have long to wait. First came the rustle of heavy boots in the dense grass, then a bright beam from a hand-held searchlight flitting across the marshy terrain. Two uniformed guards appeared on the ridge, silhouetted against the dwindling light of the western sky, automatic rifles slung over their shoulders, one with the cumbersome manpack on his back. He held his breath as the light swung back and forth, narrowly missing him on successive passes. Then they were moving again, back over the rise he had retreated from, and conversing. His Arabic was not good, but his ear picked out a key phrase—"... that same accursed dog!"

He remained stock-still until their sound subsided into the distance, then began to inch his way again toward the top of the small hillock. More slowly this time—to trigger the detection device again might prove fatal, and he knew it was sensitive to motions in excess of one meter per second. But he must reach his vantage point before the light was completely dissipated. Identification of the new weapon would be vital to the success of the Israeli strike force. There might not be another chance.

The climb up the short slope seemed endless, the sensation of darkness closing in like a shroud almost palpable. But when at last he peered over the crest, the outline of the SAM installation was still dimly visible. A time exposure on the sensitive film would capture it.

There was no sign of the guards anywhere below. He set up the low tripod and mounted the camera atop it. With some difficulty he located the missile launcher outline in the telescopic viewfinder and centered it. Despite the diminished light, the scene through the telephoto lens was clear and sharp. From this much closer vantage point he could now discern four distinct silhouettes of slender, conical snouts poking skyward.

Setting the timer for ten seconds, he pressed the trigger and sent up a silent prayer that the ticking of the timer would not be picked up by hostile ears. He listened intently for a few moments after the ticking stopped. Nothing. Re-zeroing the viewfinder on the radar silhouette, he took a second time exposure. Moments later, the camera packed away in a shoulder-slung case, he began the tortuous retreat back down the slope. Care still had to be taken not to move too rapidly. The Doppler device would trigger on receding targets as well as approaching ones.

Caution was already giving way to elation as he reached the bottom of the slope. He had done it! He could picture the surprise on the faces of the general staff members and the military intelligence people, could already hear the congratulations of his section leader. Rivalry between the civilian and military intelligence agencies was intense. This would be a real coup. But more important, he reminded himself, it would permit the Israeli attack force to select weapons and tactics that would defeat the new missiles and ensure the destruction of the atomic weapons arsenal.

He was certain that by now he was beyond the effective range of the antipersonnel radar. They were essentially short-range devices and would be further impeded by the intervening terrain—the low hill behind him. He stood up and began to move more rapidly, under cover of the pervading darkness that was now almost total. He must retrace his steps, exit the same way he had entered, just in case there happened to be mines. It was unlikely that they would go to the trouble and expense of mines. But it wouldn't hurt to be cautious.

There was no moon, and though the stars looked brighter than he could ever remember, they shed precious little light on the landscape. All the safer for me, he told himself. His eyes adjusted well to the darkness, but the marshy terrain looked eerie and unfamiliar in the starlight. He thought he recognized a clump of cattails that he had used as a landmark and bore to the left. It was less than one kilometer to the point where his confederate waited with the rented car. Soon they'd be speeding back toward the airport.

His mind turned to the spectacle of the impending air strike against the nuclear plant. He could picture the F-16s thundering in at ground level, their low-altitude drogue bombs splashing into the diabolical structure, ton upon ton of TNT blasting it to kingdom come. And the SAM batteries standing by helplessly, defeated by some top secret electronic countermeasure he could only speculate about. Or would they destroy the missiles first with a defense suppression strike, as they had done with the SA-6s installed by the Syrians in Lebanon's Bekáa Valley? God, what he wouldn't give to see it!

But for Itzhac, a seven-year veteran with Israeli Central Intelligence, better known as the Mossad, there would be no such opportunity. The darkness that caused him to lose his way in the Iraqi fen also served to obscure the tiny wire strung a few centimeters off the ground across the path in front of him. With an ear-splitting roar that supplied all too realistic sound effects for the scene of destruction his mind's eye was still envisioning, the ground beneath his feet blew away.

A battered camera fell back to earth and lay half buried in a clump of marsh grass. The dust of Mesopotamia settled slowly over it, sifting down upon the crumpled form nearby. In only moments, the shattered silence of the starlit night was restored. Nothing moved or breathed to break that stillness.

CHAPTER
1

The Mossad public relations man dried his hands meticulously, casting an appraising look at the image in the mirror. He ran a comb several times through the wiry mop of brillo-pad hair with no visible effect. Picking up a manila folder, he stepped out of the men's room. He paused at the water cooler to fill a small paper cup.

It wasn't like him to dawdle. But this was the part he hated most, informing the next of kin. And what he had seen in the folder made him relish it even less. The young woman waiting in his office was already an orphan, having lost her father to the Arabs in the Yom Kippur War, her mother to cancer scarcely a year later. And now he had to tell her that her closest surviving relative, her older brother, was missing and presumed dead.

He could see her through the window of his office, sitting in the chair next to his desk, her hands in her lap. Her appearance was not exactly reassuring. She was a pretty thing, dark haired, light skinned, soft and feminine. And vulnerable. There would be no way to break it to her gently.

Entering the office, he introduced himself and got the bad news out in a hurry, bracing himself for the histrionics that were certain to follow. But the only sign that she had understood him was the slow nodding of the head, the immense brown eyes, unmoistened, continuing to regard him with the same penetrating look.

"Of course," she responded in a calm, well-modulated contralto that was much too big a voice for the body that went with it. "Why else would you have gotten me down here? Now tell me the rest of it, please. How was he killed? Where did it happen?"

"I'm afraid we're not at liberty to reveal—" He stopped himself in midsentence of the customary disclaimer, realizing that he would have to level with her on several particulars. Among other things, he would have to explain why there would be no body to claim.

"I can only say this much. Your brother was killed in line of duty in a foreign country. Unfortunately, because we do not have

6

diplomatic relations with this country, there is no procedure for returning the remains. He was in the country illegally, you see. He was aware from the beginning that if anything went wrong, we would be forced to deny that he was one of ours, that we had sent him there."

"What you're telling me is that he was killed by the Arabs in one of the countries where he was sent to spy." At his raised eyebrows, a note of impatience crept into her voice.

"That is what you do, isn't it? Spy on Arabs? So the question is, which Arab country?"

Her intensity and directness were too much for the PR man. He avoided her eyes.

"No, I didn't really expect you to answer. I have a pretty good idea what country it was and why he was there."

The eyebrows shot up again. "My dear Miss—"

"Oh, don't worry. Itzhac didn't tell me. My job in the government, you see; it gives me some insight into— But you could never get anything like that out of my brother."

Her tone softened again. "He believed in what he was doing. He believed that what he did would save the lives of others. You can't live a better life than that, can you? Or die a better death."

He watched the first tears stud the dark eyes, saw her blink them away impatiently. "You can be very proud of him," he said. "He gave his life for Israel. He'll be decorated for it."

"How?" she asked. "There won't even be a grave to decorate." She bit her lip.

"Can you at least tell me how he died? Was he shot, stabbed, hanged—?"

He hesitated, but finally acquiesced. "Blown up, we think."

"Oh, God! Those bloodthirsty—!" A shudder wracked her small body. "I don't know why I asked that. What I really wanted to know was whether his mission was successful—that it wasn't all for nothing." She searched his face.

"Young lady, I couldn't tell you, even if I knew. The issue is apparently still in doubt. I've been instructed to ask for your cooperation in keeping your brother's death a secret. We don't want the enemy to know that we are aware he was killed, at least not for the moment. We're asking that any memorial services and any overt expression of mourning be postponed. Will that be difficult for you?"

"Not really," she answered. "I'll sit Shiva alone, in my apartment. There are no other close relatives anyway; no one to say the kaddish. I was all he had."

And vice versa, her tearstained eyes added. He pushed a form toward her. "I'll need your address, and your signature. There'll be a small pension check coming to you. And certain personal effects to be forwarded."

She scrawled out the address and signature and got up to leave. He stood up with her. "If there's anything we can do—I can do—"

She shook her head, moving toward the door. In the doorway she hesitated, then turned back.

"Perhaps there is one thing."

"Yes?"

"Can you tell me, please. How does one go about applying to become a Mossad agent?"

"This way, Mr. Llewellyn. The President will see you now." The presidential aide was not a tall man, but neither was he as short as he appeared beside the visitor he was escorting. If it hadn't been for the touch of premature gray at the temples of his dark, wavy hair, the visitor could have passed for an Ivy League athlete. The striped tie and casual cut to the suit smacked of Harvard or Princeton, the drape of the suit coat revealing a lithe, yet muscular frame beneath, with a breadth to the shoulders that would have made padding superfluous. There was a bounce to his step that bespoke boundless energy within, bottled-up energy waiting to be released.

David Llewellyn had been in the Oval Office only once before. It had been years ago, on a White House tour arranged by the Department of State for some of the more promising newcomers to the diplomatic corps. He remembered it as something of a letdown. Without a live president sitting there it had been like a room in a museum, impressively ornate but stuffy, sterile, devoid of personality. No ghosts of presidents past had exuded from its filigreed woodwork, and the awe he had felt at visiting "the place where the buck stops" had quickly dissipated.

But this time was different. As he was ushered into the West Wing sanctuary, a flood of impressions and emotions rushed to the surface, triggered by the sight of the Chief Executive at the massive desk across the expanse of lush, flag-blue carpeting with its imbedded presidential seal in gold. For the face of the man who rose to greet him was even more familiar to him than the likenesses of the presidents etched on U.S. currency; the face of a man whose friendship he and his family had cherished since his school days. The newly elected forty-first president of the United States—about to assign him to what could be the most important post of his diplomatic career.

"David, my boy!" The President took his hand in both of his own and shook it warmly, the tired campaign lines in the corners of his eyes crinkling with affection. "How long has it been?"

"Just over two years, Mr. President. The dinner in London."

"Yes, yes. Dinner at Claridge's, the theater. You had Katherine with you, and I was batching it. What was the name of that show—?"

The President caught the warning glint in Llewellyn's eye, and some of the sparkle went out of his own. "Sorry. That was just before it happened, wasn't it." He put a hand on the other man's shoulder. "There's no forgetting someone like Katherine. Trudy and I speak of her often. What a tragedy it was—"

"Tragedy?" Llewellyn's lips formed a tight, grim line. "'Travesty' would be a better word. A travesty on everything this country stands for, that an innocent life can be snuffed out with such—impunity."

The President avoided the smoldering eyes. "They never caught up with the killer?"

"The man who pulled the trigger?" Llewellyn shrugged. "He was only a tool—manipulated, programmed by their spooks, just as ours tried to program me. Before I told them where they could—"

He looked away, his face guilt-ridden. "Those bullets were meant for me, you know. Because of my infernal past affiliation with those—"

"Come on, now, David." The President tightened his grip on the muscular shoulder. "Blaming yourself won't bring her back. It's time to let go. You have the rest of your life, a promising career, ahead of you. Why don't we zero in on that?"

The President motioned him onto a silk brocaded sofa and sat down on its twin, facing him. "You've been making quite a name for yourself in Stockholm. I've been reading your file, the reports of some of your superiors. The former Swedish ambassador's—I forget his name—was positively glowing."

"Sorenson." David supplied the name of the little bald man with the big smile and bigger heart who had treated him like a son during his stint in Stockholm. Attending Sorenson's funeral two months ago had been like losing his father all over again.

"You've learned all the Scandinavian languages," the President went on, staring at the floor as though reading from an invisible resume. "You speak Swedish like a native." David's hopes soared. The post of ambassador to Sweden was a coveted one. He had been performing it in an acting capacity ever since the ambassador's death. All the President had to do was make it official.

"I'm not sending you back there," the President announced abruptly. "I need you somewhere else."

Motioning for David to follow, he strode to the giant map projection of the world built into the curved wall of the Oval Office. "The Middle East is going critical. What's happening there may be the biggest challenge faced by my administration." His forefinger found a spot on the map. "This is where I need you, David. Right here."

David's face fell as he stared incredulously at the designated point on the map. "Israel? But I'm not Jewish. I can't even read Hebrew."

"You'll learn, son, you'll learn. And meanwhile, I'll have a personal envoy in place, an envoy I can rely on to size things up for himself and express his own point of view."

"But Mr. President—"

"You'll be the number two man in our new embassy in Jerusalem. Ambassador Abrams is already in Tel Aviv to take over the reins of the outgoing ambassador and make preparations for the move. He's a fine man. You've met him?"

David shook his head, fighting back the bitterness of his disappointment. Israel, of all places! With all the candidates to choose from, why would he be picked for such a post? It didn't make any sense. Unless—

"I know you two will hit it off. He's been a staunch supporter of Israel, knows the country well and has many friends there. But he's going to need all the help he can get. We're planning a new peace offensive in the Middle East. We need a go-getter like you to hammer away at the rough spots, get through to some of the dissident elements, make things happen."

"Mr. President," David interrupted, "we've known each other for a long time. We've always been able to talk frankly and openly. There must be dozens of others better qualified for this position than I am. So why me? What are you holding back?"

The President's initial frown of displeasure gave way to a long, appraising look.

"All right, David, I'll level with you. I was perfectly sincere in my assessment of your talent for handling the diplomatic end of this assignment. But we also need someone with your demonstrated ability to get a certain other kind of job done. An extremely delicate kind of job that would be impossible if certain parties suspected you were there to do it. You have the perfect cover, a diplomat with an established track record, eligible for reassignment and promotion."

"Spy work—spook business! You know how I detest that whole scene! And you know why I got out of it, swore I'd never go back—"

"Wait, David! Hear me out." The President put a restraining hand on his shoulder. "I know how you feel about undercover work; I respect those feelings. If the situation weren't already desperate, I wouldn't ask this of you." He lowered his voice. "We have a crisis in Israel. There's a leak at the American embassy; someone is funneling top secret information to the other side."

"So? You've got professional plumbers that handle leaks of that sort, a whole raft of counterintelligence types to choose from—CIA, DIA, NSA. What's wrong with Consular Operations? They must have at least one agent in the embassy."

The President nodded. "Yes, yes they do. But so far he's failed to turn up anything. Apparently he's too well known to the mole; he's being screened out. As for alerting the bigger agencies like the CIA, that might be counterproductive. We're trying to keep knowledge of this situation contained. The worst thing that could happen right now would be for the Israelis to find out about this leak."

"Why?" David queried. "They're our allies, aren't they?"

"Exactly. And we want to keep it that way. There's a struggle for power going on behind the scenes in Israel right now, a militant faction within the present government who want to break all ties with America, go it alone. If they were to learn that certain Israeli secrets have been compromised by this leak at the embassy, it would give them a big club to use on Shamir."

"Israeli secrets? What kind of secrets?"

The President looked at him warily. "That's something I'm not at liberty to reveal. Suffice to say that it concerns Israel's nuclear weapons program."

"What nuclear weapons program? I didn't know they had any."

"Oh, yes, they have one, all right." Again the President lowered his voice, his jaw tightening. "I'll be frank with you, David. If I had known beforehand what I learned in just one day of national security briefings on taking office, I might have had second thoughts about staying in the race. There are things happening behind the scenes in the Middle East that could make the Lebanese War, or any other war between Jews and Arabs, look like a Sunday school picnic. The bomb! That's the ultimate danger over there, the potential of a world-threatening nuclear catastrophe! Both sides have it, or are on the verge of getting it. And when they do—"

There was something in the President's eyes that David had never seen before. He was somewhere else, far from the Oval Office, witnessing something unspeakably distasteful, as he stared at the blank wall facing him.

"Have you ever seen the results of a nuclear explosion on a populated area? No, of course you haven't; you're too young. It was forty years ago. Even among older Americans, relatively few have seen it, except perhaps in newsreels or newsphotos at the time. And most of those have erased it from their memory banks by now. But if you'd been to Hiroshima or Nagasaki, witnessed it with your own eyes soon afterward, there'd be no erasing it. Ever."

"You were there, Mr. President?"

"Right after the war ended. I was with a military inspection team. By then a lot of the rubble had been cleaned up, but the smell of death still hung over the place. Whole city blocks were missing—leveled. And you couldn't clean up what happened to the populace. The hospitals were still full of the critically injured, the mutilated, and the dying. But worst of all were the walking wounded, with disfiguring sores that no known medicine could heal. The walking dead."

The President turned back toward David, fixing him with an urgent stare. "We can't ever let that happen again, anywhere in the world. That's the awful responsibility that hangs over this chair, this office. Whoever occupies it can't afford to be caught napping. He has to know what's happening, be on top of every potential flash point in the world that could set off the fuse to another Hiroshima. And at this moment, my young friend, the most critical of those flash points is a small country at the eastern end of the Mediterranean Sea, where a security problem in our own embassy could provide the fatal spark. End of speech."

The President waited for the younger man's reaction. Llewellyn was profoundly moved. A nuclear arms race in the Middle

East, the U.S. caught in the middle. The prospect was chilling, the urgency undeniable. But he still had reservations about what was being asked of him.

"So you want me to unearth this mole in the embassy, plug the leak. Isn't that like locking the barn door after the horse is gone? If this sensitive material is already in the wrong hands, it's too late, isn't it?"

"Not necessarily. You see, we're not really sure what information was leaked, where it went. The only way we can find out is to catch the mole and interrogate him. But the main objective is to stop him and put him away, before he deals off any more secrets. We'll give you all the help we can, alert Cons Op that you're coming on board and have their man in the embassy fill you in—"

"No!" Llewellyn interjected. "They're not to know. Nobody in the embassy is to know I'm wearing any other hat than my diplomatic one. I'll only agree under those conditions. I freelance. I'm on my own."

"Done!" The President jumped to his feet, extending his hand. "I knew I could count on you, David." He took a card from his pocket and handed it to Llewellyn. "Call me on this number a day or so after you get there. I'll be interested in your first impressions. That's a direct line to the Oval Office here—avoids getting hung up on the notorious White House switchboard. It will always be open to you."

He shook David's hand again. "Always remember one thing, my boy. The country I'm sending you to is one of our staunchest friends and allies. Amid all the posturing and maneuvering you diplomats have to go through to exert influence on a friendly government, that consideration should be foremost in your mind, even though that government, at times, may seem intractable and exasperating."

David nodded emphatically. "I couldn't agree more, Mr. President. But perhaps the CIA could use some instruction on that point. I've heard some rumblings—"

"I've heard them, too." The President's voice hardened. "Leave the CIA to me."

The male aide reappeared and David was ushered out of the office, the President's parting words still echoing in his ears. Words that had a familiar ring. Another president, more than two decades earlier, had said virtually the same thing. John Fitzgerald Kennedy.

Sergei Brastov walked down the ramp from the Al-Jumhuriya Bridge and into the little park that meandered along the east bank of the Tigris. He was on his daily late afternoon constitutional and stepped out briskly, mindful of his physician's injunction to exercise his heart at an accelerated pace several times weekly. The park was his favorite spot in the Iraqi capital, the only spot that reminded him even remotely of home. There was something universal about the smell of grass and flowers and the sound of children at play, even though the tongue they spoke was strange to his ears.

Visions of the parks of Moscow crept into his mind's eye—Dzerzhinski, Izmailovo, Sokolniki, and his own favorite—Gorky—long and narrow, like this one, and stretching along its own river. He felt a touch of the nostalgia that had permeated those first homesick weeks a year and a half back, ushering in his mission to Baghdad. But the sensation lasted only a moment. The parks of Moscow would be frozen now, filled with snowdrifts, swept by chilling winds. But here—wonder of wonders—a January day that was like spring.

The playground nearest the bridge was alive with children, shrieking their enjoyment as they swarmed over the slides and swings and climb-ons. As he ambled by, drinking in their pleasure with a vicarious thirst, they paid him scant notice. It had been different when he first came here. He could still remember their staring eyes, making him feel like something from outer space. Were they used to him now or was it something to do with himself, something inside himself that had changed and adapted, making him somehow less conspicuous? There was no fathoming the ways of children, he decided, wondering why the myriads of staring faces had bothered him so at the time. A man so used to being stared at in his own native land.

Khrushchev. People kept mistaking him for Nikita Khrushchev. But that, too, had largely subsided now that the former premier was no longer in the public eye and his image was fading from the people's memory. Sergei Brastov now admitted something to himself that he never would have acknowledged in those days. He had secretly enjoyed being taken for the head of state. The physical resemblance was undeniable, though he had tended to downplay it at the time. Of course the premier's face was more pudgy and cherubic-looking than his own; the ears far more protruding; the thinning, closely cropped fringe of white hair above the balding forehead sparser. But the look in the unwavering steel-blue eyes was the same. In his heyday Nikita Khrushchev had been regarded as a dynamic and innovative leader—a crafty tactician, a wily foe to his enemies. All characteristics that Brastov liked to believe applied to himself.

His own self-image had profited immensely from the likeness, and in turn, his career. A light colonel in military intelligence, he had risen to the rank of brigadier general before the premier's luck ran out and he was retired to his dacha outside Moscow. Retired? Banished would be more accurate. Put out to pasture. Brastov's own career seemed to have taken a downturn since then. No more promotions. And he had no doubt that his rivals regarded his assignment to this obscure, second-rate country as a kind of banishment. Fools! Couldn't they see that it was the chance of a lifetime? An opportunity to carry off one of the truly great coups in the Middle East chess game that the Soviet Union played with such skill and cunning.

A lifetime student of the game of chess and an accomplished player, Brastov habitually drew analogies between his intelligence machinations and the strategies and tactics of the chess board. The opening moves in this international game had been particularly crucial and difficult. Relations with Iraq, once a staunch USSR ally liberally supplied with aid including arms shipments, had waned, hitting rock bottom during the war with Iran. The Soviets had chosen to hedge their bets and play both sides of the street, secretly furnishing weapons and other aid to the Iraqi foe.

When Brastov had arrived on the scene, he had encountered a bitter wave of anti-Soviet sentiment fed by recent disclosures of the extent of Soviet aid to Iran, which made his job at first seem impossible. But the protracted war with its neighbor had left the Iraqi exchequer in a sorry state, compounded further by the oil glut; the timely influx of much-needed monetary assistance with the promise of new weapons had helped reverse the anti-Red tide. His own efforts to cultivate the policy makers and military leaders were finally bearing fruit. He was at last being listened to, and the minister of defense, whom he had courted the hardest with "beyond the call" efforts that included teaching chess to the painfully slow-witted man, now treated him like a close friend.

He sighed, thinking of his investment of time and energy into this project. And sacrifices. Not that his separation from his family was such a big sacrifice. Katya had long since lost interest in the sexual aspects of connubiality, though she dutifully sought to hide that fact from him. He had no doubt that she found a welcome respite in the forced separation. Her letters were happy, filled with news of their son and daughter, both married now with children of their own. He missed them, but he had never been too comfortable in the doting-grandfather role—too reminiscent, he supposed, of the lateness in his life and approaching retirement, which he dreaded. Anyway, Katya made up for it with enough doting for two grandparents.

Other deprivations were harder to take. The company of friends, the good times, with conviviality and vodka flowing freely together. Franz and Sasha and Yevgeny, his three closest friends. Now they were only chess boards in his Baghdad flat, three boards set up with pieces, on which he conducted his correspondence chess games with each of them. It was the only time he drank any more, sipping his vodka in the privacy of his own room as he moved the pieces and plotted his own answering moves, reminiscing about his absent friends. There was no one in Baghdad he wanted to drink with anyway. And no one to play chess with who could give him a game.

It was beginning to get dark. Brightly colored lanterns blinked on along both sides of the pathway, bathing the lush foliage in hues of red and yellow and green. He had passed all the playgrounds and was approaching the area where cafes and fish restaurants lined the shore, neon signs beckoning in gaudy Arabic script. He paused for a moment beside a railing to watch the fish turning on spits over open wood fire pits, the smell wafting up to him on the light breeze off the river. *Mezgoof*, grilled carp from the Tigris dispensed an aroma when being cooked that promised a delicious treat. But the actual taste, the one time he had stopped to sample it, had been disappointingly flat and flavorless, and he had left most of it on the plate. Like many other things in life, he reflected, turning to retrace his steps, the enjoyment was mostly in anticipation, not in the fulfillment.

Would it be so with this Iraq project that he had poured so much into? Would there be any sweetness in the taste of victory, when it came? Or was the pleasure all in the game itself, the excitement of matching wits with a worthy adversary, the cerebral exhilaration from the encounter? In his chess victories, the actual mate or resignation of his opponent was invariably anticlimactic. The supreme thrill was felt at the moment when his mind seized on the key move or sequence of moves that assured success. And in the Iraq/Israel match, that moment had already arrived.

Everything revolved around the Osirak atomic reactor facility in a small suburb twelve miles southeast of Baghdad. The reactor had been built for Iraq by the French, part of a multibillion-dollar assistance package that also sent aircraft, missiles, and other weapons to Iraq in exchange for cash and a much-needed influx of Iraqi oil. The reactor was ostensibly for scientific research. But it was no secret that the design of "Tamuz 17," the code name for the reactor project, called for the use of highly enriched uranium suitable for conversion to weapons-grade plutonium. When a crew of Italians was later brought in to construct a "hot cell" on the same premises for the extraction of plutonium from the spent fuel, the worst fears of various Iraq watchers were realized.

Like his government, which was a signatory to the nuclear nonproliferation pact, Brastov had serious reservations about the long-term implications of Tamuz 17. But neither he nor his government was inclined to let those reservations stand in the way of more immediate opportunistic capital to be made at the expense of the West. There was no question about the Iraqi intentions. Nor about the retaliation their actions would continue to bring down upon their heads. His mind ticked back over the early history of the Osirak venture.

When Iraq, early in 1980, had negotiated a deal with Brazil for large quantities of highly enriched uranium, a chain of sordid events had followed. The Egyptian-born head of Iraq's nuclear program, Yahia El Meshad, had been bludgeoned to death in a Paris hotel room. A possible witness to the event had later been killed by a hit-and-run driver. Then in September 1980, some months after hostilities had broken out between Iran and Iraq, two Iranian Phantom jets had tried unsuccessfully to bomb Tamuz 17.

It was at this juncture that Saddam Hussein, the dour Iraqi president, had put his foot in his mouth by trying to reassure the Iranis that they had nothing to fear from the atomic facility, that any forthcoming nuclear weapons were intended for use not against them but against "Zionists." A few Zionist ears must have been tuned in. In August 1981, just as Tamuz 17 had been about to come on line, it was inundated with Israeli bombs in a daring daylight raid. The reactor core had been crumbled by an almost direct hit, crashing into the cooling pool. A top French physicist, Damien Chassepied, had been killed in the raid.

It had been conservatively estimated that the plant would require three years to rebuild, even if the French agreed to continue their participation in the project. But François Mitterand, newly elected French premier, had dragged his feet before reluctantly agreeing to honor the commitment of his predecessor, and the facility was only now starting to produce plutonium. Brastov's government agreed with the Iraqis that Israel was certain to attempt another air strike against Tamuz 17. But this time they would be ready. The defenses that had secretly been prepared for them with the newly developed USSR SA-10 missiles, camouflaged to prevent their discovery by spy planes or satellites, had been Brastov's own idea, and he had been instrumental in making the necessary arrangements with the Soviet military assistance bosses.

It had not been difficult to persuade them. Russia's military experts were still smarting from the embarrassment suffered during the Israeli incursion into Lebanon, when their supposedly superior weapons in the hands of the Palestinians and Syrians took a sound pasting. Their newly deployed SA-6 missiles, installed to provide air defense in the Bekáa Valley of Lebanon by the Syrians, had been wiped out en masse by Israeli warplanes and artillery, with negligible losses. The Soviets were looking desperately for a way to recoup, and Brastov's proposal had come at the right time.

The SA-10 missile had been a well-kept secret. While its existence as an advanced technology developmental weapon was known to the NATO nations, its performance and range of capabilities were not. Kept under wraps during its test phase in Siberia and not yet deployed elsewhere, it was a big question mark to the West. But not to Brastov, one of the Soviets in the know. The test results had been dramatic. The SA-10 was the best surface-to-air missile ever, surpassing anything the U.S. had in production. The ambush at Osirak seemed tailor-made for its debut.

The actual preparation of the defenses was not under Brastov's direct jurisdiction, anymore than the rebuilding of the atomic plant had been. But as the ranking officer in the Soviet military mission to Iraq, he considered himself nominally responsible for the entire operation—an opinion not shared by the Russian army colonel in charge of installing the SA-10 missiles. After an initial encounter in which his authority was questioned, Brastov had decided to back off and leave the colonel to do his job. His own interests lay in the grand strategy, the orchestration of the total event or series of events about to be set in motion. For in his mind the ambush of the Israeli bombers by the lethal SA-10 missiles was only a prelude to an even more devastating move tied to the inevitability of a second Israeli air strike against Osirak.

First, he must formulate his plan, a plan that was airtight, with every alternative thought completely through to the end, every detail ironed out. And second, he must sell the plan—to the

Iraqis and to his own military intelligence chain of command.

The latter, he knew, would be considerably easier if he already had the Iraqi acquiescence to his plan. So he had concentrated on his good friend, Amahl Zahadi, minister of defense. It was Zahadi who had triggered his thinking when he had inadvertently divulged the existence of an Iraqi agent in the Israeli air force. Careful and tactful probing had eventually elicited that the agent was a flying officer, a trained F-15 pilot, certain to be in on the Osirak strike and hence privy in advance to the day and hour the strike would occur—vital information to alert the Iraqi defenses. The germ of an idea had begun to sprout in Brastov's fertile and devious mind, eventually developing into the plan for a daringly ingenious gambit. The more angles he examined, the more details he checked out, the more certain he became that the plan would succeed.

It was only within the last week that he had exposed the plan to the defense minister, with limited success in persuading him of its merits. But tonight he would get another chance. Zahadi had agreed to call a meeting of his closest advisers and general staff members to consider the plan.

Brastov reached the ramp leading back up to the bridge and quickened his pace. With so much at stake, it wouldn't do to arrive late.

The youth movement within the Israeli high command was apparent in the look of the men seated around the U-shaped table at the regular Monday meeting of the General Staff in Tel Aviv. Gone were the seasoned faces, familiar and comfortable as a favorite pair of old shoes reluctantly consigned to the trash heap, each time-worn crease evoking a memory of those early, crucial battles for survival. The oldest of those on the current General Staff appeared to be scarcely into their forties, including the man in the four-star general's uniform at the head of the table. He was the army chief of staff and chairman of the Joint Chiefs, a former battalion commander in the 1973 Yom Kippur War, who had distinguished himself in the Sinai campaign. His name was Yigal Tuchler.

General Tuchler's soft-spoken and patient manner of conducting a meeting was deceptive, as all around him were well aware. He was still every bit the tiger he had been in those decisive days more than a decade before when he led his tank battalion over the makeshift bridge thrown up by the army engineers across the Suez Canal, turning that seesaw war into a rout. He listened attentively as the two-star general two seats to his right described the plan for the forthcoming strike at the rebuilt Baghdad nuclear plant. Tuchler was under heavy pressure from the minister of defense to get the operation under way.

The Likud coalition of Menachem Begin, now led by his successor, Itzhac Shamir, was in trouble. Since the retirement of Begin, the government had become more and more faction-ridden, its popularity waning as Israel's inflation problems continued. It was badly in need of a shot in the arm. And he knew that the minister of defense, his hawkish boss, would not brook any further delays.

"It's not going to be that easy this time." The air force general was tall and blond, with boyish good looks. As the campaign ribbons above his left pocket testified, he was also much decorated. "The first time, in 'Operation Babylon,' we had the element of surprise completely on our side. We were able to fly from our base in the Sinai and bypass the main Jordanian and Iraqi defenses. When our aircraft were finally detected over hostile territory, our ruse worked perfectly—pretending to be Jordanian pilots on a training exercise, speaking in Arabic and using Jordanian frequencies and call letters.

"The same tricks are not likely to work again. And this time they may be expecting us. Then there is the problem of the AWACS in Saudi Arabia, which we did not have to contend with last time in our crossing of the North Arabian Desert."

The chairman of the Joint Chiefs nodded. "Then I take it, General Lansburgh, that you are not proposing a carbon copy of the 1981 Osirak strike. You have a different plan for the use of the F-16s this time?"

The blond general smiled. "Quite different. We don't plan to use any F-16s at all."

General Tuchler's eyebrows rose, along with those of most of his staff. "No F-16s? But that's our first line strike aircraft. You're not thinking of using those war weary F-4s of yours?"

By way of an answer, General Lansburgh was already striding toward the enormous backlighted map on the wall facing the conference table. He picked up a pointer and flicked on the light, the soft translucent colors depicting the Middle East countries coming instantly to life. Israel was a characteristic strip of cerulean blue along the eastern end of the Mediterranean, looking minuscule compared to the large patch of chartreuse that was Iraq and the even vaster sepia expanse of Saudi Arabia.

"We have a problem with the F-16," General Lansburgh explained, leveling his pointer at the southern boundary of Israel, where the color of the Sinai Desert had been changed from Israeli blue to Egyptian orange. "Our detour to the south, around Jordan, staging from this base in the Negev instead of our former base in the southern Sinai, will add over two hundred kilometers to the length of the mission. Even with external fuel tanks, the sixteens cannot make it back without in-flight refueling, and that would be an extremely vulnerable operation over hostile territory." He replaced the pointer in its rack and turned toward his expectant audience. "So we propose to use F-15 Eagles instead."

Exclamations of surprise escaped several General Staff members. Tuchler's forehead knitted into a puzzled frown. "The Eagles normally provide air cover for the strike aircraft. You propose to bomb with them as well?"

"We have always had that option with the F-15, sir, though we don't ordinarily like to risk our first line air superiority fighter in bombing missions. But now we have a configuration with a much extended strike capability." The blond air force general pressed a button, lowering the screen for the slide projector. From the projection booth behind the conference table a yellow beam materialized, flashing a blurred aircraft image on the screen, which quickly snapped into focus.

"This is the new multirole fighter version of the F-15, the so-called 'Strike Eagle.' It is not yet operational in the United States, so you may not know of it." He pointed to the underside of the fuselage. "The chief modification to the fighter version is the addition of these conformal fuel tanks, called 'Fastpaks,' strapped on beneath the aircraft here between the two engine nacelles and, in effect, becoming part of the fuselage. They extend the range of the Eagle appreciably without significantly altering its flight characteristics. And in addition—" he paused for emphasis before delivering the clincher, "they contain bomb racks from which we can hang two Mark 84 one-ton bombs on each Eagle—the same armament used to take out the Osirak plant in Operation Babylon."

General Lansburgh turned to face his audience, arms folded across his chest. "Gentlemen, we have a dozen of these aircraft, equipped with the new conformal tanks and bomb racks, ready to go."

There was a general murmur of approbation from around the table. As impressed as the others, Yigal Tuchler could still not refrain from some mild chiding. "General Lansburgh, you know how I hate surprises. Why was I not informed of this development?"

"Sir, the order for the Fastpaks was placed several years ago. For obvious reasons, we didn't feature the bombing aspect—the procurement was justified as a simple extension of the fighter version's range by means of additional fuel tanks. We chose to keep the refitting and training exercise under wraps until we could confirm that we had an operational viability for this mission with the modified Eagles. We have only just established this."

Somewhat mollified, the chairman pressed on. "You are telling us that these—these Strike Eagles can carry the full bomb load, reach and destroy the target, and return without in-flight refueling?"

General Lansburgh nodded affirmatively. "The squadron has been training for months to do just that, sir."

"But you will need other, standard F-15s to fly cover, in case some of the Iraqi fighters are scrambled?"

The tall, boyish air force boss shook his head. "That is one of the added dividends of the new Strike Eagle. As a multirole fighter, it is able to defend itself. Each Eagle will carry two Sparrow missiles in addition to its bomb load, making a separate fighter escort unnecessary and allowing us to carry out the raid with a smaller, less detectable force than that used in Operation Babylon. By the way, we propose the code name 'Fiery Furnace' for this one."

This brought smiles to the faces of those around the table who appreciated the irony invoked by the reference to Nebuchadnezzar's biblical revenge on the Children of Israel, which had also backfired. But Tuchler's mind was on less esoteric matters.

"The Iraqis have more than 200 MiG-21 and MiG-23 fighters based within range of your route to Baghdad. You mentioned the threat posed by the Saudi AWACS. If it detects your formation over northern Arabia, it will alert the entire Iraqi defense network. How do you propose to avoid this?"

General Lansburgh was obviously primed for this one. "With great care," he responded, drawing a few smiles, but a frown from Tuchler. He hastened to explain.

"While it is true that the AWACS maintains surveillance over the North Arabian Desert, it does so only sporadically. There are presently four AWACS aircraft, based near Riyadh, providing around the clock surveillance. Priority is given to the area around Southern Iran and the northern end of the Persian Gulf, including the oil fields from Bahrein to Kuwait. The AWACS almost invariably flies the same pattern—a straight leg of up to five hundred miles north-northeast from Riyadh, then retracing its path in the opposite direction before turning north again." He returned to the lighted map display and picked up the pointer, tracing out a long oval emanating from just west of the Persian Gulf and running parallel to the border between Saudi Arabia and Iraq.

"It is only near the end of its northbound leg that its coverage extends far enough northward to become a threat to us. Less than halfway back along its southward flight path it loses contact with Northern Arabia and Iraq—for something over an hour."

"And is the timing of its turn from north to south predictable?" the chairman broke in.

"No, sir. It varies from day to day—hour to hour. We are relying on a well-placed agent to alert us by radio at the exact time the southward turn commences. We will scramble our strike force accordingly."

"Hmm," mused the chairman. "How long will your aircraft be in the zone of AWACS coverage?"

"For approximately one hour after lift-off."

General Tuchler whistled softly. "That calls for almost split-second precision."

The handsome air force boss smiled confidently. "We are noted for it, sir."

"And on the homebound flight?"

"The AWACS will pick us up somewhere near the Iraq-Arabia border. Too late to scramble hostile aircraft that have any chance of intercepting us."

Tuchler nodded, apparently satisfied on this point. "What of the Osirak terminal defenses?"

"Sir, we have had consistent reports from military intelligence corroborating earlier Iranian reports of SA-6 missiles encountered during their unsuccessful 1980 strike at Osirak. In Operation Babylon we encountered no SA-6 launches whatsoever. Only some scattered bursts from conventional antiaircraft that did no damage. In any event, the SA-6 should pose no threat to us if we adhere to the same low-level delivery tactics we employed in the last strike. It is simply too slow to react. By the time our jets pop over the horizon it is already too late."

"What are the chances, General Lansburgh, that these local defenses have been strengthened? Do we have up-to-date reconnaissance?"

Lansburgh turned toward a balding, bespectacled officer to his left. "Perhaps General Falcovitz would care to comment."

The chief of Aman, the Central Forces Intelligence Corps, stood up and advanced toward the projector screen, signaling to the projection booth as he did so. A black and white aerial photograph appeared on the screen and General Falcovitz used the pointer to call attention to the lower left-hand corner of the slide.

"This is the latest U.S. satellite photo of the Baghdad region, obtained just last Thursday. The next slide is a blowup of the area here at Osirak, to the south and west of the Iraqi capital."

The image of the second slide materialized, a grainy, blurred picture typical of overmagnified reconnaissance photos. "That is the Osirak nuclear reactor plant in the center of the slide. Two SA-6 sites are visible, one here to the west of the plant, and another here to the south. From close up one can make out four tracked vehicle launchers in revetments at each site, and in separate revetments the radar tracking and control unit for each site on its own tracked vehicle."

The intelligence general's pointer flew about, singling out blobs on the fuzzy slide that were barely discernible to the staff officers at their distance from the screen. "Closer examination reveals that the launchers are the three-rail 'Gainful' configuration and that the controller exhibits the characteristic double dish antenna of the 'Straight Flush' radar. In short, there can be no doubt that we are looking at SA-6 missile sites, which, as General Lansburgh has explained, can be readily circumvented by our strike force with appropriate tactics."

Falcovitz replaced the pointer and started back to the table.

"One moment, General." The chairman held up his hand and the intelligence general halted. "Have you compared this latest reconnaissance photo with previous photos to determine whether there have been additional alterations to the landscape around the atomic reactor site, alterations that might signal added air defenses, perhaps camouflaged from your 'eye in the sky'?" It was a loaded question, a dirty trick to play on poor Falcovitz. But Tuchler had an objective.

"Yes, sir," was the response. "We do that routinely. There have been extensive changes to the surrounding terrain over the span of time since the last raid, as the Iraqis tightened their local security and strengthened the fortifications around the perimeter. We believe these are mainly to protect against surface penetrations. But there were several suspicious blotches showing up on our last infrared satellite photo, which could, indeed, be camouflage nets. Such nets are commonly used to cover antiaircraft artillery. We therefore notified General Lansburgh to be prepared for ZSU-23-4 weapon emplacements at these points, the Soviet armament most likely to be deployed there."

"Those guns will not be a factor," Lansburgh volunteered. "So long as we approach from low altitude, there is inadequate time for the gun-laying radar to develop the necessary tracking accuracy."

"I am wrestling with a somewhat different concern," Tuchler interjected. "Tell me this, General Falcovitz. Why do you suppose the Iraqis would go to the trouble of camouflaging their gun emplacements, but leave their much more lethal missile sites fully exposed to view?"

"It is standard practice to camouflage artillery emplacements," the military intelligence general replied blandly. "They are relatively compact and easily hidden. An SA-6 installation is a very different proposition. The equipment may be spread over an acre of ground. Camouflaging it would be totally impractical."

The chairman nodded. The explanation sounded plausible enough. But something still nagged at him. He turned to the man in civilian clothes at the end of the table.

"Mr. Shilo, what is your opinion? Is there something other than harmless popguns waiting beneath those camouflage nets to bite us?"

The Mossad deputy's response was guarded. "Possibly. That suspicion was, of course, our reason for sending a man in. Unfortunately, as you know, he didn't make it back out. His assignment was to obtain close-in photographic evidence. He had plenty of time to do so according to his partner, who was waiting for his return when he heard the explosion. We assume that our agent was returning when a land mine detonated and killed him. Whatever secret he may have unearthed he took with him. The second agent attempted an on-the-spot reconnaissance, but was unable to get anywhere near the site, by then swarming with security police. Since then the guards have been tripled. Sending in another man is out of the question."

"What do you suspect was on your agent's film?" Tuchler probed. "Would you care to hazard a guess?"

"No, sir," the intelligence director answered promptly. "We are not in the guesswork business. Our job is to remove the guesswork."

Tuchler drummed his fingers on the tabletop. This was like

pulling teeth. But it paid to be overly patient with this man, the only one at the table who did not report to him. As director of the Central Institute for Intelligence and Security, better known as the Mossad, Mordecai Shilo's pipeline went straight to the prime minister. He tried another tack.

"According to your report of the incident, it was almost pitch-dark at the time of the explosion, and your agent had been absent for well over an hour. Let us ask ourselves, what could have been of such overriding importance that he would place his own life in jeopardy by remaining so long in that heavily patrolled corridor?"

Shilo still hesitated. "As I said, General, pure conjecture on such things is out of my province."

For the first time, exasperation showed in the chairman's expression. The Mossad director was holding something back. He made a mental note to contact Shilo privately and worm it out of him. He turned back to the air force commander.

"General Lansburgh, the time is growing short. I am expecting a go-ahead at any time from the Prime Minister. Operation 'Fiery Furnace' may now be considered to be in the final countdown. You will have your forces poised and ready to go on an instant's notice."

CHAPTER
2

David Llewellyn shifted uncomfortably in the wicker chair, making a crackling noise that drew a quick glance from the Israeli foreign minister. This was ridiculous. Why was he so uneasy? A man of the world, a seasoned hand in the U.S. diplomatic service, who had been through any number of these "changing of the guard" affairs. But never on an assignment where so much was at stake, he reminded himself; never where the odds were so stacked against him. The first non-Jewish envoy in the forty-year history of the Jewish state. And charged with a secret mission, in the bargain, with no one he could turn to for help.

At the moment, the secret part of the job was taking a back seat to the diplomatic part. If he was to function effectively in his role as a special envoy, it was important to get off on the right foot with the foreign minister, who would be his primary interface with the Israeli government. So far in this initial meeting he had listened a lot and spoken very little, content to let the other American do most of the talking—the outgoing envoy, who should already be fading out of the picture. But Martin Singer, he realized from an association going back many years, was not the fading type. Marty didn't even know the meaning of the word.

He studied his flamboyant former associate, marveling at how little his appearance had changed in the six years since they had last worked together in the U.S. embassy in Sweden. The lustrous face radiating vitality, darkly bronzed, as always—even in Stockholm it had somehow managed to retain its tan. Piercing blue eyes that had always reminded him of Paul Newman, flashing and giving off sparks as his words and gestures became more animated. No, Marty Singer was not about to go out like a lamb. It was his last opportunity to get a few things off his chest, and he was just getting warmed up.

"Not that it hasn't been an interesting eight years, Si. But I'm afraid the disappointments far outweigh the accomplishments.

My government and I had such high hopes of finding a solution to this mess over here. We thought our peace initiative had a good chance of making it. But what happened? Your government spat on it, turned their backs on us while accelerating their plans to colonize the West Bank. For God's sake, when will you realize that you can't go on like this—surrounded by enemies and biting the hands of your only friends?"

David Llewellyn squirmed and braced himself for the foreign minister's reaction. But Shimon Kedar was a cool customer. He smiled and turned toward the new envoy.

"You must forgive Martin, Mr. Llewellyn, and not be embarrassed by his outburst. We are good friends, you see, which gives him the right to speak to me like a Dutch uncle. A right of which he avails himself most freely. But I am no less candid with him. I will be candid now. While our people wholeheartedly embrace the friendship of America, they also recognize that some of the actions taken by the American government, though perhaps well intended, are not in our nation's best interest. The sale of weapons to our enemies is particularly galling, and the surest way to poison the relationship between our governments. Yet that was almost the first official act of the administration that sent Martin to us eight years ago."

Martin's sudden flush was perceptible, even under the heavy layer of suntan. "All that fuss over the sale of the AWACS to the Saudis, a purely defensive system containing no weapons whatever. I could never figure out why you were so damn vehement about it. You didn't make half as much fuss when the Carter administration sold them F-15s."

The little man with the bushy gray brows smiled grimly. "Those Saudi Arabian F-15s were also billed as 'purely defensive' weapons. Even when your military were persuading your congress of this, they were aware of adaptations that already existed to turn these aircraft into deadly bombers. We were not to be fooled by a similar story on the AWACS. But in spite of all our protests you went ahead with it, and AWACS is there, now, a giant eye in the sky that can stare across our borders to spy on us and inform our enemies of our activities. And we perceive that it is quite capable of directing a horde of converted F-15 bombers in our midst."

At this Martin snorted and threw up his hands in a gesture of appeal to higher authority. The foreign minister turned again to the new envoy.

"And what are your views on the subject, Mr. Llewellyn? We have high hopes that the nation that has been our most steadfast ally is ready to move quickly back in step with us—if campaign promises to the American people can be taken seriously."

Smooth, thought David, sizing up his new opposite number. And very adroit. Anyone who could outtalk Marty Singer had his instant admiration. But he also knew the importance of a show of solidarity, and decided to sidestep the wedge that the foreign minister sought to drive between him and Martin.

"The President certainly believes in maintaining a close relationship between our two countries, but I'm not sure you'll notice any real shift in policy," he responded, noting the approving gleam in Martin's eye. "Our concern will continue to be finding peaceful solutions in the Middle East and avoiding weapons proliferations and confrontations that could blow the lid off this powder keg and lead to World War III. Keeping in step works both ways. Our administration will not take very kindly to any more 'surprises,' such as the invasion of Lebanon and the strike on Baghdad."

Instantly, he regretted making the last statement, perceiving that Kedar was stung by it. But the foreign minister's icy calm prevailed.

"Mr. Llewellyn, I will be patient with you, more patient than I sometimes am with Martin, because you are new here, and—forgive me—not a Jew. When you mention confrontations, do you not see that our very presence here is a constant confrontation to the Arab nations, who regard us as a festering sore in their midst? We are on 'friendly' terms only with Egypt, and only because we subdued them in several successive wars and made them realize we are here to stay. Certainly this confrontation is a 'powder keg,' but is it any more so than that between your country and the Soviet Union, backed up by countless nuclear warheads in intercontinental rockets trained down each other's throats? How can you believe in a policy of arms parity in that situation and not see that it also applies to us? Were the Arabs to gain access to nuclear weapons, it would be a disaster for us. We have no choice but to take the steps ourselves that will maintain the weapons parity, as we did against the nuclear plant in Iraq. That is the grim game of survival that we must continue to play."

"And sending spies to steal our secrets from us—that is also part of the game?" Martin had reentered the conversation with a vengeance. It was Kedar's turn to color.

"You seize on an isolated incident, an admitted mistake. One which has been duly redressed by our government and laid to rest."

For Pete's sake, Marty, tone it down! said the look from Llewellyn. But Singer was building a head of steam that wouldn't be arrested.

"So you admit that spying on us was a mistake. What about your Lebanon blitzkrieg? That was your most colossal blunder, and I've never heard you acknowledge it. All those innocent bystanders killed—what threat were they to the sovereign nation of Israel? Are we any better than the Nazis when we adopt their methods? Moses must be rolling over in his grave at the breaking of his commandments by 'God's chosen people'!"

Kedar stared back at him, their eyes locked together. "Of course," he responded in a quiet voice heavy with sarcasm, "you would be the expert on the breaking of the commandments, wouldn't you?" Singer flushed once again as the foreign minister spun on his heel, turning his back to them. David was alarmed; Marty had gone too far. It would be devastating if the foreign minister walked out of the meeting.

But "Si" Kedar was not walking out—not before he had the last word. He turned, resting his hands on the table, and David watched the muscles working in the strong face beneath the graying temples. He was a little man no longer; his presence was huge and dominating.

"I need no lessons from you on the Ten Commandments," he began evenly. "But let me instruct you, both of you—," his eyes held David's for a long moment, "on another commandment that wasn't on those clay tablets, yet was just as surely handed down from Yahweh to Moses and imparted to his people as the other ten. Commandment Number Eleven. The reason the Jews are still around after the countless persecutions and pogroms down through the ages—the inquisitions, the holocausts. The unwritten commandment, unspoken, because it need not be spoken, it is so deeply ingrained. The overriding commandment, taking precedence over all others. 'Thou shalt survive!' "

The Jaffa Gate entrance to the Old City was bustling with the traffic of tourists and pilgrims, cars and buses disgorging their occupants around the oval drive facing the western wall. "Come on!" shouted Martin, who was several yards ahead and setting a stiff pace.

As they pushed their way through the crowded portal, David stared up at the parapets of the Citadel, the stone fortress built by the crusaders. It was his first visit to the Holy City and he was not in a mood to rush things. As long as he had known Marty Singer, he reflected, the man had been in a perpetual hurry.

"What's the rush?" he inquired, catching up with Martin and tugging on his sleeve.

"Company," Martin answered offhandedly, without slackening his pace. "We're meeting someone for lunch, didn't I tell you?"

"You know damn well you didn't tell me." David's response was lost in the crowd noise. As he hurried to keep up, he wondered what his mercurial friend might have up his sleeve.

Leading into the heart of the ancient city from Jaffa Gate, David "Street" proved to be more like a narrow alley. The transition from new city to old was at first jarring. From a modern, clean, and orderly environment he was plunged into what appeared to be an exclusively Arab enclave, unkempt, malodorous, and almost unbearably noisy. The sheer volume of crowd sounds, intensified by merchants hawking their wares at the top of their lungs from the abundance of shops that lined the crowded thoroughfare, reminded him of the bazaars and flea markets of several Muslim cities he had visited. And so did the prickly perception of danger lurking there, the feeling of being secretly observed, of unseen eyes boring into him.

He had invariably felt uneasy in such places before. But here in the Arab quarter of Jerusalem the sensation seemed heightened. He had an overwhelming intimation of being shadowed, but fought the impulse to look behind him. What foolishness! Nobody in Jerusalem could know of his undercover assignment.

The sense of danger subsided; he found himself caught up in the infectious excitement of the scene. He couldn't remember ever seeing so many different garbs or hearing such a variety of languages and dialects in one place before. Jews and Arabs, businessmen in coats and ties, clergy of assorted denominations in their formal robes of office, tourists from all parts of the world in more casual attire. Packed together in a river of humanity that somehow maintained its uninterrupted flow through a passageway now and again constricted by encroaching walls and medieval archways or blocked by a donkey cart unloading its merchandise. Generating its own music as it paraded on, music free of the harsh western street sounds of auto traffic. A resounding symphony of human voices raised in conversation, argument, and exhortation, in tongues both familiar and foreign to his ears. Street vendors and shopkeepers, vocally contending for the attention of the passing throng from stalls lining both sides of the narrow alleyway, stalls stocked with jewelry and carpets and sheepskin coats, meat carcasses and rosaries and Palestinian dresses.

Arabs seemed to be the most numerous here, the men in predominantly western dress, jackets and sweaters and shirts open at the neck; the traditional headdress, the *kaffiyeh*, was the only visible tie to their heritage. These appeared in assorted colors and designs, plain white and checkered, one a vivid pink-red with white polka dots. A few more wore fezzes or Arab caps instead —light-colored skullcaps resembling the Jewish yarmulke. Muslim women were scarcer, attired in long, flowing gowns and shawls or head veils, some faces completely covered. Plain black predominated, though some of the Palestinian women wore colorful skirts with floral and embroidered patterns.

A blind Arab was swept past, attired pitifully in an assortment of old rags, his cane tap-tap-tapping as he was carried along by the stream of onrushing humans. Two Hassidic Jews went by, pale men with side curls and scraggly gray beards, wearing long black coats and wide-brimmed hats, totally absorbed in their own conversation and oblivious to the glut of humanity surrounding them. A bakery boy wearing a colorful western T-shirt dodged through the crowd, a platter full of sesame-covered disks of Arab bread balanced precariously on his head. The mouth-watering aroma of the freshly baked bread reached David's nostrils, drowning out for the moment the less appetizing smells of donkey dung trampled into the cobblestones and bodies perspiring in the desert heat.

He felt a tug on his arm. "This way." Martin steered him off to the right, through an archway that led up a picturesque, vaulted corridor that was almost deserted.

"Where are we?" David asked, as the crowd noise began to subside.

"This is the Armenian Quarter. My favorite restaurant is here."

"An Armenian community—inside the walls of Old Jerusalem?"

"Only for the last few centuries—about fifteen, to be more exact." Martin plunged through a narrow archway beneath a multicolored sign suspended from a wrought-iron bracket that protruded from the stone wall. David followed, unable to read the name emblazoned in illuminated letters of the Cyrillic alphabet. He found himself in a small enclosed courtyard paved with rough, irregular stones. Tables and chairs were spread about the opposite side of the courtyard, the small tables covered with white linen and sparkling with silverware and crystal.

The heavily mustachioed majordomo, attired in a colorful native costume, welcomed Martin like a long-lost relative, bowing and smiling. Martin returned the conviviality, introducing David as the new American envoy and employing a few words of Armenian with a horrendous accent that made the other man break up.

"Great sense of humor, Armenians," chuckled Martin as they were seated at a table alongside a giant, ornate espresso service of polished brass.

"I must say, you seem to be in excellent spirits after the dressing down you just received." David had been relishing a post-mortem on the meeting with the Israeli foreign minister and this seemed as good a time as any.

"Dressing down? That was mild. You should see Si Kedar when he really gets up a head of steam. As you undoubtedly will. Yitzhac Shamir, who had the job when I first came here, was a pussycat compared to Si. He's formidable." Martin used the French pronunciation of the word for emphasis.

"He certainly was impressive." David could still see the foreign minister's face and hear his powerful voice. The look in those eyes that had captured and held his own so intently was burned in his memory. "His personality is overpowering. He makes you feel what he's feeling, as if by osmosis."

"Or hypnotism. Don't be taken in, my friend. That performance was mostly for your benefit. Si knows I'm a lost cause, and leaving in the bargain. You're new grist for the Kedar meat grinder. He's already trying to soften you up. Notice how he lost no time in singling out your non-Jewishness? He'll try to capitalize on that, lay a guilt trip on you so you'll bend over backwards."

"Maybe so. But you were the one who triggered his outburst. There were sparks flying between you two that had nothing to do with me. Something much more personal than the Law of Moses and the transgressions of the Likud government."

Martin looked at him with new respect. "Why, Davey! You caught that, did you? But that will all explain itself in due course, when our guest arrives." He glanced impatiently at his watch.

"She should have been here by now. Ah, there she is."

David looked up to see a slender, smartly dressed young woman entering the courtyard. She was picking her way carefully across the cobblestones in her high heels, staring concentratedly at the rough pavement, and had not yet seen them. Dark, almost raven black hair fell in soft rivulets to her shoulders, emphasizing the contrasting whiteness of the face it framed, a face seemingly untouched by the searing sun of the desert.

"Daniella—over here!"

She looked up, removing her sunglasses, and David was struck with her natural beauty. Dark, flashing eyes joined the full, unrouged lips in a smile that radiated inner warmth. Then quickly the smile faded, like the sun going under a cloud.

For at that moment the heart of Daniella Zadik was anything but warm. She was feeling desolate, though determined not to show it. What was the other man doing here—why had Martin brought him to "their place" at a time like this? A time that might be their last time here together. Her insides were a jumble of conflicting emotions as she sized up the tall, distinguished-looking man who had risen from the table at her approach and was staring at her, their eyes meeting briefly before she turned her gaze on her lover. Her late lover. Suddenly, she knew what Martin was up to and her eyes flashed fire.

The look was not lost on Martin, who moved quickly to her and caught her in a perfunctory embrace. "You bastard!" she murmured into his ear through clenched teeth.

"Be good," he whispered back. "I'll explain later." Her look, as they separated, told him he needn't bother.

"Daniella, may I present my good friend, David Llewellyn, the new U.S. envoy. David, this is Daniella Zadik from the foreign minister's office. Daniella has been my right arm here in Jerusalem."

"And a lot more," thought David, sensing the electricity between them. Electricity powerful enough to have generated some of the sparks in the Kedar meeting. He waited for her to extend her hand, noting the hesitation. Then the cloud lifted and the smile was back. She shook his hand vigorously.

"Welcome, Mr. Llewellyn. We've been expecting you. The foreign minister is looking forward to a close working relationship with your new government. You met with him this morning?"

David nodded, returning the smile. "I was most impressed

with him. Strong personality and intellect. Remarkable presence."

"Yes. And warmth. For such a strong man he is also very kind and gentle. He is like a father to me."

"Daniella lost her father in the 1973 War," Martin explained. "Daniella is a sabra, born and educated here, a native Israeli."

David couldn't take his eyes off her. "What do you do in the foreign minister's office, Miss Zadik?"

Her short laugh had a musical quality. "A little of everything, I guess. My official title is Special Assistant to the Foreign Minister. Actually, I'm just a notch above what you in America would call a 'girl Friday.'"

"She's being far too modest," Martin interjected. "No one in that office can get things accomplished the way Daniella can. Si absolutely relies on her. And so will you, David. That's why I wanted you two to get together." He glanced at his watch. "We'd better order. I have to get back to Tel Aviv and finish packing."

Her face fell, and for an instant David saw a different Daniella, unmasked in her misery. But only for an instant.

"Why don't you order for us, Martin? You always know what's best." David saw Martin look up sharply from the menu. But her placid expression belied any intent of irony.

"That drive back and forth from Tel Aviv is such a grind," she continued evenly. "At least, Mr. Llewellyn, you'll be spared that, now that your embassy is moving to Jerusalem."

"And sleeping in the cool night air of the Judean hills instead of the miserable suffocation of Tel Aviv's humidity." The note of envy in Martin's voice sounded genuine. "We should have done it sooner. Now that the oil glut has taken all the teeth out of the Arab bloc's threats against countries that have embassies here, they'll all be moving back. The only sensible thing. Trying to do business with the Israeli government from Tel Aviv is like making love by remote control."

An unfortunate choice of metaphors, thought David, watching Daniella's reaction out of the corner of his eye. But she gave no outward sign of offense. Martin motioned to the waiter who was hovering nearby and ordered their lunch in his broken Armenian. Almost instantly a tray of appetizers and carafe of rosé wine arrived. While Martin filled their glasses, Daniella turned to David again.

"Was there some altercation in your meeting with the foreign minister? He arrived back just now terribly out of sorts."

"Oh? I'm sorry to hear that. It could be that we were a trifle overly—outspoken." David looked at Martin.

"Hell, Daniella, you know how it is with Si and me. We speak our minds, always have. Besides, he loves debating. It gets his juices flowing. He's at his best when he's aroused."

He raised his glass. "To absent friends, past and present."

David caught the wistful look in Daniella's eyes and it came to him that she had been anticipating a much more personal toast, a much more intimate "last supper." She had expected to be alone with Martin. Suddenly he felt like an intruder. But he played along, clinking glasses with Martin.

"To old friends. And to charming new ones," as he turned to Daniella, who had not yet raised her glass.

"Yes," she responded, "I would be most happy to call you friend, Mr. Llewellyn." Her manner was pleasant but cool, like the rose-tinted wine in the clear crystal goblets that rang with a perfect tone as she touched hers to his. He watched her raise the glass delicately to her lips, avoiding his eyes.

"If the truth were known, old Si probably agrees with me more than he's willing to admit," Martin chuckled, picking up the thread of the earlier conversation. "He knows full well that if the government continues its hard line, its unilateral, provocative actions—continues to alienate the few friends it has left in the free world—there'll come a day of reckoning. And that day is fast approaching." He popped an appetizer from the tray into his mouth and continued on unabated, chewing intermittently. "One thing I'm sure we agree on is the seriousness of the threat to Israel and the volatility of the situation. There are a dozen potential fuses that could set this thing off at any time."

"What would you have us do?" Daniella protested. "Sit and wait for it to happen? Do nothing while the Arabs develop nuclear weapons to use against us?"

Martin withdrew an olive pit from his mouth and tossed it carelessly onto the cobblestones. "Damn it, Daniella, you know you can't continue to go around shooting up the place like a bunch of Wild West vigilantes. The free world will eventually hang you, even if the Arabs don't. The United States is committed to keeping peace in the Middle East. That's why we're trying to make friends with the more moderate Arab countries, spread the 'spirit of Camp David' around."

She shook her head vehemently. "There are no moderate Arab countries, as far as we are concerned. They are all dedicated to our downfall, our ultimate withdrawal or destruction. And as for your spirit of Camp David, instead of courting Jordan and Saudi Arabia you'd be better off doing some fence mending in Egypt. Since we gave back the Sinai, whatever spirit there was seems to have died."

"Bravo," thought David, admiring her forthrightness. Though his orientation on the subject was much the same as his predecessor's, he enjoyed seeing Martin get as good as he gave.

But Martin wasn't through quite yet. "You're evading the main issue. What will you do—fight the whole world? Fight us? It could come down to that, you know. We have military missions now in three Arab countries. If a war broke out, our people there would be caught in the middle."

"Then they shouldn't be there. Peace in these times in the Middle East is an illusion. How can we possibly guarantee their safety?"

"I have a brother in Riyadh—my kid brother, actually, the baby of the family." David was staring fixedly at the wine carafe at the center of the table from which the face of an adolescent boy stared back. It was the way he still thought of Richy, now a grown man in his midtwenties. "He's an engineer, working on the AWACS. He even flies in it. Are you saying he might be in danger?"

Martin and Daniella exchanged glances. "I wouldn't worry." Martin dismissed the matter lightly. "The AWACS support contract has only a few more months to run at most. He'll probably be out of there before anything happens."

David sought Daniella's eyes for affirmation, but they were fixed on the table, her expression noncommittal. "I haven't seen him for over three years. I've been thinking of running down there to look in on him."

The waiter approached to announce that the main course was ready to be served, but Martin told him to hold off, ordering more wine. "I have to find a telephone," he announced, excusing himself. "Enjoy the wine and the rest of the hors d'oeuvres. I'll be back momentarily."

He strode off across the courtyard, Daniella's expression looking daggers into his back. David felt uncomfortable. "Look," he said, "I'm in the way here. I didn't know—Martin didn't tell me—"

"That he was shacking up with a sabra?" Fury leapt from her dark eyes, and it seemed to David to be now directed at him.

"Are you so blind? Don't you see what he's doing? It's so obvious. He's throwing us together. You're to be his proxy, so that his conscience will be clear and he won't have to worry about abandoning his little 'rose of the Negev.' He's even arranged things so he'll be spared any tearful good-byes."

He looked at her in disbelief. "Surely he wouldn't—"

"Oh, yes, he would. It's just like him. I don't know how well you know Martin, Mr. Llewellyn. I know him very well—too well. Despite his charm, Martin is a moral coward. He'll only give so much of himself and runs away from any situation that cuts too deep. I was only an interlude in his life and now he'll go back to his wife and pretend it never happened."

She rushed on, the anguished torrent of words spilling out of her. "Oh, I've known all along it couldn't last, that it had to end some day. I had even made up my mind that our parting would be joyous, a final scene to remember. I had myself all prepared. But not for this! Not to be handed off like a sack of flour!"

Tears stung her eyes and she dabbed at them with the clenched fist of her right hand. He pushed back his chair. "I'll leave you alone with him. I'll just—"

"Wait." Her hand found his, restraining him. She dabbed at her eyes again, regaining control. "If you leave now, before he returns, he'll be certain I drove you away."

Her voice was much calmer now, the tone softened. "You can help me salvage something out of this. When Martin returns, tell him you have to leave immediately. Make up some excuse—anything. I need some time alone with him. I won't be cheated out of it."

"Of course," he agreed.

For the first time she seemed to take note of his crestfallen look. "I'm sorry. Forgive my outburst. I'm afraid you are the innocent bystander that is always getting run over."

She met his solicitous gaze, reading the sympathy in the gray eyes. "One thing, Mr. Llewellyn—a word of advice. I wouldn't delay too long on that trip to Arabia to see your brother. He means a great deal to you, yes?"

He nodded wordlessly.

"Yes, I could tell that. I could see it in your eyes when you spoke of him. Then by all means plan your visit immediately."

"He is in danger, then! You know something you're not telling me!"

She shook her head. "Nothing that specific. Just call it

woman's intuition. But I advise you to see your brother soon, Mr. Llewellyn. Don't put it off."

By any standard, the defense minister's residence was luxurious to the point of opulence. By Iraqi standards, it was palatial. Scion of one of the wealthiest families in this formerly impoverished land—only recently rejuvenated through its OPEC oil revenues—Amahl Zahadi had furnished the pink stucco Moorish mansion with the creations of Araby's most skilled artists and master craftsmen. The Oriental carpets rivaled the best that Brastov had seen in the oil-rich emirates to the south. The gleaming copperwork in the samovars and giant planters, he had learned from a previous visit, was of local origin, created by bearded artisans in the teeming bazaars of Baghdad.

He was led by a servant into the spacious waiting room that adjoined the minister's office and private quarters. The room was deserted; he was the first to arrive. Lush damask divans were placed against three of the four walls, and he settled into one, leaning back to admire a heavy gilt-framed landscape by one of the old masters covering a large expanse of the opposite wall. It was one of the few examples of western culture to be seen in the Zahadi residence, but Brastov knew that there were others, kept out of sight—refrigerators and ice makers, televisions and washing machines—all the trappings of western consumerism. The defense minister had the latest models, including a shortwave radio set that could tune in to half the world, its antenna disguised as a stucco-encrusted minaret.

A sudden bustle in the hall outside announced the arrival of the defense minister and his entourage. Moments later he swept into the drawing room, followed closely by the presidential interpreter and the top presidential adviser, known in some quarters as the "assistant President." The uniformed army and air force chiefs of staff, both major generals, were not far behind. They were large men who dwarfed the fifth attendee, Hammud al Fawzi, Director of Intelligence—an imposing title for a man who stood scarcely five feet tall.

"Ah, General Brastov." Amahl Zahadi advanced smilingly toward the Russian, who stood up and bowed slightly from the waist, accepting the warm handshake. "You are punctual, as always."

The interpreter began to translate, but Brastov brushed him

away, answering in Arabic. "The business at hand is of crucial importance to both our governments."

"Indeed." The defense minister nodded, the smile on his face receding into a thin line below the small mustache. He was a handsome man, young for so responsible an office. He looked to be in his midthirties. Unlike the other three civilians, who wore the conventional white cotton ankle-length robes, he was dressed in a business suit and tie, the plain white headdress worn above it his only visible concession to tradition. "Shall we meet in my private study?" He moved toward the door on his left.

Brastov trailed the others into the elaborately wood-paneled room, studying the backs of those ahead of him. Halim, the interpreter, was young and intelligent, his eyes gleaming with raw, undisguised ambition. He was not to be trusted, an opportunist who would alter a statement to suit his own ends. Concern over this had caused the Soviet emissary to redouble his efforts to master the difficult Iraqi dialect of Arabic.

The generals Brastov knew only slightly. They spoke for the two major military arms of the country and would have a vote on whether or not to lay the plan he was proposing in front of a president. But they would not have the deciding vote. That honor would belong to the tall, gaunt man in front of them.

As usual, Brastov surmised, Ali Mustafa would be the key. President Hussein absolutely relied on him. He was the closest thing to a soothsayer or grand vizier left in the former kingdom-turned-republic. The presidential adviser was of keen mind and kept his own counsel until he was sure of his ground. When Mustafa spoke you could be sure that a great deal of thought lay behind his words and that he had weighed all the arguments, adding fresh viewpoints of his own.

"So this is the lineup," thought Brastov. It was about what he had expected. His first objective was to get rid of the interpreter. He whispered a few words in the defense minister's ear and Halim was promptly excused, shooting Brastov a dark look as he left the room.

Zahadi opened the meeting by asking al Fawzi for an intelligence update on the Israeli plans to strike the Osirak nuclear plant. Wearing a white fez with a red tassel, the little man strode importantly to the map case on the facing wall and pulled down a large color map of the Middle East. Brastov had little use for the so-called director of intelligence. The man was a pompous ass, pedantic in the extreme when giving a briefing. His whole manner conveyed his high opinion of himself as the see-all and know-all of the arcane dominion over which he held sway. Brastov, whose private sources of information usually kept him several steps ahead of the self-important little man, had difficulty controlling his patience when al Fawzi had the floor. But on this occasion the intelligence director proved to be one up on him.

"Before discussing the Zionist strike plan, let me bring you up to date on the recent attempt by a Zionist agent to penetrate the Osirak defense zone." Brastov's heart skipped a beat. He had been fearful of just such a move by the Mossad, but had not been apprised of any such occurrence.

"As you have no doubt been informed," al Fawzi continued, "the attempted penetration, which occurred yesterday evening, was unsuccessful. The agent was killed by an antipersonnel mine while still in the restricted zone. We have since developed the film taken from his damaged camera, which proved to be close-up silhouettes of the new missile installations. The Zionist agent carried no walkie-talkie or other means of communication. Immediately following the detonation of the land mine, the entire area was swept by our security forces. There were no signs of any confederates. We are now certain that the agent was operating alone and that his secret died with him."

Brastov heaved a sigh of relief. Premature Israeli discovery of the SA-10 could jeopardize the entire operation. The defense minister's next question anticipated his remaining concern.

"What measures have you taken to thwart any further attempts to learn our secret?"

"We have doubled the number of guards and extended the perimeter," the little man responded. "We have also installed additional electronic surveillance devices. It would be impossible for anyone to get that close again."

Back in front of the map, the intelligence director launched into his exposition on the Israeli air strike plan. "We expect them to use the F-16 fighter-bombers again, carrying 2,000-pound bombs, with F-15 fighters flying cover. Probably the same size force—eight bombers and six fighters. It will be a daylight raid, as before, to assure the desired bombing accuracy. They will skirt around Jordan again to avoid the heavy air defenses south of Aman, proceeding across the North Arabian Desert. The 1981 raid was staged out of an air base in the Sinai—since returned to Egypt. This time they will originate from this base in the Negev Desert." He used the pointer to indicate a spot some hundred kilometers to the south of Jerusalem. "This will increase the distance of the flight, including the return leg, by several hundred kilometers. When they near our border they will descend to low altitude to escape detection by our radar, and remain low until they reach the target area.

"There you have it." He replaced the pointer and extended his hands palms up. "A repeat performance in all respects. Until we reach the end game, of course." He smiled knowingly.

"Not quite." The air force chief of staff was shaking his head dubiously. "Those extra hundreds of kilometers may change things significantly. Our data on the F-16 indicates that it would run out of fuel on the return leg."

"Perhaps in-flight refueling?" the intelligence man ventured.

The two military men looked at him as though he were crazy. "Over hostile territory?" the army chief snorted. "With fighters from three nations on alert for them and our ground radars tracking their tankers? That would be suicide."

Brastov decided it was time to take the floor, hoping that his improved command of Arabic would hold up under fire.

"Perhaps they'll find a way to increase the range of the F-16 —extra fuel tanks, for example. That question doesn't concern me as much as one other. How do they sneak through Saudi Arabia without being detected? The AWACS is now on continuous air alert. One of the four aircraft is always airborne."

The two officers exchanged glances, while the intelligence man burrowed into his notes and background material. He came up for air moments later, waving a diagram and looking triumphant.

"The AWACS flies an oval 'race track' pattern that concentrates its coverage over the oil fields—Dhahran and Ras Tanura —and the northern end of the Persian Gulf. The North Arabian Desert is searched only sporadically, when the aircraft reaches the northern terminus of its oval flight path. With prior knowledge of this search plan the Zionists could time their crossing of Arabia to coincide with the time at which that territory is not under surveillance."

Brastov nodded. "Very likely that is what they plan to do. But since Baghdad will know from its agent in the Israeli Air Force the exact timing of the raid, it would be possible for your government to alert the Saudis so that they could alter their AWACS search schedule and be in the right place at the right time to detect the Israeli strike force."

The intelligence man stared at him, uncomprehending. With the exception of the defense minister, who knew what was coming, the others wore puzzled looks.

"But why would we do that?" The air force chief of staff voiced their common demurrer. "We are laying a trap for them—an ambush. We want them to get through to Osirak."

"I had in mind an additional trap—a different kind of trap." Brastov stood up from the conference table and walked to the massive desk across the room, on one corner of which stood a gleaming black and white chess set reflecting highlights from the warm yellow glow of lamps scattered about the study. The handsome set had been his gift to the defense minister. Its board of purest white alabaster was inset with squares of obsidian. The pieces were of polished ivory and ebony.

"If Your Excellency will permit—"

Zahadi nodded his assent, and the Russian carried the chess set back to the table and set it down in front of the others. Deftly, he rearranged the pieces in the classic form of the "King's Indian Defense."

"White is on the attack. We, the black forces, know they are coming. We wait for them, preparing our defense. On the surface, it looks like a classic defense, something they have seen many times before. But we have a surprise in store for them, a key move held in reserve until the white forces are too fully committed to back off."

"The SA-10 missiles, of course." The army general was something of a chess enthusiast himself. "We destroy their bombers while they are in their low-altitude approach run and helpless—unable to escape."

"And then what?" Brastov swung around, facing the general. "The bombers are but pawns. So we capture a few pawns, but the game continues. Anyone can still win—the Israelis can replenish their warplanes from the Americans. We will have won only a momentary advantage, a small moment of triumph. And will have missed the supreme advantage, the master stroke."

He spoke with unusual intensity and directness. The general flushed. "I don't see—"

"Look." Brastov began moving the pieces in rapid succession, the white pieces marching down the board to threaten the black king, the black pieces scattering with no perceptible pattern or sense of purpose. Several white pawns were lost in the process, but white ended up with a commanding position, the black king surrounded and in danger of imminent checkmate.

"The loss of a few pawns didn't bother white too much, eh? He has a mate in one move."

Those at the table who understood the game studied the board and nodded. The Soviet adviser smiled slyly. "Only it is not white's move. It is black's." He snatched up one of the black knights and moved it onto a square where it placed the white king in check but was in danger of being immediately gobbled up by a white pawn. "Check! And also, en garde!"

Prior to the move, the black knight had been interposed between the white queen and one of black's bishops, which protected it from capture by the queen. The diagonal was now open between the black bishop and white queen, the bishop unprotected by any other piece. White could capture it with his queen except for one small detail—his king was in check. His only recourse was to capture the knight, removing his king from check. At which point he would lose his queen to the black bishop.

"A dramatic turnaround, was it not?" Brastov picked up the white king and turned it on its side. "On the threshold of victory, white has lost his queen, his position is now hopeless, and he is forced to resign. Why? Because he was so intent on administering a quick coup de grace that he did not perceive the trap being set for him. His queen was back on the seventh rank, relatively unexposed. He felt secure.

"This is the kind of trap I propose, gentlemen. We do not settle for a few pawns. We go for the queen!" He looked from one face to another, but only the defense minister's showed signs of comprehension.

"Think, gentlemen. What is the most powerful piece the Israelis possess, the piece without which they have no attack and no defense, without which their position is hopeless?"

"That's easy," blurted the army general. "Their one powerful ally, the United States. We were crushing them in '73 until the American president Nixon intervened and resupplied them with his airlift." He regarded the Russian's grinning face and nodding head with a deepening frown. "What are you proposing? How does one go about capturing the United States of America?"

"You take my little chess example too literally." Brastov caught the first glimmer of understanding in the eye of Ali Mustafa and concentrated his attention on the "Grand Vizier." "We do not have to actually capture the U.S. queen to deprive Israel of her use. We can do so by creating an incident so distasteful to the Americans that it will drive a permanent wedge between them and their Zionist ally. Relationships between the two governments have been steadily deteriorating. The new U.S. president promised a reconciliation, to assure himself of the Jewish vote. A second honeymoon, eh? We will make it a very brief one."

He had all their attention, now. They were hanging on his next words. "Your undercover agent on the Israeli strike force is the key. I congratulate you, that was a brilliant accomplishment." He threw the Iraqi intelligence man a few crumbs before sweeping them away again. "You have placed him well, but you do not use him well—only for information on the timing of the raid. How must he feel about being forced to take part in an air strike against his homeland? You can spare him that and divert him to a much more rewarding assignment. One which can change the balance of power and pit our adversaries one against the other."

Brastov walked to the map and picked up the pointer. "Your F-15 pilot takes off from the Israeli airfield somewhere in the Negev to fly protective cover for the F-16 strike aircraft. He will be armed with four heat-seeking Sidewinder missiles and two radar-guided Sparrows. Somewhere above the Northern Arabian Desert he leaves his formation and pretends to turn back. On whatever pretext—engine trouble, faulty radar. Out of sight of the strike force he turns southward, accelerates under afterburner, and heads for a rendezvous with the AWACS, which is traveling northward in response to an alert received from your government. He will have no trouble finding it. Its prolific radar emissions can be picked up on his homing and warning receiver hundreds of kilometers away. When he is within range, he launches his two Sparrow missiles in a single salvo. They can hardly miss—the AWACS is a gigantic radar target. But if necessary, he moves in closer and finishes the giant plane off with his Sidewinder missiles. And then he simply—disappears."

A gasp came from the air force general. "Did I hear you correctly? Shoot down a Saudi Arabian AWACS—are you mad?" The others stared at him in wide-eyed amazement. Except for Zahadi and Mustafa. The latter appeared lost in thought.

"Think about it," the Russian continued. "American civilians will be on board. Technicians and engineers. Israel will of course be blamed. Once the world learns of their second attempt to bomb Osirak, there will be no doubt that the AWACS was destroyed by an Israeli fighter to prevent it from sighting the Israeli

strike force and sounding the alarm. The Americans will be furious—doubly furious that their willful ally did not confide in
them and showed blatant contempt for the loss of American lives.
A hue and cry will be raised in America, even among Jews. It
will be the turning point that all Islam has been waiting for, the
U.S. at last stripped away from Israel, leaving her exposed and
isolated."

"But the Saudis," protested the army general. "They are fund-
ing our nuclear program. If they learned it was we who destroyed
their AWACS, we would never see another riyal from them."

"There is no need for them to find out. The pilot, as I said,
will simply disappear. No one else beyond those in this room,
except of course your President, need be informed. But even if
the Saudis should eventually learn of it, don't you think it would
be worth it to King Fahd and his brothers? Begin's legacy, the
present hard-line Israeli government, continues to frustrate their
attempts to negotiate a Palestinian state on the West Bank and
return the shrines of Eastern Jerusalem to Arab control. That
government is certain to fall, and the path will be cleared for a
Saudi-sponsored Palestinian refugee plan to succeed. Besides,"
he added, again speaking directly to the presidential adviser, "the
AWACS still officially belongs to the U.S. It won't revert to
Saudi Arabia until it passes its acceptance tests. The Americans
will have to stand the loss and replace it at no added cost to the
Saudi government."

He looked for a reaction in Mustafa's deadpan face but could
read none. The two generals were speechless. The intelligence
man, still frowning, contributed his own measure of cold water.

"I'm afraid you underestimate the Zionists. They are sure to
discover our agent's identity, once he deserts with his valuable
aircraft. They will inform the world that the AWACS killer was
an Iraqi agent."

Brastov laughed. "Who will believe them? Surely not the
Saudis. Without the pilot they will have no evidence. And as for
the Americans, they will be reminded of the *Liberty*, the American spy ship deliberately sunk by Israel during the 1967 War,
which the Israelis also sought to blame on their enemies."

Silenced for the moment, the intelligence director looked toward the defense minister for guidance. Amahl Zahadi's face remained impassive as he studied the reactions of those around
him. It was Ali Mustafa who broke his own prolonged silence.

"Extraordinary! You are most eloquent, General Brastov, and

you have done your homework well. Your plan appears to have great merit; it is a very bold and daring plan, indeed. I have several questions on some of the details, but they will keep for now. If the Defense Minister concurs, I will arrange for an audience with our esteemed President. Only he, of course, can commit our nation to an operation of such momentous consequence."

Zahadi nodded. "That would certainly be the appropriate next step. If we're all agreed, then?" Without waiting for a response from his own staff he rose from his chair, signifying that the meeting was concluded. There was a sudden buzz of voices as the inevitable second thoughts and yet unspoken reservations began to fly. The defense minister turned back toward the table and motioned for quiet.

"One word of caution. It is not yet decided that we will pursue the proposed course of action. But if we should, it is imperative that our secret be protected at all cost. Those of you in this room are the only ones privy to this secret plan. Your are to discuss it with no one. If there is a leak, it will be on your heads."

Brastov was elated. He shook hands with Zahadi and Mustafa and thanked them, then drifted toward the door. From the corner of his eye, he saw Ali Mustafa tug on the defense minister's sleeve and detain him as the others left the room. So there will be a rump session without the rest of us, he thought. He would have given a lot to be able to listen in.

"President Saddam Hussein is a very suspicious man." Ali Mustafa sipped from the demitasse of strong black, sweetened coffee as his host nodded knowingly. "His first question will be, 'What's in it for us?' His second will be, 'What's in it for the Soviets?'

"The first question I think I can answer more than adequately," the gaunt Arab continued. "If the American reaction to the apparent destruction of the AWACS by the Zionists is, indeed, the one predicted by our Russian friend—and I have no reason to doubt it—then we will at the very least be rid of the government installed by that terrorist Begin. President Hussein despises the man and blames him personally for the supplying of arms to Iran, the air strike on Baghdad, and the invasion of Lebanon.

"In the longer term, the Zionist enemy will be severely weakened by the loss of American support and must ultimately fall prey to a concerted Arab offensive, whether by economic and political means, or military. The fact that Iraq cannot immediately take credit among our brother nations for bringing this about should not deter us. The frosting will still be ours—the destruction of the Israeli bombers by our missiles—and the taste of it sweet in our mouths while we await the day when we can devour the rest of the cake."

The defense minister smiled, savoring the thought along with the bittersweetness of the rich Arabian coffee, as Ali Mustafa continued.

"There is another aspect of this strategy which bears even more directly on the future of the Iraqi Republic. If we can succeed in alienating the Americans from the Zionists, it will solve a problem that presently weighs heavily on our President and the members of the Revolutionary Command Council. Eventually, the world is bound to learn what the Israelis cannot yet prove: that our nuclear plant has the capacity to extract plutonium from the enriched uranium ore shipped in from Brazil, and that we are but a short step away from possessing multiple kiloton warheads. Our risk would be great, indeed, if the United States were to react by agreeing to supply Israel with fissionable material to restore the arms parity in the Middle East. There can be little doubt that they already have the technology to convert these materials rapidly into bombs. We cannot permit this to happen. The Russian's strategy is timely and would seem tailormade to create the desired rift between the U.S. and the Zionists that would forestall any such development.

"But the Soviet's motives puzzle me." An uncharacteristic frown wrinkled the placid forehead of the presidential adviser. "Not that the urge to make trouble for the Zionist nation is out of character for them. They have always been rabidly anti-Zionist and outspokenly critical of Begin and his ilk."

"Much of which is for our benefit," the defense minister observed dryly, "to court the favor of Islam and place a stigma on the Americans for aiding the Zionists."

"Precisely. So why would they propose a plan which might ultimately remove the stigma and bring Islam and America closer together, thereby diminishing their own influence here? That would seem to play into the hands of the Americans."

Amahl Zahadi shrugged. "I'm afraid I don't have that answer."

"Nor I, my friend, at the moment." The "Grand Vizier" drained his demitasse and carefully replaced the tiny porcelain cup in its delicate saucer. "But that point will bear some further thought. A great deal of thought, before we allow ourselves to become fully committed to this Brastov plan."

"Where is that fucking Llewellyn?" The big, dark-browned man in the olive drab fatigues checked his watch and glowered at the tow-headed younger man sitting at the desk facing his. "The inconsiderate bastard is probably still in the sack."

The other man, bent over his desk in concentration, made no response and did not look up. This only heaped fuel on the fire.

"Christ, Hanson, I can't work out this shit by myself. You're supposed to be in charge of this mother-fucking operation. If you want your fucking AWACS to fucking track, you'd better make that son of a bitch cooperate."

The blond man looked up wearily from his work. "Hauser, you've unquestionably got the foulest mouth this side of Piccadilly. I gave you seventy-two hours to clean up your act before our lady engineer arrives on board." He looked at his own watch. "You've got exactly forty-two minutes left."

"Don't change the fucking subject."

A sudden blast of wind made the frail Quonset hut quiver as if caught in the grip of a palsied giant, accompanied by the abrasive staccato of thousands of sand particles driven forcibly against the corrugated metal walls. Both men glanced apprehensively out of the tiny window at a landscape stained brown by clouds of blowing sand. The blond man stood up and walked to the window, staring out at the bleak scene. The three giant E-3A aircraft, parked less than a quarter of a mile away on the apron of the concrete runway, were all but invisible.

"Saudi-fucking-Arabia," he muttered under his breath. "What a godforsaken spot to try to pull off one of the miracles of modern science."

Hauser was not to be put off. "What about Llewellyn?"

"He'll be along. Beethoven's Fifth was already booming out when I knocked on his door. Guess he didn't hear me."

"High-toned fucking bastard. He thinks he's better than us. Thinks he's King Shit."

Hanson walked back and stood in front of Hauser's desk. He leaned down on his palms, his face a few inches from the other man's. "He *is* King Shit. It's *his* radar, a radar he knows like the back of his hand. And on AWACS, my friend, the radar is the center of the universe. Not your computer. Not even my airplane. But his radar. We can't possibly get this job wrapped up without him. So unless you want to spend another year or two in this dismal hole, you'd better resign yourself to getting along with him."

"He'd be a lot fucking easier to get along with if you'd kick his ass once in a while, Hanson. But you're too gutless—you always take his side. Boeing should have known better than to put a fucking kid who isn't dry behind the ears in charge of a job like this."

Hanson bit his lip and sat back down at his desk. Fucking kid. Except for Hauser, who was in his thirties, and one older technician, they were all kids out here. Field service engineers were generally young and single, some hired directly into these jobs fresh out of school. It was good hands-on hardware experience, and the field allowance and per diem made their starting paychecks look a lot bigger. Older, married engineers were reluctant to commit to a long-term assignment in a spot where they couldn't take their wives and families. And God knew this was no place for a wife.

The thought of his wife made him feel like chucking the whole thing for the umpteenth time this month. Christ, he missed her. It had been more than six months since his last furlough. He wouldn't get home again until the job was finished, which it should have been by now. Many of the support group had already left for home. But, as usual, Murphy's Law had taken effect. Unforeseen problems had developed in the later stages of the flight testing, anomalies that hadn't shown up in any of the earlier AWACS test programs. Nothing they couldn't work their way out of, he was certain. If he could only hold his small flight test support group together, keep them from self-destructing. But how? He had so little authority over them. A Boeing engineer, nominally in charge because he represented the prime contractor, trying to work his will over engineers and technicians whose paychecks came from Westinghouse and IBM and Northrop.

His personal charisma—the wit and charm that had carried things off until now—were wearing pitifully thin. His little band were on the ragged edge of exhaustion from working nights and weekends. You could keep that up only for so long. He had given them today, Sunday, off—except for the two group heads, Hauser and Llewellyn. IBM and Westinghouse. The computer and the radar. That interface was the heart of the problem. Something had fallen into a crack between the two and the finger-pointing, each blaming the other, was endless.

He couldn't really fault Llewellyn. The man was a technical marvel, the best he had ever seen. He had participated in the NATO trials in Germany that had preceded the Saudi deployment and knew the system better than anyone. It was unusual in Hanson's experience to find an engineer whose skill at software matched his hardware knowledge. Llewellyn was that rare combination and had personally written new code that had gotten around some of the difficulties. If only he would work more closely with Hauser. But Hauser was hard to take, and he had his own reservations about the man's competence.

He laughed aloud, a somewhat bitter laugh, remembering his own naive pre-Hauser image of the IBM engineer. Gentlemanly demeanor, quiet competence, white shirt and tie, buttoned-down collar, buttoned-down mind. Ha! Hauser had not just tarnished that image, Hauser had destroyed it. Several times of late he had been tempted to request a replacement from IBM, but was deterred by the thought of breaking in a new man at this late juncture. And now, ironically, he was about to be saddled with the job of breaking in a woman engineer. That was all he needed. She would probably turn out to have no experience and a language barrier to boot. Come to think of it, it might be better if she didn't speak English. The profanity and ribald humor of his men would be tough to take, and he had no illusions of breaking them of it overnight.

Emerging from his reverie, he noted that Hauser was about to lay into him again and decided to beat the big man to the punch. "If I kick anybody's ass, Hauser, it'll be yours. It's your computer that keeps dumping when we're up there doing intercepts."

Hauser's obscene rejoinder was drowned out as the door suddenly burst open, the accompanying gust of sand-laden wind blowing the papers atop Hauser's desk halfway across the room. "Close that fucking door!" he shouted, making a dash after the scattering pages.

The figure framed in the open doorway appeared in no particular hurry to obey the irate command, pausing momentarily to enjoy the comical scene of the heavyset, fatigue-clad engineer scurrying across the floor in pursuit of his windblown paperwork. Wearing an amused look, the face peering from the hooded warm-up suit was a more youthful version of his brother, the diplomat's, the figure somewhat slighter and less developed but just as tall. Almost languidly, Richard Llewellyn reached for the doorknob that the wind had wrested from his grasp and forced the door back in place until it latched.

"Fucking lamebrain!" Petulantly, Hauser sorted and smoothed the rumpled sheets of paper.

"If my brain is lame, Hauser, yours must be paraplegic. Your million dollar computer is falling apart before our eyes and you don't even know why. Or does that frantic scramble to retrieve your notes mean that there are finally some answers there?"

Hanson couldn't suppress a grin at the barb delivered by the radar man. Llewellyn wasn't a particularly sarcastic person; sarcasm was a refuge he took only when criticized or threatened. But on those occasions he could really dig it in and twist it. Hauser was no match for him.

"Fuck you, too, Llewellyn!"

"Hauser, you disappoint me. It isn't your profanity, per se—an accomplished swearer can be a true artist with words. But yours are so predictable and repetitious. If you must refer constantly to the same act, at least throw in a few synonyms for variety, like fornicate and copulate."

"There's nothing worse than a fucking know-it-all," muttered Hauser, looking like he could strangle the man with his bare hands. But Richy had already turned away and was unzipping the jacket of his purple jogging suit as he approached Hanson's desk.

"Westinghouse to the rescue again," he announced, extracting a fat envelope from inside the jacket and tossing it dramatically into Hanson's lap.

"What in the hell's this?" Hanson undid the catch on the envelope and inverted it over his desk. Several reels of magnetic tape fell out, accompanied by a sheaf of computer printouts on tractor paper. Puzzled, he looked at Llewellyn for an explanation.

"I had these flown in from Geilenkirchen. They're the Westinghouse tapes we used in the initial NATO trials, when we did the tracking in the radar processor. Before the Boeing and IBM software was ready. They worked like a charm. And we still have more than enough memory in the radar."

Hanson's expression grew more perplexed. "What good will that do? We can't give this program to the Saudis. It hasn't been cleared. Besides, all the system logic is geared to a central processor tracking solution."

"I realize that." Richy's voice reflected a studied patience. "But we have to fly tomorrow, right? And we're being monitored —we need a successful tracking demonstration. Besides, these tapes can help us isolate the problem. If the program runs and we successfully track multiples, it will establish once and for all that the problem is not in the radar but in the computer or software. We can program these same algorithms to run on the central processor and—"

"Oh no you don't!" Hauser, who had been eavesdropping on the conversation between the pair, now asserted his rights. "Not on my fucking computer!"

They were interrupted by a loud beating on the door and muffled voices raised in profane demand for immediate entry. Realizing he had inadvertently set the latch when he slammed the door against the wind, Richy sprang up to release it. "What the hell, it's Raunch and Paunch," he announced, as two beleaguered forms in hooded parkas swept in on another blast of sand-drenched air. "I thought you gave them the day off."

"I thought I did, too." Hanson watched the pair remove their parka hoods and shake off the loose sand. "You chose to spend your first day off in five weeks with us? We're deeply touched."

"We ain't staying." The smaller of the two spoke with a Brooklyn accent through teeth stained brown with tobacco. The Sperry technician, formerly known as "Brownsville" after the rough-and-tumble Brooklyn district where he was spawned and spent his formative years, had been renicknamed by Hanson after he teamed up with his much plumper sidekick. "Raunch" fell somewhat short of doing justice to the sleazy stories favored by the dark, wiry little technician, whose repertoire consisted of only the most graphic, humor being incidental. He seemed to have an inexhaustible supply. Llewellyn, who grimaced along with the others during the frequent performances, couldn't remember hearing the same story twice. Raunch's real name was Jules Berger. He had changed it legally to "Julius Bergstrom" to circumvent the Saudi screening of support personnel rosters for Jewish names.

"Paunch" was his inseparable companion and greatest fan. While the others groaned at the little man's stories, Frank Waterhouse belly-laughed and applauded unabashedly. An affable Texan transplanted to California, where he had hired in with Northrop as a field engineer, Paunch had retained his taste for country and western music, which he inflicted on the others with a stentorian voice that was usually off-key and a battered guitar, played badly. Richy's own taste ran to classical; he wouldn't have relished the country renditions even if delivered with perfect pitch. Still, entertainment was scarce in Arabia and the incongruous pair provided comic relief from the humdrum diet of support work. His own appellation for the two, "Corn and Porn," had finished a close second to Hanson's.

"We're here to meet the Persian broad," Raunch continued in his Brownsville gutterese, "and kinda—you know—welcome her aboard."

"Ha!" bellowed Hauser. "Some welcoming committee. One of your raunchy stories will shock the fucking pants off her."

"Exactly what I had in mind," the little man responded, grinning obscenely at Hauser. His partner felt compelled to explain.

"We have this little bet, see? About the new lady engineer. We figured we'd come over and get introduced and get the bet settled. Julie, here—," he glanced amusedly at his diminutive sidekick, "is positive she'll turn out to be a living doll. He don't know what dogs they are, these female engineers. I've met a whole bunch of different ones, and they was all dogs."

"Not this one." Raunch shook his head emphatically from side to side. "My horoscope's never wrong. On today's date I'm slated to meet a gorgeous Pisces. Who else could it be?"

"You really believe that astrology shit?" Hauser laughed derisively. "Paunch is right. She's sure to be a dog. How much you betting? I'd like a piece of that action."

"Twenty bucks?" The Sperry technician extended his hand. The other seized it. "You're on."

Raunch pulled himself up to his full five feet five, smiling craftily. "What you don't know is, I already seen her."

"What? How—?" Hauser sensed that he had somehow been had—suckered into betting against a sure thing.

"He means in his fantasies," Paunch explained. "Julie is always fantasizing. He's screwed half the movie stars in Hollywood."

"This wasn't no fucking fantasy." Raunch sounded defensive. "It was a bony-fide dream. I seen her face in this dream, see? And dreams don't lie. Ask any brain doc, that's what they'll tell yez. Right, Hanson?"

The blond engineering manager ignored the question. He had a sinking feeling things were already getting out of hand.

"Now look, all of you. Miss Razmari could be walking through that door any minute now. And you're talking about her as if she were some kind of common tramp. You've all been briefed on Islamic women. They're not like American broads—they've led sheltered lives and haven't been exposed to crude goons like you. And they're not used to being ogled. So for Christ sake don't leer at her like you were mentally taking her clothes off. And watch your language. That goes double for you, Hauser. And you, Raunch—none of your stories, not even the one-liners. Especially not the one-liners. I know how hard up you guys are, but try not to take it out on some poor, defenseless native girl."

From the back of the room, where he was pouring coffee, Llewellyn applauded Hanson's speech loudly. He had been listening to the conversation with an amused expression on his face. Now for the first time he entered in.

"Right on, Hanson—protector of Islamic womanhood. And anyway—," he now addressed himself to the others, "that bet of yours is ludicrous."

"Whaddaya mean?" Raunch's little black eyes darted defensively in his direction.

"Dog or nondog, how will you decide? You're all so sex starved, anything wearing a skirt will look good to you. You might as well pay Raunch off right now."

"Hey, he's right." Hauser glanced at the others. "We gotta have an impartial judge. What about Hanson? He was the last one to go on leave. He'll be the most objective." Raunch and Paunch quickly voiced their affirmation.

"Oh, no!" Hanson protested as Richy smirked. "I'm not getting involved in any such asinine—" He was interrupted by the sound of a vehicle screeching to a stop outside the Quonset hut. Raunch led the rush for the tiny window.

A covered jeep was parked in front of the door, its occupants not yet visible. A tall man with a mustache wearing a Saudi Air Force uniform unfolded himself from the cramped confines of the jeep's interior and walked around to the other side.

"It's Colonel Foo-ad," yelped the excited Raunch. "What's he, her bodyguard?"

"That'd be like a fox watching the chickens," laughed Hauser.

"Shh!" hissed Paunch, elbowing in for a better view. "She's getting out!"

"I don't believe it." Hauser's voice sounded almost reverent. Richy found himself at the window, craning his neck along with the others. He had been halfway expecting a heavily veiled, dark-gowned figure resembling the Bedouin women encountered on his infrequent trips into the city, and was totally unprepared for what he saw extending through the open door of the jeep—a pair of shapely legs in designer jeans over high-heeled leather boots. The balance of the skintight Calvin Kleins proved to be filled out just as nicely, as Miss Razmari emerged into the dust-streaked sunlight, her hair bound up in a brightly colored scarf wound several times around her head for protection against the blowing sand. Her loose-fitting blue denim vest, left unbuttoned over a tightly tucked white blouse, did little to hide the ample bosoms beneath. Richy could not make out the face, still in shadow. Then she closed the jeep door and turned.

"It's her! Jesus, it's her!" Raunch blanched and looked like he might pass out.

Hauser emitted a low whistle. "What a honey!"

"We don't need no judge for that." Paunch reached for his wallet and extracted a greenback. "Here you go, pal. It's worth it."

He handed the bill to his awestruck partner, who accepted it, still looking dazed. "I got goose bumps—look at my fucking arm!"

"Knock it off, you creeps, they're coming in." Hanson moved toward the door. "Get away from the window and try to act civilized."

Colonel Fuad burst through the door first, Miss Razmari in his wake. Richy felt he would never get used to the reverse etiquette that placed men ahead of women in this topsy-turvy Arab world.

"Ah, good morning, Colonel Fuad." Hanson disliked the pompous officer, but tried not to show it in his greeting. The colonel was his official interface with the Saudi Air Force, and good relations were important, especially with his project problem ridden and behind schedule. Saluting him wordlessly, Colonel Fuad walked stiffly to the front of the room, as the young lady paused just inside the door, uncertain of what to do. Hanson smiled at her reassuringly, and she smiled back.

Standing in front of Hanson's desk with his back to the small blackboard, Colonel Fuad removed a folded sheet of paper from his pocket and proceeded to read from it in a strong voice that reflected a good command of English—British English, not American. His manner was formal, his expression deadly serious. The man doesn't have a funny bone in his body, thought Richy.

"Mister Hanson, and other members of the American support group, allow me to present Miss Roxana Razmari, who has been assigned to work as a member of your group for the duration of your stay in our country. Miss Razmari is a well-educated and highly qualified computer expert who holds the degrees of bachelor of science and master of science in computer sciences. Because of Miss Razmari's qualifications and the need for experienced personnel to continue the flight support effort when your group retires, our government has waived the restriction against a woman working in the same office with men. Though not a native of our country, Miss Razmari is to be regarded as a representative of our government in the E-3A integration effort. We consider the transfer of knowledge to our representative highly important, and you are instructed to cooperate with her and assist her in every way possible. Are there any questions?"

With only a brief pause, suggesting to Richy that he really wasn't in the mood to answer any, Colonel Fuad folded up his speech and repocketed it. "Very well. If I can be of any further assistance in this matter, please notify me." Another formal salute and he was striding toward the door, for the first time deigning to glance in the direction of the object of his prepared speech. The twitching of his thin mustache and faint expression of distaste, looking down his long aquiline nose, left no doubt in Richy's mind about the colonel's displeasure with her attire. Then he was gone, and she was left alone in their midst.

She had removed her head covering, and her dark auburn hair hung loosely at her shoulders, framing a face devoid of makeup —that needed none. Hanson, nearest to her, extended his hand and introduced himself, as the others crowded around. She shook hands enthusiastically and smilingly as she was introduced. Richy was last. He was impressed with the strength of her grip and the way she looked directly into his eyes. This was no shrinking violet, no shy, sequestered Arab's daughter. This one had definitely been around. What was it in the dark eyes that sparkled so? The promise of intelligence, certainly. And the hint of something slightly mischievous?

"I want very much to get to know all of you," she assured them in a lilting soprano. There was a faint, undefinable accent, but no trace of British in her otherwise perfect English. "Please call me Roxana. And please don't give me any special treatment. I just want to be one of you, a part of your team. Please try to forget that I am a woman."

"That," piped up Raunch, "ain't going to be so fucking easy." Hanson glared at him, but Roxana Razmari took it in stride, joining in the general laughter without so much as a blush or downcast eye.

CHAPTER 3

When the phone rang, David Llewellyn was sleeping so soundly that it took a while to penetrate his consciousness. It had been a long and frustrating day. Impatient to get on with the undercover assignment, he had risen at dawn to drive the hundred miles to Tel Aviv and check in at the American embassy. The moment he had set foot in the door, he knew he had made a mistake.

In the process of relocating to Jerusalem, the embassy had proved to be a shambles, offices stacked high with packing boxes and furniture crated for shipping, their occupants nowhere to be found. Of the people he had planned on meeting, he had been able to cross only two names off his list. Weary and frustrated after the drive back through heavy traffic, he had resigned himself to the prospect that his detective work would have to wait until the entire cast was reassembled in its new Jerusalem location. He had stretched out his long frame on the bed, still in his street clothes, for a few minutes' rest, and promptly fallen asleep.

The staccato jing-jing of the telephone was coming from the ambulance that hurtled through his dream, the vehicle's side panel emblazoned with a blue Star of David in place of the accustomed red cross. Who was the casualty inside the ambulance; himself, perhaps? He awoke not knowing, still faintly disturbed by the dream and its possible significance.

"I suppose I'm the last person you expected to hear from," answered a melodious and vaguely familiar voice to his sleep-befogged "hello." It took several seconds to register. "Hello, are you still there?" inquired the solicitous feminine voice. Daniella's voice.

"Yes—yes, I'm here. I—must have dozed off."

"At nine in the evening?" Her giggle was a pure delight. "Mr. Llewellyn, that will never do for an envoy. Much of the real business of diplomacy is conducted after dark."

He pondered her meaning, his brain just beginning to come

around. "You're right. I didn't really expect to hear from you again, after——"

"After the way I treated you. I know. You have been on my conscience. I'm calling to apologize. And to try to make amends."

"No apology necessary." What did she mean by "making amends"? "Did you have your——," he searched for a diplomatic way of phrasing it, "your private final scene with Martin?"

"Yes, thanks to you. It was a much shorter scene than I had envisioned," she added hastily. "I turned out to be the one who walked out. But not until I'd gotten a few things off my chest."

"Good for you. He had it coming."

"Yes. Well, that's a closed chapter." The initial note of gaiety in her voice had given way to one of resignation. She hurried on. "I said some terrible things to you, unfair things. What must you think of me? I had no right to take my feelings out on you."

"Forget it. Your reaction was perfectly understandable. I was ——in the way."

"No," she said, "I want you to know that I'm not really like that——I wasn't myself. Please try to forget my behavior and let me start fresh."

"It's forgotten." He was wide awake now and already relishing the prospect of a fresh start with the girl with the musical voice. And the lyrical name. Daniella.

"Tomorrow is the Sabbath," she continued. "I know you are interested in seeing the Old City. I thought I would volunteer to be your guide if you wanted to spend some time exploring. There are places off the beaten track," she added by way of inducement, "that tourists seldom find."

"Splendid!" He needed no inducement other than her company. Besides, it would take his mind off the irritating delay in getting on with his time-urgent assignment. "But I have to spend an hour or so at the embassy here in the morning."

"And I at the synagogue. Shall we say noon, then? I can come by the embassy."

"Noon it is. This is awfully good of you, Daniella." The name felt good, rolling off his tongue.

"Not at all, Mr. Llewellyn. Consider it part of my atonement."

"Please call me David. Mr. Llewellyn is my father."

She laughed. "Your father is not the U.S. envoy. In the diplomatic service, protocol must be adhered to, mustn't it? Until tomorrow, then——Mr. Llewellyn?"

"Till tomorrow, Miss Zadik," he answered with mock formality. As he hung up the phone, he resolved that by lunchtime tomorrow their relationship would be on a first-name basis.

He had promised the ambassador that he would look in on the new embassy and make sure that the move was progressing smoothly. The relocated U.S. embassy was on Rachel Imenu Street, a wide and stately tree-lined boulevard in New Jerusalem. The elaborate four-story mansion had been built by the Netherlands in the mid-1970s as their embassy, the Dutch architect using rough-hewn blocks of native limestone to construct the most imposing edifice on embassy row. Under the threat of an Arab oil embargo in 1980, the Netherlands had reluctantly packed up and moved to Tel Aviv. The United States had just negotiated a long-term lease agreement beneficial to both countries.

As David mounted the stone stairs leading to the entry facade, he filled his lungs with the crisp, pine-scented air of the Judean hills. It was a glorious winter morning. At the top of the staircase he turned to look back and discovered the holy city spread out below in breathtaking panorama. The sun's rays were just beginning to penetrate the lower reaches of the wakening city, weaving a magical tapestry of light and shadow, the uneven texture and hilliness of the walled dominions heightened by the three-dimensional effect of the horizontal light. A valley running north and south through the middle of the city still slept in almost total darkness, while the higher ground to either side blazed forth in brilliant sunlight.

His eye was caught and held by a dazzling halo of light near the eastern wall, where a burnished golden dome thrust upward from a wide, elevated plateau much higher than the surrounding terrain. It must be the Dome of the Rock he had heard so much about. Site of the ancient stone monolith sacred to three religions. To its right, a smaller silver dome glistened like a companion piece in the same bejeweled setting. That would be the famous Mosque of Omar, third most holy in all of Islam, after those in Mecca and Medina.

The spectacle held him spellbound, the excitement of discovery and impending exploration coursing through him. It was almost eerie, the sense of suspended animation created by the rising sun. He watched the featureless void in the low eastern sector of the city come to life as spires and rooftops and jewel-bright windows were popped onto the canvas by the unseen artist with the deftest of brush strokes.

With an effort he tore himself away, continuing on. Pushing through the revolving door, he was pleased to see the guard on duty at his station inside. The man offered a cheery "Good morning, sir," as he checked David's credentials. But the entry foyer proved to be a magpie's nest of crates and packing boxes and furniture lying helter-skelter, the cleanup crew nowhere to be seen. He checked his watch. They should have been on duty an hour ago. He walked back toward the guard.

"I expect you're looking for the furniture movers." The guard pointed toward the staircase, leading to the basement. "The other gentleman has them in tow, working down on the lower level."

"What other gentleman?" David hadn't expected anyone else. The embassy was officially closed until Monday, when most of the new personnel were due to arrive.

"Mr. Abernathy, sir. He was already here when I opened up this morning."

Of course. The intelligence man. He would have to see to his special security equipment and coding apparatus. David had only just met the man on the previous day's trip to Tel Aviv and already disliked him. If he thought he was taking over the cleanup crew, he could think again. He took the steps down the basement stairwell two at a time.

Though he had never set foot in it before, the basement of the new U.S. embassy had an all-too-familiar look about it. Its uncarpeted hallways and windowless offices were typical of the territory allocated by embassies to the ever-expanding enterprises of security and clandestine operations. This netherworld he now trod would soon be the domain of Consular Operations, the intelligence-gathering arm of the Department of State.

The coldness and starkness of the surroundings were most appropriate, he reflected. A twinge of the old feeling of revulsion stole over him. It was a part of his past he hated to be reminded of, his erstwhile role in the clandestine world that operated between these walls. An episode in his life that he had sought to bury, along with Katherine, in his bitterness toward the unfeeling, faceless organization he held responsible for her death. But it refused to stay buried; it had come back to claim him again. Because he couldn't say no to a president who was also a lifelong friend.

It was easy to find the furniture crew's whereabouts. An un-

godly racket was coming from a large office just off the main
corridor, with Abernathy's voice leading the uproar.

"This way, this way, turn the corner. Easy, easy! Don't drop
it, you bloody wogs!" Four bedraggled Arab youths struggled
and grunted under a large crate that must have contained a heavy
safe of some sort, from the way they were sweating.

From Abernathy's manner of speech, David had at first
thought him English, but had subsequently learned that he was a
native American formerly attached to MI-6, the British Secret
Service, at various locations in the Middle East. Odd, how some
people unconsciously picked up the inflection and idiom of new
surroundings—often the most reprehensible of each, David reflected.

"No need to talk to them that way," he admonished, as the
hapless movers prepared to set down their unwieldy cargo.

"Oh, hello, Llewellyn." Abernathy barely looked at him.
"Who, the bloody wogs? Don't worry about them. They don't
understand a bloody word of English. Or much of anything else.
Careful! Ease it down, ease it down! If it cracks open, I'll have
your backsides flayed bloody!"

Fearful of having hands or fingers trapped underneath, the
porters dropped the load and sprang backwards. The heavy safe
fell the last foot or so with an impact that shook the whole building and splintered the wooden cross ties on the bottom of the
crate. The Cons Op man swore loudly, the youthful Arabs looking at him apprehensively, dusting their hands and breathing
hard. They were a motley lot, wearing sandals on their feet and
dressed in rags, remnants of T-shirts and nondescript jeans.

"In Tel Aviv you get decent labor—Jews, who understand
English. Here you get wogs!" Abernathy shook his head disgustedly. "It's got to go farther back, all the way against the wall."
He gestured with his hands, then went through a pantomime of
lifting the safe and moving it against the wall. "Like this, you
bloody dimwits!"

One of the group, probably the foreman, spoke a few words of
Arabic and gripped the bottom of the crate. Reluctantly, the
others joined him. Together, they wrestled the ponderous object
into place.

"I'd like my crew back now, if you don't mind." David tried
to keep the animosity out of his voice.

"All in good time. Security first, you know. I have some

crypto equipment and a few file cabinets left. After that they're all yours."

Abernathy stood with his hands on his hips, a supercilious smile on his face, awaiting David's reaction. His tone made it abundantly clear that he wasn't taking orders from the envoy. As the number two man in the embassy, Llewellyn outranked him. But the Cons Op man reported directly to the ambassador. Like the organization he represented, he made his own rules. This little episode would come under the heading of putting one of the lesser diplomats in his place. David made a quick decision.

"Okay, keep half the crew until you're finished, but make it fast. There's a huge stack of furniture in the foyer that has to be moved and I only have until noon." He tapped the foreman and the youth next to him on the shoulder and motioned. "You two come with me." "Wog one" and "wog two" followed him obediently down the hall, only too happy to escape from the clutches of the abusive English-American. David could picture the intelligence man standing there with his mouth agape, but he didn't look back.

Grainger, the office manager, had promised to arrive by mid-morning with a room-by-room master plan. David set his crew to breaking open crates and concentrated on finding the ambassador's furniture. By 10:30 there was no sign of Grainger, and the two-man crew had barely made a dent in the vast pile of crates and boxes. Abernathy was taking his own sweet time about returning the others.

When the office manager walked in shortly after eleven, David was fuming. He had Grainger call the moving company for reinforcements, then checked off the ambassador's furniture against the master list. By noon, the ambassador's office was at least presentable, but the rest of the building was a shambles. He gave his subordinate some hurried last-minute instructions, then dashed back to the foyer. Daniella was already there, in a white sheath dress that knocked his eyes out. And she had company—Abernathy—fawning over her and acting as though they were old friends.

"You didn't tell me who your 'nooner' was with, Llewellyn," he whined, with a leer that matched the suggestiveness in his voice. "No wonder you were in such a rush."

David ignored him, taking Daniella's hand and welcoming her to the new American embassy. "I'd show you around, but things are in a bit of a mess, as you can see. Next week would be better."

"Oh, I've been here before, several times. We have quite a lot of business with the Dutch."

"And about to get in Dutch again, by the look of it." Abernathy chuckled at his own witticism. David gave him a sharp look. The obnoxious little man just did not know when to back off.

Daniella took his arm. "Shall we go?"

They walked out through the entrance and down the stairs. "I detest that man," Daniella whispered, "and everything he stands for."

So she knew about his job. "How do you come to know him?" he asked.

"Through Martin. It's rather a long story. Can we talk about something more pleasant?"

"Sure," he agreed. "Like where we're going for lunch. All that unpacking has given me an appetite. Not to mention a thirst."

"I have a recommendation. Fink's Bar. It's a Jerusalem institution, one of the must places to visit."

"Fink's Bar," he repeated dubiously. "Not a very auspicious name. What's so special about it?"

"It's an authentic English pub, started years ago by David Rothschild, who has the distinction of having turned Dr. Kissinger down when he wanted to take it over for a private party during one of his shuttle diplomacy visits. And," she provided the persuader, "it's one of the few places in town where you can get a drink before sundown on Saturday."

"That settles it." He grinned and squeezed the bare arm clinging to his. "Fink, here we come."

Out of the corner of his eye David saw a drapery move in the foyer window of the embassy. Part of a head appeared, then disappeared again behind the drape. The Cons Op agent was still observing their departure.

The afternoon sun was warm against his skin, complementing the glow that he felt inside. A glow produced only in part by the good malt scotch. Fink's Bar had proved to be an effective icebreaker, though Daniella had disdained the alcoholic offerings, favoring the strong black coffee. On account of the Sabbath, he assumed, remembering the wine that had flowed at their luncheon with Martin. For Daniella, alcohol would have been super-fluous, anyway. She was lively and animated, caught up in the excitement of showing the new American envoy her city, ac-quainting him with its fascinating history and incomparable heri-tage. He was greatly impressed with her knowledge and had been surprised to discover that she was as well versed in the Muslim and Christian background as in the Jewish.

As one who fancied himself a student of history, he had dis-covered that he was woefully deficient in his knowledge of the Holy Land. He had always thought of the Crusades as a period from the dim, distant past, an era almost too remote to contem-plate. She was amused at his observation.

"The Crusaders were—how do you say in America—'John-nie-come-latelies.' They were preceded by the Jews, the Baby-lonians, the Persians, the Greeks, the Syrians, the Romans, the Byzantines, and the Muslims. By the eleventh century, when the first Christian Crusade began, the city founded by David had been conquered no less than a dozen times, most of the con-querors believing themselves 'Crusaders.' The Temple of Solo-mon had been rebuilt twice before its final destruction by the Romans."

Her eyes turned sad. "It will never be rebuilt. That's why we cling so desperately to its only remnant, the Wailing Wall—the western rampart of the Temple Mount. It proved too sturdy for even the Romans to destroy. Like the Jews, themselves. Conquered, burned out, banished, and enslaved over the three thousand year history of the city of David, we have always come back."

He was reminded of the Israeli foreign minister's eleventh commandment. Daniella's history lesson had driven the message home. It was more than a people's instinct for survival. It was a profound belief in their destiny and indestructibility as a people, springing from their faith in one benevolent superbeing.

Impulsively, and he was sure, unconsciously, she had touched his arm several times during her impassioned recital of the attri-butes of her beloved city. At one point, her hand came to rest casually on top of his. The intimacy of her touch excited him. Quickly, and just as casually, he had covered it with his other hand. She had not withdrawn it. Now they stood side by side holding hands unabashedly in the sunlit reaches of the Jewish Quarter, mesmerized by the vista that opened up before them.

Directly ahead lay a great square paved with honey-colored stones, sloping downward toward a wide, sheer, sixty-foot cliff that rose majestically at the farther end. The western wall of the Temple Mount, atop which once stood the ancient temple, conceived by David, built by Solomon. For centuries, the traditional site of mourning for the lost temple and city of David; then, with the end of the mandate and departure of the British after World War II, inaccessible to the Jews. Until the Six Day War liberated it. Ahead to the left, a massive golden hemisphere seemed to float above the wall—the same Dome of the Rock that had captured his eye that morning from the embassy steps.

Hand in hand, they walked in silence down the slope toward the Wailing Wall. The giant square was virtually deserted, except for the area directly in front of the wall, a beehive of activity. In one corner a Bar Mitzvah was culminating in a joyful folk dance, the young boys singing gaily as they moved like a serpentine toward the exit, hands on the shoulder of the boy ahead. Hassidim in their long black robes and broad-brimmed hats were oblivious to the disturbance, standing close to the wall or leaning against it, lost in prayer. Others sat in chairs as if rooted to the spot, immobile except for their bobbing heads. A bearded rabbi in long white robes and a white yarmulke conducted a service for a small congregation from behind a portable black prayer table. Nearby, a young man and an older man stood praying under a single fringed prayer shawl, the strong family resemblance leaving little doubt that they were father and son.

As they drew nearer to the wall, David was struck by the incredible size of the individual blocks of stone that made up the massive structure. Small wonder that this wall, like the people it symbolized, was indestructible, he reflected, marveling at the manual labor it must have taken to stack the monoliths atop one another. Time had etched character into the wrinkled face of the ancient monument, corners and edges of the blocks eroded away to form deep crevices between them. Closer, now, he noticed that each crevice within arm's reach of the paved surface seemed to be stuffed full of what looked like folded or wadded bits of paper. He turned a questioning glance at his guide.

"Prayers?"

Daniella nodded. "*Kvitlachs*—petitions. They believe the Wall will carry them straight to God."

He noted her smile. "You don't believe it?"

"Oh, yes," she answered quickly, "I believe in prayer, all right. But not necessarily in special delivery."

His appreciative chuckle was answered by her own spontaneous laugh, a bright, delightful break in the reverent mood with which she had approached this hallowed shrine. They reached the bottom of the slope, where a low chain fence fringed the level quadrangle in front of the wall. Daniella turned toward him, releasing his hand.

"This is as far as we can go together. If you want to go closer, we'll have to split up. The men's entrance is there on the left. You can borrow a skullcap from the official in the booth."

A flimsy-looking fence made up of woven plastic panels separated the area immediately in front of the wall into two sectors, the larger directly ahead, the smaller to the right. For the first time it dawned on him that there were no women to be seen in the larger compound into which he had been looking. The area beyond the flimsy low fence was apparently reserved for them.

"No thanks," he answered, recapturing her hand. "I'd rather stick together. Besides, don't we have a lot more ground to cover?" His eyes sought out the golden dome, but it was blocked from view, now, by the proximity of the high wall.

She nodded, her white teeth flashing in a sudden smile. "But I was dying to see how you'd look in a yarmulke."

She led him to a pathway off to the right that ascended on a broad ramp to the base of a long flight of stairs. The stairs disappeared into an arched passageway through the wall. It was a long climb. Halfway up, the Dome of the Rock reemerged above the wall, drawing his eyes like a magnet.

Daniella followed his gaze. "Fascinating, isn't it? At the top of these stairs we will pass through a wall most sacred to the Jew and step immediately onto hallowed ground of the Arab. Their Haram-as-Sharif—Noble Sanctuary—site of the ancient rock from which the Muslims believe Muhammad ascended to heaven. The same rock on which the altar of the Temple of Solomon stood. And also the spot, many of our people believe, on which Abraham offered his son Isaac in sacrifice to show his total obedience to God."

David marveled, the significance of her words sinking in. A Biblical rock sacred to Jews and Muslims alike, pivotal in the history of the ancient world, dating back four millennia or more. His sense of anticipation made him forget the discomfort of the sudden ascent, and he quickened his pace. They reached the apex of the stairs and moved into a short, darkened tunnel through the wall, emerging into partial sunlight, shaded by a fragrant grove of pines and cyprus. It was only then that he realized how heavily he was breathing.

Daniella, showing no visible effects from the sustained climb, regarded him amusedly. "Would you like to rest for a minute?"

Sheepishly, he shook his head. "I'm fine. A little out of shape is all. Let's press on."

Through the trees they caught glimpses of the dome. Then, suddenly, they were in an open clearing and it towered over them, serene, majestic, and overpowering. For the first time he glimpsed the building in its entirety. The dome's base was a perfect octagon, its exterior emblazoned with multicolored Persian tiles in which aquamarine predominated. The effect was dazzling —a giant box inlaid with jewels and capped with gold. The Jewel Box of Islam.

But the genuine jewel was that which lay inside—the priceless rock of antiquity. Under an archway of mosaics engraved with verses from the Koran, they entered between massive bronze doors. Two rings of blue-veined marble columns with gilt capitals formed a double concentric pathway around the interior, the innermost columns supporting the mammoth dome. The outer ring was carpeted with Oriental rugs of a deep green hue, the inner with deep crimson.

"Look up," she whispered. His eyes traveled upward to the top of the dome and a breathtaking spectacle. The interior of the seventy-foot cupola was decorated with mosaics of gleaming golds and reds in intricate and interlocking Oriental patterns. Subdued light from exquisite stained glass windows set into the lower part of the dome illuminated the shimmering ceiling and filtered downward toward the rock.

"It's customary to walk clockwise around the rock," Daniella whispered, pulling on his hand.

"Wait a moment. I want to look at it first." They walked through the inner ring of pillars and peered over the low parapet.

The immense expanse of grayish brown stone covered almost the entire area beneath the dome. David stared at the ancient rock, hypnotized by it. Its scarred and chiseled features testified to numerous mutilations at the hands of its many and various custodians down through the ages, imbuing it with a sense of life of its own drawn from the countless lives lived around it. Daniella waited in silence, touched by the awe and reverence that she read in his eyes. When he came out of it, she squeezed his hand.

"Our people continued to pray here at the rock for centuries, even after the temple was destroyed. Until the Christians took over Jerusalem, under the Byzantine Empire. They considered this polluted ground and converted it to a dung heap." She smiled at his shocked reaction. "When the Muhammadans conquered Jerusalem in the eighth century and Caliph Omar searched for the site of the rock on which to build his mosque, he found it covered with dung and refuse. He was furious with the Byzantines. Some historians say he made them clean it up with their bare hands."

They moved onto the red carpet and began the traditional circumambulation of the rock, David still lost in thought. "How ironic that the Jews and their sworn enemies would both revere this same chunk of rock."

"Not only the rock, but many of the Jewish patriarchs, as well. Noah, Abraham, Moses. The Koran draws heavily on the Bible. Even Christ is revered as one of the true prophets."

"Then—then Allah is the same God—the God of the Bible, the God of the Jews!"

"Yes, of course. Allah, Elokim, Yahweh, Jehovah. All the same, all one. That is what Muslims believe. That is what the Koran teaches."

He shook his head. It was too much for him. "How can they declare holy war on a people who believe in the same God?"

"Ah, but we are still infidels, just as you Christians are. We do not believe in the true and final prophet, Muhammad—the other teachings of the Koran. And we have taken by conquest this third holiest of all the shrines of Islam. This is the ultimate insult, the desecration that cannot be forgiven."

"But I understood these grounds were administered by the Arabs, themselves—that your government relinquished its authority over this area to Muslim control."

"Yes," she answered, "that is what we agreed to soon after the Six Day War." They exited through the south portico, known as the Mecca Gate, Daniella pointing toward a building near the western boundary of the compound.

"The Supreme Muslim Council is headquartered right here on the grounds. They administer the Haram and have charge of everything, including security. But we are always blamed when something goes wrong. When an Australian fanatic set fire to the Al Aqsa Mosque in 1969 it was laid at our doorstep. As though we had planned it as a deliberate desecration."

They walked southward down a flight of steps toward the plain-looking rectangular building whose sole external distinction was the silver dome at its farther end—striking, but only half the size of its golden companion that spanned the venerable rock. The Al Aqsa Mosque—the legendary Mosque of Omar. "Only Muslims are allowed inside," Daniella explained, "unlike the Dome of the Rock, which is open to all visitors. But we can look in from the outside if you'd like."

It was not yet time for the midafternoon prayer and there were few worshippers in the compound. They passed the ablution fountain where several Arab men busied themselves, perched on stone seats, removing shoes and headdresses and carefully bathing hands, heads, and feet prior to entering the mosque. Standing within a few yards of the entrance, they peered inside through Gothic arches in the marble facade that covered the front of the mosque. The high-vaulted ceiling was supported by parallel rows of stone arches that reminded David of Roman aqueducts he had seen in parts of Europe, except that these arches were buttressed by exquisite marble columns that gleamed in the reflected light from the side windows. Hundreds of Oriental carpets of a deep mulberry shade covered the floor. The interior seemed immense, the scattering of kneeling occupants lost in its vastness. He commented on this, and Daniella smiled.

"On holy days the Aqsa Mosque is packed to overflowing. It seems hard to believe. The entire compound is filled with pilgrims"—she motioned toward the paved expanse surrounding the Dome of the Rock—"all on their knees, facing south toward Mecca. They come from all over the world. But the leaders will not come, the heads of state and royalty of the Arab countries. They have sworn an oath not to pray here so long as they must get Israeli approval to enter Jerusalem. Only Sadat broke that pledge and prayed here. They could not forgive him for that. They killed him for it."

He looked at her in disbelief.

"Oh, yes, Mr. Llewellyn—David. I can assure you that was the main reason. This spot you are standing on still is capable of arousing passions and hatreds as violent as those that launched the Crusades. For forty centuries this land has been fought over. Jews and Arabs continue to die. There is no sign that it will ever stop."

There was no bitterness in her voice, only sadness and resignation. He took both of her hands in his, staring into her moistened eyes.

"You don't hate them, do you? The Arabs killed your father, but there's no hatred inside you!"

"Look again, Mr. Llewellyn. You have to look much deeper. My hatred is reserved, you see, for those who deserve it. The fanatics, the terrorists, the schemers and instigators in the Arab countries who will resort to anything to drive us from our land. But these pathetic souls?"

She freed one hand and swept it toward the ragged procession of worshippers entering and departing the mosque. "Just look at them. They are such a pitiful lot, dressed in rags, for the most part, destitute. Many have lost everything, including their pride and self-respect. Even hope. They seem to have nothing left— except their religion. How can you hate them, feel anything but pity for them?"

"Pity for the Arabs? From a sabra?"

"You think we are without compassion, just because we were born and educated here?" The arched brows over the pensive eyes made her face even more beautiful. "Do you know where the name 'sabra' comes from? It is the fruit of the cactus, hard and spiny on the outside, but soft on the inside."

Impulsively, ever so lightly, he kissed the petulant lips. "This one feels pretty soft on the outside, too. You're an amazing woman, Daniella. You've opened my eyes today, made me see what's at the center of things here. Better still, made me feel it."

"Then you must be a feeling person, a caring person." She kept her face close to his. He could feel her warm breath against his lips. "How different you are from Martin. It wasn't possible to share such things with Martin. He was always so—independent. And restless." Tears came into her eyes, and she bit her lip. "Why do I keep bringing him up, why can't I get him out of my system?"

He put his arms around her and she leaned against him, oblivious to the disapproving stares of Muslims entering and exiting the mosque. "You know what I'm doing," she whispered into his ear. "Just what I said I wouldn't do. I'm using you. I'm using you to get over him."

"Shh!" he whispered back, savoring the feel of her vibrant young body against him, more than a little intoxicated by the fragrance of her hair in his nostrils. "So what are you supposed to do when you lose the person closest to you? Drop out of life? Shun people? Crawl into your shell? Take it from me, it doesn't work. I tried it."

She leaned back in his arms and looked into his face. "Who was it? Your wife?"

He nodded. "She was killed two years ago. I've never stopped missing her."

She gave him a little final squeeze and extricated herself, taking his hand. "Suddenly I'm feeling a little tired, David. We'd better put off the rest of the tour until another day. Would you take me home, please? We can get a taxi at the Damascus Gate."

Daniella lived alone in one of the newer high-rise apartment buildings that dominated the New Jerusalem skyline in massive clusters to the north and west of the Old City. "Cliff City," thought David, as the taxi approached the hulking forest of towers and was swallowed up in the total shadow of a jungle all but impenetrable to the sun. The contrast with Old Jerusalem was jarring, reminding him of another city of cliffs that had encroached on his boyhood home in Queens, New York, when block upon block of identical twelve-story apartment buildings sprang up to alter forever the stately character of the Forest Hills landscape.

The taxi halted in front of the unimposing entrance to one of the carbon copy buildings. Would she invite him up, or should he invite himself? He wasn't ready to be separated just yet, to lose the special feeling of closeness engendered by the incomparable afternoon in her company. She must have felt the same, for when he paid the taxi driver and sent him on his way there was no objection from her. She took his hand. No words were spoken as they walked together toward the entrance. He felt a bond between them, a tacit understanding. He opened the door.

"I'm on the tenth floor. I usually walk up—for the exercise."

"Fine," he said, restraining a groan.

"But let's take the elevator. We're both tired from walking."

Relieved, he waited with her until the elevator droned to a stop, then held the door open for a heavyset, elderly woman who had been waiting ahead of them. She lumbered into it, then turned and eyed them sharply, a look of disapproval written across her heavy-jowled countenance.

"Shalom, Geveret Shmuel." Daniella managed a smile, not letting go of his hand. The woman returned a "shalom" that was more of a grunt than a meeting, then looked away. She got off at the third floor.

"Yenta!" Daniella giggled as the elevator picked up speed.

"She's the apartment busybody and chief gossip. By tomorrow we'll be an item all over the neighborhood."

"Will that embarrass you?"

"Not in the least. I do as I please. She doesn't know who you are, so there can't be any diplomatic repercussions."

In front of apartment 1023 she took the latchkey from her purse and unlocked the door. He held it open and she started in ahead of him. Closing the door, he heard her little scream of alarm, and she ran back, throwing herself into his arms.

"Oh, David! Somebody's broken in! My beautiful apartment!"

Over her shoulder he could see an overturned lamp on the floor. He latched the door behind him. "Wait right here until I make sure they've gone."

The apartment was a complete shambles. It had been thoroughly ransacked—furniture upended, cushions, articles from shelves, and drawer contents strewn about by an impatient and extraordinarily untidy intruder. There was no sound and no other sign of the culprit. He checked the bedroom, bathroom, and small kitchenette to make sure before returning.

"Whoever it was has gone. The windows to the fire escape are locked from the inside. They must have had a key. Or picked the lock."

She shook her head in bewilderment. "I can't imagine who—or why. There's hardly a thing of any real value, except to me." Still shaken and clinging to his arm, she walked back with him into the smallish living room, surveying the wreckage in disbelief. A shiver ran through her.

He patted her hand reassuringly. "It's all right. They won't come back now." He removed his jacket and wrapped it around her shoulders, then set about righting the furniture. "Why don't you see if anything's missing? Then we'd better call the police."

She made a hurried check. The small, antiquated television set was still on its stand. She found her meager collection of jewelry intact in its padded leather case among the objects scattered about the bedroom floor. A quick inspection of the kitchen produced a wooden tableware chest that had been knocked to the floor, her grandmother's initialed silverplate still inside. Daniella came back to the living room and collapsed into the easy chair he had just set back on its feet.

"Nothing seems to have been taken. Why would anyone have done this?"

"They must have been looking for something." He sat down

on the floor next to her chair. "Something to do with your job in the Foreign Office, perhaps? You must handle classified material. Do you bring papers or work from the office home with you?"

She shook her head. "Nothing classified. It's not allowed. The Foreign Minister is very strict about that. If we have something to finish up, we work late at the office."

He rose and picked up the telephone book from the table next to her chair. It was printed in Hebrew. He handed her the book. "I can handle the numbers okay, it's the letters that throw me. How do you spell 'police' in Hebrew?"

"Here—give me that!" She shook her head in feigned disgust. "An envoy to Israel who can't even read Hebrew!"

As she looked up the number, he pushed the telephone toward her. He was about to hand her the receiver when her hand stopped him.

"David, why don't we wait until morning? We're both very tired, and if they send someone over tonight, we'll have to wait for them and answer a lot of questions. It doesn't seem so urgent now. After all, nothing was taken."

He nodded his agreement. "I'll help you get the rest of this mess cleaned up."

He finished the living room while she tidied up the kitchen. She returned looking much brighter. "Only two dishes and one glass were broken. I thought it would be much worse."

She looked over the living room, nodding approvingly. "I wasn't sure where things belonged," he apologized. "I'm afraid I put them back just any old way."

"It's fine. In fact, I think you've improved it." She stood facing him, her warm brown eyes filled with gratitude. "I—I don't know what I would have done if you hadn't been here. It's sweet of you to stay and help."

He smiled and patted her hand. "Think nothing of it. We've still got work to do. The bedroom is a total wreck."

The mattress lay upended on the bedroom floor amid a jumble of twisted blankets, clothing from the closet, and articles from bureau drawers. Daniella groaned. "I can't face it in these tight clothes. Turn your back for a minute, please, David."

He followed instructions. But the mirror on the vanity in front of him made it difficult to avoid peeking. A velvet smooth, lightly tanned back was revealed to him with a patch of white where the bra had been removed. As she reached for a robe in the closet, a plump white breast with a pink eye peeked out around one side of the tawny back. The stirring in his groin reminded him of how long it had been since he had gone to bed with a woman.

"That's better." She heaved a loud sigh of relief. "Now you can look."

She had slipped into a pale green velour robe with a belt that hugged it tightly to her slender waist. In her bare feet she was inches shorter, looking suddenly petite and vulnerable. He had the momentary sensation of scooping her up and feeling her feather-light in his arms.

"Shall we get on with it?" Her self-conscious smile made him realize that he had been staring.

She knelt on the floor and began picking up the perfume bottles and cosmetics scattered about. He knelt beside her. "What shall I collect?"

"Why don't you start with stockings and lingerie. They go back in the dresser."

On all fours, he moved about the floor, accumulating a little pile of sheer hosiery and undergarments. He was about to ask her how she wanted them folded when the absurdity of thc scene struck her and she burst into a fit of uncontrollable laughter.

"The new American envoy to Israel picking up the traces of his new job," she stammered, gasping for breath. "Oh! Ow! If I only had a picture of this. What the newspapers wouldn't give for it!"

Somewhat ruefully, he joined in the laughter at his own expense, sensing the ridiculousness of his appearance. "Here," she chortled, "let me show you what to do with those."

She crawled in front of him and began folding the garments into neat little squares. The robe was loose about her shoulders and he found himself looking down at a very inviting patch of bare skin below the nape of her neck. Unable to resist, he bent down and pressed his lips to it.

"Oh!" He felt a shiver run down her spine, but she didn't protest or pull away. He moved his lips farther down her back, sliding them over the silky skin. A low moan escaped her. He kept going, his hands loosening the belt of the robe, allowing the movement of his head to continue down her back, pushing the collar of the robe ahead of it and stripping it from her shoulders. His tongue thrust out to sample the taste of her skin and she moaned again, her legs collapsing gradually until her stomach pressed on the floor. His lips reached a small indentation at the base of her spine, his tongue darting hungrily into it. With a little squeal, she rolled over on her back, the robe falling away completely.

Her eyes were closed and she was moving sinuously, a horizontal belly dancer. She certainly had the body for it—he stared in fascination as he unbuttoned his shirt and stripped off his trousers. In a single, perfectly coordinated motion he fell to his knees as she reached up for him. Then the belly dancing began again, slowly at first, sliding him exquisitely back and forth within her. Unbidden, his own pelvis joined in, picking up the rhythm and adding velocity. The beat increased, building to a frenzied pitch. The sensation of total pleasure was irresistible, overpowering.

Her sobbing brought him back. A strange kind of sobbing—her eyes were dry. And then she was smiling. And kissing him. And holding him tightly against her, so that he couldn't withdraw. As if he ever wanted to.

It was dark before he reached the embassy. He paid off the taxi driver and started toward the rear of the building to retrieve his car, then changed his mind. Might as well check on the progress of the unpacking crew, as long as he was here.

The guard was just going off duty, setting the locks and alarm. He reminded the envoy to depart by way of the rear exit. David inquired about his assistant, Grainger.

"Left half an hour ago, sir. Everyone's out except Mr. Abernathy."

The mass of furniture in the vestibule had melted away, but its residue remained, an unsightly pile of fractured packing crates and wrapping littering one end of the giant waiting room. He cursed aloud into the echoing emptiness. He had left instructions to stack the debris in the rear of the building, out of sight.

He trudged up the semicircular staircase that rose gracefully from the vestibule to inspect his own office on the second floor, feeling the tiredness in the calves of his legs. His footsteps echoed eerily in the deserted, dimly lighted corridor. Well, at least Grainger had gotten something right. His furniture was all there, arranged as he had directed. He collapsed into the comfortable leather swivel chair that had followed him halfway round the world and spun around to survey the night view from his office window.

Lights sparkled up at him from below in the direction of the

Old City. Could it have been only this morning that he had watched the sun's first rays set it on fire? It seemed more like days ago than hours. His mind began to retrace the day's adventures, re-absorbed into the richness of experience and spectacle. He was back under the spell of the City of David—under her spell.

"Back so soon? The first date must have been a bust." He started, wheeling around in the chair. Where had the man come from? He had heard no footsteps in the hall and suspected Abernathy of deliberately sneaking up on him. Ignoring his icy stare, the Cons Op agent settled himself on one corner of the desk, tugging distractedly on an ostentatiously oversized meerschaum pipe.

"Look, Abernathy, let's get something straight right off. What I do outside the embassy is strictly private and none of your affair. Do I make myself clear?"

"Oh, yes, perfectly clear." The intelligence man pursed his lips and bobbed his head slowly up and down. "A predictable reaction. The same one I got from your predecessor when I tried to warn him."

"You warned Martin? About what?"

"About his private life not being as private as he liked to think. About the danger of consorting with a known agent of the Mossad."

"Agent of the—what? You can't mean—Daniella?"

Abernathy nodded, a glint of triumph in his eyes at the discomfiture his revelation was causing the other. "It's true. I have the proof. Daniella Zadik is an agent of Israeli Central Intelligence."

David stared at him. "You're crazy! She's no agent. She works for the Foreign Minister."

"A most effective cover. It opens a lot of doors." Abernathy blew a perfect smoke ring and watched it rise languidly to the ceiling.

"I don't believe it." David got up out of the chair and strode irately across the room. The other man's eyes followed him.

"We've suspected her for some time. Her brother is a long-timer with the Mossad. We've just gotten positive proof of her own involvement. I'd be happy to show you the evidence."

Evidence. A bell rang in David's brain. "Abernathy, you bastard! You're the one that ransacked her place today. You knew she'd be out for the afternoon—out with me!"

"Nonsense." The intelligence man remained cool, ignoring the vehemence of the accusation flung at him. He pulled on his pipe reflectively as the new envoy continued to stare him down in angry confrontation. "So she's had you to her flat already. She's a fast worker. Did it ever occur to you that she might have torn it up herself to make it look like a break-in?"

"Tear up her own apartment? Why the devil would she do that? You're covering up, Abernathy. What were you looking for? Why are you persecuting this girl?"

The agent made no immediate response, staring back from his perch on the desk, puffing steadily on the outlandish meerschaum. The smoke was beginning to irritate David almost as much as the man's obnoxious personality.

"You're unreal, Abernathy. You and your melodramatic little spy games. Are we spying on the Israelis, now? Have they suddenly become the enemy?"

Abernathy chose to take the question seriously. "One never knows, in this business." He stood up from the desk and emptied his pipe of its spent contents, clanking it several times against the ceramic ashtray for emphasis. "You might equally well ask why the Israelis are spying on us." He paused, letting the point sink in. "Now let me ask you a question. How far has this gone between you and the girl? Has she seduced you yet?"

The man's impertinence and bluntness were too much for David. "Out! Out of my office! And keep your filthy nose out of my affairs. I won't have you snooping around behind my back. You have no such authority." He moved menacingly in the smaller man's direction.

Abernathy beat a hasty retreat, but paused at the door. "On the contrary, I do have the authority. Much more authority than you realize. Some day you'll understand what's really happening here. In the meantime, I'm only trying to protect you—perhaps save your career. If you'll just agree to work with us, help us learn from the Zadik girl what—"

"Out!" He advanced toward the doorway, the agent disappearing swiftly through it, closing the door behind him. David stood staring at the closed door, fists clenching and unclenching, his sense of outrage vitriol in his throat. The man was a contemptible liar. Had to be. Daniella was genuine. He knew this—felt it—with every bone in his body. He would never believe there was anything false or deceitful about her.

Seduced. That was the word Abernathy had used that had so

infuriated him. What had happened today between him and Daniella had been beautiful and natural. Nothing artificial, nothing programmed. If there had been any semblance of seduction, it was the other way around—it was he who had done the seducing.

But a thin edge of doubt began to assail him as he thought back over the episode in her apartment. The apparent break-in had certainly been convenient—an icebreaker, a way of bringing them closer together and an excuse for his staying on. And her hesitation at calling the police. Could she have staged it, as Abernathy implied? No. He couldn't believe it. The honest, direct, open Daniella he had discovered this afternoon would not have resorted to such a subterfuge.

Yet, as much as he despised the man, there had been something in Abernathy's manner just now that was also believable, that belied any attempt at deception. Something different about the man, something more earnest, that he couldn't quite put his finger on.

Then he had it. The British accent. It had been totally dropped. Abernathy had been conversing with him in pure, unadulterated Americanese.

CHAPTER
4

Sergei Brastov had seen Saddam Hussein only once before, and never up close. But he was intimately familiar with the Iraqi president's background and rise to power. Hussein had been the strongman in the Baathist party coup of 1968 that had overthrown the Arif government and installed Ahmed Hassan al Bakr as president.

A "bloodless" coup, it had been called, since the deposed head of state and his henchmen were spared the customary head-rolling. But the extensive head-knocking that had paved the way had been engineered by Saddam Hussein, the former army general, who succeeded to the presidency in 1981 when al Bakr stepped down because of ill health. The "Republic" of Iraq, pending formal enactment of a permanent constitution, was still in its transitional phase. Presidents were not elected; they ruled by decree.

Brastov found the appearance of the Iraqi strongman no less intimidating than his reputation. Standing a head taller than the Russian, Hussein was attired in a forest green army uniform, the shirt open at his thick bull neck. Bushy black brows glowered down at the Russian above a grim streak of mouth surmounted by a heavy black mustache that turned down slightly at the corners. The president did not offer his hand, and Brastov felt awkward for a moment, then clicked his heels together and bowed slightly by way of salute, mouthing a few traditional words of Arabic that he had thought suitable for the occasion.

"Ah," said the president, black eyebrows dancing momentarily over the slate-gray eyes, "you speak our language. That is a good sign." He looked significantly from his defense minister to his personal adviser, then motioned toward the three chairs that surrounded the massive desk of highly polished teak, behind which he settled himself. Characteristically, he got right down to business.

"Comrade Brastov, I have already been briefed on your proposal by these two gentlemen. I will tell you my first reaction. Your suggestion that we deliberately set out to destroy one of the most prized and costly aircraft belonging to our close Islamic neighbor and benefactor is nothing short of preposterous! A most risky and perilous course of action to embark on—an action that could lead to disaster for us if the secret got out or if anything went wrong."

The Russian's face fell at the apparent rejection; he was conscious of beads of perspiration forming on his forehead. The cold slate eyes held him in their inexorable grip.

"But on further examination," Hussein continued, "the spectacular results projected make this preposterous plan worth considering." Brastov brightened. Perhaps there was hope after all.

"I have a few questions that I hope you can clear up," the president went on in a nondialectic Arabic that was purposely slow and deliberate so that the Russian would be sure to understand. "First of all, I presume that this proposal of yours has been cleared with your superiors in Moscow and has their concurrence?"

Brastov nodded emphatically, as Hussein continued with scarcely a pause. "Is there any danger of a breach of security from that quarter?"

The Russian hastened to reassure him. "None whatsoever. The plan carries our highest security classification and has been reviewed only at the highest levels."

The president nodded slowly, the brooding look deepening. "Then my next question is—why?" Brastov was taken aback, acutely aware of the eyes boring into him. "Why was this risky proposal advanced, approved by your superiors? What is your purpose?"

The blunt question carried a pronounced overtone of accusation. The Russian glanced away from the dark countenance of the president to the faces of Zahadi and Mustafa, sitting to his left. Had the two put his plan in a bad light? Both avoided his eyes. He was on his own; it was his move. And the best defense, as always, was to attack.

He stared directly back into the penetrating eyes. "With due respect, Your Excellency, I should think the answer is obvious. Surely you are aware of my government's stance in this matter. We share your revulsion over the excesses of the Israelis, the massacres in the Palestinian camps, the wanton rape and destruction of Beirut. We have a common objective to weaken Israel and bring about the downfall of the regime instituted by Begin and still in power under—"

"Silence!" Hussein's hand shot out, its fat, stubby fingers extending themselves across Brastov's line of vision. "We do not repeat those names within these walls. We do not dignify the country that is a noncountry by giving it a name. Nor the person that is a nonperson—a nonhuman—an accursed, unspeakable dog!"

With relief, Brastov sensed that the Iraqi president's rage was directed not at him but at the hate object whose name he had been so thoughtless as to invoke. On his feet, now, Hussein continued his tirade, storming angrily about behind his desk.

"A city of a million people reduced to rubble, an incomparable city that was once one of the brightest, fairest jewels of all Islam. Thousands upon thousands of innocents slaughtered, whose only offense was to be living there. Murdered by this power-drunk maniac, this former Irgun terrorist. Where will he and his henchmen stop? Beirut was only an appetizer. They are secretly stockpiling atomic weapons that could wipe out all of our cities."

He laughed bitterly. "And he calls me a meshug—meshug—"

"Meshuggener." The presidential adviser supplied the elusive Hebrew word.

"Meshuggener," Hussein repeated. "Yes. Crazy. That is what he called me, in front of his spineless, rubber-stamp parliament, after his unprovoked and criminal bombing of Osirak. Well, if it is crazy to want to defend oneself—to prepare to defend all Islam against this barbarous and malignant power—then he will find out just how meshuggener I am!"

Calmer now, the Iraqi president returned to his seat behind the desk. "Every Arab state, every single Islamic country supports us in this. Since the Beirut massacre we are getting more money for our nuclear project that we can spend on it. Our progress has been astounding. We are gaining on these Zionist madmen. We will overtake them. We will bury them!"

For punctuation, the beefy fist banged down heavily on the hardwood desk. Brastov shuddered inwardly. Proliferation of nuclear weapons within the Arab countries would escalate the destructive potential of this Middle East tinderbox to world-shattering proportions. How to stop it was an item on the still-secret agenda of his government's forthcoming summit meeting with the United States. He mentally washed his hands of the subject, so totally beyond his control, waiting for Hussein to get back to the project at hand.

"I have only one more question for you," the Iraqi president resumed in a much quieter tone, recapturing the Russian adviser with his deep-set eyes. "Will it work? Will this trick of yours really bring about the results you predict—the split with America, the fall of the Zionist government?"

Brastov returned the stare, warming to his favorite scenario. "If your agent in their air force is as good as I've been led to believe, it will work like a charm. He will find the AWACS a fat hen ready for plucking, undefended and helpless. Here is how it will happen.

"Your pilot will encounter the AWACS when it is six or seven hundred kilometers north of Riyadh, a region in which there are no nearby airfields. Their radar operator will detect the approach of an unidentified aircraft from a long way off on his radar screen. When your pilot subsequently turns on his radar, the AWACS will use electromagnetic identification to discover that his aircraft is an F-15. This information will be relayed to Ground Control, which will quickly verify that there are no Saudi F-15s operating in the vicinity. The deduction will be simple. Only one other country in the Middle East has fighters of this type, the—"

He caught himself just in time. "The Zionists. By now, your pilot is closing on the AWACS at an extraordinary rate of speed —more than twice the speed of sound. Interceptors will be scrambled from the nearest base, and the AWACS ordered to turn back. But long before they can arrive, your pilot will overtake the lumbering craft, and it will fall from the sky like a flaming meteor, carrying all aboard, including the Americans, to their death.

"The F-15, bearing its country's markings, will turn up after a forced landing in the Sinai, its pilot nowhere to be found. The hue and cry by Saudi Arabia will draw world attention to the incident. Once the Osirak connection—the motive—is established, America will have no doubts that the attack was deliberate and flagrant. Their president will be given no alternative to severing relations with the present government, assuring its downfall."

Saddam Hussein remained silent for a time, digesting what he had heard. The Russian waited, pondering whether he should volunteer to clarify certain points, get into further details of the plan. What had the other two told Hussein? They had uttered scarcely a word in his presence. His instinct told him he had said enough, to wait the man out.

Abruptly, the president stood up and extended his hand. "That will be all for now, Comrade Brastov. You will be notified of our decision. In the meanwhile, you are directed to refrain from discussing this matter with anyone outside of this room, including your government."

"But the preparations—time is growing short." The look of dismay on Brastov's face said it all.

"We will make all the necessary preparations—if we decide to pursue it. It is better for your government, as well as ours, that you not be directly involved. Let us make sure that there is no way of tracing this action back to you."

Disappointed, the Russian shook hands perfunctorily with Mustafa and Zahadi and left the president's office. He had visualized being a part of the exercise, manipulating the pieces, as it were, from behind the scenes. He didn't trust the Iraqis to make all the right moves. Yet, he told himself, he shouldn't be surprised. Hussein, characteristically, would want to take all the credit. There would be no breath of any Soviet involvement in the affair within the Islamic community.

Still, those in the know would be aware—his own highly placed Soviet contacts with whom the proposal had already been cleared. And certain others. The credit for masterminding the operation, in those circles that most mattered, would be his.

Suddenly he felt much better. Hussein's reaction could only mean that he had already decided. He was sure of it. The AWACS plan—his plan—was going full speed ahead.

There was no direct flight from Israel to Saudi Arabia—probably would never be, David mused. The only Arab country serviced by the Israeli airline, El Al, was Egypt, a bona fide fringe benefit to travelers as fallout from the Camp David Accords. To fly to Riyadh, you boarded their daily flight to Cairo, where you changed planes and airlines. The connections were terrible; a five-hour layover, catching the late-afternoon Pan Am 747 nonstop to Riyadh, was the best he could do.

The Cairo flight left Ben Gurion at seven in the morning. It was listed as a one-class flight, which invariably meant tourist class, which on El Al, he knew, would mean narrow seats and no service, meals, or refreshments. At least he was traveling in style as far as the airport. He was comfortably ensconced in the posh hindquarters of Black Beauty, Ambassador Abrams's chauffeur-driven limousine, a long, sleek Lincoln, its diplomatic flags flying taut and proud above the front fenders. A token of the old man's goodwill toward his new special envoy, as was his approval of David's whirlwind trip to Riyadh to look in on his kid brother.

"No time like the present, Llewellyn," the ambassador had counseled, when he had broached the subject on Monday. "Best do it now, while we're shifting gears to get relocated. In this business you never know. Tomorrow the roof might fall in and I couldn't spare you."

The same observation, David reflected, could be made about his other piece of business, the assignment to which the ambassador was not privy. His search for the mole was stalled until the embassy cast was reassembled in Jerusalem. They would be straggling back in for the rest of the week. The earliest flight reservation he could get was Wednesday morning. He had decided to grab it.

With an effort, he turned his thoughts back to the purpose of his trip. It would be good to see Richy again. The brother eight years his junior, child of his parents' old age—the "menopausal miracle" of the family, as Richy cynically referred to himself—held a special place in his heart. Until finding Katherine, he had never felt closer to anyone. That feeling of closeness remained, somehow, surviving the long separations that careers in different foreign service enterprises entailed. It was hard for anyone else to understand.

"How can you say you're close when you seldom see each other anymore?" Katherine had pondered. "You almost never write or even talk to each other on the telephone."

"Closeness is a matter of feeling," he remembered answering, groping for the right words, not fully understanding, himself. "When you're really close to someone, you don't have to be physically close. There's a sense of the other person—an awareness—that reaches across the distance in between."

He could see her tossing her head, in that beguiling way of hers, asking if he felt the same thing with her; and acting a little hurt when he answered, no, it was a different kind of closeness, and besides, he and she had never been separated. Dear Katherine! If only she knew. Now that fate had separated them permanently there was never a day that he didn't think about her.

But still, it was different with brothers. Did Richy feel the same way as he, he wondered?

A nagging concern for his only brother's well-being, a sense of unease that he couldn't explain, had prompted this sudden flight to Riyadh. A decision encouraged by Daniella, who had communicated her own uneasiness and sense of urgency. Daniella; what on earth had become of Daniella?

After his encounter at the embassy with Abernathy on Saturday night, he had tried to phone her. When there was no answer, he assumed she had stepped out to run an errand. He had tried again minutes later, kept trying off and on for two hours before turning in. Was she all right? Could the intruder have returned? Unable to sleep, he had thrown his clothes on and driven to her apartment. He could see the light under her door, but there had been no sound from within and no answer to his ring.

She had been weary, he knew, from the long day's activities, the shock of returning to find her flat ransacked. Could she have dropped off to sleep with the light on, a sleep so sound that the ringing of the phone and the doorbell hadn't awakened her? He had pounded on her door, shouted her name. The only answer came from the adjacent apartment, a muffled protest in Hebrew, the words unintelligible, their meaning unmistakable.

He had driven back to his own lodgings, telling himself that he was foolish to worry, that she could take care of herself. But when morning came, there was still no answer. He had phoned all day Sunday, driven by her flat again. There was still no sign of her. On Monday he had called the foreign minister's office, talked to a secretary. Miss Zadik was on holiday this week, he was told. Had she gone away somewhere? he inquired. The party didn't know.

Funny, if she'd been planning a vacation, that she hadn't mentioned it. He had tried again to reach her each succeeding day, tried again this morning. Where was she? What could explain her three-day absence?

It had started out rather like a spy novel—the phone call at the stroke of midnight, just as she was drifting off to sleep. The voice had said simply to report for duty at once. Excitement coursed through her and she forgot her tiredness. Yitzhac, dear Yitzhac! Here I go, picking up the traces!

But that was hours before. Hours spent filling out forms, followed by periods of waiting, that had dulled the sharp edge of her resolve, the gray mantle of fatigue slipping back over her. The Mossad, it seemed, was not that different from other institutions of her acquaintance. Even here, the God of Paper ruled supreme. Fill this out! Fill that out! Hurry! So you can sit and wait. And wait. And wait some more.

The young clerk in charge of the paperwork returned after a prolonged absence. "What am I waiting for?" she demanded, exasperated.

"Your control," he responded. "He should be along any minute."

Minutes were turning into hours, and she had nodded off several times before the door to the cell-like waiting room opened and a short, middle-aged man entered. At least she took him for middle-aged, by his stooped posture and grizzled beard. But that was before she saw his eyes. They were young, alert eyes, radiating raw intelligence.

He was studying a file—her file, she quickly concluded—and did not look up from it as he made his way to a chair across the table from her and sat down in it. She watched the restless eyes devour the material in front of them, the face expressionless, fingers riffling the sheets of paper. Among them were the forms and questionnaires she had filled out during the early morning hours; but there were other pages, also, that she didn't recognize.

It was a full minute before he looked up, finally acknowledging her presence. It seemed much longer. What passed for a smile registered fleetingly behind the bushy beard, supplanted by a sudden explosion of words.

"Okay. Miss Zadik. Daniella. A pleasure. It appears we can use you. I am Baruch Shmona. It's not my real name, of course. I'm to be your control. You know what that means?"

He didn't wait for an answer. "It means that I will be your contact with the Institute—your only contact. You will receive your instructions through me. You will report to me on a regular basis. Whatever intelligence you glean from your assignments will be passed directly to me. In short, from this day forward, as far as you are concerned, I, Baruch Shmona, am the Institute. Understood?"

She frowned. "I thought there would be some sort of training, a school for new agents. I know next to nothing about—"

He shook his head emphatically, a condescending half-smile on his face. "Oh, Daniella! The misconceptions that people have about this business! If we put you all in some 'spy' class together, you would immediately know one another's identity. Any possibility for effective cover would go right out the window. No, Daniella, I will teach you all you need to know. I will be your instructor."

"Then I'm to start immediately?"

"In fact, you have already started, though you may not have been aware of it. By coincidence, you embarked on your initial assignment several days ago, before we had completed our screening of your candidacy."

"I—what?" Her brain struggled to grasp his meaning. "What assignment?"

"Let me be candid, Daniella. While you bring a number of potential assets to this job, your present usefulness to us derives in no small part from your well-placed position in the Foreign Minister's office and the contacts that this position opens up."

"You're asking that I spy on my—on the Foreign Minister?"

"Hardly, Daniella, hardly that. We're not reduced to that, as yet, spying on our own. No, I was referring to your contact with the American Embassy; in particular, your relationship with one of the recent arrivals there, the new special envoy."

"David!" The name exploded out of her, before she could suppress it.

"So it's 'David,' is it? Good, good. This liaison came to our attention just yesterday, prior to conducting our deep sweep of your apartment. We want you to—"

"You!" Her astonishment quickly gave way to indignation. "It was you who ransacked my apartment!"

"Not I, personally, I can assure you. We have agents who are trained for that. It's standard procedure for all new candidates."

"Are they always so neat?"

"Oh, that. Yes, I understand they did leave your place in a bit of a mess. My idea, actually. I thought it might provide a conducive environment for strengthening your relationship with Llewellyn. The protective instinct of the male aroused—"

She was almost too furious to speak. "How dare you presume! My private life is my own! How dare you meddle—!"

He took her outburst in stride, waiting out the storm. "From now on, my dear Daniella, you will have no private life. Not private from the Institute, at least, while you are working for us. We must know everything, every detail you can learn about this man Llewellyn, what his mission here really is. We have reason to believe—"

"No!" she broke in. "I refuse! I will not spy on friends. I volunteered to work against our enemies, not our friends. America is on our side."

"Americans, my dear young lady, come in all shapes and sizes, some on either side. Your Mr. Llewellyn may not be quite what he seems; we are not sure, yet."

"Then let me reassure you. He is exactly what he appears to be, a diplomat with a special portfolio, a personal friend of the American President, sent here to improve relations with our country and pave the way for a new Middle East peace initiative. The Foreign Minister will verify that what I'm telling you is true."

The man called Shmona studied her earnest expression for several moments, weighing his response.

"What I'm about to tell you is in strictest confidence. It may not be divulged by you to anyone, including your Foreign Minister."

He extracted a yellow form from the pile of papers in front of him and waved it at her. "Your signature is on this. You have sworn an oath of secrecy, and been apprised of the possible penalties for breaking this oath."

She nodded, swallowing hard.

"Secrets are the main commodity we deal with in the Institute, you see," he continued. "Their secrets, our secrets. A great deal of our time goes into discovering the secrets of our enemies. Our own, we seek to protect. Some of our secrets—very sensitive secrets—are shared with our American ally. The U.S. Embassy is a repository for some of this sensitive information, charged with its protection. Information which could compromise our government, threaten our country's very existence, if it got into the wrong hands."

"What has this to do with Ambassador Llewellyn?" she broke in impatiently.

"I'm coming to that. We had already picked up some signals, disquieting signals, that something was amiss at the embassy, that certain leaks of sensitive information have occurred. But there is, as yet, no hard evidence."

"Again, what can that have to do with David? He has only just arrived."

"Precisely, Miss Zadik, precisely. It is his arrival at this particular moment that has escalated our concern. You see, we have unearthed certain secrets about Mr. Llewellyn's background.

While his diplomatic credentials are perfectly genuine, we have learned that he spent a period of his career some years ago as an undercover agent for the State Department's counterintelligence branch.

"In short, the new American President has sent a trained counterspy to the embassy in Israel. We want you to find out why."

Richard Llewellyn looked up from his paperback novel to inspect the runway below for signs of an incoming 747 with Pan Am markings. Nothing. The flight from Cairo was considerably overdue. Not that this was unusual here in Riyadh. Sometimes flights were hours late. You could never find out from the airlines. Your only option was to come to the airport on time and wait.

It wasn't the most comfortable spot to wait in, he reflected. The posh cocktail lounges indigenous to major airports around the world were of course anathema here, where the taboo on alcohol was zealously enforced. But with all the petrodollars sunk into the Riyadh International Airport, you'd think they could have afforded some upholstery. He shifted his weight on the unpadded hardwood bench and tried to concentrate on the small print.

It was no use. He was too keyed up, an undercurrent of excitement inside him in anticipation of seeing his brother again after —how long had it been? More than three years. Ironic that their first reunion in so long a time should be in a foreign country—and countries didn't get much more foreign than Saudi Arabia. But since taking the job with Westinghouse in Baltimore, he had spent most of his time overseas, introducing the AWACS first to the NATO nations, then here in Arabia. His several vacations back at the old homestead in Forest Hills had failed to overlap visits by brother David on his own foreign service furloughs.

Three years! Would he look the same; or had Katherine's death changed him? Richy formed a mental picture of a tall, debonair, dark-haired man in his late thirties bouncing lightly down the gangway from the plane. He had always taken pride in his brother's appearance, pride in David's accomplishments. God, it would be good to see him, to talk seriously and also kid around, like they had in the old days. He had been so busy, of late, so wrapped up in his own work, he hadn't realized how much he missed the guy. Face it, there was still a strong bond there. Hell, don't mince words. You love the guy.

It hadn't always been that way. For one stretch of time, in the troublesome sojourn from puberty through adolescence, he had harbored a smoldering feeling of resentment for the paragon older brother that bordered on hate. David had been a top student, good at sports and everything else, popular with everyone. After eight years, he was still remembered at the Forest Hills junior high and high schools, where Richy ran the gamut of his brother's former teachers and coaches, being constantly compared to his successful sibling and expected to measure up.

The same pressures were at work at home, where his parents drew inevitable, though more restrained, comparisons. He recalled with a sudden twinge of the shame he had felt afterwards, his outburst that had so alarmed his mother and enraged his father, when the dam had burst and he could hold it back no longer. "I can't be David! I'm somebody else! Can't you get that through your heads?"

Getting it through his own head had been the hard part. When he had given up trying to measure up on the David yardstick and begun to follow his own instincts, develop his own interests and specialties, the big brother shadow began to subside. He had discovered an appetite and aptitude for things technical and scientific, an area that had not been one of David's strongest suits. He had taught himself electronics, practicing by repairing the home TV, and had mastered the subject years before he took his first college course. While still in high school, he had built a home computer from a kit and learned to program it. By the time he had entered college, computers and software were second nature to him. In his sophomore year, he was already casting about for a specialty. He had found it in radar.

From a scientific curiosity fresh out of the laboratory in World War II, radar had evolved into an ultrasophisticated marriage of high-powered radio elements with high-speed digital processors and displays, all under computer control. It was openly acknowledged by radar supply houses that their offspring had become so elaborate that they had outstripped the ability of any single individual to understand the radar system in its entirety. As a recent engineering graduate assigned by Westinghouse to their highly complex AWACS radar, Richy had set out to prove them wrong.

In the space of one short year he had mastered the entire radar system, including a working knowledge of every element, from the ultrapowerful transmitter to the rotodome antenna array to the vast complex of processing hardware and displays. But his major achievement was his facility with the software, the hundreds of thousands of lines of program code that made these elements play together as the world's most advanced surveillance system. Before he was sent overseas as part of the team that would introduce the AWACS to the NATO nations, he had personally written much of the code; he understood every line of it. He was no less a marvel than the system on which he had become the world's expert and in which he took such pride.

"Wait until David sees it!" he thought. He had been planning the demonstration since the first word of a possible visit by his brother and had completed all of the necessary arrangements to take the American diplomat through one of the AWACS aircraft. Somehow he needed to see the impressed look on David's face, the awe that he had seen in the eyes of other visitors when confronted with one of the technical wonders of modern time. It was important to him—for one who had lived so long in awe of his older brother.

There was another treat in store for David, a dinner party this evening at the Tangier, the closest thing Riyadh had to offer in the way of a cozy supper club, but still, regrettably, sans alcohol. It would be just the three of them, Roxana making up the third.

He and Roxana had been hitting it off very well. It was his job to teach her the basics of the radar software, and she had proved to be a fast learner. It was unique in his experience to encounter a natural beauty with such intelligence, to say nothing of technical smarts. They spoke the same language, which extended from computerese to literature and classical music. He already felt that he really knew her; it was hard to believe that it was barely a week since she had come on board.

This would be their first real date, not counting part of an evening in his room sampling his record collection and his private hoard of Scotch whiskey, smuggled in aboard AWACS aircraft number three with the help of a Boeing friend in Seattle. A platonic evening, as it turned out, though a highly stimulating one. He knew that he was using his brother's visit as a kind of catalyst to get their relationship into high gear, and he sensed that it wouldn't hurt his chances with Roxana if a little of David's glamor rubbed off on him. Which one was he trying to impress the most, he wondered; his big brother, or the lovely Irani?

In Richy's mind, the diplomatic world in which his brother moved was a totally glamorous one, replete with gala dinners and parties and bevies of beautiful, well-dressed, accessible women. A handsome, unattached envoy was bound to make out like a bandit. Though he hadn't seen his brother since the tragic death of his sister-in-law, his imagination filled in the blanks.

In point of fact, he now realized, he and David had had very little discussion at all on the subject of women and sex. Not since an event that was vividly etched in his memory—the "facts-of-life" session more than a decade ago, with David pinch-hitting for his father, who shied away from such responsibilities. It occurred to him that the brother who had opened his eyes to the joy of sex had never seen him in the company of a woman, probably thought of him as some kind of monk. Well, this dinner tonight with Roxana would dispel any such notion.

"Pardonnez-moi, avez-vous une cigarette?"

He turned around to explain to the Frenchman that he didn't smoke. It was David, grinning down at him like a Cheshire cat. How in blazes had he missed seeing the plane land?

He jumped to his feet and started to shake hands briskly, then found himself caught up in a crushing bear hug. Hugging back just as fiercely, he felt the hot tears, unbidden, steal into his eyes.

The rented Simca was tiny but adequate. David's single large bag took up most of the back seat. Richy pulled out into the stream of departing traffic, just ahead of a chauffeur-driven ivory-white Rolls, and turned south, toward the city.

"I thought we'd get you checked into your hotel, then come back out to the base. I've laid on a little personally guided tour of the AWACS. That is, if you're interested."

"Extremely," David enthused, curious to see, firsthand, the aircraft that Begin had made such a bone of contention when the new Reagan administration began pushing the sale to the Saudis.

"And this way, you'll get to see something of Riyadh before dark," Richy continued. "It's kind of a modern wonder of the world—a high-rise city of more than a million where there was little more than an overgrown baked-mud village a couple of decades ago."

"It's hard to believe," David concurred. "I got a view of the skyline, flying in. All those skyscrapers in the middle of the desert. And this airport. It's humongous!"

"The largest in the world," Richy volunteered. "That is, until the Saudis finish the one at Dhahran."

"Dhahran will be even bigger?" His brother was incredulous.

"I'd heard that the oil glut was forcing some cutbacks."

"They're starting to feel the pinch a bit," Richy acknowledged. "Only it's more of a slowdown than a cutback. The major projects are still going ahead. But they're a little less reckless in the way they throw money around. A few years ago there was no way they could spend it all."

Traffic, which had been relatively light around the airport, began to thicken noticeably as they drew closer to the city. David noted a preponderance of taxicabs and an inclination by their drivers to blow their high-pitched horns at the slightest provocation.

His brother laughed. "They couldn't drive without their horns. A lot of cabbies are Arabs; it's one of the few menial jobs Saudis are willing to perform. They hate hard physical labor, consider it demeaning. That kind of work is done by outsiders, mostly from neighboring Islamic countries. There's been a huge influx. I'll bet over half the population of Riyadh are foreigners."

"Doesn't that create a lot of problems?"

"It's starting to. Crime, for one thing. The rate of crime here was the lowest in the world, until recently. Most of the crimes are committed by foreigners. The Saudis are ingrained with the concept of capital punishment, but it takes the newcomers a while to catch on. Thieves have their hands cut off. Murderers are beheaded—right in the public square. There was an execution here in town just the other day, with thousands of Saudis watching."

David recoiled. "Watching? Are they that bloodthirsty?"

"Not at all. They consider it their patriotic duty, an important element of the anticrime program."

Noting his brother's expression of distaste, he smiled. "The Saudis are a little hard to understand at first, but they have many fine qualities. They're a really special people."

David looked skeptical. "I'll have to take your word for it. The only one I've met since my arrival was too intent on ransacking my suitcase to say a civil word."

"Ah, yes. Customs. They're very thorough here; I should have warned you. They were probably looking for dope and booze. And magazines."

"Magazines? You mean pornography?"

"Not necessarily. All magazines and newspapers are censored. Usually they just tear out the liquor ads and pictures of scantily clad women."

"But," protested David, "what's the object? What are they trying to prove?"

"The object is to protect their own people from the excesses of western civilization. The House of Saud considers itself the champion and defender of the Islamic faith, the strict interpretation of the teachings of Muhammad and the Koran. They recognize that they need us here, need our skills and technical expertise to modernize Arabia and prepare it for the future. But they're determined that their subjects will not be westernized in the process, in a materialistic sense. Liquor and movies and other forms of frivolous entertainment such as dancing, are strictly outlawed. Segregation of the sexes is still pretty rigidly enforced. And you won't see any low-cut dresses or short skirts on Saudi women, though the face-veil code has been relaxed."

"You'd think the younger generation would rebel. What about college students?"

Richy chuckled. "That's the funny thing. Some of the college kids seem to be the most vocal about the dangers of westernization. Many of them go abroad for their education, and no doubt kick up their heels a bit while they're away. But when they return, they revert back to type and conform. And there's no visible women's rights movement, even though women are still subjugated in many ways and not permitted to pursue some of the more glamorous careers."

David fell silent, sorting out what he had heard, staring out at the passing scenery. They were in the city now. What a weird city! So different from any he had visited before—from the city he had just departed. Jerusalem and Tel Aviv were modernized cities, also, carved out of their own desert. But they were embedded in the lush greenery of an oasis cultivated and irrigated by an industrious, caring populace. And they were conspicuously clean and tidy.

The contrast with Riyadh was striking. Piles of rubble and refuse littered the grounds of tall buildings already completed and occupied, dust and sand everywhere, obscuring newly constructed walkways. There was an unkempt, uncared-for look about this miracle city that had sprung so suddenly from the empty desert, a harshness of scene he found jarring and disquieting after the harmony of the Israeli surroundings. All contributing to the sense of malaise he had felt since stepping off the plane and encountering the hard-nosed, unfriendly customs personnel.

A prickly sensation on the back of his neck made him turn and look back. The white Rolls from the airport was still behind them, the Arab chauffeur inscrutable under his native headdress and sunglasses, any occupants to the rear invisible behind the opaque glass divider. Why was he so jumpy? No one but the ambassador knew he was coming here today; the notion of being followed made no sense. He shook it off. But the uneasy feeling, the sense of a hostile environment, remained. Imagine what a Jew must feel coming here, he thought. Imagine how Daniella would feel.

"This is my baby, right here—number C-103." Richy pointed to the tail number on the nearest E3-A aircraft, pride mingled with excitement in his voice.

David stared up at the gleaming white fuselage tattooed with the black Arabic markings of the Royal Saudi Air Force. So this was the AWACS, the weapon system that had raised such a furor of protest from the Begin government. He had been expecting something far grander.

What he saw was a very ordinary-looking, average-sized jet transport, its lines reminiscent of, if not identical with, a Boeing 707, the first commercial jetliner to go into service, almost three decades ago. A jetliner outmoded, now, by the wide bodies and the new airbuses; next to its own sister ship, the 747 jumbo jet, a virtual dwarf. Its sole mark of distinction was a peculiar appendage projecting skyward just in front of its tail—a giant horizontal disk suspended high above its aft fuselage on two flimsy-looking struts, giving it an ungainly, humpbacked appearance. This, he quickly realized, must be the radome, housing the wide, squat, rotating antenna that scanned the skies in all directions, searching for hostile aircraft.

Mounting the access stairway, he wondered about another notable departure from the airlines' 707 configuration; there were no windows or portholes cut into its sides. The reason became clear as he followed his brother inside. Darkness was apparently the milieu of the men who made the AWACS do its thing.

In the subdued light of the cabin's interior, multicolored symbols on enormous video display consoles sparkled like jewels in an onyx setting. Replete with control panels and digital keyboards and countless switches, knobs, and auxiliary displays, the row of consoles seemed to extend all the way into the tail of the airplane. Each console was manned by a uniformed operator hunched down in concentration in his upholstered cubicle, head encircled by earphones with attached mike, hands busy at the controls. Their rapt expressions, eyes riveted to the blinking, perambulating blobs of iridescent color, were reminiscent of teenagers vying mightily inside a video games parlor.

Against the background noise, the steady hum of the aircraft alternator, and the sporadic jabberings of the operators into their microphones, Richy sought to explain what was happening.

"Saudi controller trainees practicing intercepts on the simulator. We run training missions in this aircraft when it isn't flying."

He pointed to a flashing red symbol on the nearest display.

"That's a known hostile. The blue triangle is a Saudi fighter being vectored to intercept by the AWACS, under voice command from the controller. His job is to bring the interceptor into visual contact with the hostile on a favorable course to make a visual identification and press home an attack."

David watched in fascination as the red and blue symbols on the giant display converged on one another. Suddenly, there was a bright flash of yellow at the point where the hostile aircraft symbol had appeared. It expanded in size for several seconds, then faded out. The red symbol had completely disappeared.

The Saudi operator turned in his seat and grinned up at them, immensely pleased. "Ka-blooey!" he exclaimed.

"Ka-blooey!" Richy echoed, nodding enthusiastically and patting the controller on the back.

"Ka-blooey?" David grinned. "What kind of Arabic word is that?"

Richy laughed. "We provide the simulated yellow flash on the screen as a payoff for successful intercepts of bogeys. The trainees love it. But it lacked appropriate sound effects. 'Ka-blooey' was my idea. I guess it caught on."

He took his brother's elbow and led him toward the forward part of the airplane, where it was somewhat quieter. David looked back at the Saudi trainee, re-engrossed in his console and oblivious.

"They're like little kids playing video games."

"Don't mistake their boyish enthusiasm." Richy's voice took on a more serious note. "When they get upstairs, into the real flight environment, they grow up in a hurry. It's quickly impressed on them that the game they're playing can turn into a very deadly one. If a force of fifty or sixty hostile aircraft should suddenly show up on those scopes, their country's survival—and their own—could hinge on their proficiency at handling multiple intercepts."

"Is that at all likely? I mean, who do they expect to attack them—the Russians?"

"Right now they're more worried about Iran and that crazy Ayatollah. That's why the AWACS surveillance has been concentrated on the northern side of the Persian Gulf. But you never know. The idea is to be ready for anything—the unexpected."

"Like what?" David persisted.

Richy steered his brother through a doorway leading off the main corridor, into a small compartment dominated by an island of displays and control panels at its center.

"Like what? You saw for yourself how the petrodollars have transformed Riyadh. Even with the oil glut, those dollars are coming out of the ground at an enormous rate. The temptation to tap into that multibillion dollar flow could become irresistible. The oil fields are lightly defended, ripe for plucking. Financially strapped or oil-poor nations, if they become desperate enough, could be sorely tempted—even Israel."

"Oh, come on, Rich! Israel?"

"Don't scoff. Somebody must be concerned about it. Our flight plans and surveillance patterns were altered less than a month ago to extend cover to the North Arabian Desert. Who else would attack from that direction?"

David thought about it. It didn't make any sense. Any disruption in the flow of Arabian crude would jack up the price of oil and throw a giant monkeywrench into the entire western economy. As had already been proved more than adequately by King Faisal's oil embargo back in '73. The Israelis would have nothing to gain from such a recurrence, would go down the same financial drain as their American friends and all the other nations tightly tied to that economy. He voiced his observations to his kid brother.

Richy concurred on the matter of economic impact on the West. "Now you know why we're here. Uncle Sam can't afford to let that happen."

"But I still don't see how a handful of these radar platforms is going to prevent it. If a country like Iran attacked with their entire U.S.–supplied air force, or if the Soviet Union decided to—"

"I'll show you how." Richy motioned him into the bucket seat of a swivel chair anchored to the floor in front of the control center. "This is my flying office, the radar control bench. I have my own separate computer here that manages the radar and talks to the big IBM machine that controls the rest of the AWACS subsystems."

He flipped a switch on the control panel alongside the giant circular picture tube. Instantly, a narrow green beam shot out from the center of the scope to its extremity and began to rotate slowly in a clockwise direction.

"The antenna is turning, upstairs in the rotodome," Richy explained, pointing to the rotating green line. "But the transmitter is off; we're not actually radiating. We have so much power that if we transmitted here on the ground, we'd cook the insides of any living thing within a few hundred feet of the aircraft that got in the way of our beam, just like they'd been in a microwave oven. So there are interlocks to prevent that from happening when we're on the ground.

"But when we're airborne, at our cruising altitude of thirty or forty thousand feet, that phenomenal transmitter power lets us operate all the way out to the horizon. Every time that green line scans out a complete circle, we've searched over 200,000 square miles, an area bigger than the whole state of Texas. Any man-made conveyance that's moving through that space, a Bear bomber at high altitude or a MiG sneaking in on the deck—even a tank or armored personnel carrier that's moving along the ground—will show up on this display and be color coded as friendly or hostile on the controllers' consoles.

"That's the key, big brother. Early warning, so you don't get surprised. And battle management, from a catbird seat where you can see the entire theater of operations spread out below you and know exactly what's going on."

David was starting to get the picture. Visibility, he knew, meant everything in the conduct of a battle. Keeping tabs on the location and disposition of the enemy, the deployment of his forces, their direction and rate of movements. AWACS provided the battle commander with a bird's-eye view of the battlefield, unobscured by clouds or haze or the ever-present pall of smoke from a shooting war, color coded to separate friend from foe and updated at frequent intervals. With such visibility, Napoleon would surely have prevailed at Waterloo. Or in a more timely example, the Egyptians could have seen the Israelis coming in the Six Day War, saved their armor from the wholesale havoc wreaked on it by the Israeli warplanes, and possibly turned the tide.

Now he understood the vehemence of the Begin regime against the deployment of AWACS to the Saudis. It represented a giant step in the art of warfare, a true breakthrough. But he had a further reservation.

"Doesn't this make your AWACS platform a prime target? You have no weapons on board to defend yourselves. How do you expect to survive one of these attacks?"

"Good question." Richy sat down on the countertop and switched off the radar, the thin spoke of green on the radarscope coasting to a stop, then fading from view.

"Here's how it's supposed to work. We can detect the incoming forces several hundred miles away. We alert the fighter aircraft at the forward air bases and vector them on intercepts of the attackers, pulling back as we do so. But of course we're not fast enough to outrun enemy fighter planes, so we're relying on the Saudi interceptors to protect our ass. And from what I've seen of them, they're damn good. The pilots are well trained, thanks to the U.S. Air Force, and they've got good equipment: F-4s, F-5s, and F-15s."

"But do they have enough of them?" David persisted. "Wouldn't a very large raid saturate your defenses?"

The radar man shrugged. "Fortunately, I won't be around to find out. I think they can handle the Iranis with the fighters they have deployed right now. If it's a much larger threat than that, they'll obviously need help from us. That's where the Rapid Deployment Force is supposed to come in. You must have heard of it."

David had. A Department of Defense crash program carried forward under the Reagan administration, most of its details were classified top secret, including the basing plan for the force. But it was no secret that a new troop carrier aircraft was under development to provide the means of intervening effectively and rapidly in global brushfire situations where the interests of the United States were threatened. And the turbulent and unpredictable Middle East was generally touted as a prime example of such a potential situation. A trouble spot where anything could happen, with little or no warning.

"Rich, no matter how fast the RDF arrives on the scene, I don't see how they're going to be in time to help that poor AWACS of yours, flying point out there against a whole horde of enemy fighters. How much longer do you have to fly in this damn thing?"

Concern edged his voice. Richy looked at him in surprise. "Why big brother, I think you're actually afraid for me! Not to worry. I don't see any war clouds gathering on the horizon, do you? Besides, we'll have this job wrapped up in just one more week of flying. Then another week or two on the ground to get it all documented."

"Only one more week in the air? That's good to hear." David was relieved. "But about those war clouds, Rich. The kind of wars they have over here, by the time you see the clouds, it's already too late."

CHAPTER
5

The dinner hour in Riyadh arrived late. Not so late as in Spain, where the main course, David remembered, might not appear much before midnight. But late enough that his stomach, unfortified with a predinner ration of gin and vermouth, was beginning to grumble impatiently.

The two brothers were seated together on a comfortable low divan, their backs propped against massive overstuffed pillows. They were into their second glassful of scalding-hot mint tea, de rigueur for a Moroccan-style restaurant, but a poor substitute for a dry martini or flute of well-chilled champagne. Still, David had to admit, the ambience of the Tangier was all that Richy had claimed for it, the rich carpets and tapestries and opulent furniture subtly illuminated by the warm glow of dimmed golden lamplight. A most restful setting, conducive to relaxation and quiet conversation, the subdued strains of Oriental strings in the background just sufficient to obscure the drone of voices from nearby tables. But his baby brother seemed anything but relaxed. His conversation was sporadic, eyes darting repeatedly toward the entrance to the restaurant. Roxana, who was to meet them here, had not yet made her appearance.

David closed his eyes for a moment and let his mind drift free. Under the spell of the exotic music, it conjured up the image of a shapely belly dancer, face hidden by a veil, her supple body swaying to the Oriental rhythm. He knew that body, knew that beneath the veil would be the face of Daniella. The image faded, and he came back to reality. There would be no belly dancers here in puritan Riyadh. Such public exposure of the female form was strictly proscribed, even in a traditional dance that was highly favored in other Muslim countries.

He felt Richy nudge him, opened his eyes, and started. A woman in black stood just inside the entrance, head and shoulders shrouded in a heavy black veil. She saw them, raised her head in recognition, and slowly began to unwind the veil as she moved in their direction.

David had an inexplicable premonition that the face about to be exposed, as in his just-concluded daydream, would be Daniella's. But a different face emerged, a fresh young face with full, rouged lips and eyes alive with vitality and excitement. The unpeeling continued, revealing bare, ivory-smooth shoulders and a neckline that plunged far below the limits of Saudi propriety.

Roxana folded the black scarf and laid it next to her purse on the divan facing them. "The veil is a drag, but it beats being stared at on the street. Or arrested for indecent exposure." Her sparkling eyes rested briefly on David, who had come up belatedly off the divan, then moved to Richy, standing beside him.

"Aren't you going to introduce me?"

"Of—of course." Richy had difficulty finding his voice. He was used to the Roxana of the Quonset hut and the E3-A, the unrouged, blue-jeaned, head-scarfed, flight-geared Roxy. This was a different Roxana, a sexy, devastating woman he had never seen before.

"Miss Roxana Razmari, may I present my brother, David. David, this is Roxana."

"Charmed, Miss Razmari." David accepted the extended hand and was rewarded with a firm squeeze. The mascara-lined, hazel-green eyes twinkled back into his as she settled herself on the opposite divan facing both of them.

"I thought Americans always used first names. The flight crew call me Roxy, but I prefer Roxana. It's not my real Iranian name, but it's close enough. Is it permissible to call an envoy by his first name?"

"Please do." David's winning smile flashed a warm greeting. "But if you'll forgive the observation, you talk more like an American than an Irani."

"Oh, that's from grad school at Cal Poly," Roxana explained quickly. "I guess quite a little bit of California rubbed off on me. Anyway, it's better to be taken for an American," she added. "Iranis are not too popular in Arabia at the moment."

"I was wondering about that," David commented. "How was it that you were accepted by the government here on such a sensitive defense project?"

For an instant, he thought he detected a glimmer of apprehension in her eyes. But if so, it was only fleeting, the friendly sparkle back immediately. "They are desperate for trained help here, particularly in the computer sciences. And I speak Arabic fluently. Besides, I haven't been back to Iran in years—since before the Ayatollah returned. I am a refugee, like many of the Iranis exiled in your country."

Richy had been following their conversation closely, eyes glistening with the gratification that comes on those rare occasions when two of one's favorite people meet for the first time and hit it off immediately. "Roxana is a topnotch programmer," he enthused, "and fantastically quick to learn. In a couple more weeks, she'll know everything I know."

Roxana laughed embarrassedly, shaking her head emphatically. "I'll never know that much about the AWACS radar. Nobody will." She returned her gaze to David. "Your brother is the world authority. It's frightening to think that one day he won't be here to answer my questions."

David nodded. "I can appreciate that. Richard ran me through a demonstration today. It was pretty overpowering. There must be an endless amount to learn."

"There is, but fortunately, I have the best teacher." She threw Richy an appreciative smile. "But I want to hear about your work, David. It's fascinating to meet a high-ranking American diplomat. I'm dying to learn how a non-Jewish envoy is received in Jerusalem—if I may turn the tables and ask you that."

"Very well, so far, thank you." The question had taken him by surprise. A direct little thing, wasn't she? "I haven't felt excluded or discriminated against, if that's what you're getting at. The foreign minister assures me his door will always be open."

"The foreign minister. That's Shimon Kedar, isn't it? Tell me about him."

A well-informed little thing, also. "Si Kedar is a little man with a big personality and intellect. You have a special interest in Israel, Miss Razmari?"

"Roxana," she reminded him sweetly. "I'm interested in knowing what's happening there; it has such an effect on the rest of the Middle East. There's a total blackout of news here in Riyadh. In America I got spoiled; we could read about it or watch it on the television news. I was in California when the Lebanon war was going on. The news coverage was good. It was almost like being there."

The words seemed to gush out of her, the sentences running together. She paused for breath. "Are there any more surprises like Lebanon in the offing?"

"Not to my knowledge." Why did he have the feeling they were sparring? "Of course, I have no direct line into the Israeli cabinet or Defense Department. I might be the last to know."

"Oh, now David." The demure smile persisted. "I'm sure you're being far too modest. Your embassies have a way of finding out these things, don't they? I mean, in Teheran—all those CIA agents in the American embassy. It was common knowledge."

The brazen little—! Did she suspect him of being an agent? No, that was ridiculous. Stop bristling! His own smile answered hers.

"My dear Roxana. I can assure you we do not make a practice of spying on our friends." The disclaimer sounded hollow and unconvincing to him, Abernathy's face insinuating itself into his mind's eye.

Their waiter, arriving with a steamy copper washbowl, provided a welcome distraction. As custom dictated, towels were dispensed first to the gentlemen, a slight not lost on the lady, whose little grimace was duly noted by the attentive Richy.

"Chivalry must be dead here," he observed.

"Ha!" Roxana exploded. "It has yet to be born here, or in most other Islamic countries. At least that's one thing the Shah did for Iran. Or rather, the Mrs. Shah."

Determinedly, she returned to the prior subject of conversation, regarding David with a playful half smile. "So, you do not spy on your friends. Most commendable. But it's so difficult, these days, to tell who your friends are, isn't it?"

In spite of himself, he burst out laughing. "Touché, Roxana! I confess, I'm not privy to what the CIA does or whom they consider their friends or enemies at the moment. We have a very simple working arrangement. I leave them alone, and they leave me alone."

He rinsed and dried his hands and accepted a menu from the hovering waiter, hoping that the subject was closed. The menu was in Arabic. Roxana translated it for them, item by item, Richy commenting on the dishes he recognized from his previous visit.

David listened with half an ear, studying the glamorous, Americanized Irani with the disarmingly direct manner and quick, inquiring mind. Had her questions been random ones, or was there a purpose behind them? He wondered just how close she and Richy had become. His brother, so far as he knew, had had little experience with women. And this one, unless he missed his guess, had been around a lot. He feared his baby brother might be getting in a trifle over his head.

Dinner at the Tangier proved to be as interesting as it was appetizing. Their waiter, Ahmad, was a born clown. He had a story to go with each successive dish introduced to the table, acting it out as Roxana laughingly translated from the Arabic. There was a paucity of tableware to eat with, because, as Ahmad observed, Allah had provided man with the ideal eating utensils —his fingers. Only the right hand must be used, however, the left being taboo for eating purposes, having, as Ahmad put it, "other uses" that contaminated it. His pantomime left them in stitches and very little to the imagination.

After the soup and the salad and couscous came a baked lamb in pastry dish, a bit on the greasy side, but succulent. Roxana, David noted, was a good eater, not at all bashful about wading in with her fingers. His own stomach, so recently famished for food, was now filled to bursting, with hardly a clean spot in evidence on his dampened bath towel, provided to each guest for cleaning the "eating utensils" between courses.

His relief was manifest when Ahmad deposited the final course on the table, a bowl of fresh fruits and nuts, and commenced pouring the thick, rich, Arabian coffee. "You must all manage at least one loud belch," he informed them through his giggling translator, "or our chef will be mortally offended." At their inability to produce even one modest-sized burp between them, he pretended to be genuinely put out. "May Allah have mercy on your souls." He turned on his heel and stalked off, shaking his head.

"Leaving us to our just desserts," Richy suggested. The other two groaned in unison, Roxana mustering enough energy to bombard him with the extra backrest pillow. It bounced off his head and rolled into the aisle, winding up in front of the neighboring alcove.

David, who was facing in that direction, had been vaguely aware of two men seated there, dining quietly in contrast to the spirited goings-on next door to them. He had noted raised eyebrows on the part of the man facing him once when the hilarity had gotten a bit out of hand, but could only see the back of the taller man, who had not bothered to turn around.

Now, for the first time, he did so, revealing a face so gaunt, the skin so tightly stretched over the hairless expanse of scalp and forehead, that the impression of a death's head was inescapable. The dark-circled, sunken eyes enhanced the effect, and when their owner smiled—a bizarre, smirking grimace exposing two rows of yellowed teeth—the illusion was complete.

Slowly and deliberately, the ungainly skeleton to which the skull was attached unfolded itself and stood up, retrieving the pillow from the floor with a deft sweep of one gangling arm, like a giant praying mantis scooping up its unsuspecting dinner. A single stride brought him in front of their table, where he addressed himself to the senior Llewellyn.

"I do believe your lovely dinner companion has lost her pillow. Kindly allow me to return it, and to introduce myself."

David blinked, momentarily speechless, the deeply resonant, cultured voice totally unexpected from the emaciated wreck that towered over him. A voice invoking an English gentry background.

"I am Sir Roger Tewkesbury-Cream." The grotesque smile persisted, as if frozen into the wasted jaws. "And you would be Ambassador Llewellyn. It is a rare privilege, sir, to meet you; a rare privilege, indeed." He extended a long, bony hand, which David accepted gingerly, anticipating the chilly touch of the pallid, fleshless digits but not the grip of steel, which made him wince.

"How do you know me?" he inquired suspiciously, certain that he had never laid eyes on the man before. He could hardly forget a face like that.

"Ah, yes, that could do with a bit of explaining." The Englishman glanced purposefully at the unoccupied portion of Roxana's divan. "Might I join you for a moment?"

Without waiting for an answer, the hulking skeleton replaced the cushion and collapsed itself onto the settee, its other occupant scooting sideways in the nick of time. David did a rapid reevaluation. The outlandish-appearing drop-in had the unmistakable air of an aristocrat. Unless he missed his guess, the modish mohair business suit that hung so limply from the scarecrow frame was Saville Row tailoring.

Roxana shrunk back perceptibly and looked helplessly toward Richy, whose face wore a faintly amused expression. He thrust out his hand. "I'm the envoy's brother. I work here in Riyadh."

"Of course. The AWACS expert." The skull shook his hand heartily. "And the beautiful young lady from Iran is one of your associates on the project, I believe."

He turned the full force of his presence on Roxana. "Charmed to make your acquaintance, my dear. My name is Roger. To some I am known as 'Jolly Roger.'" The chilling smile broadened.

Roxana suppressed a shudder and could not bring herself to accept the repulsive hand extended toward her. Instead, her hand found Richy's under the table, her gay mood of minutes before noticeably dampened. It frightened her that this eerie stranger should know who she was, know anything about her. What did he have to do with her? What did he want?

David was wondering the same thing; the preliminaries had gone on long enough. "You seem to know a lot about us, considering that none of us has ever laid eyes on you before. Just who are you, Mr. Cream, and why are you here?"

"Tewkesbury-Cream," the Englishman corrected. "We English have a habit of hyphenating surnames, don't you know. But please call me 'Sir Roger.' It sounds so much more friendly."

He settled into the comfortable back cushion and beckoned to the waiter. "Would anyone care to join me in a spot of tea?"

David's patience was wearing thin. "I think we'd all prefer to hear what you have to say." And then get rid of you, he added to himself.

Sir Roger sighed. "I see that you're a man who likes to get directly to the point. Permit me to do so, then. The fact is, I've been trying to catch up with you all afternoon, since learning from a mutual acquaintance in Jerusalem that you were here in Riyadh to visit your brother."

"What mutual acquaintance?" David challenged. "Only the Ambassador knew—"

"Someone else in your embassy," the Englishman responded. "One of our sources; it's not important."

"It is to me. I don't like leaks." Heightened hostility showed in the envoy's eyes. What did Sir Roger mean by "our sources"? Was this some kind of spy caper? Had Abernathy found out about his trip and tipped off one of his old British cronies?

"Ah, but this is purely a diplomatic matter," the skull hastened to assure him, reading the change in his expression. "You see, sir, I am representing a prominent member of the royal family here, the House of Saud. While recognizing that your visit here is unofficial, my client is most anxious to meet with you while you are here in Riyadh. It isn't often that an American envoy to Israel gets down this way," he added wryly.

"Meet?" David's frown deepened. "To what purpose? I have

to get back. I have an early morning return flight."

"Yes, yes I know. But after all, sir, the royal family. My client is available this evening. He is, in fact, standing by at this very moment, awaiting your response."

David was not exactly overwhelmed by the mention of royalty. The so-called royal family of Saudi Arabia was a sizable one. He had heard that several thousand Saudis claimed that distinction. "Just who is this royal client of yours?" he demanded.

The Englishman hesitated. "I should not like this information to go beyond the three of you." The obsidian pupils of the sunken eyes darted from face to face, underlining the warning. He lowered his voice to a conspiratorial whisper.

"We are speaking of no less than one of the sons of the late King Faisal."

He produced an envelope from the inside pocket of his stylish suit coat, handing it to David. It was addressed to "Ambassador Llewellyn" and bore a red wax seal with the impression of crossed swords beneath a palm tree. He broke the seal. The brief note was in English, and he read it aloud.

"I should like very much to meet with you during your stay in Riyadh, on a matter of utmost urgency to both of our governments. Signed, Prince Turki al Faisal."

If David wasn't impressed, his companions certainly were. Roxana tugged on Richy's sleeve, leaning across the table to whisper in his ear. "He's Director of Foreign Intelligence, one of the most powerful men in the government. Your brother must see him."

Richy agreed. "It sounds important, Dave. Don't hesitate on our account."

David was also aware of Prince Turki and his position in the government. It reinforced his suspicion that the American intelligence community, known to be thick with their Saudi counterparts, might be trying to involve him in something. His initial reaction was to avoid the meeting. But could he afford to do that? He had yet to discover his first clue to the identity of the embassy mole. Anything that might uncover such a lead should be pursued. He decided to play along, agreeing to accompany the bizarre go-between to the audience with Prince Turki.

Sir Roger immediately dispatched his companion to telephone the news to the Saudi prince. "The meeting may run quite late," he warned Richy. "I'll see that your brother is returned to his hotel at its conclusion." He hurried off to collect his limousine.

Richy stared after him. "What a creepy dude!"

"Hardly your typical PR man," David agreed.

"Why on earth would a Saudi prince use someone like that for a front man?" Richy pondered.

"Good question. Perhaps this meeting with Prince Turki will provide the answer." And a few others, he hoped. He clamped a hand on his brother's shoulder. "Sorry about the change in plans. Why don't you join me for breakfast tomorrow?"

He turned to Roxana and took her hand. "Sorry I have to run off. You've been a charming dinner companion, beautiful and witty. Best of luck in your new career; I know you'll do well. And take good care of the kid here."

"I intend to," she replied, squeezing his hand before releasing it.

He looked for the check, but Richy had already picked it up. The Englishman beckoned from the door. He stood up to go.

"Till tomorrow, then; breakfast at my hotel. I hope I haven't ruined your plans for the rest of the evening."

Richy grinned. "I'm sure we'll think of something. Right, Roxy?"

She nodded, returning his smile, and David noticed that the mischievous sparkle was back in the dancing eyes.

After the first kiss, Richy knew he was about to get laid, and the realization shot through him like an electric shock, setting his whole body on fire. He had never been kissed like that before, by a mouth seeking out his mouth with understated passion, by lips that felt their way inside his own until a perfect coupling was achieved. When her tongue at last sought his, imparting its unmistakable invitation, it seemed the most natural thing in the world.

Kisses, in Richard Llewellyn's limited experience, had been clumsy, disappointing preludes to further disappointments. Making out with women, he decided early on, was simply not his bag. You needed supreme self-confidence, the kind of brazenness that broke down resistance. He couldn't muster it; he realized that his inherent shyness was a debilitating impediment.

Not that the world knew him as a shy person. If you were born shy, you strove to compensate for it. You forced yourself to be outgoing and gregarious, developed a shell that disguised as well as protected your hypersensitive insides. No, shyness wasn't something you showed the world; you did your best to cover it up. Just as you covered up the fact that you were still a virgin, until that first, unsatisfactory deflowering.

But suddenly everything was different. Here, halfway around the world from his birthplace, a woman who was everything he had ever dreamed of was in his arms, inviting him to make love to her. Roxana, the most desirable of women, vibrant, intelligent, lovely beyond words—and she wanted him! He could hardly believe his good fortune. Self-assurance coursed through his veins. With a strength that surprised him, he swept her up and carried her onto his bunk.

"You are very strong." The glittering eyes were smoldering, now, communicating a desire that matched his own. Tenderly, he raised her head and back off the bed and found the zipper on the low-cut gown. Milk-white breasts spilled out of the built-in bra; spellbound by their beauty, he bent to kiss the tiny rosebuds at their centers. She peered up at him dreamily through half-closed lids as he carefully removed her gown and slipped off the filmy hose and sheer, brief underpants. "And also very gentle."

His own clothes were on the floor in a matter of seconds. "And also very ready," he whispered into her ear, as their disrobed bodies came together in the first exhilarating contact of naked skin. God, was he ready! A lifetime of being ready.

"And also I am ready," she whispered back. It was the last time either spoke, their mouths otherwise occupied. The feel of her satin-smooth thighs sliding against his own was overpoweringly provocative. Their young bodies clove together, a single writhing, pulsating form, his hands and lips everywhere, exploring, caressing. He couldn't get enough of her, his body aching to possess, devour hers. He needed more hands, another mouth.

And then her own delicate hands became busy, touching, fondling, then guiding him unerringly, the exquisite sensation that ensued lighting a fuse within him that burned all too rapidly beyond his control. Too short a fuse, he thought helplessly, before abandoning himself to the excruciating pleasure of the explosion. But Roxana's uninhibited cries of fulfillment told him otherwise.

The light touch of a single fingertip gliding slowly back and forth across his lips brought him back. He awoke to see her sitting on the side of the bed, clad only in his T-shirt that she had retrieved from among the hastily shed garments he had scattered about the floor. She smiled at him, and he yawned and sat up.

"I thought we were both going to take a little nap."

"You men! You can fall asleep at the drop of a hat. I'm much too excited to sleep."

The nipples stood out prominently where her breasts bulged against the white T-shirt, their beige-pink rosettes clearly visible through the thinly knit fabric. "I'm excited, too," he said, reaching for her.

She submitted to a lingering kiss before slipping free of his arms. "I mean, the whole evening has been exciting. I guess I'm still flying high. Meeting your brother—what a charming man! Dinner was so much fun. And then that hideous Englishman, Sir Roger What's-His-Name, appearing out of nowhere. And the note from Prince Turki. Do you realize David is meeting with the prince at this very moment? Aren't you curious to know what's happening?"

Richy stretched and threw his legs over the side of the bed to sit beside her, recapturing her waist in the crook of his arm. "I'm curious, all right—curious about you. I want to know everything about you, everything I've missed by not knowing you sooner. Who the little girl was that grew up to be so bright and beautiful."

He kissed her neck tenderly. She patted his hand. "I'm sure you'd find it very dull. I'd rather talk about your brother's audience with the prince. Don't you have any idea what it could be about?"

He shrugged. "Couldn't it just be a formality—diplomatic protocol, or something of the sort?"

She shook her head. "I don't think so. Faisal's youngest son is not a diplomat; Prince Turki's business is protecting his country from its enemies. No, there's something important going on, I can sense it. Hasn't David mentioned anything about his work that would give you a clue?"

"Not really. He's not exactly a chatterbox when it comes to talking about his job. Besides, he was as surprised as we were at the invitation." He looked at her curiously. "You're really turned on by all this, aren't you? How do you know so much about the Saudi government?"

"I don't, actually," she answered. "But I'm greatly interested in it. Living in a foreign country can be a marvelous opportunity to learn about it firsthand. This country is just emerging from long centuries of slumber. The changes within the last decade have been unbelievable. We're seeing history in the making."

"And I thought you were just a computer grind in her pretty little lady engineer cocoon," he laughed. "I'm discovering all kinds of things about you tonight." He rolled back onto the bed and pulled her toward him. "Let's discover some more."

She resisted halfheartedly. "Richard, invite me to breakfast with you and your brother tomorrow. I'm dying to know what happened."

"Okay, fair enough. You spend the night with me, I buy you breakfast."

"Silly," she giggled, snuggling up to him. "I have to get back to my own room. Do you want me to have to wear my evening gown to breakfast? That would be a dead giveaway."

"Okay," he agreed, "no evening gowns. The T-shirt you're wearing will do just fine."

David Llewellyn was beginning to wonder what had possessed him to go along on this venture. The drive seemed to be taking forever. As if it weren't spooky enough to be riding along in the semidarkness sitting next to Boris Karloff, the limousine had left the relative comfort of the city lights and was now immersed in the blackness of the desert night. Was the meeting with the prince all a hoax—was he being taken for a ride? The letter from the prince had looked authentic enough, but now he realized that it could have been a forgery. Kidnapping in a foreign country was an ever-present danger that American diplomats were continually warned against. His curiosity, his excitement at the prospect of a possible lead to the identity of the embassy mole, had influenced his judgment. The first glimpse of the limousine awaiting him in front of the Tangier should have been a sufficient dissuader.

It was an ivory-colored Rolls, looking identical to the one that had stuck so closely to their rental car all the way into town from the airport. It confirmed his suspicion that he had been expected, followed continuously since first setting foot in Riyadh.

Had he been set up? If so, who had leaked his travel plans to Riyadh? Surely not the ambassador; Abrams was no more anxious than he to have it known that the second-ranking diplomat in his embassy was off on a visit to a country hostile to Israel. The only other person who had known of his plans in advance was Daniella, who had since dropped out of sight. Was there some connection; was she somehow involved in this? No, that was absurd. Even supposing for the sake of argument that Abernathy's accusations about her Mossad affiliation were on target;

that was all the more reason why any liaison with the Saudis from that quarter was totally illogical.

Abernathy. The finger of suspicion somehow kept pointing in his direction. He was in charge of embassy security; there could have been a tap on the office phone on which David had personally called in the flight reservations. Or Abernathy could have learned the flight plans from the ambassador's chauffeur in time to inform his former MI-6 cronies, of whom the weird escort sitting beside him was almost certainly one. But to what end; what did they want from him? Was it connected to the secret mission to Jerusalem laid on him by the President? Had Abernathy somehow learned of it? If Abernathy was the mole, this midnight ride could be a scheme to get him out of the picture. Permanently.

As if to allay any such fears, his traveling companion proceeded to maintain his lively line of chatter. "It does seem a long way, doesn't it? But it's not a great deal farther. Prince Turki, like many of the royal family, much prefers the tranquility of the desert to the congestion and clamor of the city. Those who are forced to live in the city make numerous pilgrimages out onto the open sands where they can sniff the freshness of the air, feel the desert winds against their skin, and commune with their nomad heritage.

"It's a great honor to be invited into the Prince's home," he continued. "I, myself, have been there only once, though our acquaintance goes back many years. The Prince treasures his privacy out here and prefers to conduct most of his business in the city."

"What makes me so important, then?" David asked suspiciously. "I've never even met the man. What business between us could be that urgent?"

"I'm not at liberty to say," the cultured Oxford voice replied. "I'm afraid you'll have to wait for your audience with him to be enlightened."

If there really is an audience with the prince, thought David, still uneasy, conscious of the hair under his collar standing on end. He hadn't really felt comfortable since arriving in Riyadh, he realized. There was something about Arabs and Arab countries that gave him the creeps.

As the limousine slowed and turned into a narrow driveway, the appearance of the residence illuminated by the car's headlights did little to reassure him. The house was anything but princely, a small bungalow, dimly lighted and meagerly land-scaped. The beam from the headlights swept out into the void of the immediate surroundings. There were no neighbors, no ad-joining houses or buildings to be seen. Nothing but sand dunes. An ideal spot for a kidnapping.

The chauffeur came around to open the door. "Come along," Sir Roger invited reassuringly, preceding him out the door. "I'll introduce you to the Prince. You'll find him urbane and articu-late. He is unquestionably the best educated of all the royal fam-ily. Prepped in your country, degrees from two American universities and one British."

David stepped out onto the recently oiled black asphalt drive. There was still no sign of life from within the bungalow. They made their way along a flagstone path set into the white gravel that covered the entire expanse of front yard—a white rock lawn in lieu of green grass. The only plants in evidence were cactus of different varieties. Water was evidently in short supply here.

There was no doorbell. Sir Roger knocked briskly on the heavy hardwood door, and it opened almost immediately. Pre-pared for almost anything, David was taken aback. Instead of a henchman or royal attendant, there stood the prince himself in his stocking feet. David recognized him immediately, the hawklike Faisal beak unmistakable. But otherwise there was little facial resemblance between the famous father and his youngest son, whose thick-lensed glasses above a scraggly, unkempt beard pro-jected the look more of the owl than the hawk. Of medium height, looking somewhat frailer than the usually hearty al-Saud stock, he wore a handsomely gold embroidered black *thobe* topped off by the traditional Saudi red and white checked kaf-fiyeh.

"Ah, Mr. Llewellyn. So good of you to accept my invitation at this inconvenient hour, and on such short notice." He shook David's hand warmly. "I have just now sent my man off to bed, but he prepared coffee before he retired. Won't you join me?" He shook Sir Roger's hand. "And you, my good friend. Welcome to my house."

The Englishman bowed deeply. "I am greatly honored, Your Highness." He nudged David, who assumed that he was expected to follow suit. But bowing wasn't his style.

"It's very good of Your Highness to receive me at this late hour," he managed. "How can I be of assistance?"

"Ah, you Americans. So direct. No beating about the bush. I

miss that." The prince motioned them toward a comfortable grouping of chairs and sofas about a low table atop which an ornate gold and silver coffee urn sent up its steamy, aromatic essence. When they were seated, he began to pour.

"There are many things about America I miss. And Britain, also, things I learned to appreciate in the years that I spent there. If we were there now, I could offer you spirits along with your coffee. But here in Riyadh we must set a good example. The House of Saud is entrusted with the protection of the Islamic covenants, the continued strict adherence to the teachings of the true prophet. If we do not personally follow them, how can we expect our people to do so?

"It is our people, you see, who are the true treasure of Saudi Arabia, the real trust of our ruling family, as opposed to the black riches buried beneath the sand." He passed the coffee around and sighed. "We try very hard to stay in touch with our people. Sometimes it takes a great deal of patience. They are slow to accept necessary changes. They oppose reforms, the education of women, for example. Much of our time is taken up holding communion with them, listening to their concerns, administering to their needs—and complaints."

"The *majlis*," volunteered Sir Roger.

"Yes, my friend, the majlis. The open court held every morning except on the Sabbath," he explained for David's benefit, "presided over by the King, himself. Any citizen can attend and present a petition or grievance. It is traditional. Here in this age of computers we are still doing it. I sometimes wonder, myself, how my uncle can continue to afford the time."

David leaned back in his chair, trying to appear more relaxed. He knew that small talk before business was normal with the Arabs. Was the prince only trying to put him at ease, or was this some kind of a snow job to set him up for something? He wished that Turki al Faisal would get to the point.

The prince sensed his impatience. "It grows late. Let me state my purpose in asking you here. As Director of Foreign Intelligence, I am responsible for the security of my country against acts of aggression or intervention by other nations. We have only recently uncovered a most serious threat to our national survival. I believe you will agree, Mr. Llewellyn, knowing as I'm certain you do of the close financial coupling between our two countries, that if any such disaster were to overtake Saudi Arabia, the repercussions in America could be very grave, indeed."

"As well as in Britain—the entire West," Jolly Roger threw in. "Banks everywhere—the World Bank—would collapse."

Prince Turki ignored the interruption, his bespectacled eyes riveted to David's face. "To avert such a catastrophe, we need your help. My intelligence organization is working closely with British and American intelligence in an effort to uncover more details of the plot against us. But at the moment we are stymied. In your capacity as the new envoy to Israel, you may be in a position to do us a great service. Will you help us to save our country?"

The prince's direct question caught him by surprise. What was going on here—what was that son of a bitch Abernathy setting him up for?

"Your Highness," he responded, more sharply than he had intended, "this has gone far enough. The man you've obviously been in touch with already approached me—propositioned me— with an outrageous suggestion that I spy for him on one of our closest allies, the country to which the President of the United States has made me his personal envoy. It's highly improper that I should even be discussing this with you—I'm surprised you would even approach me. Such matters should be handled at Cabinet level—the Secretary of State, the National Security Adviser. But since you brought it up, let me make it clear to you, once and for all, that I would never consider doing any such thing."

"Even if it meant averting a major catastrophe and saving half the world—your own country included—from financial ruin?" If the prince had taken umbrage at this disrespectful outburst, he disguised it well. "Mr. Llewellyn," he continued coolly, "I cannot go through your State Department channels on a matter such as this. There would be inevitable delays—and leaks—and we cannot tolerate either. In the interest of time and expediency I have no choice but to come directly to you and appeal to your own conscience and sense of patriotism. Your own intelligence people are prevented by strict U.S. security regulations from divulging to you the nature and severity of the threat that we face. But here in Arabia I am not bound by those contraints."

Prince Turki seemed to consider for a second, then rose from his chair. "Kindly remain seated," he admonished, as the other two got to their feet. "I'll only be a moment." He padded briskly out of the room. David looked questioningly at the Englishman and noted the glint in his eye.

"You're in for a bit of a shock," he whispered. Almost immediately the prince was back, bearing a thick manila folder.

"Before showing this to you, I must ask that you pledge your strict adherence to the tightest possible security measures concerning this information. This document was originated by the government of Israel. You will note the highly classified markings on its pages. To divulge the existence of this document or any of its contents to any unauthorized person would be considered the most serious of felonies by both our governments. The extreme sensitivity of the information will become clear to you as you peruse it. Do I have your pledge?"

David stared back into the owl eyes and nodded, his pulse quickening. Could this be one of the "leaked" documents the President had referred to? If so, it had to have left a trail, one that might be followed back to the source, the embassy mole. He reached for the manila folder. Turki al Faisal handed it over.

"You will see that there are two documents. One, in Hebrew, is a photostatic copy of the original. The second is an English translation by your CIA, the accuracy of which has been authenticated by my own language specialists in Foreign Intelligence. You do not read Hebrew?"

David shook his head, trying to keep the disappointment from registering in his expression. A CIA translation, supplied through CIA channels to British and Saudi intelligence. That would seem to rule out any connection with the mole as the source. His eyes scanned the Hebrew manuscript, the only intelligible words those stamped across the top and bottom of each page, presumably by the CIA—TOP SECRET—NOFORN. The latter classification, prohibiting any foreign release, struck him as not only unusual but ludicrous, the document having been originated by one foreign government and obviously already distributed by the CIA to at least two others, the English and Saudis.

He moved quickly to the English translation, which carried identical classification markings plus a combination of letters and numbers that he recognized as a code classifying the manuscript as a CIA "black" document. The first page also bore the date of publication, July 4, 1987; the place of publication, Jerusalem; and the identity of the originating organization, the Office of the Israeli Minister of Defense.

Page two, the title page, was a stunner, and David's gasp was audible as he read:

CONTINGENCY PLAN FOR THE OVERTHROW
OF THE HOUSE OF SAUD AND TAKEOVER
OF THE SAUDI ARABIAN OIL FIELDS

Self-propelled, his eyes raced over the pages that followed. There was a listing of conditions under which a military takeover of Saudi Arabia might become a recommended option to an Israel with its back to the wall, among which he noted: oil starvation of Israel by the tightening of the OPEC oil embargo to cut off present supplies; threatened financial collapse brought about by the possible loss of U.S. financial aid due to deterioration of Israeli-American relations, accompanied by the deployment of a U.S. Quick Reaction Strike Force in a hostile Middle East country; possible sanctions imposed against Israel to enforce the establishment of a Palestinian state within Eretz Israel; and Saudi-sponsored proliferation of nuclear weapons into the hands of hostile Arab nations.

The takeover plan described on succeeding pages was a summary but nevertheless quite detailed. Phase One entailed preemptive air strikes against Saudi military installations located on an accompanying map. He noted that these were chiefly air bases, including the air force headquarters at Riyadh, where AWACS was based, plus the naval bases along the Persian Gulf and Red Sea. Phase Two would commence with the daring night landing of commandos in troop transports at Dhahran, the largest airport in the world, gas flares from the adjacent oil fields lighting the way. With control of the major oil fields quickly established, coordinated early morning landings of paratroops at the airports outside Riyadh and Jedda and in the oil enclaves of Qatar and Ras Tanura would follow. There was reference to an accompanying action, "Operation Bright Sun," not apparently described further here or elsewhere in the document.

The third and final phase was referred to simply as a "mopping up exercise." The royal family and its representatives in government would be interned and a provisional government set up, drawing on "dissident elements" within the kingdom. Petroleum production experts would be brought into the oil fields to guarantee minimal disruption in the flow of oil. Aramco would be taken over and administered by the provisional government, with assurances to all consumer nations and participating oil companies that a "fair" distribution policy would be upheld. Sheik Yamani's recent replacement would in turn be replaced by a designee of the new government as Arabian oil minister and OPEC representative. The plan said nothing about pricing policy. It didn't have to. By controlling the price of almost half of the world's oil, Israel would have at its mercy the financial solvency of every major country with the possible exception of Russia.

David looked up from the document into the two pairs of eyes intent on his reaction. Sir Roger's face wore its intense and bizarre "jolly" look in anticipation; Prince Turki's was a model of expressionless calm.

His first reaction was one of skepticism. "Where did this come from?" He wouldn't put it past the CIA to resort to a forgery for the furtherance of their own ends. It wouldn't be the first time. "Can anyone vouch for its authenticity?"

"We have positive proof that it is genuine," the Prince replied quickly. "I cannot divulge the source, but I can give you my personal assurance that it is authentic."

"But—it's too preposterous!" David shook his head, still unbelieving. "The sheer audacity! How could they even dream of being able to pull it off? The armed might of the entire world would be against them."

The prince permitted himself a slight smile, which as quickly vanished. "Timing, Mr. Llewellyn. The element of surprise. They have the tools and they are masters at it. The quick strike without warning. Once in possession of our oil fields they could blackmail our country—all of the Western nations—into submission."

"But you have AWACS. You would see them coming and be able to alert your air bases, your militia—the U.S. Rapid Deployment Force."

"True, AWACS would be a problem for them. But it has certain weaknesses that could be exploited. We cannot afford to gamble that they would not find a way to neutralize it. And as for your Rapid Deployment Force, it has a few shortcomings of its own, I am afraid, though your government, in concert with mine, is working hard to correct these. But at this moment the Rapid Deployment Force might be compared to the Holy Roman Empire, which was once described as being neither holy, Roman, nor even an empire. I'm afraid your so-called Rapid Deployment Force has turned out to be none too rapid in its response, not yet fully deployed, and a questionable force to be relied on."

David pondered for a moment, his frown deepening. "I can't believe they'd really risk it. Unless they were completely backed

into a corner. Even then—the odds against them, the consequences of failure." He thumbed back through the document to
its title page. "Contingency plan. Lots of governments make military contingency plans and never carry them out. Are you sure
you're not overreacting?"

Just the whisper of a frown rippled the forehead between the
two thick lenses. "I do not believe that I overreact, Mr. Llewellyn. Any more than my father overreacted in 1974 when a previous contingency plan surfaced for the conquest of our oil fields
by a foreign power. Do I need to tell you which government
generated this plan? Our good friends, the United States of
America, Mr. Llewellyn. The plan was purposely leaked by your
State Department to intimidate King Faisal into lifting the oil
embargo. A most ill-considered and clumsy bluff. It angered my
father, who had already made the decision to end the embargo in
the interest of better relations between our two countries. But in
the end he did not take it seriously. It would have been totally out
of character for your country, you see."

"But not for Israel?"

"Precisely, Mr. Llewellyn. More specifically, not out of character for the Begin regime and their successors. They have made
it abundantly clear that they consider it their right to go anywhere
and do anything in the Middle East that they conceive to be in
their own best interest, world opinion be damned. And thanks to
the bountiful aid from America, they have the third most powerful war machine on earth with which to carry out their objectives."

"But would they dare to use it so flagrantly, knowing that it
would mean the end to all such aid, the alienation of their last
remaining friends in the world?"

"That is a gamble we can ill afford to take. It is our country,
you see, that is on the line." The prince stared thoughtfully down
at the table for a moment. "Do you play poker, Mr. Llewellyn?"

"Occasionally."

"Would you bet against a sure thing, a hand you knew to
contain a winning hole card?"

"Of course not." What was the prince driving at?

"We believe that Israel holds such a card, Mr. Llewellyn. It is
referred to in the document you hold in your hand. You noted,
did you not, the reference to 'Operation Bright Sun'?"

David nodded.

"That is a new code name to us," the prince continued, "one

that we have not yet positively broken. But of the nature of the operation we have no doubt. It is, in short, some form of nuclear blackmail.

"Don't look so startled, Mr. Llewellyn. Such tactics are hardly new to the Jewish state. Surely you are aware that the threat of nuclear weapons was employed against the Syrians and Egyptians to halt their advances in the early stages of the October War, when Israel was losing. The fact that such weapons were not actually used is beside the point. We do not question that they possess them. Their factory at Dimona in the Negev has been turning them out steadily for more than a decade."

David was stunned. "I'm aware of the nuclear reactor at Dimona, of course. But actual weapons—what proof do you have of this?"

Prince Turki shrugged. "What proof is necessary? The warning delivered to Egypt and Syria speaks for itself. I first learned of this directly from Anwar Sadat, and later from President Hafiz Assad of Syria. Both men believed that the threat was genuine and that nuclear weapons would have been employed had not the war turned in Israel's favor."

A nuclear war in the Middle East, the very scenario invoked by the President! The color drained from David's face as the President's words came back to him. A vivid enactment of an all-too-possible holocaust flashed before him, the oil resources of half the world obliterated overnight, atomized by all-consuming white-hot fireballs leaving nothing but giant mushroom clouds in their wake. And the nightmare consequences, the financial chaos that would inevitably follow one of the milder ones compared to the threat of nuclear escalation that could eventually engulf the entire planet. The ingredients were all there, dry tinder waiting for the spark to set it off. A spark that must be avoided at all cost.

His eyes came back into focus, the death's-head countenance of the Englishman providing grim punctuation to his vision of horror. He looked back into the face of the Saudi director of foreign intelligence. Could he trust this man? Was this prince of Arabia as sincere as he pretended to be, dedicated only to the preservation of his country and people? Behind the thick glasses, the face was noncommittal, a mask.

Don't trust anyone, said the voice inside him. *Just play along*.

The newly appointed American envoy to the state of Israel heaved a heavy sigh. "What is it you want me to find out?"

CHAPTER
6

As his taxi sped north on Dizengoff Street, the Tel Aviv cabbie felt a hand on his shoulder and turned his head questioningly.

"I'll get off here."

The hard-bitten cabdriver cursed under his breath and slowed in preparation for fighting his way through two lanes of heavy traffic to reach the curb. "I thought you said—"

"I did. I changed my mind."

Horns blared from behind as the taxi maneuvered between the fast-moving vehicles, its driver responding with a well-chosen imprecation in Yiddish as he searched for a place to pull in to the curb. His fare sprang from the cab with the easy grace of a natural athlete. He was not a tall man, but solidly built, dressed in the royal blue uniform of the Israeli Air Force and wearing captain's bars on his shoulders. He thrust two folded bills through the half-open window.

"This should do it. Shalom."

Blind at close range without his reading glasses, the cabbie held the currency at arm's length, squinting his eyes. Two ten-shekel notes. A good tipper, for a serviceman. "Shalom," he answered, plucking the well-chomped cigar from his mouth and looking back out the window. But his fare had already vanished into the crowd.

Captain Zev Lieb paused for a moment, ostensibly to inspect the opulently decorated windows of Gucci's. Their reflective surface provided a panoramic view of the street behind. Satisfied that no other vehicle had followed the cab, he stepped out smartly, turning west down the first side street, then slackened his pace. There was no rush, he reminded himself; he was quite early. The Namir Center along the Mediterranean shore would be at most a fifteen-minute walk. After the ride in from the air base, the stroll would do him good. It was a fine day, as ideal for walking as for flying. He glanced up at the blue sky with its delicate scattering of lacy white cirrus, feeling somewhat like a truant schoolboy. That was where he should be right now, with the rest of his squadron—where he had planned to be. Until the letter had reached him.

Extracting the envelope from the breast pocket of his uniform, he removed the note inside and unfolded it, revealing a scant two columns of letters and numbers commingled. To the uninitiated eye it would appear to be an innocent chess-by-mail communication, a sequence of moves recorded in the standard shorthand of the game. 1 e4 d5—opening king's pawn moves. 2 Nc3 Be3— white advancing king's knight and black, king's bishop. But Capt. Zev Lieb's eye was better trained. Months before he had memorized a code that translated the sequence of numbers into the date and hour of a meeting, the letters into one of a number of designated locations and the identifying code for the rendezvous. The chessboard set up in his room at the officers' quarters was only a cover; he barely knew how to play the game. And Zev Lieb was not his real name. He was Adnan Ibrahim al Amiri, Iraqi citizen and undercover agent. His code name was "El Aurens."

Without slowing his pace, he scanned the note again and went through the mental process of deciphering it. He had made no mistake. The date was indeed today's, the hour 11 A.M., and the place the Kek Csillag, a Hungarian cafe in the Namir Center— the collection of shops and eateries along the beach, near the marina. He wondered at the time of day they had selected, chafing a bit. Why couldn't they have made it in the evening, when he would have had no trouble getting away? It had not been easy to get the morning off. Training for the upcoming action had intensified, the start of the countdown apparently nearing. He had had to feign a severe toothache to be granted an emergency visit to his dentist here in the city. There'd better be a good reason.

"They." That was the other thing. There was no indication in the message of whom he was to meet. There never was, the procedure "don't find us, we'll find you." In the previous meetings there had been several different contacts. He had no idea who they were, except that they had used the proper identifying code and obviously knew who he was, and he assumed that the reason for anonymity was to protect them against subsequent exposure. The procedure struck him as slipshod. Not knowing his contact certainly made it easier for some counterintelligence agent to slip in and gum up the works. If the enemy were ever to discover his identity—

But that was something he refused to dwell on. If it happened, it happened, and he would somehow find a way out. He enjoyed what he did, savoring the salty taste of danger, addicted to the adrenaline high that went with putting his own life at risk. It seemed that his entire life since childhood had been a series of perilous adventures, brushes with death part of the menu. He had survived each one and in the process developed an aura of his own indestructibility. Ever since the crash of the primary trainer that had almost killed him, early in his flying career, he had been obsessed with the notion of a special relationship with his creator. Allah was his shield and protector. Allah would watch over him.

Flying was his first love and still the pursuit that gave him the greatest pleasure. Doing it covertly as a member of the enemy's air force only added spice to the experience. And with the Israelis he was going first class, flying the best fighter in the world, the F-15, instead of some cast-off MiG fighter from the Soviet Air Force, the best his own country could offer.

It had not been easy. The masquerade as an Israeli had been, if anything, the least difficult part. After all, he had trained for it most of his life, consciously or unconsciously. He had spent his youth in Haifa, growing up in their midst. An orphaned Muslim in the most squalid of orphanages, bitterly resentful of the relative affluence of the Jewish children and hating them for it, hating his own miserable existence there. Until he had escaped and found his way to the birthplace of his parents. It was the reason he had been selected for an assignment like this, groomed for it continuously since the time shortly after his arrival in Baghdad, when his background had come to the attention of the authorities.

First the battery of tests, establishing his basic intelligence, his raw qualifications to meet the exacting demands that would be placed on him. Then the cramming, the catching up on basic disciplines and academics woefully neglected in the minimal schooling provided by the Haifa orphanage. He was sent to Hebrew school with a number of others to brush up the language they had grown up with, then sent to live with renegade Jews who put on the finishing touches. When the flight training began, he had shown an unusual aptitude, which had been the clincher. Culminating in a new identity, Zev Lieb, complete with forged Israeli birth certificate and college degree, dropping him back into their laps. With an arrangement that he be accepted as a flight candidate in the air force cadet training program, through what combination of bribery and string-pulling he could only speculate.

Making it as an air force fighter pilot had been the real challenge. The Israeli standards were exacting, the competition keen. Only the very best made it, the others "washed out," sent back to their families or kibbutzim to pursue other less glamorous careers. He had found the academics the most demanding, the actual flying a piece of cake. Until that day when the rudder of his trainer locked, sending it into an uncontrollable spin. He had managed to bail out, prevailing, somehow, against the almost overpowering combination of gravity and centripetal force and parachuting safely to earth.

The loss of the trainer, he had feared, would be sufficient cause for failing him. But a postmortem on the crashed plane verified the malfunction of the rudder assembly through failure of a critical part and he was exonerated, becoming in the process something of a folk hero among his fellow pilots and officers, who were even then beginning to recognize his exceptional flying talents. Talents later proven under fire in live skirmishes with Syrian MiGs, the small black silhouette painted on the nose of his F-15 testifying to the kill for which he had received credit.

He had been surprised at the degree of satisfaction received from that kill, the absence of remorse over the taking of the life of a fellow Muslim. But at that time his country had considered Syria an enemy, its president, Hafiz Assad, an outspoken critic of the Iraq government of Saddam Hussein, openly promoting his downfall. And after all, hadn't the destruction of the Syrian jet been part of his cover?

How far would he go to protect that cover? If it meant shooting down a MiG-23 with one of his countrymen at the controls, could he perform? It might come down to that in his fighter escort role over Baghdad. With a mental shrug, he dismissed the disturbing thought. He would know what to do when the time came. If it came.

Close enough to the beach now to smell the salt air and hear the sound of the rolling surf, he began to speculate on the reason for today's meeting. He had sent no message of his own requesting such a contact or indicating a need to pass new intelligence, still awaiting the announcement of the date and hour of the Osirak strike. The implication was that they had something to tell him, some piece of important information or change in orders. What could it be, and who would bring it? His last contact, the fat businessman type with his air of self-importance and ridiculous, oversized sunglasses that he insisted on wearing even while indoors? Or the ascetic-looking younger man who had preceded him, dressed in Levi's, T-shirt, and tennis shoes, the casual attire that had become the unofficial uniform of Israeli youth? Or one of the others—or someone new? They had followed the unwritten law of agents in cover, speaking only in Hebrew to avoid undue attention, and he had been unable to decide whether they were actual Jews or imitations, like himself.

A sea of masts protruded above the railing just ahead of him. He had reached the eastern boundary of the small marina. The Iraqi agent stared over the railing at row upon row of pleasure boats bobbing restlessly up and down at their moorings. They epitomized the soft life of wealthy Jews, a reminder of his deprived youth and the contrast between his arduous, half-starved existence in the orphanage and the well-fed, coddled Jewish children he had observed in the homes nearby. There was little activity in the marina, only a few of the boat slips empty. They don't even use them, he thought contemptuously. What a waste. They were only status symbols, something for one rich Jew to show off to another.

He moved on, toward the immense swimming pool dug into the sandy shoreline. If this were summer it would be teeming with Israeli youth, the clamor of their boisterous play filling the air. But it was quiet now, almost deserted, like the adjacent beach, where only a few hardy souls in bathing attire appeared to be taking advantage of the sunny January day.

The Namir Center, too, was quiet at this hour, only a scattering of window-shoppers to be seen strolling between the rows of shops and boutiques with their brightly colored signs and intriguing storefront displays. Farther along, the restaurant section languished in the lull between breakfast and lunchtime, some not yet open. There were all types, from Jewish delicatessen style to Armenian, European, even Chinese, waftings from their diverse cookeries blending in a mouth-watering amalgam of aromas. He spotted the Hungarian place beneath a star composed of blue light bulbs at the far end on the beach side, outdoor tables arrayed across a patio that fronted on the beach.

A woman in a colorful apron was sweeping up the entryway as he approached. "We're closed," she announced. "Come back at eleven-thirty."

Great planning, he thought disgustedly. It was not yet eleven.

He sat down at one of the outdoor tables. "All right if I wait here?"

The woman shrugged and went on with her sweeping. She was raising a cloud of dust. He was relieved when she finished and went inside. The table he had selected was in shadow; he moved to a sunlit one and turned his chair away from the beach to avoid the glare off the ocean. The sun felt good on his back. It made him feel drowsy.

He hadn't heard the man approach and was surprised when he appeared suddenly sitting across the table. He had come from the beach, dressed only in bather's trunks, walking silently on bare feet. A habitual sunbather, by the look of him, one of the sun-worshipping breed who wouldn't let a sparkling winter day like this go to waste. He had the suntan to prove it.

"Mind if I join you?" he inquired in a Hebrew abundantly laced with some foreign inflection. He was wearing sunglasses and carried a small, brightly striped beach bag. "It looks like we're in for a bit of a wait. I'm famished—missed my breakfast this morning."

"Please." The Iraqi had trouble placing the accent. It certainly wasn't from any of the Arab countries. Nor were there many blond Arabs. More likely, he was European. The man must be his contact. Should he initiate the identifying sequence, or wait? He decided to let the other go first.

"Cigarette?" The bronzed sunbather produced a silver cigarette case from the small beach bag he was carrying. It was a timeworn overture, an overworked spy movie cliché. But a very effective one, nonetheless. A natural enough act, one that would appear innocent to any uninvited observer, casual or otherwise. The code could be transmitted in any number of ways that such a spectator would have difficulty in detecting—the initials on the cigarette case, the brand of cigarette, a certain ring worn on the offering hand, the words exchanged subsequently. Only insiders would know the proper code and response preselected for this specific meeting.

The Iraqi looked for it and found it—the blond man's thumb-nail atop the cigarette case, as he extended the opened case across the table. One edge of the nail bore an ugly purple bruise, as though struck with an errant hammer blow.

"Thank you." The Iraqi extracted one of the cigarettes with his right hand, his left removing a lighter from his trousers pocket. "Light?" The thumb that flicked on the flame bore a similar black and blue crescent on its nail, one that he had painted on with a laundry marker that morning before leaving his quarters at the air base.

"Let's get down to business. I have a lot to tell you. There are new orders. They are quite explicit and involved; we'll have to go over them carefully." The blond man spoke in a normal voice. There was not a soul within earshot, the other outdoor tables deserted at this hour. The sound of the pounding surf would prevent his voice from carrying to stray ears. A well-planned rendezvous after all, admitted the Iraqi, his attention riveted by the mention of new orders.

As the other man proceeded on in the same monotone, he listened silently and attentively, his eyes gradually widening in disbelief. Finally, he could no longer restrain himself.

"But that is madness, utter madness! We throw away everything that we have worked to achieve, my cover blown, my usefulness destroyed! And for what?"

"It is not your role to question these orders, but only to carry them out." The blond man's voice was calm but firm, an authoritative voice, used to issuing commands and having them obeyed. He was not, the Iraqi suddenly realized, just another messenger. "Your leaders are well aware of the unique strategic benefit of your present placement. They would hardly be ready to sacrifice this if they were not persuaded that the potential gain was worth it—the creation of an incident that will bring the Zionist nation to its knees."

"I don't understand." Somewhat chastened by the rebuke from the other over his initial reaction, the pilot struggled to perceive the bigger picture he was attempting to paint.

"Just hear me out. The brazen attack on the defenseless aircraft will be blamed on the Israelis. There are Americans aboard the AWACS. The American deaths will not be taken lightly by a nation already wavering in its support of the present regime. They are counted on as the final straw that will cut off American aid and topple the Likud government."

The calm voice paused to let the message sink in. "You will have made a singular contribution, to the benefit of all Islam. And your usefulness will not be, as you say, destroyed. On the contrary, you will return to your country, where your skill as a pilot and inside knowledge of the enemy's air power will be put to excellent use."

The latter statement did wonders for the Iraqi flier's outlook.

He could picture his triumphal return to Baghdad, a hero and lauded military expert—a spy in from the cold, no longer facing the spy's inevitable fate for exposure. Only the informed few would know the whole story, of course. But that would be enough.

"I have been instructed to ask you only one question," the blond man continued, "and it is a strictly technical one. From your standpoint, is the plan on a sound technical footing? Will it work—can you shoot down the AWACS?"

The Iraqi considered only briefly, his white teeth flashing in a sudden smile. "It is a gigantic target. And it is completely defenseless. I cannot miss."

His contact, he noted, did not return his smile. The pilot's eyes searched the expressionless face, seeking to penetrate the mask behind the dark glasses. That accent. And something else about the man. Of course. That was it.

"Now I have a question for you," the fighter pilot countered. "Why does an American join us in a venture such as this—a mission that will end up killing other Americans?"

The blond man's only response was to remove his glasses, the steady gaze of the piercing blue eyes providing the Iraqi with no semblance of an answer. "Shall we go over it one more time for good measure?" asked Martin Singer.

Martin Singer watched the receding figure in blue until it was swallowed up by the burgeoning lunchtime crowd in the Namir Center. The Iraqi walked with a lightness of step and muscular grace reminiscent of a predatory feline. He must also possess a good measure of the cat's instinct for survival, thought Martin admiringly, to have maintained his dangerous masquerade for so long a time. There was no doubt in his mind that the agent would be successful in his deadly undertaking. What a magnificent animal! What a pity that it would have to be destroyed.

But the Iraqi could not be allowed to return to his native country, where his reappearance could arouse suspicion, speculation—the odd chance that he would be recognized by the wrong person and the plot to throw blame for his act on the Israelis exposed. No, there was too much riding on this one. The plan called for the Iraqi flier to disappear after the AWACS attack, and disappear he would. Permanently. When he approached the remote recovery base in the Sinai, expecting that the way had been paved for a friendly reception, he would meet with an unfortunate accident. Egyptian jets, their pilots alerted only to the event of an Israeli fighter plane violating their airspace, would blast him out of the sky. The necessary arrangements were already being made through Singer's confederates there, including follow-up actions to ensure that the charred remains in the burned-out shell of an Israeli F-15 were incapable of being subsequently identified.

This part of the plan was, of course, unknown to the Iraqis, who would have been terribly upset at the prospect of losing their invaluable, highly trained pilot-agent. Upset enough, perhaps, to pull out of the whole affair if they learned of it in advance. To say nothing of what they would do if they found out that their trusted agent and informant of four years, the former American envoy to Israel, had in fact been working for the CIA all along.

His career as a double agent had been at the behest of the Company, with the objective of infiltrating the Iraqi intelligence establishment. It had begun with bits of secret Israeli defense information furnished to Iraq from embassy files, with the full knowledge and concurrence of his CIA superiors, but not of the Israelis—or of any higher U.S. authority, he was later to learn. When the intelligence proved valid, he had progressed to more and more responsible assignments. For more than a year now, from his cover in the American embassy, he had been operating as the central communication link and chief local coordinator for a handful of undercover agents in Israel being run by remote control from Baghdad.

Strange bedfellows, he reflected. An American Jew conspiring with Arabs against the Jewish state. Or so it would appear to the uninitiated world out there if they ever found out—the open, nonclandestine world. The real world? Martin saw it the other way around. The real world was the largely invisible one he lived and moved in, a world of determined, dedicated men. Informed men, aware of the ever-increasing threat to the continued existence of any kind of world if the dominoes kept falling one on top of another until the final catastrophe was triggered. Motivated men, believing that they could push back on those dominoes, break the pattern, make them fall in a different direction. And using every means at their disposal to do so, bedfellows be damned. For this was war, a war of survival. Not just for the good old USA, or the young nation of Israel that had received his total support, blind support, for so long. In this war the enemy was Armageddon.

Martin Singer did not see himself as just another soldier in that war, one of innumerable pawns out in the field manipulated by a faceless CIA. He knew his superiors and was in on the big picture, consulted regularly by the Company's policymakers. He concurred wholeheartedly in the Middle East scenario that had begun to shift priorities within the Company away from Central America. The conclusion was obvious, inescapable—the crucial confrontation was building near his home turf in Israel. Since the drastic escalation of the price of oil a decade ago, the financial center of gravity of planet Earth had been concentrated in a region no larger than a few tens of square miles along the western shore of the Persian Gulf. A region containing half the oil reserves of that planet, generating a billion dollars of new capital each day for the country whose flag flew over its derrick-dominated landscape. If you made a plot of value per unit area versus defenses per unit area for each spot on the globe, as CIA technicians had done, it hit you right in the eye. The Arabian Gulf region fell so far off the curve it wasn't even on the chart. A plum so vulnerable, so lightly defended, that it literally cried out to any foreign power sufficiently strong and unscrupulous to come and pluck it.

The result would be world chaos—the threat of global nuclear war. It couldn't be allowed to happen. His country was spending billions to make sure that it didn't, developing the most potent mobile defense unit ever assembled, the 200,000-man Rapid Deployment Force. At the first outbreak of hostilities, marines, rangers, whole airborne divisions could be ferried in overnight aboard newly developed supertransports specially designed to land on short runways.

But unforeseen logistics problems had developed. To be fully viable, the RDF needed a permanent base of operations within Saudi Arabia, one that could be prestocked with all of the ammunition, support gear, and supplies necessary to wage a successful military campaign. A secret site for the base in the Rub' al-Khali, the vast "Empty Quarter" of central Saudi Arabia, had been designated and successfully negotiated with the Saudis. To ensure that no word of the secret base would leak out, it was being conducted as a spook program, the CIA put in charge, given responsibility for the site preparation and its subsequent operation. It would be the biggest program in the history of the CIA, and Singer had been personally selected to manage it.

But now the government of King Fahd was having second thoughts, worried over the prospect of continuing to keep the existence of the American base a secret from its own people. There was increased distrust of Americans among the populace, largely feeding off the continued American aid and arms deliveries to Israel in the face of the stalled Palestinian autonomy talks due to the Likud government's intransigence. The ground-breaking had been postponed indefinitely. Perhaps later, the Americans were now being told. Meanwhile, time was slipping away.

The Company was not noted for sitting on their hands and waiting. Their top agent in Israel had been ordered to find a way to move things off dead center. To Martin Singer, veteran diplomat who had spent his last eight years in the American embassy at Tel Aviv working with the Begin government, the first step was an obvious one. The hard line of the Likud coalition was poisoning Saudi-American relations. There would have to be a change of government.

One domino at a time, falling against the next. The first being an incident that would topple Likud, paving the way for the opposition government to reopen the Palestinian talks. But how? A chess communication that came by diplomatic pouch a week previously while Singer was still at the embassy had provided the answer. As he deciphered the message, the envoy had become increasingly excited. This would do it! The plan would work. Unfortunate that the lives of a few fellow Americans might have to be lost in the process. But the greater good justified the sacrifice.

As the ranking Iraqi agent in Tel Aviv, he was in charge of the communication network that linked the half dozen local operatives with their Baghdad control. He had deliberately inserted himself as the Iraqi pilot's contact to size up the man while relaying his orders. He was impressed with what he had seen and heard. There would be no slipups from that quarter.

He was more concerned about some troublesome counter-espionage activities that might tip off the wrong people before the operation was sprung. It was inevitable from the onset, of course, that the leaks of secret information from the embassy files would eventually be discovered. But that discovery had come at an awkward time. Weeks before leaving the embassy, he had been aware of the investigation launched by the Cons Op man, Abernathy. It hadn't worried him much, at the time. There was no reason why he should be suspected; his tracks were well covered. And Abernathy was singularly inept.

But word had just reached him from the Iraqi agent in Jerusalem that the old fool was beginning to make headway after all, that his own name had surfaced in the investigation. Plus another disturbing bit of news. His ex-girlfriend was playing footsie with the Mossad, and there were indications that the Israeli intelligence organization was also aware that certain of their documents had been compromised through U.S. embassy leaks.

His string was beginning to unravel. Could he hold it together until the crucial AWACS incident was consummated? He had to! Abernathy and Daniella. It could be disastrous if the two should happen to get together and compare notes. The pupils of the penetrating blue eyes narrowed. Something might have to be done about that.

For what must have been the dozenth time in the last hour the traffic-clogged artery between Tel Aviv and Jerusalem constricted again, bringing the taxi to a sudden halt. At the exasperated sound from the back seat the driver threw up his hands in a gesture of helplessness. In the gathering darkness David Llewellyn squinted at his watch, trying to make out the position of the hands. Too late now to catch the ambassador before he left the embassy. He could only hope that Abernathy was still there. He had some things to get off his chest that wouldn't keep well overnight.

The return trip from Saudi Arabia had been a nightmare. What should have been a half-day trip at best had taken from dawn till dusk. Beginning with a bomb scare at the Riyadh airport that had delayed the departure for two hours while all of the luggage was removed from the plane and meticulously searched. He had missed his connecting flight in Cairo by only minutes and been forced to languish there for several more hours until the late afternoon flight departed. By the time he finally reached Ben Gurion International, the ambassador's limousine, programmed to meet him four hours earlier, was nowhere to be seen. His message from Cairo, advising of the change in arrival time, had apparently gone astray.

There had been no alternative but to stand the expense of a taxi, his only chance of reaching the embassy before everyone left for the day. He was already chafing over the continued delay as the cabbie crawled out of the congested main terminal area, its crosswalks choked with pedestrians. Funny, he could have sworn that one of those pedestrians was his former diplomatic colleague and predecessor in the Israeli envoy job, who supposedly had returned to America several days previously. But when he had wound down the window of the barely moving auto and called out Martin's name, the blond man in the dark glasses only a few paces away had looked at him without recognition and moved on. Could he have been mistaken? He didn't think so; not unless Martin had an identical twin.

Traffic on the expressway was starting to move again, showing signs now of breaking out of its doldrums. Finally! He had eaten nothing since breakfast, and the churning in his empty stomach did little to improve his disposition. His brain was churning also, the revelations of the Saudi prince turning over and over in his mind. Back amid the more familiar surroundings of the Jerusalem environs it all seemed so unreal, so unbelievable. He couldn't swallow it, he realized now, any more than he could believe that Daniella's relationship with him had been in any way devious, her motivations those of a Mossad agent. There had to be another explanation, a bigger picture that this all fit into, that would also explain why Abernathy, that underhanded son of a bitch, had set him up with the Saudis. He would confront the Cons Op agent tonight and force the truth out of him. And then he would find Daniella.

When the lights of the American embassy at long last swept into view, he motioned the driver toward the rear of the building, where he had left his car. Could it have been only yesterday morning? God, it seemed more like a week ago. There it was, right where he had parked it, in one corner of the nearly deserted lot. There were only two others to keep it company. He recognized the dark blue Fiat and felt his pulse accelerate. It was Abernathy's.

The transfer of the luggage completed, he tipped the driver generously; the cab drove away, and he strode rapidly toward the rear entrance. No use trying the front. The guard would be long gone. At the door he hesitated, trying vainly to recall the code he had memorized only two days earlier. He made a deliberate effort to relax his mind and it came to him. He punched the numbers into the digital keyboard on the lockbox device, and the double door clicked open.

The pervading silence of the deserted embassy and tomblike quality of its dimly lighted interior invoked the mood of his night visit of the previous week: the night of that first confrontation with Abernathy, when the man had sneaked up on him and surprised him in his new office, sowing his seeds of doubt about

Daniella. He would turn the tables now, force some answers out of the obstreperous agent. Suddenly aware of his echoing footfall breaking the stillness, he deliberately dug in his heels, accentuating the clicking sound of the hard leather against the polished stone. *I'm coming for you, Abernathy. And when I want to talk to a man, I don't sneak up on him.*

The thick carpeting on the stairs interrupted the staccato message. In the basement corridor the incandescent lighting of the embassy's upper reaches gave way to the cold, unearthly glare emitted by a sparse array of fluorescent fixtures attached to the low ceiling. The stark illumination supplied an appropriately eerie touch to the sanctum sanctorum of Consular Operations, he reflected; an atmosphere conducive to the weird, clandestine schemes that were hatched here.

There was no sound from Abernathy's office as he approached, but he must be there. The office door was open, and he could see the light from inside spilling out into the empty, dimly lit corridor. A sudden loud noise made him whirl around, his heart pumping. Then he realized it was the sound of the rear entrance door slamming. Someone had left the building—probably the driver of that third car in the parking lot. He took a deep breath. Why was he so jumpy?

Two steps from the office entrance he smelled it, and his heart shifted back into high gear. The fragrance reminiscent of sandalwood, combined with some other exotic ingredient. Her fragrance—Daniella's. He couldn't be mistaken. It was too deeply ingrained in his memory, inseparable from that unforgettable afternoon in her company, her essence that pervaded his thoughts, his dreams. He dashed through the door.

Abernathy was waiting for him, sitting bolt upright in his high-backed chair, the inevitable meerschaum clenched in his teeth, eyes staring expectantly at the door. David looked about the room for Daniella, but there was no sign of her, except for the delicate after-scent that lingered behind. There was no question in his mind that she had been here. He turned angrily back to the embassy security man.

"Where is she? Where's Daniella? What in the devil is—"

Something about Abernathy's appearance arrested him. The man had not moved. The staring eyes were too staring, too vacant, focused not on him but on something happening far away —an infinity away. The Cons Ops man was not going to answer any questions for him. Or for anybody. Not ever.

Suddenly the pipe detached itself from the mute jaws and clattered noisily onto the desktop. His feet frozen to the floor, David watched in horror as Abernathy began to tilt, almost imperceptibly at first, slipping slowly sideways in the chair. As the movement increased, the head slid from the leather headrest and the corpse spun from the chair, disappearing behind the desk as it thudded to the floor. David advanced tentatively, peering around the desk. The body rested on its chest, now anything but lifelike, the head grotesquely twisted halfway around so that the vacant eyes still stared upward at him.

He shuddered, bending down to relieve the awkward posture, turning the head to a less unnatural angle. A silly thing to do. The corpse wouldn't know the difference. His hand came away with blood on it; the back of Abernathy's head was matted with it. Revolted, he recoiled, straightening up abruptly—and ran right into the massive blow that came from behind.

A blinding flash of lightning crackled through his skull, and his head exploded with searing pain. He grasped for the desk on the way down, missed it, and floated like a feather the last hundred feet to the floor. Floated on an evanescent wisp of perfume that buoyed him and softened his landing.

Out of the dense mist, through a collage of psychedelic lights, Daniella's face swam toward him, her eyes dark with concern, wet with tears. Her lips formed words, words he could not understand, soundless words he struggled in vain to read. He fought for comprehension, fought his way back to consciousness.

"Don't try to move yet. Just lie still." The musical voice was strangely subdued, playing in a minor key. He hadn't been hallucinating. She was really there, the swollen, throbbing balloon that his head had turned into cradled tenderly in her arms. He disobeyed the solicitous instructions and instantly regretted it, a wave of dizziness and nausea engulfing him. Concussion. He knew the symptoms. He let his head sink back gratefully into the soft, cool arms and closed his eyes.

"Where did you come from? Where in God's name have you been?" His own voice made a hollow, echoing sound as though emanating from the bottom of a deep well.

"Shh! Don't talk, just lie still," she soothed, rocking him gently in her arms. "I saw the body there at the desk. It was horrible. I ran out of the building. Then I saw your car. I came back."

He waited for her to go on, but she left it at that, as though her words explained everything. Or anything. A hundred questions inside of him were crying out for answers all at once, as his head began to clear. Then one question of paramount urgency popped to the top.

"The killer—the man who slugged me. Did you see him?"

She shook her head. "I didn't see anyone. The corridor outside was deserted. There was no sign of anyone upstairs."

He sat up, fighting back the nausea. "He may still be here, in the basement somewhere. One of the other offices along the corridor. There's no other way out. We've got to—"

"Whoever was here has gone," she interrupted. "Right after I found you here, I heard the door slam upstairs. He must have hidden somewhere while I made my way down the corridor."

David groaned, struggling to his feet. His head reeled, and he sat down abruptly in Abernathy's chair. "We've got to notify the authorities, the ambassador. Get this place sealed off. You haven't called the police?"

"No." She rose from her sitting position on the floor and smoothed her dress where his head had lain. There was no sign of blood, he noted with relief. "David, I need to ask a favor of you—a big favor. It's important that I not be involved in this. My position with the Foreign Minister is very sensitive. I could lose my job."

Which job? he wanted to ask, Abernathy's words of warning about her Mossad involvement echoing in his ears. A warning that somehow took on more credence, now, with its purveyor lying dead on the floor in front of him. Daniella had a lot of explaining to do.

"What were you doing here?" he demanded. "Why did you come here? And how did you get in with the place locked up tight?"

"I was invited here. By Abernathy. He gave me the code numbers to punch in. He said he was on to something, that it was vital that we exchange information. He hinted about a plot against the government."

"I thought you couldn't stand Abernathy. Why did you suddenly trust him?"

"I didn't. But I decided to come anyway. On the chance that I might learn something that could help my—my country."

David thought it over. It didn't wash. It was only days earlier that the Cons Ops man had spoken to him about Daniella, branded her as dangerous. Why would he suddenly decide to confide in her?

She read the doubt in his eyes. "You don't believe me."

"It doesn't make any sense. Why would he call you? If it was a matter involving the Foreign Office he'd have gone directly to your boss, Kedar. Or worked through the ambassador."

She hesitated for a moment before answering, studying his face. "I'm afraid there's something I haven't told you about my job."

So here it came. True confession time. He felt sick again, nothing to do with the effects of the concussion this time. Daniella was one of them, a goddam spook. She'd been playing games with him, all along. The whirlwind romance had all been a charade.

"I wanted to tell you before, but you see they made us swear never to divulge it to anyone, not even to . . . family. For me that posed no problem, since I had none."

She hesitated. She was having difficulty getting it out. He'd save her the trouble. "Don't bother explaining," he interjected dully. "Abernathy already told me. He was on to you."

Her eyebrows arched in astonishment. "Told you what?"

A short, hollow laugh escaped from somewhere inside him. So the game playing was to continue. "That your position with the Foreign Minister was only a cover," he continued in the same listless tone. "That you're a secret agent, working for the Mossad. That part of that job was to spy on us, your American friends."

She stared back at him, wide-eyed and speechless, looking suddenly fragile and forlorn. Part of him wanted to fold her in his arms, tell her it didn't matter. But another part, a prouder part, held back.

Daniella found her voice. "No, David, no! You can't believe that. It's not true." There was desperation in her voice. She reached for his hand, seeking to reassure him through the warmth of physical contact, a reassertion of the intimacy that had passed between them. His own hand accepted hers passively, the warmth unreturned. He avoided her eyes.

"You were probably spying on Martin, too." There was bitterness in his voice. He plunged on, unable to restrain himself. "That business about him dropping you. It was the other way around, wasn't it? He was no use to you any more. But I was."

Daniella gasped. "David! Stop it! How can you—"

"By the way, if it's any consolation, your lover didn't go running back to his wife after all. He's still around. I caught a glimpse of him in Tel Aviv today. But you probably knew that."

"What?" The genuine shock in her voice drew his eyes back to hers. They were round and open, the tears prompted by his stinging words arrested by the impact of his revelation. "Martin? Are you sure? But that means—David, we've got to warn—"

The rest of her words were drowned out by the stentorian voice of a bullhorn in the corridor outside, its volume turned up to peak amplitude. The torrent of Hebrew was unintelligible to David, but he saw Daniella cringe, the apprehension in her eyes. Then the message was repeated in English and he understood why.

"This is the police. You are under arrest, on suspicion of murder. The building is surrounded and you cannot escape. Throw your weapons out through the door. Then crawl out on your hands and knees. Now!"

The inky blackness directly ahead became gradually suffused with a pale glow emanating from the faintly discernible horizon. Martin Singer watched the aura of whiteness expand itself and grow in intensity. The lights of Tel Aviv. Ben Gurion Airport must be somewhere just ahead.

He craned his neck, searching the darkness below on both sides of the airplane. There it was! Da-dit-dit-dit da-da-dit. As his straining eyes recognized the flashing light code of the airport beacon, the tenseness inside him began to drain away. Night flying was not his bag. Too easy to get disoriented, lost, even on a short hop like this one.

He banked the light plane to the left and began his letdown as the welcome sight of the airport lights appeared ahead under his right wing, rows of blue perimeter lights flanking the brighter yellow ones that outlined the runways. Blue and yellow lights, reminding him of Hanukkah. The Festival of Lights had never looked lovelier.

For the first time since his unexpected sighting by David Llewellyn that same afternoon at the airport, his mind began to relax. A most unfortunate encounter, he had thought at the time. It had forced his hand, forced him to accelerate a plan that had not fully jelled. He couldn't risk the chance that the other American had recognized him and would mention his whereabouts— his continued presence in Israel—at the embassy, which would have alerted Abernathy and placed him on his guard.

But Llewellyn's spotting him had turned out to be a stroke of luck. It had spurred him to act immediately, to reach the embassy ahead of Llewellyn. A day's delay, even an hour's, would have been disastrous. Abernathy was ready to blow, armed with just enough circumstantial evidence and fragments of data to shoot down his whole operation. The meeting with Daniella would have done it, would have confirmed Abernathy's suspicions and also, through Daniella, tipped off Israeli counterintelligence. He couldn't let that happen.

He switched on the radio to contact the tower. "Ben Gurion tower, this is Cessna A7744Y requesting clearance to land. Over." He spoke in Hebrew, imparting a guttural quality to his voice that was more like the speech of the plane's owner. If necessary, he knew that the man would swear it was he who had piloted the plane tonight.

"Clearance granted," the radio crackled back. "Use northwest runway, heading zero four two. Barometer setting thirty point one four. Wind north northwest at zero twelve knots." He entered the traffic pattern, flipped the landing gear switch to down, and turned on the landing lights.

No, there had been no choice. Too much at stake; Abernathy had to be silenced. Regrettably. Don't play the hypocrite, he told himself, you know you could never stand the officious little bastard with his silly affectations. He had made the decision the minute he saw Daniella's small roadster pull into the embassy lot ahead of him. For a moment he had feared that he would have to kill her, also. Now that would have been regrettable. But she had conveniently stopped off at the ladies' room, giving him time to surprise Abernathy and get the job done. Neatly. A single bullet in the back of the brain, death instantaneously.

The appearance of the Cons Op man propped up in his chair, dead eyes open and staring, had had the desired effect on Daniella. A stifled scream, and she had bolted from the building, giving him time to search the desk and office for any material that might put his operation in further jeopardy. Insufficient time, as it turned out. He had barely begun when there had been another untimely arrival—Llewellyn's—announced in advance by his heavy tread on the marble floor of the embassy vestibule above.

Retreating to his hiding place behind a file cabinet, he had waited for his chance, using the butt of his automatic to buy more time for the completion of his search. Forcing a locked drawer in the desk, he had found what he was looking for—an envelope containing a record of the Cons Op agent's personal investigation into the source of leaks from the top secret files in his custody. An envelope that now lay next to him on the copilot's seat. He would peruse it later at his leisure. There had only been time to leaf through it hurriedly, but he had seen enough. He had recognized only too well the names of documents believed to have been compromised. And he had seen his own name prominently recorded on several of the later pages.

The Cons Op file cabinets had looked virtually impregnable. There was one file in there that he really would have liked to get his hands on. He had been considering an attempt at blasting the locks with his silencer-equipped automatic when the click of high heels on the floor above dissuaded him. Hiding in an adjacent office until Daniella passed down the corridor, he had decided on the delay-and-confusion ploy—an anonymous tip to the police. Arrest under suspicious circumstances might compromise Daniella's sensitive cover, keep her occupied and off balance. Anything to delay the unraveling process that tonight's killing was certain to set in motion. Until it was too late for anyone or anything to interfere.

As the light aircraft descended he watched the floodlit runway out ahead move toward him, slowly at first, then faster, rushing up to meet him. He eased back on the control column, reducing the throttle gradually. How high was he now—twenty feet, fifty? It was almost impossible to judge distance at night. If the plane stalled out too high above the runway—!

With a screech, the front wheels made contact, the tail wheel settling smoothly onto the concrete as he pulled the stick into his lap and rode the rudder pedals. A two-and-a-half-point landing. Not bad for an occasional weekend flyer.

His flying ability was a well-kept secret, unrecorded in the copious files and dossiers kept on all U.S. diplomatic personnel. Even the CIA was unaware. He had done it on his own while in Israel, stealing an afternoon here, a morning there from his job at the embassy until he had his pilot's credential. It had cost him, he reflected—was still costing him. The arrangement with the owner of the Cessna was not inexpensive. But it had paid off tonight.

Reaching the end of the runway, the light plane turned toward the private aircraft parking area and pulled into an empty slot between two tethered Aero Commanders. The engine sputtered and died, the sudden silence startling. Martin Singer opened the canopy and took a deep gulp of the cool night air, letting it out slowly. It was over. He had been forced to act on impulse; there had been insufficient time to reach either his CIA superiors or his Iraqi contacts. No need for them to know now. This one was on him.

The Iraqi *slik* had only recently been moved. It was now located in the back of a kosher meat market. Singer smiled at the irony. "Slik" was a Hebrew word for a secret hiding place. Sliks had been used in Tel Aviv decades ago by the Haganah's intelligence service, Shai—the Hebrew syllable always uttered in a whisper—to hide their secret records from British snoopers during the latter days of the Mandate. They had gone to elaborate lengths, creating false walls with spring-actuated panels to conceal the existence of the clandestine rooms within. The British had never found them.

This latest Iraqi slik would have done the Shai proud. A small, invisible door behind the racks of meat hanging in the cold-storage locker led to a hidden compartment just large enough for a desk, chair, file cabinet, and shortwave radio. The meat market was owned by an Iraqi butcher who was also an agent, posing as an Israeli. The clerks who waited on customers in the front of the store were never allowed in the storage locker, which was locked when not in use. They were used to the occasional meat inspectors and wholesalers that the butcher ushered into its confines.

There was only one clerk behind the counter at this hour, waiting on a lone customer. Shuffling the official-looking sheaf of papers in his hand, Martin entered the shop and inquired after the butcher. The hulking proprietor appeared immediately, wiping his hands on a blood-besmirched apron. He looked at Singer, then at his watch.

"You're late tonight," he grumbled. "We're about to close."

Martin shrugged his shoulders and grinned. "So I should make a reservation? You know our policy. We drop in unannounced, any old time. It's better you shouldn't know when we're coming."

The butcher snorted. "I don't know what you're expecting to find. My beef is only the best grade. Not like that horse butcher on the next block." He winked at the clerk and late customer, both of whom were smiling. "Well, come along then." He held open the waist-high door that led behind the counter, then motioned the "meat inspector" through the curtained doorway toward the meat locker entrance.

"You're lightly dressed. It's cold in there."

"I'll survive. I'm used to it." The pair disappeared inside the locker and the heavy insulated door slammed shut.

"A letter came for you today," the butcher informed him in a low voice. "That special kind, in the square envelope. It's inside, in the mail folder."

Singer started. "Why didn't you call me? You know I said—"

"I tried," the other interrupted. "Your landlady has the message. She said you hadn't returned all day." He disappeared behind a row of carcasses suspended from a heavy rail by meat hooks and reached a beefy hand up toward the bracket holding the rail to the wall. Almost noiselessly, the subdued whirring of a precision electric motor barely audible, the wall began to slide away, revealing a low opening just large enough for a man to enter if he stooped and bowed his head.

The butcher stepped to one side to let him through. "I'm going back and close up. Buzz me when you're ready to leave."

Singer stepped into the hidden compartment, pushing the button that simultaneously turned on the light and activated a microswitch to close the door behind him. His heart was racing as he dialed the combination on the file cabinet lock. The "special" square envelopes were used by the Iraqi pilot-spy. Would this be the message announcing the final countdown for the operation known as "Fiery Furnace," specifying the date and time of the raid and the other critical details? He jerked the file drawer open and snatched the letter from the mail folder, ripping away the envelope.

The message encoded in the Iraqi chess cipher was disappointingly brief. His eye jumped immediately to the final three moves, which comprised a pattern he recognized on sight, requesting an immediate meeting. Hungrily, he deciphered the earlier part of the message. The result was not too enlightening. "Change of plans. My role altered. Strike imminent. Details in meeting."

Good news and bad news. He pondered the latter. What could the change of plans be, the altered role? Something that could derail his carefully planned operation? He would just have to wait for the meeting with the Iraqi to find out. Impatiently, he seized a sheet of paper and set about drafting the encoded reply that would set up the time and place. His mind focused on the other two statements. "Strike imminent. Details in meeting." The time for the strike had been set! There must be too many details to convey in a coded message. Much more practical to do it in person, obtaining verbal confirmation that all was understood.

Martin Singer completed his reply and addressed the envelope that he would personally hand carry that same evening to the air base message office. Then he picked up the microphone and flicked a switch on the master panel above an assortment of black boxes that comprised the shortwave transceiver set. A very special set of black boxes that would scramble his voice and transmit it to Baghdad in a "spread spectrum" of frequencies undetectable to the Israeli listening devices. The ready light flashed on, and he began speaking in a halting Arabic.

"Abu, this is Akhiwiya. Father, this is little brother. The ram is being readied for the slaughter. The lost sheep has been found and returns to the fold tomorrow. Then the rest of the wool will be shorn and sent home."

CHAPTER
7

When the phone call came from Defense Minister Zahadi's residence, Brastov was in the bathroom, shaving. It was shortly after midnight. He would normally have been fast asleep at this hour. Instead, he was fully dressed.

An emergency session of the Defense Advisory Board would convene in one hour, the male secretary's voice announced in a condescendingly slow Arabic. "I shall be there," Brastov replied, and hung up abruptly without giving the caller the satisfaction of the puzzled inquiry he was probably expecting. Which would no doubt have been parried by some haughty rejoinder pointedly reminding the Russian that such weighty matters could not be discussed over the public telephone.

The overly pompous secretary was only a message boy, Brastov perceived, and would not be in the know. But the Russian was. A call from one of his own sources had alerted him more than a half hour earlier, providing him with just enough details in a simplistic, prearranged code to prepare him for what was coming. Over that same public telephone.

Returning to the bathroom, he picked up the gleaming straight razor and scraped the remaining lather from his face, then wiped it clean with a fresh, steaming towel from a silver chafing dish. The earlier message had both disturbed and stimulated him. Those Israelis were certainly unpredictable. They were forever coming up with something new, just when you thought you had them in a corner. A worthy adversary, they could always be counted on to give you a decent game.

News of their change in strategy had only served to firm his own resolve, whetting his appetite for the fast-approaching contest. But would that news have the same effect on the Iraqis? Or would it shake their faith in his AWACS plan? Calling an emergency meeting in the dead of night testified to a certain degree of alarm. Would they panic and back away? He put the question to the shrewd eyes that stared back from the mirror. The plump, cherubic face, baby pink from the effects of the piping hot towel, had no immediate answer.

Same cast of characters, noted Brastov, seating himself at Amahl Zahadi's sleek ebony conference table. Same setting. Same plot? His thoughts returned to the evening session in the defense minister's study only a few weeks previously, where his performance had won acceptance of the daring AWACS gambit. He looked at the faces of the two individuals he knew to be already informed, Zahadi and al Fawzi, the intelligence director. There was uncertainty in both, their eyes eluding his. If there was any backsliding, he would have to nip it in the bud. He slipped his feet out of the too-tight oxfords. This one might call for some old-fashioned table banging, Khrushchev style. Hard leather heels on polished wood.

This time Zahadi wasted no time with preliminaries. "I've summoned you here at this inconvenient hour because we have a critical decision to make, and very little time in which to make it. Only hours ago we received an urgent message from our chief operative in Tel Aviv. He had just returned from a meeting with El Aurens. We are in possession of the entire attack plan of the Zionist enemy. The raid on Tamuz 17 is set for Friday—this coming Friday, gentlemen! Three days from now!"

Excitement ran through the defense panel like a shock wave. Brastov was infected by it, even though to him the revelation was old news. He watched the reactions and listened to the invective that flew about the table in the resulting hubbub.

"We will destroy them!" cried the air force general. "They are all dead men!"

"The Sabbath!" bellowed the outraged army chief of staff. "They are attacking us on the Sabbath!"

Zahadi held up his hand for quiet. "Yes, general, the Sabbath. It was somewhat predictable that the strike would come on a Friday, our Sabbath, when attendance at the Osirak facility would be minimal. Avoiding the outcry that came over the loss of life from the last strike, especially from the French, who lost one of their top scientists. That strike, if you recall, came on the Christian Sabbath, Saturday. The Zionists could not be expected to make that mistake again."

"If it was a mistake." The army general's tone was reinforced by angry mutterings from several of the others. Again the defense minister signaled for order.

"There is much more to report—developments that could significantly impact our carefully laid plans. Kindly permit me to present this information to you, and then we will discuss it. We have very little time. President Hussein has been notified and expects a firm recommendation today, immediately following the noon prayer."

An anticipatory hush fell over the group as Zahadi continued. "I will summarize, then ask the Intelligence Director to fill you in on the details. The changes in the Zionist plan that most affect us are two. First, the attacking aircraft will not be F-16s, as we were anticipating, but specially modified F-15 Eagles carrying more internal fuel. These 'Strike Eagles,' as they are called, will each carry a pair of two-ton bombs, as well as missiles to provide their own air cover. Only twelve planes will be used in all, to minimize the chance of detection by our radar. A small force, gentlemen, but not to be taken lightly. Need I remind you of the devastation wreaked before when a single one of these massive bombs found its way into the heart of our reactor building?"

"Not this time!" shouted the army chief. "Fifteens or sixteens, it makes no difference. We are ready for them. They won't get near Tamuz 17 this time. Our missiles—"

"One moment, Hammud." Ali Mustafa, seated next to the army general, placed a restraining hand on his shoulder. "You spoke of two changes in the Zionist attack plan," he addressed the defense minister. "May I inquire as to the second?"

Zahadi nodded glumly. "This may represent more of a problem for us. The Zionists have perceived that our defenses around Tamuz 17 have been strengthened. They suspect that the Soviet SA-8 missile is being employed. Their attacking aircraft will be equipped with special jamming devices intended to neutralize our missile control radar."

Consternation gripped the two uniformed attendees, their shocked looks testimony to the respect held for the Israeli countermeasures equipment. "Those accursed jammers are trouble!" exploded the air force boss. "They knocked out the Syrian SA-8 missiles in Lebanon."

"How did they find out about our missiles?" the army chief of staff demanded. "We were assured that strictest security would be enforced!" He looked accusingly at the diminutive intelligence director, whose face began to redden.

Brastov was tempted to jump into the fray, but held back. Better to let the jittery Iraqis blunt their spears on one another first.

"Gentlemen, gentlemen!" Zahadi threw up his arms to quiet them. "I stated that Dr. al Fawzi would cover the intelligence report in more detail and answer your questions. He now has the floor."

The intelligence director slid back his chair and rose, drawing himself up to his full four feet eleven inches. His jowly face still reflected the resentment he felt at the challenge flung at him by the military man, but he controlled it, responding with a haughty composure.

"There is no occasion to panic," he began acidly. "There has been no security leak. The enemy knows nothing. If he did, he would hardly be sending in weapons that are outmoded and ineffectual against the real missiles deployed around Tamuz 17—the SA-10." He looked toward Brastov for corroboration. "Am I correct, Comrade Military Adviser?"

Brastov could have kissed the feisty little man. "You are entirely correct, Comrade Intelligence Director. The SA-10 overcomes all of the shortcomings of the SA-8 and goes far beyond it. Its radar is totally immune to the Israeli jammers that proved so effective in Lebanon against the SA-8. This was demonstrated conclusively during the qualifying tests in Siberia."

"But still undemonstrated operationally." The man in air force blue was still not persuaded. "Why should we take chances? We know now when they are coming. My jet fighters can intercept them much earlier, before they get anywhere near the nuclear plant."

Brastov had his reply ready, but the toy bulldog beat him to it. "Oh, yes? And just how do you propose to locate them? We have no concrete information on their route, but are informed that they will fly very low and sneak in underneath your radar umbrella. These new Strike Eagles are equipped with—," he read from his notes, "a terrain-following radar mode that permits them to hug the ground while penetrating at high speed." He looked up archly at the air force man. "Unless your radar blind spots have suddenly healed themselves, you have precisely the same problem you've always had. The bombers will be on top of you before you know where they are. By the time you flush your fighters, they will be over Baghdad."

"Search aircraft," the man in the blue uniform countered. "We could put up our own scouts, have them patrol the entire perimeter—"

"And announce to the enemy that we are waiting to ambush them—that we have had advance warning of the strike?" This time it was the army chief who took issue with his air force opposite number. "The minute they spotted your patrol craft, they would simply turn back and wait for another chance. And they would realize that they had a mole in their midst. We would be signing El Auren's death warrant."

"Precisely." The tiny intelligence director fairly glistened with vindication. "We should not allow ourselves to be put off from our original plan. Last-minute changes always create problems. The trap we have set so painstakingly with the help of our Russian friends is as sound as ever and ready to spring. No changes are necessary."

The air force general was silent, looking thoughtful but no longer openly hostile. There appeared to be no other dissenters. Brastov breathed easier. Hurdle number one seemed to have been successfully negotiated. He was personally elated over the news that the Strike Eagle would be employed in lieu of the F-16. There had been only fragmentary intelligence about its progress in America and no mention at all of Israeli participation in the program. But one thing was clear from the scant intelligence he had perused. Strike Eagles would eventually be the top of the line in the U.S. Air Force—aircraft that combined the best fighter characteristics with an in-weather ground strike capability superior to anything else in the world.

Now they would get an early test in the hands of the able Israeli pilots, a baptism of fire from the superlethal SA-10 missiles waiting to destroy them. The best going against the best. His superiors back in Dzerzhinski Square would be overjoyed. The lost prestige from the dissappointing showing of Soviet weapons during the Lebanese invasion would be recouped in one sudden and dramatic confrontation, world opinion reversed overnight. For Brastov had no doubt about the outcome. He had been in Siberia, had witnessed with his own eyes the destruction wreaked upon target after target by the Soviets' overpoweringly swift and maneuverable new weapon.

"I have a few additional questions, Dr. al Fawzi." All eyes shifted again to Ali Mustafa, whose concurrence was mandatory in any course of action decided upon. "Here it comes," thought Brastov, bracing himself for the crucial test.

"We have not yet spoken of the other part of our plan," continued the gaunt presidential adviser, "the attack on AWACS, in which our agent, El Aurens, is to play the principal role. The six F-15s flying fighter cover have apparently been scrubbed from the enemy's attack plan. You have not yet informed us of a most crucial point. Is El Aurens still in the picture—is he to fly one of the twelve Strike Eagles?"

"I was just coming to that," the spy boss replied somewhat defensively. "We may have to cancel that AWACS business. El Aurens is still on the roster for the Osirak operation, but only as a first alternate, in the event of illness or injury to one of the other twelve."

The Russian felt his stomach convulse; he had not been apprised of this development. His brilliant coup was in danger of going down the drain!

But Mustafa, too, was committed to the AWACS venture. It was his plan now; it was he who had sold it to Saddam Hussein. "Hmm," he mused. "Illness or injury, you say. That shouldn't be too difficult to arrange. Your agent is resourceful, and the other pilots conveniently accessible to him, yes? They assuredly train together, dine together, sleep in the same quarters. Why not simply order El Aurens to make arrangements for one of the other pilots to be—indisposed?"

The little man stared back at the presidential adviser, not knowing quite what to answer. He looked toward the defense minister for guidance, but received no help from that quarter. "There are other problems," he protested. "The armament—the air-to-air weapons carried by the attackers have been drastically reduced." He checked his notes. "The gun has been taken out. And instead of six missiles—two Sparrows and four Sidewinders—they will carry only two."

"Which two?" The question was out of his mouth before the Russian realized it. The point could be significant. Two Sparrows were more than adequate for the job; two of the smaller Sidewinders might be somewhat marginal.

Once again the director of the spy agency referred to his notes. "It must be here somewhere." He riffled through the papers in front of him, his forehead wrinkling with annoyance. He read from the notes.

"Two air-to-air missiles will be carried by each Strike Eagle." His eyes searched the copy, then narrowed in frustration. "It doesn't say which type."

"I gather from your question, Comrade Brastov, that you regard the armament type as pivotal?" The presidential adviser fixed him with a steady gaze, awaiting his answer.

Brastov cursed himself for his rashness in flagging the issue. The plan must go forward, regardless of which type of missile was carried, as long as there was an opportunity to kill the AWACS and lay the blame on the Israeli government.

"I would prefer the Sparrows, with their larger warheads, of course," he answered. "But my Soviet ordnance experts assure me that either missile would be adequate. Against a soft target like AWACS, a salvo of two Sidewinders should be more than sufficient."

"Nevertheless, I recommend that we request a clarification on the armament question from our man in Tel Aviv." Mustafa looked toward the defense minister for assent, as did the intelligence director, who had finished his report and now relinquished the floor.

Amahl Zahadi nodded his head. "By all means, and as quickly as possible. You'll take care of it?" At al Fawzi's sign of acquiescence, he addressed himself to the group as a whole.

"We are all in agreement, then? We press forward with the same basic plan adopted at our last meeting. There is no necessity to alter our plan in any significant way, except to instruct our agent, El Aurens, to take the necessary steps to ensure that he will be at the controls of one of the twelve attacking aircraft." He caught al Fawzi's eye again. "You will relay that instruction to him?"

"It is as good as done, Excellency."

"We are agreed, then?" The defense minister scanned the faces around the table for any sign of dissent. Brastov held his breath. Al Fawzi had obviously deferred to Mustafa's judgment. But what about the two generals? The army chief appeared thoughtful but resigned. His air force counterpart was staring down at the table, a frown on his face. Brastov watched and waited, the silence becoming unbearable, broken at last as the general looked up.

"I still don't like it. There is always a chance that any weapon will fail. I have seen it happen many times in the field, even with the superior ordnance manufactured in your country, Comrade General." The air force chief gave Brastov a meaningful look.

"If those two missiles, whatever type they are, turn out to be duds, there is no longer a backup weapon with which to finish off the AWACS. We will have sacrificed our best-placed agent for nothing."

The defense minister and presidential adviser exchanged glances. It was Zahadi who eventually responded.

"General Haddad, was it not you, yourself, who suggested that El Aurens's days might be numbered anyway—that we should get him out before he is discovered, tried as a spy, and executed? That would truly be a sacrifice, for we would lose him permanently, and all the knowledge he has gained of the enemy from his years in their service would die with him.

"But the plan we propose to follow entails retrieving our valued pilot-spy and bringing him safely back to Iraq. His knowledge, the secrets of the Zionist Air Force operations and strategies, will be yours, and you will have a genuine hero to inspire your men and spur your enlistments."

Mollified, the air force general held his peace. The defense minister looked around the table.

"If there are no further questions, we will proceed accordingly. Later today I am to brief our president on these latest developments and our concurrence to proceed. Let us all pray to Allah for the success of our grand venture. The meeting is adjourned."

Brastov breathed a heavy sigh. The "grand venture"—his grand venture—had weathered yet another storm. The final storm, he felt certain. The die was cast. Friday was but three short days away.

"Our President never ceases to amaze me." Ali Mustafa held the door open for the defense minister as they departed the ultramodern glass and steel tower that housed the executive offices of the Iraqi government.

"Unpredictable, as always," Zahadi agreed. "But this morning he outdid himself. What a marvelous twist to our plan! Why did we not think of it?"

"Because, my friend, we were thinking defensively: hold the line, keep to the plan at hand. Saddam Hussein is a tiger. He saw the opening, and all of his instincts said 'attack!' That is why he has leapfrogged us."

"Out-boldened us. And I was afraid we were too bold, to begin with." The defense minister chuckled. "What would the Russian do, if he knew?"

Mustafa smiled, in turn, then turned serious, grasping the

other's arm for emphasis. "He is not to know in advance, our President made that clear. And Amahl—these particular orders to El Aurens—they are not to go through our man in Tel Aviv. A special courier must be used this time. You can arrange this?"

Zahadi frowned. "It can be done, of course," he shrugged, "but it seems like a lot of trouble to go to when we already have a perfectly secure pipeline set up. What are you afraid of? Do you suspect—?"

"Nothing specific, my friend. Probably just an old man's sixth sense going wild. But I've learned over the years to indulge such notions. And since this is the President's own brainchild, it won't hurt to take special precautions, will it?"

The young Israeli detective in the black turtleneck and Levi's was all business as he arrived to take charge shortly after the body had been photographed and removed. He introduced himself as Lieutenant Ziffer. His first move was to separate the two suspects so that they could be questioned individually and their stories compared in the standard police fashion. Daniella's eye caught Llewellyn's briefly as she was led off to an adjacent office by a uniformed policeman. He caught the urgent message. "Don't tell on me; don't blow my cover!"

She needn't have worried. He wasn't about to tell the police anything he didn't have to. They were on questionable ground here; technically, the embassy was U.S. territory.

"Now tell me, please, Mr. Llewellyn," the lieutenant began, "what were you doing here tonight?"

"I work here," he answered shortly. "This is the American embassy. It's my job to be here."

The sarcasm wasn't lost on the police detective, but he took it in stride, his voice losing none of its smoothness. "Are you always here so late, then?"

"I was returning from a trip. My car was parked here. The taxi from the airport dropped me off."

"And the young lady, Miss Zadik. She accompanied you?"

He shook his head.

"Then what was she doing here?"

"You'll have to ask her."

"We shall, Mr. Llewellyn, we shall. But you are acquainted with her, are you not?"

Llewellyn nodded. "She works for the Foreign Minister. Our embassy does a lot of business with that office."

"So you know her only in a professional capacity? You have not met her socially, dated her?"

"That's none of your business!" David exploded. "And furthermore, you have no jurisdiction here. I'm not answering any more questions until I talk to the ambassador."

The police lieutenant handed him the phone from the adjacent desktop. "Do you know the number?"

Without answering, he dialed the number of the ambassador's residence that he had memorized before leaving on his Saudi trip. As the number rang, he heard a click in the receiver. One of Ziffer's men would be listening in on the other end of the conversation.

A befuddled Abrams, roused from sleep in the earliest morning hour, listened incredulously to Llewellyn's terse account of the situation at the embassy in the aftermath of the death of its security officer at the hands of persons unknown. The ambassador promised to rush right over. He instructed his subordinate, in the meantime, to cooperate with the authorities in every way possible.

The lieutenant spoke briefly with someone outside the door, then resumed his interrogation. He abandoned the line of questioning about Daniella, for the moment, zeroing in on the trip from which the envoy had just returned. When informed that the destination was Saudi Arabia, he reacted sharply, as though this, in itself, constituted a crime.

The kid gloves were off now. His manner grew more and more aggressive and hostile, some of the questions thinly veiled accusations. David stood it as long as he could, answering evenly, trying to keep his cool. But when the interrogation shifted back to Daniella, he had had enough.

"Let's clear up one thing, Lieutenant. Am I a suspect in this murder? Is Miss Zadik a suspect? Are you arresting us?"

"That will be determined in due course," responded the detective, "after we have gone over your statements."

"Lieutenant, you're a damn fool! Did you find a murder weapon? Of course not! The killer took it with him. While you fritter around here, he's getting away. We are entirely innocent of any wrongdoing; Miss Zadik's statement will corroborate my own. I demand that you release us immediately!"

He got up from his chair. The detective jumped to his feet,

livid. "Mr. Llewellyn, you will sit back down! You will—"

The confrontation between the two was interrupted by the arrival of the ambassador. The sight of his glistening bald head emerging from the cheerless fluorescence of the basement corridor was a welcome one to David. Abrams was influential and persuasive. He could be counted on to get Ziffer and his men squared away so they could all go home.

He couldn't remember ever feeling so dragged out. The bump on the back of his head was throbbing incessantly, swollen to the size of a walnut. He longed for the sanctuary of his own apartment, the hot shower that would wash away the accumulated dust and sweat of the Saudi trip and its shocking sequel, if not the lingering sensation of blood on his hands where they had contacted the back of Abernathy's head. First a hot shower, then the coolness of the sheets on his own bed, where the throbbing in his head would subside and he would be able to think. He had a lot of thinking to do, questions to answer for himself. Different questions from those being flung at him by the Israeli detective.

Some questions were easier than others. The precipitous arrival of the police had baffled him. How had they learned so swiftly of Abernathy's murder? How did they gain entry to the tightly secured embassy? Now that he was permitted a moment of undisturbed reflection as the detective and the ambassador conferred, the answer leapt out at him. The killer, of course—an anonymous tip. He must have informed the police to throw suspicion on the two bystanders who would be discovered with the body, thus delaying his own pursuit. Leaving the rear entry to the embassy propped open for the police would ensure their timely penetration to catch the pair "red-handed."

The identity of the murderer—that was the all-important, all-consuming question now. For in Llewellyn's mind, the killer of Abernathy and the mole he was searching for had merged into one. Everything pointed to it. The murder was obviously an inside job; whoever had been there that night had access to the embassy and knew his way around. There was no indication of burglary as the motive for his actions. Abernathy, David was convinced, had been killed because he had found out something that put the killer in jeopardy. And that something figured to be the source of the leaks that had become a grave security matter for the U.S. and its Israeli ally.

But who was this killer-mole? With Abernathy dead, he hadn't a clue. Or had he? Suddenly he recalled Daniella's reaction at his mention of Martin Singer's continued presence in Israel. The abrupt arrival of the police and their protracted interrogation had temporarily put it out of his mind. She had been on the verge of telling him something important. If only he could talk to her!

Could Martin be mixed up in this? No, that made no sense at all. He had known Singer for years. He was a totally up-front guy; there was nothing devious about him. Obnoxious, at times, to be sure, but not underhanded. Martin an undercover operator? It just didn't figure. Besides, hadn't he himself seen his friend more than thirty miles away, shortly before the murder took place?

The voice of Ambassador Abrams broke into his stream of consciousness. "Come on, my boy, you're going home." He put a hand on David's shoulder, his nearsighted eyes squinting behind tortoiseshell spectacles at the bump behind the left ear.

"That's a nasty one! There might have been a concussion. Lieutenant, why wasn't this man given medical attention?"

"He didn't request it, sir. But we can take him to the dispensary now if you like."

"No!" David exclaimed. "It's all right. I just want to get some sleep."

"You're not dizzy, or nauseous?" the ambassador persisted.

"No, sir, I'm fine. Just bone weary." He stood up and started for the door. The detective restrained him with uplifted palms.

"I'm releasing you in Ambassador Abrams's custody. But we may need to talk to you again soon. Under no circumstances are you to leave the country. There'll be no more trips to places like Saudi Arabia, or anywhere else, until our investigation is completed. Is that understood?"

David nodded, his head aching afresh from the sudden rise from the chair. The room was starting to swim around him; all he wanted was to get out of there, away from the fouled atmosphere of the murder scene, into the fresh air. But wait; what about Daniella?

"Daniella—Miss Zadik. You're not holding her, are you?"

The lieutenant shook his head. "She was released a half hour ago. The Foreign Minister himself appeared and escorted her home."

Relieved, David moved toward the door. "I'll drive you home," the ambassador offered.

"No, thank you anyway, sir. My car is parked outside."

"One moment, Mr. Llewellyn. Your personal effects." The detective left the office and returned immediately with an envelope, which he inverted over the desk.

"You'll be needing these." The billfold, passport, and key ring removed from his person when the police first arrived tumbled onto the desktop.

David picked them up one by one, dropping the keys and billfold into his trousers pockets. As he slid the passport inside his jacket, a folded slip of paper fell out of it and fluttered to the floor. He retrieved it casually and scanned the brief handwritten note inside.

"Must talk to you. Breakfast King David, 8 o'clock." It was signed with the single initial, D.

Alfresco breakfasting at the King David Hotel was a pleasant prelude for tourists in the know to the exploration of the Old City that would follow. From their table on the terrace, they could stare across at the western wall of the ancient metropolis and the intriguing array of spires and domes protruding above it, anticipating the sights and discoveries that awaited them. Despite the earliness of the hour, a substantial number had already congregated by the time David arrived, savoring the sight of the battlements and ramparts of the crusader-built citadel over luscious fresh fruits and breads, blintzes and eggs, and pickled herring and lox.

He found a small table for two set off by itself in a corner, under a potted palm, and sat down where he could watch the entrance and the view at the same time. It was a fine, sunny winter morning with just the whisper of a breeze that bore the promise of spring—a romantic spot for a rendezvous with a beautiful woman. But there was no romance inside of him, at the moment. There was only anger, an anger fed by the painful wound at the back of his head and the urgent compulsion to apprehend its perpetrator. The same man, he was now convinced, that he had been sent here to find and unmask.

As for Daniella, his feelings about her were too confused, at the moment, to put into words. Abernathy's diatribe against her, identifying her as an Israeli agent, had come back to him repeatedly, culminating in the man's caustic insinuation that her every response toward him had been a sham. The indictment of a man now dead, which somehow gave his words added credence. Part of him was still unwilling to believe it. But last night, when he had confronted her with the accusation, she had not denied it.

He glanced impatiently at the watch on his left wrist: 8:10 already; she was late. He wondered idly if this was habitual with her. She had been late for that first memorable meeting, the farewell luncheon with Martin.

From his seat on the terrace he could make out the contours of the Jaffa Gate, through which he had entered the Old City on that first occasion, and the adjacent walls of the crusader fortress past which he and Singer had walked on their way to the luncheon rendezvous. He was reminded of the infectious excitement that had gripped him as he was carried by the torrent of diverse humanity through the constricted and colorful passageway leading toward the center of the venerable city. And his surprise at discovering an Armenian Quarter, with its little open-air restaurant tucked away off a hidden side corridor. Then that first sight of Daniella, picking her way with care across the cobblestoned courtyard in her high heels to join them.

He looked back toward the entrance, and started, the sensation of reliving the moment almost eerie. She was wearing the same smart two-piece suit she had worn that first day. She had stepped onto the terrace and was peering beneath her sunglasses, searching the tables, that familiar frown of concentration on her face that he remembered from his first sight of her. And the same smile of recognition lit up her face as she discovered him beneath the potted palm.

He waved and stood up, watching her glide toward him, high heels clicking their way across the terrace, the sunglasses removed now, revealing those wide, alluring brown eyes. Damn! She was magnificent. Was she an actress, or was she for real?

"Shalom, David." Her hand was soft and cool, its firm pressure in quest of an answering squeeze that wasn't quite there. She searched his eyes, but there were no answers there, either. He bent down to pull the chair out for her, and she saw the small bandage at the back of his head.

"Oh, David! Your poor head! It must hurt terribly. Did you have a doctor attend to it?"

"No," he said. "There wasn't time for a doctor. I bandaged it myself."

"You should see a doctor," she urged. "I'd be happy to recommend one. He could prescribe something to ease the pain."

"No, thanks," he responded. "There's only one thing that will ease the pain—catching up with the guy who did it."

She looked at him in alarm. "You're not thinking of going after him yourself? That—killer?"

"That's exactly what I'm thinking about." The glint of determination in the steady gray eyes told her that he meant it. "In fact, it's about all I've been able to think about since last night."

Her concerned look persisted while the waitress arrived with their tray, unloading the coffee that David had ordered for them, and a plate full of assorted hot rolls. Daniella waited until the waitress was out of earshot.

"But, David, that could be very dangerous. The murderer is still armed, probably wouldn't hesitate to kill again. Shouldn't you leave that kind of thing to the proper authorities?"

"Like Ziffer and his Keystone Cops?" He laughed contemptuously. "They couldn't find a clue if it jumped out and bit them. Do you realize, you and I are their prime suspects?"

He saw the instant alarm that swept over her face. "You didn't tell them—"

"No, you needn't worry." The sarcasm in his voice was unmistakable. Was that her urgent reason for this morning's get-together—just to make sure that her precious undercover job hadn't been compromised? He was suddenly incensed.

"Besides, what could I tell them? What do I really know about you? Other than the fact that if you really are one of them, you're damn good at it. You sure had me fooled."

"You still think that I—?" There was pain in her eyes. Her hand grasped his. "No, David! I won't have you believing that! It isn't true!"

He pulled his hand away. "You deny that you're an agent of the Mossad?"

She looked behind her concernedly. But the patrons at the nearby tables were more intent on their generous breakfasts and the spectacle of the Old City than on snatches of conversation from the table in the corner. "Please don't talk so loudly," she pleaded in a subdued voice. "You know that if I were one of them, I'd have to deny it, be pledged to keep it a secret. Otherwise, it could destroy my usefulness to them."

"Blow your cover, you mean." He laughed scornfully. "You don't have to say any more. You've already confirmed what I suspected."

"No, David, please listen!" She seized his hand again, a note of desperation in her voice. "When I was with you—that glorious afternoon and evening; that was before—"

She stopped herself, biting her lip, her face reflecting the struggle going on inside her. She could see the hurt, the lingering doubt, in his face. She made up her mind.

"I'm going to tell you a story—a true story—about someone whose name I won't mention. Call her a friend of mine. She is a sabra who became a struggling career girl after she left the kibbutz, working her way up to a responsible position with a high government official."

"The Foreign Minister, by any chance?" he interjected.

Her nod was almost imperceptible as she hurried on. "She had only one sibling, a brother, who meant the whole world to her, her only close surviving relative. Their parents were both dead, the father killed in one of the Arab wars. That brother served his country passionately in a highly secretive and hazardous capacity. He knew the danger he was in; he made sure his sister knew, also. He wanted to prepare her for what might happen.

"But you can never be prepared for a thing like that. When the news of his death reached her, she reacted in an unexpected way. She went down and volunteered—enlisted—in that same 'branch of the service.'"

David grasped her arm in a grip of steel. "When?"

"Just two days ago, while you were away on your trip."

"Then she wasn't—you weren't—"

"No, not then; not until after." She smiled reassuringly, tenderly, feeling the tenseness drain out of his grip on her arm, watching the hard eyes soften.

"That explains what happened to you—why I couldn't reach you. You must have just gotten the news." He took her hand in both of his. "I'm sorry about your—about your friend's brother."

A tear stole into each eye; she brushed them away. "The worst of it is, she can't let on. His death has to be kept a secret, her mourning has to stay bottled up."

She wiped her eyes on her napkin. "We should eat our breakfast. The coffee's getting cold." She freed her other hand from his and poured the fragrant liquid from the carafe into the china cups.

He clinked his cup against hers, looking into the soft brown eyes until they came back to his. "It's corny and trite and this isn't champagne, but I'll say it anyway. To us."

"To us, then. For better or worse." She clinked back. They sipped in silence for several moments, totally absorbed in each other, under the spell of their reconciliation. He was the first to break it.

"That wild man, Abernathy! He warned me about you, you know, said your job with the Foreign Minister was just a cover, that you— He had it all wrong. I told him I didn't believe him."

"Guilt by association. He probably discovered my brother's affiliation, assumed the rest."

His hand gripped her arm again. "He must have discovered something else—something that did him in! What was it? What were you about to tell me, just before the police barged in?"

Her face clouded over and she turned away, avoiding his eyes. "Nothing. I thought for a moment—but I was mistaken."

"Daniella, come on!" Why was she suddenly being evasive? He reached across the table and grasped both her shoulders, turning her back to face him. "It was when I mentioned spotting Martin at the airport. You said—"

"I know what I said. I was overreacting. Martin behaving so suspiciously, deceiving everyone into thinking he was out of the country. It wasn't like him. It came to me all at once that there might be another side to Martin, a darker side that I was never shown. It would explain why Abernathy contacted me, the connection—my former relationship with Martin, which he knew about." She shook her head slowly from side to side. "But I was wrong."

He let go of her shoulders and slumped back into his chair. "The same thought crossed my mind. But it didn't make sense to me, either. I've known Martin a long time. He was never into anything devious or sub-rosa. And besides, he was miles away when Abernathy was murdered."

He leaned forward again, taking her hand in both of his. "Let's try again. Exactly what did Abernathy tell you?"

She frowned. "He wasn't telling—he was asking."

"Asking what? Sometimes a question can be full of answers."

She shook her head. "Not this one. The question concerned me, what I was doing on two specific days in the last two months. It was an outrageous thing to ask me. I told him so before I hung up on him."

Now it was David's turn to frown. "He suspected you of something?"

"At first that's what I thought. He came on so strong, you know, in that way of his. But when he called back, he was more conciliatory. He said it had nothing to do with me, that I was not being investigated, but that my information might be crucial in staving off a major threat to the security of our two countries."

"What threat? Did he give any particulars?"

"No," she answered. "I tried to get more out of him, but he said he couldn't go into it on the telephone. He instructed me to come directly to the embassy. Then he gave me the punch code for the rear entry."

"What did you do then?"

"I called my control, informed him of the contact, and asked for instructions. He told me to keep the appointment and report back to him afterwards."

"Which you did, no doubt, after you were released by the police."

She nodded somewhat ruefully, and he couldn't suppress a wry smile. "That must have been a shock for him. Two days on the job, and his new charge is involved in a murder." A new thought struck him. Could the Mossad have been responsible, taken Abernathy out for some unknown reason? No, nothing pointed to that; he was grasping at straws. He might equally suspect the CIA. His first gut feeling had been the most reliable. The murder had to be connected with the security breach at the embassy. The mole he was searching for was almost certainly behind it.

Evidence, clues. So far there seemed to be very little to go on. What had the murdered man stumbled onto? "Let's get back to Abernathy's question," he suggested. "Those two days that he was inquiring about: were you able to reconstruct what you did, whom you saw?"

"Not until this morning. I don't keep a diary. The closest thing to it is my day-by-day appointment pad. But that was in my office, and I didn't have access to it last night. I was wracking my brain as I drove to the embassy, trying to remember anything out of the ordinary that happened on those two dates, which were both working days. I couldn't come up with a thing."

"Let's get that memo pad!" he exclaimed, starting up from his chair. She restrained him with a hand on his sleeve.

"I have it right here in my purse. It's the reason I was late. I stopped by the office this morning to pick it up."

"May I see it?"

"Yes, but you needn't bother. I've already scanned it. There's absolutely nothing noteworthy on either day. They must have been two of the most empty and uneventful days in my whole life. No important meetings or interviews or briefings. I didn't even get to see Martin. Our standing luncheon date was off on both days. He was either out of town or at some conference, as I recall."

She noted the disappointment in his face. "That's what finally convinced me that my little intuitive flash about Martin being involved was on the wrong track, you see. Neither of the two dates mentioned by Abernathy has anything to do with him."

"Unless—" His eyes were suddenly on fire. "Daniella, don't you see? That could be it, the fact that he's *not* mentioned, that he *wasn't* with you!"

She stared back at him vacantly, not comprehending.

"Suppose Martin was using you for an alibi for something. Abernathy could have been checking it out!"

She frowned, still skeptical. "Then why didn't he just ask me if I had lunch with Martin, or dinner, or whatever, on those two days?"

"That's easy. You might have informed Martin that he was under suspicion. Abernathy wouldn't have taken a chance like that."

A scenario was building in his mind, based in part on a preembarkation briefing, the details of which he had memorized. "The two dates—what were they?"

"December 15 and January 10. Are the dates significant?"

"Maybe." There was no maybe about it. The dates invoked by Abernathy each fell within time spans during which two specific documents from the embassy's top secret files were believed to have been compromised. Supposing that Abernathy's investigation had narrowed down those time windows to a particular hour on those two days when the files were unattended or unaccountably left open. He would have been doing exactly what his contact with Daniella suggested: determining the whereabouts, at those specific times, of embassy personnel who might have had access, running down their alibis. And Martin Singer's wouldn't have checked out.

He looked up from the table and their eyes met. Her face wore a somber look.

"A false alibi. I should have thought of that. I guess I just didn't want to believe Martin could be implicated. Could we have both been so wrong about him? Could Martin possibly have—?"

"There's one way to find out." He held up his hand to signal the waitress for the check. "My taxi drove directly to the embassy from the airport last night, and we were driving as fast as we could in the heavy traffic. If Martin got there ahead of me, starting after I did, he must have flown. A private plane, a helicopter. Either way, there'll be a record of it at Ben Gurion Airport."

He scanned the check and dropped some bills on the table. Daniella looked at her watch. "I'm afraid you're going to be late for work."

"Quite late; I may not show up at all today." He stood up and pulled back her chair.

"You're going to the airport now? Then I'm coming with you."

He shook his head. "No need for both of us to play hooky. Besides, what would your 'fairy godfather' say? You're already in Dutch with him for his having to bail you out last night."

"The Minister doesn't expect me until later. And I am not, as you put it, in Dutch with him. He was very understanding. He gave me the morning off."

She put a hand on his arm. "Don't forget, I have a stake in finding the murderer, too. I'm still a suspect, just as you are."

"Well, okay, if you want to tag along. But it doesn't figure to be that exciting. Just some routine legwork. We'll take my car."

Arm in arm, they pushed their way across the tourist-glutted terrace toward the hotel lobby. It was a long shot, he was thinking. Martin Singer a murderer? Martin Singer the mole? But it had to be pursued until it was proven or disproven, both questions resolved. And he had to take care not to reveal to his lovely companion the true objective of his search. Let her continue to think that his motivation was one of revenge and the need to clear himself—themselves—of the murder.

Daniella Zadik was preoccupied at the moment with her own little deception, her conscience far from clear. She had disobeyed orders, violated her pledge by informing David of the death of her brother and her subsequent induction into the Mossad. But she had not told him everything.

She was spying on the man she loved, sticking closely to him, as her Mossad control had directed. David Llewellyn had a secret. It was her job to find it out.

CHAPTER
8

The multistoried Flight Ops building, on top of which the control tower was perched, was located near the geometric center of the Ben Gurion terminal complex. As he circled the small parking lot, searching for a vacant stall, David Llewellyn began to have some misgivings about the task he had set for himself. Getting the information he was after might not be as straightforward as he had envisioned. There was an armed guard posted at the entrance to the building; he was checking the badges and credentials of everyone who entered.

"We're going to need a cover story," he observed, "one we can support with official-looking credentials."

"Why not just tell the truth?" Daniella suggested. "You're the American envoy, and you're trying to trace an associate whom you lost track of here at the airport last night. You think he might have hired a private plane to fly him to Jerusalem."

He nodded. "That sounds okay, but I don't want to use Singer's name or identity. Let's just say he's a visitor from America. If they ask for a name, I'll have to give them a fictitious one. And what about you; where do you fit in? If they don't speak English, you'll be doing the talking."

"The truth, again," she answered. "I'm from the Foreign Minister's office, as my identification will confirm. In the interest of Israeli-American relations, I'm helping out the new U.S. envoy, who doesn't speak Hebrew."

Getting by the sentry proved the easiest part. Bedazzled by Daniella's smile, the young Israeli soldier inspected her government card, listened briefly to her story, then held the door open for them, waving them through to a reception desk inside.

The matronly woman behind the counter was a different matter. She was strictly business, her manner curt and unfriendly as she checked Daniella's credentials and sized up the tall American beside her. Midway through Daniella's spiel, the receptionist interrupted her.

"The gentleman's identification, please." Her English was heavily accented, but he could understand her. Her tone left no doubt who was in charge here. She was some tough cookie. He presented his State Department card, turning on some charm of his own.

"Your English is very good. I wish I could say the same about my Hebrew. I'm trying to learn, but it's very difficult."

"I vas alvays good at langvitches." The woman's manner brightened somewhat as she studied the card with his picture on it. "An envoy—zat is a high position?"

"Number two in the embassy, just below ambassador." Apparently unimpressed, she handed the ID card back to him without comment. He reproduced the smile she had seen on its photograph.

"Perhaps you can help me. I'm trying to trace another American who arrived here at the airport yesterday evening. His destination was Jerusalem. We think he may have flown there from here."

The receptionist frowned. "Zair are no scheduled flights to Yarushalem. Everyvon goes by car or bus."

"Yes, I know. But this man was in a hurry. He may have hired a private plane to fly him there."

Meshuggener Americans! said the woman's look. "Vat this man's name is?"

"Marcus." He pulled the name out of the air. "Ben Marcus. I must find him; I have an urgent message for him. His wife was in a serious auto accident. If I could just get a look at the control tower's flight log—"

"Za control tower?" The receptionist shook her head vehemently. "Not possible. Und anyvay, you vould not find him zair. Ve keep no names of passengers, only numbers of za planes. If zis Marcus is missing, you must go to police. Zey vill help you."

The woman was exasperating! "I've already been to the police," he lied; it wasn't a total lie. "They won't do anything for forty-eight hours. They say that missing people usually turn up by then. But I can't wait that long. The man's wife is dying."

He looked at her imploringly. "If I could just check the tower's log, see if any flights left here for Jerusalem between 7:30 and 8:00 last night, I'd at least have some clue to go on."

"Clue—shmoo. You Americans all sink you are Kojak,

Nancy Drew. Zis is not TV. Take my advice. Go back to police. Zey are very good at finding people."

His further remonstrations were preempted by the entrance of two men who approached the counter and signed the visitor sheet. David waited impatiently as the receptionist checked their identification, supplied them with visitor badges, and gave them some sort of directions in Hebrew. They moved off toward the elevator, and she turned back to his side of the counter.

"I am sorry. Is regulations. Vizout police order I cannot send you upstairs. You vill have to—"

For the first time she noticed the absence of his companion and erstwhile translator. "Za lady zat came viz you—vair ist?"

He turned. There was no sign of Daniella. He was careful to disguise his own surprise.

"Got tired of waiting, I guess. She must have slipped out when the two men came in. She could see that I didn't need her to translate, since you speak English so well."

He reached across the counter to shake her hand. "Thank you for listening to my problem. I'm going to take your advice, let the police handle it."

The phone at the end of the counter rang, and she moved over to answer it. He made for the door, trying not to appear excited or in too much of a hurry. He opened the door. "Ah, there you are, Miss Zadik."

There was no one there but the guard, who shrugged and smiled self-consciously, assuming that the American was addressing him. "No English," he apologized.

Llewellyn smiled back, saluted, and walked to the spot where the green Simca was parked. He unlocked the driver's side, got in, and slammed the door.

"Good girl!" he shouted aloud to the unresponsive upholstery and simulated wood paneling. If Daniella was where he thought she was, Kojak and Nancy Drew might soon be off and running on their first real lead.

A half hour later he was squirming and fidgeting. What was taking so long? He got out of the car and stretched his legs. A refreshment vending truck pulled into the parking lot and drove up to the entrance to the building, its driver tapping out three short blasts on the horn to announce his arrival.

David ambled toward it, searching his trousers pockets for coins. A cup of coffee might help alleviate the agony of waiting.

The driver opened up the back of the truck. It was self-service; he was the first customer. Wordlessly, he filled a paper cup from the giant coffee urn and offered a handful of coins to the driver, from which the man selected two.

A moment later, the entrance to the Flight Ops building erupted with noise as workers on their morning break burst through the door in high spirits, hurrying toward the refreshment truck. Daniella! This would be her golden opportunity to get back past the formidable receptionist undetected.

He stood back in the shadow of the truck and watched the faces of the employees streaming out the door. No Daniella yet. But he saw another face he recognized and quickly moved away from the truck, into the shelter of cars parked nearby. It was the receptionist, herself, coming out for coffee. As she queued up with the others, intent on her midmorning snack, he saw a slender figure slip out through the entrance and hurry off toward the spot where the Simca was parked.

He raced her back to the car. "Did you see the log? Did you find anything?"

She nodded, trying to catch her breath. Climbing hurriedly into the passenger seat, she swung around to look back toward the building. "Let's get out of here!"

He slammed the door and got in the other side, hitting the starter and gunning the engine. The Simca sped out of the parking lot, its tires squealing through the sharp turn onto the access road.

"Nobody's chasing you, are they?"

"No," she answered. "I don't think so. I just don't want to be around when that dreadful woman discovers I got by her and talked to the people upstairs. She could make trouble."

"What did you find out?" he demanded. "Were there any private flights to Jerusalem last night that could have gotten Martin there ahead of me?"

She settled back in the seat, breathing easier. "At first I didn't think so. There were several departures logged within a half hour of when you left here, but none with Jerusalem listed as the destination. I asked the clerk if there was any way to tell if one of those pilots had changed his flight plan. He said they do it all the time. He suggested looking at the incoming flight log to see if any of the planes had returned." She smiled. "He was very helpful. And cute. I have a date with him tonight."

"Get to the point," he urged. "You found something, didn't you?"

She brushed back a wisp of hair, feigning disappointment. "You're not the least bit jealous, are you? I may keep that date after all."

"All right, all right," he conceded, "I admit to being jealous. Now, cut the suspense, will you?"

"Only one of the aircraft showed up on the incoming flight log," she continued. "The same tail number that was logged out by the tower at 7:49 returned at 9:20. Its destination was listed as Haifa. But my new boyfriend said it was questionable whether its pilot could have landed at Haifa, delivered a cargo or passengers, and returned in that short a time. He could have changed his destination, flown to Jerusalem instead."

"A 7:49 departure? That could be it! Did you get the tail number and description of the plane?"

"I did more than that. I got my new friend to look up the registered owner in the civil aeronautics index. They have it all computerized. He punched in the tail number, and out came the owner's name. The plane is a two-engine Cessna, registered to Dov's Charter Service, located right here at Ben Gurion."

He slammed on the brakes, maneuvering the Simca onto the right shoulder of the service road, preparing to make a U-turn. Her hand on his arm restrained him.

"No, David. It's not back there. It's on the other side of the field, in the private aircraft area. The clerk pointed it out to me from the tower. We keep going until we reach the divided road at the airport entrance, then turn left."

He edged the Simca back out onto the road, his eye on the traffic, his mind elsewhere. If the false destination had been a cover-up, there would doubtless be others. They needed a game plan.

"We can't just go barging in there. The charter people might not give us the time of day without some strong justification. We need to beef up our story."

"Why not try the same story we used with Flight Ops?" she suggested. "It persuaded the clerk, even if it didn't work on the receptionist. We might find a more sympathetic ear this time."

"Not strong enough. It's too easy for them to say no, fall back on client confidentiality. We need a club of some kind, something to hold over them." He brightened. "What about your Mossad?

That should be a heavy enough club. Do you carry an ID card of some kind?"

Daniella was horror struck. "David! I can't go around announcing to the world that I'm an agent. I'm operating under cover. The identity card is strictly for emergencies, a last resort. My control was very emphatic on that point."

"You don't think this is an emergency? We're suspects in a murder we didn't commit. The real killer may get away if we're not successful."

"Yes, but—I still can't compromise myself with the Institute."

"All I'm asking you to do is flash your Mossad card at the proprietor of this charter service, so he'll cooperate with us. How does that compromise you?"

"Isn't that obvious? If he reads my name on the card, writes it down or remembers it, the fact that Daniella Zadik is an agent of the Mossad will no longer be a secret."

"Then we'll change your name!" He braked the car sharply, pulling off to the side of the road. "Let me see that card."

"It's in Hebrew. You won't be able to read it."

His extended hand was insistent. Hesitantly, she produced a wallet from her shoulder bag and fished a card out of one of its compartments.

He examined it carefully. The card was encased in heavy, clear plastic. The color photo of Daniella, staring back through it, didn't do her justice, he noted. Just below the photograph was her name; he had seen it often enough in Hebrew to recognize it. The caption across the top of the card in heavy block letters must be that of the Mossad, itself—the Central Institute for Intelligence and Security. That should throw a proper scare into the Dov's Charter Service proprietorship.

He turned off the engine and withdrew the key from the ignition, opening the tiny penknife that dangled from the key chain.

"What—what are you doing?" Daniella protested. "You're not going to cut into it?"

"Just separating the plastic a little, so we can doctor up the name." His fingers worked the thin blade skillfully between the layers of plastic, prying them apart.

"There. Now we need to locate a phone booth with a telephone directory and find you a new name."

"We just passed one, back at that last terminal building." She looked concernedly at the mangled ID card. "My control's going to kill me."

He started the car again and swung it across traffic and into the left-turn lane. It was less than a mile back to the building where Daniella had seen the telephone. He double-parked nearby, and they both ran to the booth.

David got there first. "Good!" he exclaimed, thumbing through the directory. "The printing's about the right size. Here, pick a name—any name."

She started at the back of the book, in the Z's. "Here's one. Zold. Racquel Zold. I always wanted to be a Racquel."

He tore the entire sheet out of the phone book and laid it on top of the book's heavy plastic cover. "Which name is it?"

She pointed to a line halfway up the left margin. With a surgeon's care, he made an incision just beneath it, then a parallel slit of the same length just above the name. "It's a good thing I keep this knife razor-sharp, or this would never work." A short stroke at either end freed the narrow strip of paper, and he used the knife's point to extract Racquel Zold permanently from her spot on page 230 of the Tel Aviv phone directory.

Back in the car, he moistened the back of the tiny slip of paper with his tongue and inserted it between the plastic sheets of the ID card, pushing it carefully into place under Daniella's photograph with the point of the penknife. "There, that should do it." He pressed the plastic edges back together and held it up for her inspection.

"Racquel Zold," she read, squinting her eyes appraisingly. "You know, it looks authentic enough, if you don't examine it too closely."

"Don't let the card out of your hands," he advised. "Hold it by the open end, so that your new name doesn't slip out of place, and flash it, just long enough for someone to see your photograph and read the Mossad caption. That way, nobody gets a chance to study it."

He handed the card back to her. She slid it carefully into its slot in her wallet. "What's my cover story? Why is the Mossad looking for Martin?"

"I wouldn't even mention Martin." He started the car and pulled out onto the access road. "You're investigating a man who eluded the authorities at Ben Gurion Airport last night. For starters, you want to know the destination of the charter flight, who piloted the plane, and the names of any passengers he carried."

"What if Martin used an assumed name? He probably would have, under the circumstances."

"Ask for a description. There can't be that many blond-haired, blue-eyed Americans in Tel Aviv that are dead ringers for Paul Newman."

That drew a smile from her. "He might have used a disguise, of course."

"If he had time to prepare one. The flight took off at 7:49. That's less than ten minutes after I saw him. It's quite possible that he had the charter set up in advance for that specific time, or—"

"Or what?"

"Or he might have decided on the spur of the moment, after seeing me. It might have been extemporaneous! After all, my seeing him there would give him a perfect alibi."

"I see what you're getting at," she nodded. "There might not have been time for a disguise. But Martin is smart. He'd have surely taken some precautions to cover his tracks."

"Yes," he mused, "I'm sure of it. It's called silent money. That's why the Mossad ploy may be necessary; we may have to scare the charter people into talking."

"And if they don't?"

"If they don't, then I'll be there to see what they do next. They might try to warn Martin that the Mossad is on his tail."

Her frown questioned his reasoning. "Perhaps so, but not in front of us, surely."

"They won't know we're together. I'll go in fifteen minutes ahead of you. I'll inquire about arranging a charter flight for some VIP, ask to see their equipment, find some reason to hang around after you leave."

They arrived at the airport exit, and he took the turn to the left onto the road that serviced the other side of the airfield. Daniella remained silent, lost in thought. He glanced across at her. She was staring out at the road ahead, her face somber.

"Nervous?" he asked. "Don't be. There's no real danger."

"No," she answered, "it isn't that. I just realized, we've been talking as though Martin really is the murderer—as though he's actually guilty. I still can't believe that. I guess I'm praying that it isn't true."

He put a hand on hers. "I know. I don't want to believe it, either. But we have to find out, don't we?"

Sometime today we *will* find out, he thought. If Martin Singer wasn't the murderer, they were back to square one. If he was, then he was something else, also: the mole that formerly operated inside the U.S. embassy, whose traffic in top secret documents threatened the security of the host nation, a ticking bomb that could wreak havoc on the relations between the two allies. One way or the other, they would know very soon.

The headquarters of Dov's Charter Service proved to be even less imposing than its name. A low, rusty metal hangar looking scarcely large enough to house a medium-sized private plane was fronted by a ramshackle wood-frame office building that was even smaller. David could see, parked on the apron of the runway, behind the hangar, several trim-looking, brightly painted aircraft. The major assets of Dov's were apparently its flyable ones.

He had parked the Simca a quarter of a mile away and walked the remaining distance, Daniella remaining in the car. No one inside the building must suspect that they had arrived together or that their visits were in any way connected. In fifteen minutes or so, Daniella would drive up in the Simca and park in front of the building.

The door to the front office was ajar; for ventilation purposes, no doubt. He could feel the warm draft of air exiting the building, aided by fans inside, their low-pitched whirring barely audible. Air-conditioning would have been a high-overhead frill for this operation. He pulled the screen door open and stepped inside.

His eyes quickly scanned the interior. It was one large room, a few desks set behind a service counter, with no private offices. The arrangement suited his purpose ideally. Standing at the counter, ostensibly occupied with arrangements for a charter, he could keep one eye on everything that occurred inside. Now if only someone here spoke English.

Dov's total work force, at the moment, consisted of two individuals. The girl at the secretary desk continued her typing and did not look up as the screen door closed with a sharp clicking noise. A fat man was lounging at the desk at her left, reading a newspaper, his feet on the desktop. He peered momentarily from behind the newspaper, then went back to his reading. David cleared his throat.

"Golda!" At the word from the fat man, the girl looked up from her typing, took stock of the tall man standing behind the counter, and got up from her chair.

"Shalom."

"Shalom," he echoed. "I'm afraid I don't speak Hebrew. I'm with the United States embassy. Does anyone here speak English?"

The girl named Golda nodded. "Yes, sir; we both do."

"Oh, that's great. My name is Llewellyn. I'm the new envoy here in Jerusalem."

He presented one of his cards to the secretary. She read the few words on it, her lips moving silently.

"What can we do for you, Mr. Llewellyn?"

"I have a VIP—that's very important person—a top American diplomat, arriving here from Washington next week, to attend a meeting at the embassy. His time is very limited, and he'll be coming in during the late afternoon rush hour. I'd like to explore the possibility of flying him directly to Jerusalem from the airport, avoiding the traffic jam on the expressway."

"Yes, Mr. Llewellyn, we can arrange such a charter." The girl stole a glance at the man behind the newspaper. "It won't be inexpensive, however. Will this be a one-way charter, or do you wish the same service on the return flight?"

"No, one way will be sufficient. The main object is to get our bigwig to the embassy before the meeting breaks up. Does this make any sense to you? Will we be saving a significant amount of time compared to using ground transportation?"

"Why, yes, I should think so." The secretary pondered for a moment. "In rush-hour traffic, the trip by limousine can take the better part of an hour. But by plane—"

She stepped over to a large-scale map on the wall and pointed to the Ben Gurion location.

"We take off from here and land at Oalandiya Airport—right here, at the northern end of Jerusalem. In one of our Cessna's, that's at most a ten-minute flight. Where is your embassy located?"

"On Rachel Imenu Street."

"That's here." She moved the pointer down the map. "No more than a ten-minute taxi or limousine ride, if that. Allow five minutes for takeoff and landing clearances, another five minutes to transfer your passenger and his luggage to our terminal from the other side of the airport; we will provide a limousine and have it waiting for him."

She wrote down the numbers and added them up, looking up triumphantly. "You could save at least a half hour in travel time."

"You mean, by taking your flight, my VIP would arrive at the embassy a half hour ahead of the time he would be there if he went all the way by limousine?" He had an ulterior motive for pressing the point.

The girl nodded. "We could almost guarantee it."

There it was! An independent assessment, supporting his own, that a man he had seen at the airport yesterday, a man with murder on his mind, could have subsequently scrambled onto a plane and beat him to the embassy with ample time to carry out his nefarious plan.

"Would you like to see our equipment?" she inquired.

"By all means." Daniella wasn't due yet; he needed to stall for another few minutes. "That's the reason I came in person," he added.

The secretary stepped out from behind the counter and pushed open the screen door. "This way."

They walked past the badly corroded sheet metal wall of the hangar toward the apron adjoining the runway, where three twin-engine aircraft were tethered. To David they looked identical except for their colors and markings. His eyes scanned their tails, searching for the number Daniella had recorded from the flight controller's log. He found it on the vertical stabilizer of the blue and white job—the plane that had taken off yesterday evening at precisely 7:49, presumably for Haifa; that could have been flown, instead, to Oalandiya Airport in Jerusalem. Had Martin Singer been on board?

"Which is the fastest one?" he inquired.

"The blue one," she replied. "I would recommend it. It does thirty knots more than the other two."

She opened the left-hand door. He climbed inside. The plane was spotless; if there had been any clues to yesterday's escapade, they had been swept away. He sat down in one of the passenger seats, ostensibly testing the upholstery.

"Very comfortable. Now, about the pilot. I'd want your best one."

"That would be Dov Gruner, the owner. I'm sure he would want to handle this personally. When we return, we'll ask him."

"The man inside the office?"

She nodded, smiling at his surprise. "Don't let his appearance deceive you. He is an excellent pilot."

Through the side window he saw the green Simca approaching the charter office. He extricated himself from the seat and climbed back out of the plane and onto the tarmac.

"A beauty, isn't she? It's our newest equipment." The secretary carefully closed and secured the door.

"Yes; yes, this one will do nicely." He watched the Simca glide to a stop behind the building, heard its door slam moments later. They walked back around the hangar. Daniella had already disappeared through the screen door. She was standing at the counter when they entered, looking cool and self-possessed. She barely glanced in his direction as the screen door clacked shut again.

The fat man, the "Dov" of Dov's Charter Service, had put aside his newspaper and was in the act of rousing himself. With an answering "Shalom," he lifted his bulk out of the chair and ambled toward the counter. Though he couldn't understand the words that followed, Llewellyn could readily guess the nature of the exchange that ensued between them. The proprietor had asked her how he could be of service. Daniella had stated that she was looking for someone. Her next act was to identify herself. She produced the doctored Mossad ID card and held it up briefly in front of Dov Gruner.

David watched the fat man's face carefully. There was something akin to fear frozen there as his eyes darted from the card to Daniella's face and back to the card again. Fear, or guilty knowledge of something? It was hard to tell.

"Mr. Llewellyn. We haven't talked price yet." The secretary was looking at him strangely. He realized he had been too overt in his perusal of the other two occupants; he would have to watch it.

"No, that's right, we haven't." He pretended to give her all of his attention. "What is the fee, then, for the services we've discussed?"

She was holding a tiny hand calculator. "I've added it up. The one-way charter flight to Jerusalem, with limousine service from the main airport to our terminal here, comes to two hundred and sixty-two shekels."

"Yes. All right. I think we can swing that." The proprietor had been jabbering steadily since Daniella had flashed her Mossad card. He had led her behind the counter and across to his desk a few paces away, for what little added privacy that would afford, David assumed. Over the secretary's shoulder he could see the corpulent Dov sitting back in his chair, his mouth going nonstop. Daniella sat facing him across the desk; she was taking notes on a small pad. Although Gruner was making an apparent effort to keep his voice down, the words were audible. Damn! If he could only understand the language!

"If you will just fill out the contract, then." The secretary shoved a form at him, supplying a ballpoint pen. "We'll also need to know the passenger's full name, the number of the incoming flight, and the time of arrival. And the date, of course."

"He'll be coming a week from Wednesday. I've forgotten which flight; it's one that arrives around five P.M., from either Geneva or Paris. I'll have to call that in to you."

He pretended to busy himself over the contract form. The secretary cast a curious glance behind her, her attention distracted by the dialogue emanating from her boss's desk. For the first time she seemed to notice that something quite unusual was transpiring, her employer undergoing some sort of interrogation by the attractive, coolly professional brunette in the smartly tailored suit. He seemed to be bending over backward to be casual and affable, Llewellyn noted. But the beads of perspiration on his forehead hadn't been there before Daniella arrived.

The secretary was openly staring at the proceedings now, tuning in on the conversation. He tapped her on the shoulder, and she turned back to the counter with a start.

"Yes?"

"Here where it says 'other conditions.' I'd like to write in the name 'Dov Gruner' as pilot. Agreed?"

"Mr. Gruner seems to be tied up at the moment," she observed. "I'll verify that as soon as he's free."

Filling in the final entries on the contract form, David continued to monitor the activity across the room. The exchange grew more animated, the proprietor doing most of the talking and gesturing. Then Daniella was gathering up her purse and tucking the notepad and pen inside. She stood up from the desk and extended her hand. Gruner struggled to his feet, a benign smile on his face as he shook her hand, his parting words disarmingly effusive. Now was the time!

He slipped the microcassette recorder out of his trousers pocket and clicked it on, palming it in his left hand with the built-in microphone exposed. Holding it just below the countertop, he watched the needle bob up and down, verifying that the volume of sound from the man's voice was sufficient for recording purposes.

The proprietor finished his speech, and David watched his

accomplice take her leave, stepping through the opening in the service counter only a few feet to his right. He searched her face for some clue to the success of the interview, but she avoided his eyes and gave him no sign to go on.

"Shalom," said the secretary sweetly. Daniella returned her smile. "Shalom." The screen door closed behind her.

"A stunning woman," the secretary remarked, looking at David for a reaction.

"Not bad," he agreed, not looking up as he put the finishing touches on the charter contract. "There, that should do it."

The secretary approached her boss with the completed contract. Dov Gruner had slumped back into his chair, the ingratiating smile no longer in evidence. He cut her off sharply, the veneer of affability suddenly stripped away. He reached for the phone.

The secretary returned to the counter, somewhat red-faced from her unexpected rebuff. "I'm sorry. He has an urgent matter to attend to first. It shouldn't be long."

"No problem."

It seemed to be taking the fat man forever to dial the number. His impatience showed in his face, mounting as he waited for the phone to start ringing, increasing with every unanswered ring that buzzed back into his ear. He slammed the phone back into its cradle.

It was an old-fashioned dial phone, Llewellyn noted; almost an antique. That accounted for the slowness of the dialing mechanism. It also accounted for his own sudden elation, despite his initial disappointment that the call was not completed and no incriminating conversation recorded.

What had been recorded might prove even more useful: a sequence of dialing sounds from a telephone executing a number that constituted an "urgent matter" for a man visibly shaken by an interrogation into last evening's charter flight. For David realized that he had only to reduce the playback speed of the recorder and make a comparison of the time duration of each digit dialed. The telephone number of the party that Dov Gruner had so urgently tried to reach would be child's play to reproduce. And where there was a phone, there was also an address.

The forest-green Simca was waiting, as planned, behind a maintenance shed several blocks from the charter line office. Sitting on the passenger side, Daniella was going over the notes she had taken during the interview with the charter owner.

He climbed aboard and immediately started the car, heading back toward the airport entrance. "You were beautiful back there," he told her. "The Mossad has got itself a really cool new operator."

"You won't think so when I tell you the results." She shook her head resignedly. "I'm afraid you're in for a big disappointment."

"No passenger name, right? No description, either."

"No passengers, period, according to Mr. Dov Gruner. He insists that he piloted the plane himself last night and carried only freight." She frowned at him. "I must say, you don't seem too surprised."

"I'm not. I expected a cover-up. What about his destination? Did he still claim to have flown to Haifa?"

"At first. But I broke him down on that." She indulged herself in a smile at the minor triumph. "I confronted him with the Ben Gurion tower records of the exact takeoff and landing times and told him we could easily check with the Haifa airport authorities. Then he admitted he had changed the flight plan after takeoff and flown to Jerusalem instead. He protested that it was no crime, that this is done all the time."

"Good girl! That must have been when he started sweating. You caught him in a lie, put him on the defensive. Did you follow up on it?"

"I tried. But I couldn't get him to change his story on anything else. 'No passengers,' he kept repeating, 'no passengers.' With that same unshakable smile."

"That phony smile, you mean. It disappeared the minute you were out the door." He patted her hand. "Good going. You threw a scare into him, all right."

She frowned again. "What good is that? We still have nothing to go on. I can't understand why you seem so pleased. Was it something that happened after I left? Tell me!"

"I'll do better than that." He slowed the car and pulled off to the side of the road. "I'll let you hear it for yourself."

He set the pocket recorder on the top of the dash panel and pushed the REWIND button. In a few seconds it clicked to a stop. Adjusting the volume, he pressed the PLAY button.

She heard the deep voice of Dov Gruner in his concluding statement, her own answering contralto as she discontinued the interview and prepared to leave. He switched off the recorder. "What was that all about?"

"He was repeating what he said before—that he had personally flown the plane, that there were no passengers. That if I had no further questions, he was a busy man. I could see there was no point in going on with it. I told him he might be called on for a formal deposition."

He started the recorder again. Shaloms were exchanged with the owner and the secretary. The screen door slammed as Daniella exited. The secretary's flattering comment on her appearance and David's understated response produced a wry smile from Daniella. "'Not bad?' Is that all—?"

"Sh! Listen." The secretary's voice could be heard addressing her boss. The pitch dropped from treble to bass, the volume rising, as a torrent of invective from the proprietor spewed out of the recorder. Daniella gasped, and he stopped the tape again.

"I see what you mean. What a change in the man! He almost bit her head off!"

"What, exactly, did he say?" he asked.

"Not to bother him. That he had an important call to make." There was the excitement of anticipation in her voice. "You recorded the phone call?"

He nodded, restarting the tape. The secretary's voice followed, in English, apologizing for the delay, with his own answering, "No problem." Then silence, except for the sound of dialing, seven successive purring sounds of varying duration, as the dial slid back to zero each time from the point to which the fat forefinger of Dov Gruner had spun it. A short period of silence following, then an angry oath, as the charter service proprietor slammed down the phone. Then—nothing. He switched off the recorder.

She looked at him questioningly. "That's it?" He nodded.

"Oh, how disappointing," she lamented, crestfallen. "No one answered. I was so sure we had something."

"And so we do. We have a telephone number, the one that Dov Gruner dialed."

He rewound the tape for two or three seconds and turned the tape speed dial counterclockwise as far as it would go. He started the tape again.

Slow-motion voices ensued in a surrealistic parody of human voices at a bass register far lower than any human voice could attain.

"Do you have a second hand on your watch?" he asked. She nodded. "Then help me time these. Write down the number of seconds taken up by each spin of the dial."

The dialing began, no longer a purring but a sequence of long, low, rasping sounds, with shorter breaks in between. The pair peered at their watches intently, recording the duration of each burst of sound.

"What have you got?" He took her notepad and compared the jotting with his own, making an adjustment or two in his numbers. "A stopwatch would have been more accurate, but I think I can make do with this."

Baffled, she watched in silence as he scribbled away intently, totally absorbed in the numbers game he was playing. "I still don't see how you tell what number—"

He waved her off. "Just a minute! I've almost got it!"

Writing furiously, he recorded seven numbers in a column, quickly adding them, recording the sum at the bottom. "That's it!" He scrawled a number across the page of her tablet, tore it off, and handed it to her.

"Three six seven, eight four nine four," she read aloud. "That's the number Gruner dialed?" She looked impressed. "How did you do it?"

"I've done it before. It's not really that difficult; you look for a common denominator. I'll show you, sometime. Right now we've got to get to a phone."

He started the car and moved back onto the road. "You're going to ring the number?" she asked.

He shrugged. "Why not? We might recognize the voice that answers. But what I really had in mind was for you to phone this number into the Mossad. I'm sure they must have access to a backward directory. They can find an address for us!"

She looked doubtful. "I could ask my control, I suppose. I know the police do that sort of thing. But I've never—"

He frowned. "We can't go to the police; they'd only try to shut us down. And I'd rather not involve your control. He might ask too many questions. Doesn't the Mossad have some sort of support activity you could call on?"

"That would be Services Division." She brightened. "Of course—I was briefed on that. They do quick turnaround research for agents in the field."

"Perfect! Do you need clearance from your control?"

She shook her head. "Just my identification number. My control will be notified of the contact, though, afterwards."

"That's okay, as long as we get there first."

He pulled into the parking area in front of the same phone

booth they had used previously. "We'll dial the number first and see what happens."

She crowded into the booth with him, sharing the receiver as he punched in the numbers. He could hear her heart beating next to his.

"It's ringing!"

It kept on ringing. When the count reached twelve, he hung up, extracting his coin and handing it to her with the number he had just dialed.

"No answer. Our party must still be out. It's your turn now. Let's see how good a spy organization you're teamed up with."

"Slow down, David, we're geting close." Daniella scanned the street numbers on her side of the street. "Seven fifty-three, seven seventy-one. It should be in the next block."

He braked the car until the speedometer dial dropped to fifteen, peering through the rain-flecked side window at the assortment of run-down shops and nondescript buildings sliding by. "This doesn't look like a residential area at all. Are you sure we're in the right place?"

"Twenty-seven . . . thirty-one. There it is, David, 833 Brandeiss Street. The one with the awning. Keep going on by, in case anyone is watching."

It looked like some kind of store. The sign suspended above the entrance oscillated languidly in the stiff breeze, its raised Hebrew lettering no help to him at all. "What is it, a grocery?"

"You're close. It's a kosher meat market."

He pulled in to the curb at the end of the block. "A meat market? What would Martin be doing in a place like that? There must be a mistake. They've given you the wrong address."

"Mossad staff services aren't allowed mistakes. We'll soon find out." Daniella opened her door. "You'd better wait here. One person asking questions will be less suspicious."

"No way!" He held onto her hand tightly. "I'm going with you. It could be dangerous for you—if Martin does turn out to be there."

She looked dubious for a moment, then smiled back at him and nodded. "All right. I can see there's no stopping you. But please let me do the talking. I have a plan."

They left the car and walked slowly back up the block. The street was not busy at this hour, only a scattering of morning shoppers in evidence. But the bakery two doors from the meat market seemed to be doing a thriving business, its few indoor tables crammed full of customers breakfasting on its freshly baked offerings, others standing at the counter. A mouth-watering aroma greeted them as they passed by the open door.

A young girl in an apron darted out of the bakery and ran by them, turning into the meat market. Perceiving that they were about to enter, she held the door open for them.

"Shalom." Daniella greeted her with a winning smile.

"Shalom, Madame." The clerk returned the smile and moved quickly behind the counter, where a somewhat older girl was waiting on a middle-aged housewife. "What will it be today, Madame?" she inquired of Daniella. "Our spring lamb is not in yet, but the beef is the best. We have a special on fresh brisket today."

"Nothing, thank you. I'm here on another matter—a matter of the heart. I'm looking for my fiancé, who has disappeared. I was told that he could be found here." She withdrew a photograph from her purse and handed it to the clerk. "Have you seen him, by any chance?"

The younger girl studied the photograph. "Look," she said to the other clerk, showing her the black and white print. "It's the meat inspector, isn't it?"

The other girl put down the package she was wrapping and held the photograph up to the light, squinting her eyes. "It surely is," she giggled, looking Daniella over. "So there's another side to him, after all. We thought he was strictly business."

"When did you last see him?" Daniella asked anxiously. "Has he been here recently?"

"Please!" interrupted the lady customer, a sharp edge in her voice. "Can I have my purchase now?" Her look of indignation traveled from the clerk to Daniella, a final censuring glance reserved for David. He shrugged his shoulders and opened his hands to signify that it was none of his affair. He had understood just enough of the conversation to realize that they had struck pay dirt; the two girls had recognized the photograph of Martin.

"Sorry, Madame." The clerk handed the package across the counter and watched the impatient customer stride out of the store. "Some people have no appreciation for romance," she sighed, turning her attention back to Daniella and returning the photograph. "Your fiancé is a nice-looking man. He comes here often to examine the goods in our meat locker. He was just here this morning."

"Was?" Daniella looked crestfallen. "Then he has left already?"

The clerks exchanged glances. "I didn't see him go," the younger one volunteered, "but I was next door on my break for a few minutes."

"He must have left," the other observed. "He never stays more than a half hour. The cold, you know."

"If there's any chance that he's still here—," Daniella hesitated. "Could I ask you to double-check for me? It means so much—"

The clerks looked genuinely sympathetic. "I'm sorry, we're not allowed inside the meat locker," the older one responded. "And the butcher doesn't like to be disturbed when he's in there. But if you'd care to wait until he comes out. It shouldn't be too long."

Daniella hurriedly explained the situation to David, speaking English. "Damn right, we'll wait," he responded. It had been apparent to him from the reaction of the two clerks that they had recognized Martin's picture. The trail was getting hot. Nothing could persuade him to leave now. "We'll wait till hell freezes over, if we have to!"

It didn't take quite that long. The sound of a heavy door clanging shut shortly alerted them to the butcher's approach. A moment later he emerged through the curtained doorway behind the counter, stamping his feet and blowing briskly on his hands.

He was a big, brawny man with heavy black brows and a ruddy complexion. An apprehensive scowl wrote itself across his features as he took in the well-dressed man and woman, so out of place in these dingy surroundings.

"Mr. Ben-Levi," the older clerk spoke up, "this lady is looking for the meat inspector." The apologetic note in her voice testified to the awe in which her stern, gruff-looking employer was held.

The butcher stepped from behind the counter, wiping his hands on a blood-stained apron. "He's not here." The dark eyes looked hostile as they swept over Daniella's face, briefly contacting her own. "He left some time ago."

"Please." Daniella managed a smile. "It's very important that I get in touch with him. Can you tell me where I can reach him?"

"The man is her fiancé," the younger girl put in helpfully. The butcher shot her a withering look, then glared back at Daniella.

"I know nothing about him. He works for the government.

You'll have to ask them. Now, if you don't mind, I'm very busy."

Charm was not going to work on this man. Daniella decided to try a different approach.

"Strange that neither of your clerks saw him leave. Could we just have a look in back?"

"Now look here! I told you, the man has gone. I ask you now to leave my—" The butcher stopped in midsentence as Daniella held up a card in front of his eyes.

"Yes, Mr. Ben-Levi. I am with the Mossad. Do you show me your meat locker, or do I have to come back with a search warrant?"

The butcher stared from the badge to the determined look in the eyes of its owner. He shrugged. "I don't want any trouble with the government. Anything to convince you. This way."

David followed Daniella and the butcher behind the counter and through the curtain, conscious of the wide-eyed clerks whispering excitedly at the new turn of events. There was something phony about this butcher—he could sense it. But would the man allow them to search the premises if he had anything to hide? He might, if he was setting some kind of a trap.

With a brass key dangling from a chain attached to his untidy apron, the butcher unlocked the heavy padlock and removed it from its hasp. He pushed the latch arm upwards to a vertical position and the massive door swung inward. A blast of frigid air assaulted their exposed faces, white, frosty vapor spilling out into the corridor. Grisly pictures of people who had been trapped in frozen-food lockers, their bodies transformed into human blocks of ice, popped into David's head. He would watch the butcher carefully, not let the man get between him and the door.

The butcher led the way inside, followed by Daniella. David entered warily, remaining next to the door as their host swung it closed behind them.

"You see?" The burly man gestured toward the expanse of meat racks with their hanging cargo. There was nothing to be seen but sides of beef, their blood-smeared surfaces covered with a hoary frost. "It is as I told you. There is no one here. Even an Eskimo couldn't stay in here so long."

David got the gist of what the man was saying. He saw no reason to doubt it; the numbing cold was already becoming unbearable. But Daniella was intent on a more thoroughgoing search. She moved toward the rows of carcasses, looking carefully behind each one of them, until convinced that there were no unexposed hiding places. Her eyes met his, disappointment written in them. He motioned her back toward the exit.

"Satisfied?" The butcher thrust up on the latch arm to reopen the heavy door, switching off the light. As he did so, a low, droning noise from the rear of the meat locker made them turn their heads. The subdued light from the single, bare standby bulb cast an eerie glow over the meat carcasses dangling from the low ceiling. A slender vertical crack of brighter light now appeared in the left-hand wall, stabbing out into the semidarkness of the vault's interior. As they watched in fascination, the shaft of light grew gradually wider, to the accompaniment of the steady whirring sound emanating from the same direction.

"No!" shouted the butcher. "Not now! Go back!"

"It's a door!" cried David. "A hidden room. Someone's coming out!"

The whirring had stopped. The light from the newly exposed recess in the wall was blocked out by a moving form, totally in shadow. Then a man's head and shoulders emerged from the truncated opening, the features undiscernible in the meager light. But David knew him instantly. The tilt of the head, even in silhouette, was unmistakable.

"Hello, Martin. How's the meat-inspecting business?"

The figure paused, squinting into the semidarkness. "Well, Davey! Fancy meeting you here. And Daniella, too. What a pleasant surprise. Only I'm afraid you picked a rather frigid spot for a reunion." Martin Singer straightened up, smoothing out his clothing.

"It wasn't our choice, Martin, it was yours." The iciness in Daniella's voice was perfectly in keeping with the surroundings.

The butcher had a message of his own for Martin. "The timing of your exit was most unfortunate. The young woman is Mossad."

David didn't understand the words, but the menace in the gruff voice was unmistakable. He spun around. The hulking figure blocked the exit, the gunmetal blue machine pistol in his hand looking enormous and ultralethal.

"I've changed my mind about leaving just yet, Isser." Martin's voice sounded calm and perfectly controlled. He blew on his hands and rubbed them together briskly. "Why don't we go back inside my little cubbyhole and talk things over? It's much cozier in there. A trifle snug, perhaps, but then the three of us are already quite well acquainted, aren't we?"

Ducking his head, he led the way through the low opening. Daniella hesitated, looking to David for guidance. The secret room looked like a dead end, a trap. Once in, there might be no way out.

It was a chance they had to take. Nodding reassuringly, he motioned her to follow Martin, the gun barrel in the small of his back an unnecessary persuader. The mole he had traveled halfway around the world to catch was within his grasp, holed up now inside his clandestine burrowings. There was no way that he was letting Martin out of his sight until he was behind bars.

"Well, now. This is much cozier, isn't it?" Martin Singer was perched atop a low safe, his back against the wall, arms folded casually across his chest. "Tell me, how did you find me?"

David sat uneasily on the edge of a small desk, facing him. It was apparent that he and Daniella were prisoners here, the sullen butcher with his murderous-looking weapon camped somewhere outside the door. His eyes scanned the interior of the tiny room, taking in its contents. A secret hideaway, an illicit spy nest of some sort, judging by the pains they had taken to conceal it. The two black boxes on the shelf above Martin's head confirmed his suspicions. He recognized the larger as a late-generation radio transmitter/receiver unit, compact and highly powerful.

"Cozy, you say?" Daniella, occupying the only chair, glared up at the man who had dropped so precipitously out of her life, only to return with a vengeance. "Cozy is what you seem to have become—with some of the wrong people. How far has it gone, Martin? Why are you selling us out?"

Her direct words made no apparent dent in Martin's aplomb. "Isn't that a trifle overstated? Selling out implies betrayal of a cause. Your cause was never mine, Daniella—blind obedience to a fanatic, a terrorist who ran your government as though he were still head of the Irgun. His party is leading you down a path of destruction—to your own destruction. They had to be stopped."

"And you have found a way to stop them." Her desperate eyes read the triumphant glint of affirmation in his. "You, a foreign diplomat, meddling in our affairs. You have no right! Who will lead us is our decision to make. The democratic process that you Americans like so much to speak about."

Martin remained unruffled. "Sometimes the democratic process needs a little help, a little push. I am simply doing the job I came here to do. Soon, very soon, you'll know the results. In the long run, the best interests of Israel will be served. It will be hard for you to see that at first, Daniella. But I'm sure that David, here, will understand what I—"

Singer's head thudded back against the wall as Llewellyn's fist caught him flush in the jaw. The smug look of moments before was replaced by one of shocked surprise.

"Understand, will I? That's for breaking my head open! I know—you were simply doing the job you came here for. And murdering Abernathy—was that part of the job, too?"

Rubbing the back of his head, Singer stared back at the other American towering over him. He tested his jaw gingerly. "Really, David, you're going to have to learn not to lose your cool like that."

"I'm just getting warmed up." David's fists remained clenched. "We want some answers, fast. This setup here, this cloak and dagger bit. Who are you working for? What, precisely, is this plot you've cooked up against the government? An assassination? Killing seems to be your style."

"My dear David, you underestimate me." The half smile returned to the bronzed face, but the eyes had turned to cold blue steel. "You see, it's not quite as simple as you make it sound. Killing Shamir would only martyr him, assuring a successor of the same ilk, or worse—probably Sharon. What we're after is a complete change of government. The Israelis must be made to see that the policies of Begin and his successor can no longer be condoned. One final, blatant excess against the country that has been their staunchest ally, and they will throw his whole gang out, replace them with a more reasonable, peace-minded Labor government. That is the brilliant stroke that we have engineered."

"And just who is 'we'? Let me guess." David pointed to the powerful shortwave radio above Martin's head. "It wouldn't surprise me if that thing was beamed straight to Moscow."

"Again, you disappoint me. My allegiances are the same as they've always been since you've known me. To my country, and to the planet it happens to reside on. I refuse to stand by and see that planet blown to bits my madmen. But you've reminded me—" He glanced at the watch on his wrist. "We're missing one of my favorite programs." He reached above him and flipped a switch on the radio's front panel.

The staccato crackle of heavy static filled the tiny room. Garbled snatches of dialogue, in a language that was not Hebrew but was equally incomprehensible to Llewellyn, cut in and out of the background noise. He looked questioningly at Daniella, who was frowning in concentration.

"It sounds like Arabic. Arab pilots, talking to one another by intercom." She shot a questioning look of her own toward Martin.

"Correction. Israeli pilots, conversing in Arabic."

Singer's enigmatic smile infuriated David. "All right, Martin, you've had your little fun. We're in no mood for guessing games. What's going on?"

"Why don't you ask your friend, here? I'm sure she knows."

Daniella's face changed expression as the explanation dawned on her. She started to speak but the words wouldn't come, held back by some inner conflict.

Singer's smirk broadened. "Apparently her lips are sealed. Very well, then, David. I'll let you in on our little secret. We're tuned in on the intercom frequency of the Israeli Air Force, in the process of scrambling their jets for a surprise raid on the Iraqi nuclear works near Baghdad. They're using Arabic to throw off the defenses."

"That was top secret information!" Her outburst rang with equal measures of shock and accusation. "Even the Mossad didn't know when it was coming. How did you—?"

"My dear Daniella. Hasn't it dawned on you yet what my true affiliation is—has always been?" There was an unmistakable note of contempt in his short laugh. "You and I are counterparts of our respective countries' most elite intelligence organizations, both using our diplomatic assignments as cover."

"The CIA! I might have known." David told himself that he should have guessed it much earlier. There was at least one in every embassy, but you never knew for sure who they were. Even Abernathy, in his State Department intelligence slot, hadn't known, it seemed. Poor Abernathy.

"Dirty tricks, meddling in other countries' affairs. It figures, all right. You're a 'Company' man. But even the Company wouldn't condone the murder of a fellow American diplomat. That was the act of a fanatic. You've stepped beyond the pale, haven't you, Martin? You did that on your own. Abernathy must have found you out. He would have stopped you, wouldn't he? So you had to silence him."

Singer's eyes narrowed, the smirk disappearing. "The fool was about to blow the whistle, tip off Washington—and the Mossad. Erasing him was the only practical way to resolve the problem. There wasn't time for a vote of the 'board': an executive decision was called for." He spoke matter-of-factly, as though discussing a routine business transaction.

"But you're mistaken about one thing. The Company would certainly have concurred, had there been time to consult them. They had too much at stake in this to allow a minor official in a rival intelligence branch, acting strictly on his own, to derail their operation at the last minute."

"And suppose Abernathy had been able to tip me off, Martin, before you 'erased' him." Daniella regarded him coldly, her words measured. "Then I would also have been expendable. You'd have had to erase me, also, wouldn't you?"

His eyes met hers, and she saw the answer written in them. "Oh, God!" She turned away.

"You're mad! You've lost your sanity, lost all sense of perspective!" Llewellyn wanted to shake the man, shake the sense back into him—rattle his bones until the whole sordid plot spilled out. "Tell us the rest of it, Martin. Just what is this Company trick to dump the government? Out with it!"

Martin read his look. "There's no need to get violent. I am telling you. The radio is telling you. Listen to it."

"The raid on Baghdad!" Daniella gasped. "They must have alerted the Iraqis. Our planes will be wiped out!"

David searched Martin's face for corroboration or denial, seeing neither. In his own mind it didn't make sense. "No," he said. "That wouldn't do it, Daniella. That would only make the people more angry at the Arabs, Likud's position more entrenched. It has to be something else, perhaps something triggered by the Baghdad strike."

"Smart boy. I always said you had promise, Davey. But I won't keep you in suspense any longer; it will happen quite soon." Martin stood up and adjusted the dial on the radio panel to tune out the static. "In just minutes from now, one of those Israeli jets you heard being launched will detach itself from the main strike force and turn to the south. A half hour later, over the Northern Arabian Desert, it will encounter a Saudi Arabian AWACS aircraft heading north. The Israeli fighter plane's mission is to destroy the AWACS before it can sound the alarm, before it can detect the Israeli strike force and warn Baghdad."

"Richy!" David gasped. "My brother's on that plane!" He looked accusingly at Daniella. "You knew—?"

"No!" she cried. "That wasn't part of the plan. It's some kind of trick, David. The Air Force wouldn't—the government would never permit it. It would be foolhardy, don't you see?"

Llewellyn turned furiously back to the CIA agent. "You son of a bitch! You knew Richy was flying on the AWACS. I told you myself."

Singer shrugged. "So you did. I'd quite forgotten. It wouldn't have mattered anyway. There's nothing I could have done about it."

"There's something we're going to do about it, right now." David towered threateningly above the other man. "I don't know how you and that infernal Company of yours arranged this, but we're calling it off. We're going to use your powerful little set here to warn the AWACS. Fortunately, I've been aboard. I happen to know its operating band and call letters."

"Don't be a fool, Llewellyn. Do you think I'd let you spoil everything when we're so close to success? The two of you are only alive right now because I got you into this room before the butcher out there could finish you off. He's not one of us, you see. He's a Palestinian and a real fanatic. All I have to do is press the button on this little cord I hold in my hand, and he'll come charging in here with that king-sized cannon of his."

"Push that button and you're a dead man." The tiny derringer in Daniella's hand looked like a toy compared to the butcher's weapon, but from close range, Martin knew, it could be just as lethal. He stared into the unwavering muzzle of the small-caliber weapon aimed at his forehead, then into the equally steady gaze of its owner. "I won't hesitate to use it, Martin. Any more than you would have, if I'd gotten in your way. Let go of the cord— that's it. Now, come over and sit on the desk, where David was. Slowly, please. This gun has a hair trigger."

Her alert eyes followed his movements carefully, the barrel of the pistol tracking his progress across the room. "All right, David, you can start sending."

He didn't have to be told. He was already in the process of punching the AWACS frequencies into the digital entry keyboard.

"Wait, Daniella, think what you're doing!" Martin Singer was the image of the cool, controlled CIA agent no longer. Perspiration beaded the suntanned forehead, the blue eyes tinged with desperation. "The AWACS band is monitored by all the Arab nations. The warning will be picked up by the Iraqis. All those fliers of yours on the way to Baghdad—you'll be sentencing them to death!"

"Shut up, Martin!" David completed the frequency selector setting and prepared to switch from receive to transmit.

"He's—he's right, David. I can't let you do it. Let go of that switch, please. Step away from the radio."

Unbelievingly, he turned to see the tiny pistol trained in his direction, its barrel leveled at his chest. "Daniella, you can't be—"

"Move!" The set of her mouth and determination in the dark eyes told him there was no point in arguing. Still, he made no move to comply, his hand resting on the transmit-receive switch.

"Wait!" Martin shouted. "Listen!"

The noisy background hum of the radio receiver had been broken again by a snatch of voice transmission in the Arabic tongue. Daniella concentrated on the words, her eyes linked to David's but alert to any sudden move by the other man. The frown in her forehead deepened.

"One of the aircraft is pulling out of the formation, just as Martin predicted. But—but the pilot says he is turning back, that he has an engine problem. What could that mean?"

Llewellyn was looking at Singer, studying his reaction. His expression was noncommittal, but there was undisguised elation —a note of triumph—in the eyes.

"I think I know what it means." David's words came slowly, the explanation still taking shape in his mind. "The engine trouble is just a ruse. He's trying to fool the others. As soon as he's out of their sight, he'll head straight for Arabia. You've got to let me warn the AWACS!"

He flipped the radio switch to transmit and picked up the microphone resting next to the transceiver unit. "AWACS C-103, this is Tel Aviv. This is David Llewellyn from the American embassy. Acknowledge, please." He switched back to receive. There was no immediate response.

"Stop him, for God's sake!" shouted the CIA man. "He's not just warning the Saudis, he's warning Baghdad!"

Daniella hesitated. "Wait, David, please. Give me time to think. The Baghdad mission is crucial for Israel. It has to succeed. My brother gave his life—!"

"My brother isn't giving his, if I can help it!" David depressed the mike button and continued transmitting. "AWACS C-103, I have an urgent message for you. Please acknowledge that you are receiving my signal. Over."

This time the static was broken by a barely intelligible voice in heavily accented English. "This is AWACS C-103. We are reading you, Ambassador Llewellyn. Proceed, please."

Daniella raised the pistol in warning. "Please, David! Don't force me to stop you!" Tears filled her eyes as she realized the man she loved would not heed her warning.

"AWACS C-103, you are in extreme danger! You are about to be—"

In the compact cubicle, the report of the small handgun was deafening, reverberating in an ear-splitting crescendo between the narrow confines of its encroaching walls.

CHAPTER 9

The startled Bedouin clung tightly to the reins of his frightened camel as the gleaming warplane thundered past only tens of feet above his head. There had been no warning, no breath of sound to announce its coming until the moment that it appeared over the top of a sand dune, swooping down upon him like an avenging angel. Then the noise had been terrible indeed, bursting upon his sensitive ears with a shattering violence that numbed his senses. His terrified eyes followed its breathtaking arc, twin tongues of flame from its glowing tailpipes emitting a final earthshaking blast as it shot overhead.

It was gone as suddenly as it arrived, the empty desert continuing to reverberate in its wake. The solitary rider dismounted, calming his still-shaken beast, and dropped to his knees, giving thanks to Allah for his deliverance.

From the cockpit of the hurtling Strike Eagle, the pilot caught a fleeting glimpse of the desert nomad below. Captain Zev Lieb, nee Adnan Ibrahim al Amiri—code name El Aurens—smiled knowingly. To the simple, superstitious Bedouin, the awesome specter overhead must seem a living thing, some truculent, vengeful creature of the all-powerful sovereign of the heavens. The Iraqi could sense this feeling, relate to it. For him, also, the Strike Eagle was something alive under him, responding with sensitivity and alacrity to his every command. Skimming over the shimmering desert at a breakneck speed just a fraction below the sound barrier, he luxuriated in the feeling. He and this magnificent beast were one; a free spirit—indomitable, invincible.

His euphoria was due in no small part to the smoothness with which his mission was progressing. The trickiest part was already over, the task of fooling his fellow pilots into believing that he had been forced to break formation because of an engine problem. His simulated flameout of the left engine of his F-15 had worked perfectly. The sudden loss of altitude as he trimmed the controls for sustained flight on the remaining engine, and the unsuccessful performance of the restart maneuver had been totally convincing. Without even having to request permission, he had been commanded by his squadron leader to turn back.

Once out of sight of the formation, he had again initiated the restart maneuver, this time cutting in the left engine throttle at the proper point in the sequence. When it roared back into action, he had begun a slow turn to the south and immediately put his jet into a shallow dive, implementing the penetration phase of the AWACS attack plan. This called for the Strike Eagle to drop down to treetop level, beneath the defensive umbrella of any probing ground radars, and cover ground as rapidly as possible, maintaining both radio and radar silence.

Treetop level. That was a good one. There was not a shred of vegetation visible to his eye in the bleak terrain rushing by below him, no greens, or even blues in this stark landscape, as though the artist had run out of every color except sienna and burnt umber. Though much of his flying had been over desert terrain, he was inured to the irrigated, planted deserts of Israel. Even the Negev had countless oases. But the land below him was nothing but windswept sand and rock, the solitary Arab and his camel the only living things encountered in the hundreds of miles he had already traversed. Nothing to navigate by, no friendly checkpoints or road junctions or river bends to pinpoint one's location. It would be easy to get lost in this void. A shiver ran down his spine, and he rechecked his compass heading. The Nafud—the vast empty quarter of Northern Arabia. It more than lived up to its name.

The insistent ding-ding-ding of his wrist alarm reminded him that it was time to turn on the TEWS—the tactical electronic warfare set. The TEWS was sensitive to any radar beam striking his aircraft and capable of indicating the direction from which the beam emanated. He was counting on this device to pick up the AWACS radar transmission and point him in the right direction to intercept the sophisticated Saudi aircraft. There were still at least five hundred miles, by his reckoning, between him and his quarry. But he knew that the TEWS was sensitive enough to detect the AWACS emanations at a distance even greater than the nominal three-hundred-mile range of the AWACS radar—the range at which his own plane would start to appear as a blip on the big aircraft's radarscope. The sooner he located it, the better. It would enable him to correct his heading and begin his climb to altitude and acceleration on afterburner, minimizing the chance of exposure to any hostile aircraft that might be sent to intercept him.

The steady background hum in his earphones announced that the TEWS was up and doing its thing. Any break in the steady tone would warn him that his jet was being illuminated by a radar signal, its transmission frequency and the direction of its source displayed. Homing in on the indicated direction was the simplest of procedures, like following a compass needle. But there was nothing audible or visible yet. It would take a while. He was aware that his low flight altitude placed him in the shadow of the earth's curvature with respect to the other aircraft. He would not detect it, nor would it detect him, until his approach brought him sufficiently close to peer over that "radar horizon." He had time to burn.

His radio was still tuned to the intercom frequency of the Israeli strike force. There had been no traffic on the channel for the last half hour. He turned up the volume until there was nothing but static in his headphones, then reduced it. Were they still under radio silence, or was he already out of range? They would be nearing the Iraq border by now, where the plan of attack called for them to simulate a Jordanian squadron on maneuvers, then drop to low altitude and disappear. It was a stratagem that had worked on the original attack on Osirak. It would work again— or seem to. He smiled grimly. Everything would seem to work— until the last moment, when they discovered what really awaited them at Osirak. Discovered it the hard way, after it was too late.

His late flying companions, his ex-comrades. How would he feel about it afterwards? Strange, he had felt no sense of loss or remorse when he had left them back there, at the moment that the finality of his act had struck home and the realization that there would be no going back had set in. That after more than four years, this part of his life was over. No regrets, only an overwhelming sense of relief.

Relief that the masquerade was finished, the pretense of being one of them while continuing to despise them. Each waking day had become a fresh torture to him, bringing with it the realization that the charade must go on. That, like the bored star, sick to death of the hit play that has run too long, he must continue to tread the boards and repeat the cloying lines. And do it convincingly. The worst of it was that the only way to be convincing was to live the part, to be the man he was impersonating. And the more he began to think of himself as Zev Lieb, captain, Israeli Air Force, the further his true persona began to withdraw, until he felt in danger of losing his real identity.

No, there would be no regrets. But in a secret corner of his mind, there would always be a cherished perception: they were the best, and he had been one of them, one of the truly elite. He had belonged.

The last weeks of intensive training came back to him with a rush, the indoctrination into the new Strike Eagle aircraft, the bombing drills in preparation for Osirak. The quintessential fighter pilot, his prior experience in air to ground weapon delivery had been minimal. He had been under the gun, his retention on the Osirak strike force conditional on demonstrating proficiency in the accuracy trials. He had found it difficult at first, the pull-up maneuver used to toss the bombs toward the target unfamiliar to him, and his first efforts dismal, the dummy bombs dropping well outside the target circle.

Stung by his initial failure, he had driven himself to the limit, logging extra flight hours of practice. When he had finally gotten the hang of it, his scores had improved rapidly, until he was besting some of the pilots who were old hands at the bombing missions. On the eve of the big operation, his late spurt had succeeded in elevating him only to the position of first alternate on the twelve-man strike team. But that was good enough. A spoonful of foreign substance introduced into a fellow pilot's soup had assured him of a spot in the starting lineup.

Air to ground. A humdrum, boring kind of mission, next to air to air. Dogfighting—that's what flying was all about. One on one with a worthy adversary, turning tighter circles than he could, outthinking him, outflying him. But when it came to winning a war, there was no question that the "air-to-mud" boys got the job done. He had learned a grudging respect for the "truck drivers" in his baptismal exposure to their kind of flying. And he had acquired their skills, skills that would stand him in good stead, once his primary mission against AWACS had been consummated. This time with live bombs, not dummies.

In his mind's eye he pictured the sleek black Mark 84 bombs he had watched the ground crew load onto his aircraft that morning, one beneath each wing, their shape resembling the darts used in the English pub game. Only these darts had been intended for a much more deadly game to be played against his homeland, their insides crammed with a full ton of high explosives. That plan had been changed, at least where these two bombs were concerned. They were earmarked for a very special target.

The intermittent signal in his headphones brought him back to the problem at hand. A radar intercept! His eyes darted to the upper right-hand corner of the control panel, the TEWS indicator. A bright strobe was visible on the small cathode-ray tube, a single line emanating from the center and extending out to the 330-degree mark on the bezel ring. Only 30 degrees off his present heading, and still a long way off, he judged, by the lack of any noticeable rotation as successive refresh strobes replaced their fading predecessors. Holding his breath, he pushed in the button marked "frequency" on the small panel beneath the TEWS display. Almost instantaneously the number 3.20 popped onto the picture tube next to the bright striation, flashing on and off in synchronism with each fresh painting of the strobe: 3,200 megahertz. S-band! There was only one radar that operated in that band in this remote corner of the world. It was the AWACS.

Banking to his left, he put the Strike Eagle into a shallow climb, pushing the throttle forward. With a sudden roar, the afterburners kicked in and the sleek jet rocketed from the desert floor up into the cloudless azure void. The Mach needle rose slowly, then quivered as the hurtling jet burst through the sound barrier. Watching the TEWS display intently, he leveled the wings, jockeying the controls to maintain the bright strobe at the twelve o'clock position—the fluorescent green strobe that marked the radar emanations from AWACS, which had already become the AWACS in his mind, the beacon that would guide him unerringly to his soft, unmissable target.

Richard Llewellyn looked up from his radar console as the spidery little technician from Brooklyn burst in on him, out of breath.

"Llewellyn, the skipper says to get your ass up to the flight deck, on the double. He tried to call yez on your headset. I see yez ain't wearing it."

"What's happening, Raunch?"

"Some kind of radio message that come in. I don't dig that R/O's lingo too good."

Richy laughed. The radio operator was a friend of his, the only member of the Saudi crew who spoke English, serving as translator for the others.

"He says he can't understand your Brooklynese at all. I told him most Americans have the same trouble."

"Natcherly." Raunch flashed his yellow-stained grin. "Yez was all victims of a deprived upbringing, away from da core of da Big Apple. Yez was never loined ta speak propily."

Feigning outrage, Richy launched an openhanded shot at the buttocks, the nimble technician eluding it easily on his way to the door.

"Stee-rike one! I bet you'd be a sucka for a koive ball."

"Screwball!" Richy shouted at the vanishing back.

He made his way along the corridor toward the flight deck, noting that Roxana was still closeted with Hanson in the next compartment. The door was ajar, and he caught a glimpse of them sipping coffee and chatting cozily. A too-familiar pang stabbed him in the belly. There was no doubt in his mind that the two of them were making it together. Since taking up with the married Boeing supervisor, Richy's glamorous understudy had dropped him like a hot potato. She was supposed to join him later in the flight for a final run-through on the radar. It would be a trying session for both of them.

As he opened the door leading to the big aircraft's elaborate cockpit, a torrent of Arabic assaulted his ears. The pilot and copilot were going at it heatedly, hands flailing the air in reinforcement of their noisy invective. Neither seemed to be paying the least attention to what their airplane was doing. Fortunately, he observed, the plane was flying itself, on autopilot.

"What's the beef?" he inquired of the radio operator, whose station was just inside the door, behind the copilot.

"A slight difference of opinion. The copilot thinks we should turn back. Here, this just came in."

The R/O handed him a sheet of paper on which a short message was hand printed. Richy stared at the radiogram in disbelief. What on earth? His brother had apparently contacted the AWACS by radio from Israel. It was some kind of warning. He reread the ending: "You are in extreme danger. You are about to be. . . ."

"Where's the rest of it?" he asked.

His Saudi friend shrugged. "That was all we received. The signal broke off. We are still monitoring, but there has been no further transmission."

Richy studied the message, wondering what to make of it. What was David trying to warn them about? The Tel Aviv origin puzzled him. "Are you sure he said Tel Aviv? The embassy has been moved to Jerusalem."

"He said Tel Aviv. It is from your brother, yes? The captain wants to know what it means."

Richy remembered David's concern for his safety during his brother's just-concluded visit. Their conversation, here in this very airplane, came back to him, and his brother's rejection of the idea that an attack might come from Israel. Had David stumbled onto some plan of theirs, been discovered, interrupted, in the act of sending his warning message?

Noting his presence, the pilot and copilot had broken off their squabble, their heads turned, awaiting his reaction.

"My brother wouldn't send a message like this unless he knew something. If he says we're in danger, we are. I agree with the copilot; we should turn back. Why does the captain disagree?"

The R/O chewed nervously on his gum, watching the pilot out of the corner of his eye. "Shortly before this message came in we were placed on Red Alert, with orders to proceed on our present heading until further notice. The captain hasn't as yet notified the rest of the crew."

"Red Alert? What's that all about?" Checking his watch, Richy realized that the northbound leg of their usual racetrack pattern had persisted unusually long; the 180-degree turn onto the southbound leg was considerably overdue.

The R/O shrugged. "Ground Control didn't say. Possibly, it's just a fire drill."

The captain broke in impatiently, and the R/O relayed Richy's comments to him and the copilot. The latter reacted emphatically, getting in a few more licks before his senior officer waved him off, jabbering a further inquiry at Richy and the radio operator.

"He wants to know if you can clarify what the danger might be that your brother was referring to. An attack by Iranian fighter planes, perhaps?"

"Or by Israeli fighters. It was something we discussed when he was here. If the Israelis were planning an assault of some kind, getting rid of AWACS could be their first move."

The R/O quickly translated his words. The captain's reaction was swift. He switched on his radio set and began talking animatedly into his head mike, the radio operator listening in through his own headset taking notes.

"He is calling Ground Control to relay your information," he explained. As he continued to record the conversation, he became more and more agitated. "Ground Control thinks there may be a connection between the Red Alert and your brother's warning. The alert came from Iraq. We have just now been informed of this. Baghdad is expecting an Israeli air strike at any moment!"

The news jolted Richy. David's warning made sense, now; the threat could be for real! He waited impatiently as the dialogue between the pilot and Ground Control dragged on, the R/O too busy recording to comment further. Then the captain signed off and the R/O came up for air, handing his transcript to the copilot.

"What is it?" Richy asked, gripping his friend's shoulder. "What was their decision?"

"We are ordered to proceed cautiously on our present heading, operating our radar continuously in its long-range search mode. At the first contact with hostile aircraft, we will turn for home."

Richy nodded glumly, the order not unexpected. It reflected the "party line" on how to defend the all-but-indefensible AWACS. At the first sign of trouble, turn tail and run. Meanwhile, continue to monitor the threat, vectoring your own fighter aircraft to its swift interception. And pray that those friendly interceptors arrive before the AWACS is blasted out of the sky.

He turned the problem over in his mind. He had been through the mental arithmetic many times. Nominally, his radar could detect approaching targets three hundred miles ahead. With a three-hundred-mile head start, it would take the fastest enemy jets the better part of half an hour to catch up with the much slower AWACS, allowing sufficient time to scramble interceptors on ground alert at nearby air bases and direct them to their targets.

But that was the catch. There were no nearby air bases in the North Arabian Desert over which they were bound. The northward travel of the AWACS had already taken it beyond the last interceptor base, northwest of Dhahran. Every minute flown on the present course put another six miles between them and their potential rescuers. Another hour of flight—perhaps even a half hour—and there would be no hope that help would arrive in time. They would literally be on their own.

The facial expressions of the Saudi crew told him that they appreciated the gravity of the situation. He turned to leave, anxious to get back to his radar station and begin his vigil for intruders from the north. A flurry of Arabic from the stern-faced captain arrested him.

"He says to keep in constant touch by intercom," the R/O

translated. "You are ordered to wear your headset at all times. He wants immediate notification of all radar contacts in the forward sector, whether hostile or friendly."

The captain added another injunction, quickly relayed. "You are not to discuss this situation with any of the other crew members."

Richy nodded his head, saluting the man in the pilot seat to confirm that the instructions had been understood. The captain was right; there was no point in alarming the others prematurely. He hurried back to his station, his mind racing, going over all the possibilities.

There was always the outside chance that the warning had been some kind of hoax, the transmission from someone else pretending to be David Llewellyn. If only he had heard the voice, he would know for sure. But how would such an imposter have known the AWACS frequency and call letters? And the timing of the message, coinciding with a possible Israeli air strike on Baghdad. No, that was too much of a coincidence. David had gotten wind of it, had tried to warn him that the wildest imaginings they had kicked around during his short visit to Riyadh were happening for real. Israeli fighter planes, made in the U.S. and carrying American-made armament, dashing toward a rendezvous with AWACS at this very minute, probably on full afterburner.

F-15s or F-16s. Those were the first-line Israeli fighters. The radar homing and warning set aboard the AWACS, the RHAWS, would eventually tell them which it was. Most likely the F-15 Eagle with its heavier complement of air-to-air weapons. Radar-guided Sparrow missiles and infrared, heat-seeking Sidewinders and the lethal M-61 Gatling gun, devastating from close in. What chance would the defenseless AWACS have against all that firepower? Slim to none.

In Hanson's compartment, as he hurried by, the intimate tête-à-tête was still continuing. He had no thought of intruding on it. Hanson would be pissed, later on, when he discovered that his radar man had been in the know and hadn't alerted him to the danger. But Richy had a lot of thinking to do, and the last thing he needed was the Boeing boss climbing all over his back.

He plunged through the door to his own compartment, his eyes riveting apprehensively to the oversized radarscope, braced for the appearance of a telltale blip near the outer perimeter of the display. But there was nothing visible in the sector up ahead, the only blips those in the aft hemisphere, reflecting friendly air traffic in the Riyadh/Dhahran/Ras Tanura triangle. He continued to watch as several fresh traces were painted on, following the slowly rotating radial line that swept around the scope in synchronism with the giant rotodome antenna suspended above the aircraft fuselage. Still nothing. But his instinct told him it would appear soon, a little green blob as harmless looking as those other blobs that represented routine aircraft operations in the commercial airlanes behind them. Only there would be nothing routine about this one, nor about the deadly cargo slung beneath its wings.

If only this Saudi version were equipped with the countermeasures package developed for the U.S. or European AWACS, there would be some hope of surviving such an attack. But in order to get the sale to the Saudis approved by Congress over the Israeli lobby, the administration had agreed to hold back all such "advanced technologies." Richy was reasonably familiar with the various countermeasures that comprised the AWACS repertoire; they were available on the NATO version of the aircraft on which he had flown during the European introduction trials in Germany. His mind ticked through the list. Threat warning receivers and computer-controlled jammers to counter radar weapons. A flare dispenser to draw off the Soviet bloc heat-seeking missiles modeled after the U.S. Sidewinder.

Signal flares—there must be some on board the AWACS! His mind leapt at the realization. They were used for emergency landings and night rescue operations, floating down on parachutes. Would they be effective against Sidewinder? They might be, if they could be dispensed at the critical time. There should be ample radiation in the three-to-five-micron wavelength region where the missile sensor operated. It was quite possible that the Sidewinder homing device could be made to transfer its track to the hotter flare target, steering the missile downward and to the rear of the AWACS where the flare was suspended, missing the aircraft altogether.

A long shot, perhaps, but certainly worth a try. But what could be done about the radar weapon, the Sparrow? Not a damn thing, he reflected gloomily. And the Sparrows were the longer range weapons. They would undoubtedly be launched first, the Sidewinders held in reserve, used later, if needed. They wouldn't be. The Sparrow carried a much larger warhead, effective even against heavily armored targets. The converted commercial airliner, thin skinned and vulnerable, would be torn to shreds by the warhead's expanding metal rods, impelled by a powerful explosive to supersonic speeds. There was no way of fooling the Sparrow's homing device short of dumping radiation at the proper frequency into its sensor's receiver to confuse it and obscure the target, which was just what the NATO jammer was designed to do. But there was no radiating equipment aboard this AWACS that even came close to the Sparrow frequency band.

Ironic, thought Richy. Here he sat with the world's most powerful airborne radar, a "death ray" capable of burning up any living thing unfortunate enough to step in front of it, and it was useless. It was in the wrong frequency band, triple the wavelength of Sparrow, seven million kilohertz from the Sparrow operating band.

Triple the wavelength! His brain seized on the phrase, the faintest ray of hope beginning to glimmer. He grabbed a pencil and paper and his hand-held calculator, churning out the initial results mentally. The third harmonic of the radar transmission would have plenty of power at the Sparrow frequency, if he could catch the missile in the main beam! But there was the off-band attenuation of the antenna and radome to take into account. He scribbled furiously, his fingers punching out the critical computations on the tiny calculator buttons. The final answer flashed into the calculator window, and he stared unbelievingly at the eight-digit number etched in green. He rechecked his calculations. The result was the same. His radar was capable of putting milliwatts of power into the Sparrow Band while it was still a mile away from AWACS. More than enough to do the job!

But his elation over this discovery was short-lived. The AIM-7F version of the Sparrow, he belatedly recalled, was equipped with a home-on-jam mode. It could readily transfer track from the weak reflected signal to the stronger, interfering one, needing only the direction of the source of radiation to steer the missile to collision with the lumbering aircraft. He was back to square one.

Realizing with a sudden rush of adrenaline that he had been neglecting to watch the scope, he turned back to it and was jolted by what he saw. In the northwest sector, somewhat farther east than he would have expected, a blip had appeared near the outer extremity of the display. Urgently, he punched a command into the console keyboard and within seconds was rewarded with the appearance of several numbers and symbols that popped onto the display in a little cluster surrounding the new radar blip.

His trained eye took them in at a glance. Mach 1.6! Whatever it was, it was coming like a bat out of hell! The altitude reading correlated with that kind of speed: 35,000 feet. And the direction indicator showed a course of about 160 degrees. It was making straight for them.

He lost no time in contacting the radio operator on the intercom. "Tell the pilot I have a radar contact. Bearing three-four-five, range two-nine-zero, speed one-six-hundred closing, altitude three-five thousand. A single blip, one aircraft. He must have spotted us already to be coming in that fast. Probably has us on his threat warning receiver."

"Roger." He had a vision of the R/O swallowing his gum at the other end. "I'll get back to you."

Richy watched the blip move noticeably closer on successive scans. At the rate the fighter was closing, it would take him only fifteen minutes to draw within weapons range. Their best strategy was to turn turtle, shut off their radar, and run for it. Why wasn't the pilot turning back?

The door opened and Hanson came bursting into the radar cubicle, Roxana at his heels. They must have been listening on the intercom, he realized.

"What's going on, Llewellyn?" There was mild resentment in Hanson's tone, but no alarm in his voice. Something unusual was happening. He wanted in on it. He peered at the display, Roxana looking over his shoulder, avoiding Richy's eyes.

Before he could answer, the intercom crackled back on. "We're not getting anything at that bearing on our RHAWS," the radio operator reported.

Richy swore under his breath. "Of course you're not. The bogey must be tracking us on his own threat receiver, maintaining radar silence. If we turn off our radar, maybe he'll turn his on. Request permission to shut down temporarily."

There was a short delay. "Permission granted, Llewellyn," the R/O relayed back.

"Llewellyn, what is happening?" Hanson grabbed him by the arm, concern showing in his face. Richy shook him off.

"Excuse me, I'm busy." He hit the red guarded detent on the master switch and the radar went into "standby"—a condition in which it was no longer transmitting but was still functioning under minimal power and could be brought on line again in seconds. The rotating strobe line on the radar display slowed to a stop, the previous scan frozen onto its face. Mentally, he crossed his fingers. The AWACS threat warning equipment, the RHAWS, would tell the story once the bogey's radar turned on, analyzing the radar signature of the unknown aircraft to make a positive identification. If it turned out to be an F-16, they at least had an outside chance. The F-16 carried no radar missiles, only Sidewinders. The flare dispenser might work against the heat-seeking missiles. But if the bogey was an F-15, they would have the Sparrow to contend with.

He tried to shut out the mental image of the scene of devastation he had once witnessed, when a war-weary destroyer used as a target had been towed back to port and docked in Baltimore harbor not far from the Westinghouse plant. The ship had sustained a direct hit from a single air-launched Sparrow missile. The bridge of the destroyer, struck by the missile, had been a total shambles, nothing left inside but twisted steel girders and buckled armor plate, wreckage strewn knee-deep throughout the large cabin that had once served as the nerve center of the warship. No human on the bridge could possibly have lived through it. And compared to the heavily armored bridge of that destroyer, the AWACS fuselage was an eggshell.

Abruptly and without warning, the big aircraft banked sharply to the left, forcing the occupants of the radar compartment to hold onto the nearest structure to avoid losing their footing. Richy breathed a little easier; the pilot was finally turning back.

"Radio operator to radar." The R/O was back on the line, his voice tense. "We have contact via RHAWS. We have positive identification. Your radar contact is an F-15 Eagle. Ground Control has confirmed that it is not one of ours."

When his TEWS display went blank, a momentary sense of panic gripped the Iraqi. It was as though he had suddenly gone blind, so intent had he been on following the brilliant green strobe, keeping it centered on the display in front of him. He had lost contact with the AWACS. It must have shut off its radar. How would he find it again?

Then he remembered the game plan and switched on his own powerful radar, his icy calm returning. The AWACS radar would surely have detected him by now, so there was nothing to lose by breaking radar silence. It was predictable that the crew would shut down their radar at some point, once they suspected that the AWACS itself might become a target, their radar used as a beacon by a marauder bent on their destruction. Yet he was puzzled; he hadn't expected the shutdown to occur so soon. By his own reckoning, the big aircraft must still be well over a hundred miles beyond the range of any of his weapons, far too distant for its crew to feel threatened.

He selected the long-range search mode and turned the range scale selector on his display to its maximum setting—160 miles. The AWACS was a huge reflector by radar standards; it should be visible to his radar well beyond its nominal range of eighty miles on fighter plane-sized targets. But the vertical trace sweeping slowly across the display from left to right revealed nothing, nothing again as he watched it sweep back in the other direction. His quarry must still be too distant. But he was certain the blip would appear soon. His own airspeed was Mach 1.6. Even if the AWACS were to turn and run, at its lumbering pace he would overtake it rapidly. Soon, very soon now, his radar would have it in its grasp.

He had mastered the use of this F-15 radar and had great confidence in it. It had served him well, had played a major role in his aerial exploits that had won him the admiration of his fellow pilots. He could only marvel at the engineering skill that had created this ingenious device, wedded it to this equally remarkable airplane. Unfortunate that the Americans were on the wrong side. Perhaps his final mission in their incomparable Strike Eagle would be instrumental in changing that.

One, two, three, four. He watched the bar indices on the radar display click up and down, indicating the elevation angle of the antenna on each successive horizontal scan. No matter where the target was flying, at whatever altitude, it would be within his field of view. The radar was searching out a pattern that extended from ground level to an altitude well beyond the flight ceiling of the AWACS.

At a point less than halfway up the display, slightly right of center, the green phosphor bloomed to yellow as the moving trace swept by. The spot persisted, blooming again a second later as the trace swept past in the opposite direction. The pilot whistled. He could not remember ever seeing a blip so large at such a range. It had to be AWACS.

From its low position on the display he quickly deduced that it had already turned away and was traveling in the opposite direction. His experienced eye estimated the present closing rate as Mach 0.8. How close was it? He moved the mode selector switch to range-while-search. The blip reappeared near the top of the display and he read its position off the range scale—150 miles. A quick mental calculation told him he would be within weapons range in fifteen minutes.

He peered back over his left shoulder toward the huge rectangular air-intake duct thrusting forward from beneath the wing. The reassuring snout of a Sparrow missile protruded below the corner of the duct; a quick glance over his other shoulder confirmed that its twin brother was also in place. The massive air scoop blocked his vision of the other underwing armament stations, where Sidewinder missiles were normally carried. But he knew that they would not be there on this mission, off-loaded to reduce weight and drag and increase combat radius. The Sparrows, it had been predetermined, would provide enough self-defense for the Baghdad run. For his present purpose, also, they would more than suffice.

Normally, he would have launched them simultaneously, in one salvo, reserving the shorter range Sidewinders for a second salvo, if necessary. But without the heat-seeking Sidewinders, he had decided to launch the Sparrows singly, monitoring the success of the first and providing for a follow-up attack if needed.

He set about the initial arming preparations now, depressing the weapons enable switch, designating AIM-7F on the weapon selector panel, and sending warm power to the starboard missile. In a few moments the ready light came on, verifying that the Sparrow selected had passed a minimal go/no-go test. Final preparations would be completed just before launch, when the radar was fully locked on and tracking the target continuously at the proper frequency for Sparrow guidance.

Plenty of time yet. He decided to leave the radar in its search mode for the moment. He was probably being monitored by the AWACS on its own radar warning equipment. It would be premature to lock on at this range and confirm to the crew what they probably only suspected at this point: that their own aircraft was a target—the target. Not that there was much they could do about it. His prebriefing had confirmed that there was no armament or effective countermeasures on board the Saudi craft, and he knew that it was presently flying well outside the protective zone where fighter support from Saudi air bases could arrive in time.

He watched the green and yellow spot move slowly down the display toward the in-range marker for the Sparrow. "Fly, pretty bird, fly," he whispered. "But you cannot escape. My Eagle flies faster." He could picture the Americans on board, trying to evaluate the situation. One of the American phrases he had learned from the Israelis came to mind. If they didn't realize it already, it would dawn on them soon. Their AWACS was a "dead duck."

Somehow the word had gotten out. Something was after them. Richard Llewellyn was besieged in his already cramped quarters as the other Americans came crowding in behind Hanson and Roxana for a look at the radar console.

"What the fuck is it?" Hauser, the last to arrive, pushed his way in rudely, craning his neck over the shoulder of the bulky Paunch.

"An Israeli F-15." Paunch, who had only just acquired that information himself, answered with authority.

Hauser blinked and elbowed in for a closer look. "It's chasing us?"

Paunch deferred to higher authority on this one. "Looks that way." The offhandedness of Hanson's answer irritated Hauser.

"What makes you think so?" he asked belligerently. "It could just be on maneuvers, couldn't it?"

"This deep into Arabia? Come on, Hauser. Besides, it seems the captain's been informed of some big Israeli operation in progress—they've got our AWACS on Red Alert. I just wormed that information out of Llewellyn here. Plus the bit about the warning that came in by radio from Tel Aviv a few minutes ago, from his big brother."

"Warning?" Hauser shot Richy a look. "Been holding out on us again, huh Llewellyn?"

Richy looked up from the notes he had been poring over. "Captain's orders. He didn't want the crew alarmed prematurely." This was getting out of hand. He had to get rid of them; he needed time to think. "My brother's message just said we were in danger. There were no particulars. Now you know as much as I do. So why don't you all just—"

"Fucking captain! What are we, cattle?" Glowering darkly, the IBM engineer peered back at the radarscope, watching the menacing blip move closer on the next scan.

"It's gaining on us! Where the fuck are the Saudi fighters? There's no sign of them on the radarscope."

"They were just alerted," Hanson answered calmly. He was determined to stay cool under Hauser's badgering. He had an example to set for the others. "They should be scrambling right now."

"But will they get here in time?" Hauser's insistent stare challenged the Boeing manager to answer. Hanson looked away.

"They won't, will they?" Beads of sweat popped out on Hauser's forehead. He grabbed Hanson by the shoulder, spinning him around. "We've got to do something!"

Hanson angrily shook off the big man's hand. "Sure, Hauser, sure. We can zap it with your computer. What would you suggest?"

"Reach the F-15 by radio, for Christ sake! Tell him we're Americans—we're his friends."

"We already thought of that. The Saudi captain said nothing doing. Proud bastard would rather go down with his ship, I guess."

"Well, I have no intention of going down with the fucking ship!" Hauser declared emphatically. "I'm getting my parachute!"

"Yes, do that, Hauser." Hanson was glad to get the irksome loudmouth off his back. "And while you're at it, why don't you distribute the chutes to the rest of us. Then we'll run through the parachute drill again." He noticed Roxana's distressed look and squeezed her shoulder reassuringly. "Just in case."

"Do it somewhere else, please." Richy's exasperation was beginning to show through. He had to get them out of there. Time was evaporating. Bailing out over the desert, to his way of thinking, was a last resort. They were inexperienced in the use of chutes; there were bound to be injuries. And in this remote part of the desert, even if they landed safely, they might never be found. There had to be another way.

For the first time, Hanson seemed to notice the scribbled notes in front of him. "What are you working on, Llewellyn?" he queried. "You have some plan to save our hides with your magic radar?"

The derision in Hanson's voice stung Richy. Their relationship had certainly deteriorated since the affair with Roxana. If it was a guilt complex, the married man was wearing it like a big chip on his shoulder.

"That may not be as farfetched as you seem to think, Hanson." He felt the other eyes focus on him, including hers. "Look, that F-15 carries two kinds of birds—radar-guided Sparrows and infrared Sidewinders. Either missile has the capacity to shoot us down, but I've thought of something that should work against Sidewinder. The AWACS flare dispenser. Paunch, you were checked out on the flare equipment, right?"

The heavyset Texan nodded, a puzzled frown furrowing his broad forehead.

"The flares should act as decoys," Richy explained, "drawing the Sidewinder seeker off target. If we get your sidekick to monitor the flash detector up on the flight deck, he can call out launch times over the intercom. You'll need to spit out flares about every five seconds after launch. Can the dispenser handle that?"

Paunch's expression brightened. "It sure as hell can. Let's go git 'em, Julie!" He looked around for his partner. "Now where'd he git to? He was standing right here. I'll go find him and give him the word." Without waiting for an okay from Hanson, he disappeared out the door.

Three down, two to go, thought Richy, frantic to get back to his deliberations. Roxana had been avoiding him. Now she spoke to him for the first time.

"The flares—will they really fool the missile?" Her voice was steady, but her eyes betrayed a frightened inner self that needed reassurance. He saw no point in overstating his hopes.

"Perhaps. I think so."

"What about Sparrow?" Hanson appeared irked at being by-passed on the flare assignment. "It's sure to be launched first. You have any tricks in your radar bag for that?"

Richy ignored the sarcasm. "If you'll just get out of my hair, Hanson, maybe I'll think of one."

"Let's go." Roxana took his arm, but Hanson obstinately refused to budge, effecting instead to look at the scope again.

"How much time do we have?"

A simultaneous call in Richy's headphone from the flight deck requested the same information. He checked his console again and was appalled at the amount of ground the bandit had covered. It had progressed more than half the distance to the center of the scope. Switching range scales, he waited for a fresh blip to appear before responding into the intercom.

"Range seventy-eight miles. Bearing one-seven-five. Closing rate five-eight-zero. Estimated time to earliest weapon release range—five minutes."

"Five minutes! Where's that goddam Hauser with those chutes?" Hanson made for the door, Roxana clinging to him.

Thank God! There was no time to lose. Frantically, Richy dug into his notes, looking for the clue that had eluded him. There had to be a way!

A commotion outside in the corridor distracted him again.

Paunch burst into the room, dragging a protesting Raunch by the collar.

"Look what I found!" he yelled, holding something aloft that could have been a portable radio or tape recorder. "It's a radio transmitter. The little son of a bitch admits he contacted the Israelis and gave them our position. He's been spying for them! I caught him red-handed!"

"Leave loose of me, ya big ape!" The wiry technician squirmed from the bigger man's grasp and shook himself like a wet rat. "I'm only trying to save your lousy hides!" He pointed to the blip on the radarscope. "This ain't according to plan, see? There's some kind of foul-up. Them Israelis ain't gonna shoot down no AWACS with Americans aboard. No way. I was calling that fly-boy to warn him, that's all. Only I couldn't make contact."

"What about earlier—two hours ago?" Paunch persisted. "You radioed them our position. You admitted it. You're an Israeli spy!"

"So what?" The little man from Brooklyn shrugged. "I don't mind yez knowing; I'm proud of it. Just don't tip off the Saudis. Yez might as well know the rest, too. We've got a big operation going. We're taking out that A-rab A-bomb plant again, the one in I-rack. Our fly-boys should be hitting it any minute now. They had to know when the AWACS turned south to time their takeoff, so's we wouldn't get in their way. Does that sound like they was planning to shoot us down? Now gimme back my radio!"

He lunged for the transceiver in his partner's hand. Paunch jerked it away and held it out of reach over his head.

"Give it to him, Paunch. It may be our only chance!" Richy's voice was authoritative, compelling. "Let Raunch try to contact the F-15 pilot again. Maybe he was out of range before. He's closer now." Too close, he added to himself, checking the display again. The fighter was nearing Sparrow range. A missile might be launched at any minute.

Retrieving his radio set, Raunch sprang into action. He switched on the set, plugged his headphones into it, and snapped an alligator clip attached to the set by a thin wire onto an exposed rib of the aircraft structure.

"AWACS C-103 calling Israeli F-15," he barked into the built-in mike. "This is agent Jules Berger aboard the AWACS. We have five Americans aboard. Repeat, five Americans. Don't shoot! Please acknowledge. Over."

He threw the switch to receive. There was no response. He tried again, this time in Hebrew. "Come on," Richy rooted silently, "answer!" But the only sound in the receiver was the low hum of background noise from the AWACS alternators.

Raunch uttered a rich Brooklynese stream of profanity. "I know it's the right frequency, and this little baby's got plenty of juice. The bastard must have his set turned off."

"Keep trying!" Richy commanded, fighting against the tide of futility that was rising inside of him.

As Raunch began again in Hebrew, the door to the compartment thrust open and a wild-eyed Hauser appeared in the doorway, Hanson and Roxana in his wake. "No fucking parachutes!" he proclaimed in his thundering baritone. "We've searched the entire plane. They're gone. All the survival gear is missing, too. Somebody made off with them before today's flight. Somebody who knew we'd be needing them."

There was a shocked silence as his words sank in. "Deliberately? What are you saying?" Paunch demanded.

"Don't you see?" Hauser looked from one face to another. "Are you all blind? It's a setup. We're not supposed to survive. Somebody out there wants us all dead!"

A setup! A deliberate trap! Richy's mind struggled with the implications. Make sure the Americans die. Create an incident. Who was the instigator? Who would benefit from such a calamity?

He was given no time to speculate on the question. The excited voice of the Saudi radio operator crackled into his left earphone.

"Alert for missile launch! RHAWS indicator shows radar in continuous track. We are monitoring for launch signature."

"Sparks!" Richy shouted into the intercom, "this is Llewellyn. I have a suggestion for the captain. Something that will make AWACS a more difficult target. Do you read? Over." Damn! Why hadn't he thought of it sooner? There might not be time enough now.

"Go ahead, Llewellyn."

"Tell the pilot to put the plane into a shallow dive, get us down on the deck as fast as possible, where the Eagle's radar will be less effective."

"Roger, Llewellyn, I'll tell him."

"Will it work?" Roxana had heard his end of the exchange; her eyes pleaded for some shred of hope to cling to.

"I don't know. It's worth a try." Would the pilot cooperate? Richy wondered. The Saudi skipper was standoffish toward the Americans, unpredictable.

His answer came with such suddenness that there was insufficient time to hold on. The floor of the AWACS dropped out from under him and he found himself floating toward the ceiling, suspended momentarily above his swivel chair before falling neatly back into it. Some of the others were not so fortunate. He saw Roxana bounce off the low plastic ceiling, then drop back to the floor in a crumpled heap on top of Raunch and Paunch. Miraculously, none of the three appeared hurt, as they scrambled for something to hold onto.

Hauser had managed to cling to the doorknob and avoid becoming airborne. "Fucking Saudi lunatic!" he fumed. "He thinks he's a fucking fighter pilot!"

"Hang on!" the R/O's voice warned belatedly through the intercom.

"Thanks a lot!" Richy gasped back, strapping on his seat belt, his stomach still hovering somewhere near the ceiling. At least, he told himself, they were getting down on the deck in a hurry, where the ground clutter might give the F-15 radar some problems.

The comforting thought was short-lived. "He's still got us," the intercom reported. "RHAWS shows radar still locked on. We're down to 1,000 feet, leveling off. Wait a minute—he's changing frequency, he's going to a higher frequency." There was an ominous pause before the R/O's voice came back, strident and shrill. "We have a launch signature! We have flash detection! He's launched a missile!"

Richy didn't have to tell them. Hauser and Paunch had their own headsets plugged in and had heard the chilling news. The others could read it from their shocked faces.

"The flare dispenser!" Paunch shouted, starting for the door. "I'll get it activated."

"Don't bother." Richy's voice sounded dead, expressionless. "He's still too far away for Sidewinder. It must be a Sparrow. The frequency change before launch confirmed it."

Roxana's face went white. "How long—?"

"Less than a minute," he answered, his voice a hoarse whisper. He checked the position of the second hand on his watch. Less than a minute to live. Unless they got very lucky. Unless—

He grabbed his intercom mike. "Sparks! Sparks! Can you hear me?"

"What is it, Llewellyn?"

"Sparks, have the pilot start a sharp turn, immediately. Tell him to really rack it up!"

There was no immediate response, as Richy fumed and waited. Then, "He wants to know which way, Llewellyn. And why? Over."

"Either way, you idiot! We have to get broadside to the direction of the F-15, then straighten out. The radar has a blind spot there. There's no time to lose! Start turning! I'm coming up there."

He undid the seat belt and leaped to his feet, the others watching him, wondering. "What is it? What's happening?" Their eyes followed him, desperate to perceive some final ray of hope.

"Just hang on tight." He dashed for the door, pushing past a dazed Hauser into the corridor.

Before he had advanced two steps along the corridor, he was thrown violently against the left side of the plane as the AWACS banked sharply to the right. Relief that the pilot had heeded his advice helped assuage the pain in his bruised shoulder. But would there be time? He looked at his watch again. The second hand had advanced thirty ticks already. Only thirty seconds left!

The force of the turn kept him pinned to the floor, the blood draining from his head and the upper part of his body, leaving him giddy and light-headed. His legs were like cast iron, refusing his every order to march. He dropped to his knees and began to crawl, pulling himself along the carpeted gangway hand over hand, his progress seeming painfully slow. He counted off the seconds, mentally calculating the turning rate for a three-g turn. It was going to be very close.

He reached the flight deck bulkhead, grasping the door handle and pulling himself to his feet. The door opened on a frenetic scene. The radio operator was shouting the Arabic equivalent of "Mayday!" into his microphone, while the copilot frantically searched the skies on his side of the plane for the telltale missile plume. The captain had his hands full just flying the unwieldy plane through its uncharacteristic high-g maneuver at low altitude, too busy, apparently, to look at the RHAWS indicator, which showed the radar strobe approaching the three o'clock position.

Richy took one look and lunged forward, clapping his hand

heavily on the pilot's shoulder. "Pull out, man, pull out!" He pointed to the RHAWS display and did a wings level maneuver with his arms. The startled captain followed suit, and Richy was thrown to his right, crashing against the R/O.

As the big plane righted itself, the copilot shouted a warning, pointing off to the extreme right side of the airplane. Richy saw it immediately, a white trail plainly visible against the pale blue sky, its right extremity a wispy tail feathering off into the distance, its left a flowing stream of freshly billowing white exhaust, defining a still-unseen object hurtling toward them. It appeared suspended there, at the same spot high on the windscreen. Was it frozen there—was time standing still? Then came the shocking realization that its very lack of apparent motion was proof positive that the missile had them in its grasp and was locked into a deadly collision course.

He checked the RHAWS again. Its single spoke of fluorescent light held steady, verifying that the radar was still tracking the AWACS, its powerful beam providing the missile its sustenance of reflected energy to home in on. The Sparrow, he knew, was tenacious, once it had hold of you; like a bulldog, it wouldn't let go. Their only chance was to dislodge the radar, make the homing signal go away.

His eyes flashed back to the top of the windscreen, as he sought to divide his attention between the radar monitoring device and the death-dealing missile. The burgeoning cloud of exhaust gases appeared much bigger now—much closer. A shimmering speck at its origin was clearly visible and growing at an incredible rate before his eyes. The form began to take shape, until he could make out the triangular, cruciform wings in the middle of the long, slender body, the sharply pointed nose. There was no mistaking its characteristics. He had seen Sparrow missiles on many occasions—lying inert on their loading gantries, slung beneath the wings of USAF fighter planes. But never one like this before, exploding out of the sky toward him at breakneck speed. Another few seconds and—

Like a sunburst, the face of the RHAWS dissolved suddenly into a dozen separate rays of fluctuating fluorescence. A break lock! They had done it! But the Sparrow seemed not to care. It was still coming, its flashing sword point a shooting star dropping out of the sky. Dropping right on top of them—nothing could stop it! The four men in the cockpit watched helplessly, bracing for the inevitable impact.

Almost faster than the eye could react, the white form streaked across their path, enshrouding them momentarily in its snowy wake. A brilliant flash lit up the morning sky, providing only an instant's warning before the big plane was rocked violently by a thunderous detonation. A detonation from somewhere beneath them, where the errant missile, losing its signal at the last moment, had plummeted into one of the countless dunes of the vast Nafud wilderness.

It took a moment for the reality of their deliverance to sink in. Then the cabin erupted with an outpouring of Arabic, as the pent-up emotions of the three crewmen boiled over. The captain turned to Richy with a "hat's off" gesture of acknowledgment for his contribution. But he knew that there was no time for self-congratulation. There should have been two missiles, not one; standard operating procedure called for the launch of two in salvo. It was obvious to him that the F-15 pilot had saved one for a follow-up attack.

"Brace for another attack!" he shouted, leaving it up to the R/O to translate. His eyes darted to the RHAWS indicator, and what he saw there made his blood freeze. The F-15 radar had them again! Their flight path had moved them out of its blind zone; the solid spoke of light radiating from the center of the scope had moved downward, pointing to the four o'clock position.

He shouted a warning, gesturing toward the RHAWS. The captain flashed a quick look at the display, reacting swiftly. He knew what to do now, a quick learner, Richy was thankful to note. The captain banked to the right and watched the bright line on the RHAWS rotate slowly back toward the three o'clock position. The strategy worked once, you could see him thinking; why not again?

Richy put his hand on the R/O's shoulder. His friend was still somewhat shaken from the ordeal of their close brush with the first Sparrow, he observed. "You watch the flash detector," he instructed. "I'll monitor the RHAWS for another launch signature." Sparks nodded his assent.

The pilot was pulling out of his turn now, the single spoke on the RHAWS settling into the three o'clock position. Richy watched for the appearance of multiple spokes on the display, which would signify a break lock. They were in the radar's blind spot again. It should happen momentarily.

He waited, holding his breath. It was taking too long! The single line on the display, generated by the radiation detected from the direction of the F-15, held solid. It was impossible—it violated the laws of physics! There was no way the radar could continue to track them in its blind spot.

When the explanation dawned on him, it was already too late. The Sparrow launch signature was flashing on the RHAWS display—the telltale frequency change just before launch. He alerted Sparks, then transferred his attention to the flash detection indicator as he racked his brain for an answer to the latest development.

It should have been obvious to him; he should have been expecting it. He had known that the F-15 was equipped with a flood horn, generating a much wider beam than the main radar antenna for situations in which the Sparrow was launched from point-blank range. In close-in "dogfight" encounters there was often insufficient time to obtain radar lock-on. The radar could be aimed by the optical sight, the pilot steering the plane to maintain the pipper in his head-up display on target, the fat radar beam assuring sufficient illumination on target for the Sparrow to home on. The F-15 would be close enough by now to use this mode; the pilot, having observed a radar break lock on the previous shot, was taking no chances with his last Sparrow.

What could they possibly do now? The situation seemed hopeless, all of his radar lore useless. The radar was out of it now, merely a slave to the pilot's eyeball. He could think of no way to break the noose that was closing around their necks. Unless the pilot screwed up, somehow, they had had it. Or the missile. Neither event seemed likely.

With a suddenness that made him jump, the flash detector lit up like a Christmas tree. "Launch! We have another launch!" shouted the R/O into the intercom. Richy could picture the consternation that this announcement would generate in the back of the airplane, where the other Americans were probably still rejoicing in their earlier deliverance. Poor Roxana.

How long did they have? Fifteen seconds, ten? He stared down into the empty desert ahead of the AWACS, his last view, ever, of the outside world? A world he would leave reluctantly, a beautiful world, even here in this parched corner of it. There were mountains in the background, but the terrain they were flying over presently was flat and smooth. The rising thermals from the hot sands worked a perfect mirage effect on the empty expanse below them, placing a shimmering blue lake just ahead. It looked so real, he had the fleeting illusion that if he could look straight down he would see the image of the AWACS reflected below, its black-striped rotodome turning slowly above its all-white fuselage.

Reflection! Image! Something in the back of his mind clicked into place. A half-forgotten conversation with a Raytheon engineer. The image problem! The Sparrow. The "chicken missile"!

"Tell him to dive!" he shouted into the R/O's ear. "We've got to get lower—as close to the deck as possible!" Without waiting for the nonplussed radioman to start translating, he pounded the pilot on the shoulder, pointing down with his finger and simulating a downward trajectory with his other hand.

The captain looked like he might protest, pointing to the altimeter, which showed that they were already below a thousand feet. But the urgency in Richy's manner persuaded him. He pushed the control stick forward, until the scintillating lake filled the windscreen and loomed ominously close, threatening to engulf them. Then he eased off, the big plane leveling out a scant hundred feet above the bogus sea. It was only then that the copilot spotted the second missile.

Richy followed the copilot's gaze into the bright midday sky. It was dropping down on them from the right side of the airplane, its fleecy train billowing ever larger. A second Sparrow missile —military designation AIM-7F: the bird that had earned the nickname "chicken missile" at one stage in its early testing against low-altitude targets over bodies of water and flat, highly reflective terrain because of its inclination to turn away from the target at the last moment, avoiding a collision. The problem had been traced to the tendency of the missile to transfer lock from the target to the radar image of the target reflected from the smooth terrain below, analogous to the virtual image from a mirror. The Narcissus of the missile world, its preference for the image had never been fully explained. Richy could not remember hearing of a fix for the problem. Now he could only pray that there hadn't been one.

They were skimming the floor of the desert, the pilot forced to concentrate on the terrain up ahead, his hands full controlling the AWACS at its risky, unaccustomed altitude. All other eyes on the flight deck were riveted on the approaching missile. It rocketed toward them, its position high on the windscreen rock-solid, holding to the collision course commanded by its internal steering apparatus. On it came in its inexorable pursuit, exploding into their vision, the identical twin of its predecessor. Closer and closer, until every detail of its gleaming white body became visible—until Richy's sharp eyes could even discern the tiny lines of demarcation around its middle that sectioned off the compartment of its ultradestructive warhead. The muscles of his body went rigid, sensing the imminent shock of impact, as though the tensing would somehow armor them against the effect of exploding steel on soft flesh. He closed his eyes and held tightly to the back of the R/O's seat, resigning himself to the inevitable.

The detonation shook the AWACS as though it were a toy. He was thrown violently to the floor and knew it must be the end as equipment and debris crashed down around him. He felt the big aircraft lurch hideously and opened his eyes just in time to see the ground disappear from view, replaced by blue sky. The flight deck was strewn with rubble but had somehow survived, the pilot wrestling with the controls to contain the runaway airplane as it bounded heavenward. Then it dawned on him what had happened. The concussive force of the tremendous ground explosion a scant hundred feet below had engulfed the AWACS, impelling it skyward. Narcissus had seen his image on the desert floor after all; the "chicken missile" had done its thing. It had missed.

Richy's eyes darted back to the flash detector display. There was still Sidewinder to worry about. They'd be better off facing it head-on—less exposure of hot engine surfaces to its heat-seeking sensor. Hurriedly, he explained the situation to a dazed Sparks, still in the process of picking himself up off the cabin floor.

The captain had successfully reined in the bucking AWACS, leveling off at several thousand feet. He quickly comprehended the translated instruction, banking steeply to the right. With one eye on the launch detector, Richy plugged in his headset and borrowed the R/O's intercom mike.

"Paunch, can you hear me? This is Llewellyn. Are you all right back there? Come in. Over."

There was no immediate answer. Then the slow Texas drawl came back over the intercom. "Whoo-ey! Looks like a back-home twister hit this place."

"Was anybody hurt?" He heard Paunch repeat his question to the others, their answers unintelligible on the intercom.

"We're pretty bruised up," the Texan's voice came back. "But it looks like we're all in one piece. Sorry I can't say the same for your radar office. It's tore up real bad. You're gonna shit little green apples when you—"

"Paunch, listen to me!" Richy broke in impatiently. "We're still not out of the woods. There's still the Sidewinder—remember? Better get to your flare dispenser station right away. Plug in your headset and call me when you get there. I'll monitor for a launch and call it for you."

"Roger and out."

The voice went away. Richy turned his attention back to the flash indicator in the middle of the instrument panel. The captain, he noticed, was also watching it intently, expecting it to bloom at any moment to announce another deadly volley of supersonic ordnance launched toward his defenseless aircraft. Though its warhead was somewhat smaller than the Sparrow's, Richy was well aware that the Sidewinder had accounted for more aircraft kills than any other missile. A salvo of Sidewinders could easily send the AWACS crashing to the desert floor.

What was keeping that pokey Texan? He should have been at his post by now. Launched from only a few miles away, the missiles would be on top of them in seconds. Once the launch warning flashed, there would be precious little time to decoy them. The flare equipment had to be cocked and ready.

"Flare dispenser power on," the drawling voice reported back finally. "Magazine loaded. We've got a ready light. Set to go. Over."

"Roger, Paunch. Remember, flares every five seconds after I call the launch."

That was a relief! He continued to hold the microphone to his lips and concentrated on the flash detector, ready to announce the event the instant it took place. It surprised him that there had been no sign of a launch signature as yet. The F-15 had to be well within the Sidewinder launch zone by now. At least in this case, he comforted himself, no news was good news.

Or was it? A warning shout exploded from the copilot as he came half out of his seat, gesturing frantically toward the center of the windscreen. Directly in front and somewhat above them, the black profile of a sleek warplane approaching head-on was silhouetted against the bright northern sky. It was in a shallow dive, rocketing down out of the sky, making straight for them! There was no question of its identity; twin vertical stabilizers jutted up like jackrabbit ears behind its sun-glinting canopy. The distinctive front profile of the F-15 Eagle was unmistakable.

"He's trying to ram us!" Richy shouted. The warning was unnecessary; the pilot could see the danger as well as he. But there was nothing he could do. It was too late for evasive action. A turn now would only play into the other pilot's hands, present him with a bigger, broadside target. If he was intent on ramming them, there was nothing that could stop him.

With the possible exception of one thing, Richy suddenly realized. A "death ray" might stop him! A death ray that worked only at short range. The only defensive weapon that the AWACS possessed. Its radar!

Was the radar still on, or had he left it in standby? He couldn't recall, it had been so long. There was no time to run back to his control station. He cursed aloud, then remembered the radar status panel in the cockpit. His head jerked toward it. Damn! The status light showed standby.

He snatched back the microphone from the radio operator. "Roxana! Can you hear me? Over!"

She came on the line immediately in response to the urgency in his voice. "Roxana, quickly! Turn the radar to ON. Set the mode switch to BORESIGHT. Hurry!"

Eyes glued to the status panel, he saw the light jump from STANDBY to ON. Good girl! Thank God she'd been an attentive student. Now the pilot of the onrushing F-15 was centered in the powerful radar beam. If he was going to ram them, he'd have to continue to fly through it. When his approach brought him close enough, it would fry his insides!

But would it be in time? Would the microwave cookery work its debilitating effect on the pilot fast enough to cause him to miss them? The rapidly closing Eagle continued to hurtle toward them, showing no signs of wavering. The death ray wasn't going to work; it was too late! They were completely at the mercy of the man in the Eagle's cockpit. What matter of man was he? Was there any mercy in him?

The answer he provided to his own question was devoid of hope. A man who had already launched two missiles at them, whose mission was to destroy them. A man apparently dedicated to some cause he prized beyond his own life, fanatical enough to sacrifice himself and his plane to carry out his orders. A man whose head he could make out now, silhouetted inside the transparent canopy, in these last seconds before impact.

The wings of the Strike Eagle waggled in a final salute. Then the streaking warplane flashed suddenly downward, the pilot's right arm completing the salute, extending upward as he disappeared beneath them. The shock wave tore into them, rocking the big plane momentarily, the noise deafening from the supersonic near-collision with the powerful fighter. And then there was no further sound from it, nor any other trace, as though the creature that had terrorized their last hours had been nothing but a phantom of their own imaginations, or of that vast desert over which they flew—nothing but a mirage.

CHAPTER
10

"My God! What have you done?" Martin Singer peered through the layers of acrid white smoke engulfing the tiny room, the report of the small handgun still ringing in his ears. "You've shot my radio! You've destroyed it!"

He ran to the smoking equipment, fanning at it with his hands. Daniella ignored him. Her eyes, filled with contrition, were on the other man.

"I'm sorry, David. I couldn't let you do it. You see that, don't you?"

He stared back at her with a dazed look, the color slowly returning to his face, the consciousness of where he was and who she was returning with it. In his zeal to warn his brother he had lost track of everything else, only subliminally aware of the gun pointed at his head. The deafening gunshot had broken his trance with a vengeance, the reality of his own danger crashing back into his consciousness. For a moment there—

She was asking his forgiveness. She didn't need to do that. There was nothing to forgive. His look, as his eyes swam back into focus, told her that. She had done what she had to do. Just as he had.

"He was my only brother." Why was he using the past tense? Was he already thinking of Richy as a dead man?

She noticed it, too. "They must have heard your warning. Perhaps they'll get away."

"Perhaps." His voice lacked conviction. The message had been incomplete. There had been no acknowledgment from the other end.

Martin was frantically throwing switches and twiddling dials. "I was counting on this radio," he fumed. "Without it, we're completely in the dark. On the AWACS outcome—on the Baghdad raid. I'll be forced to—"

A loud pounding on the door interrupted him. Daniella spun

around, her still-smoking weapon trained on the door.

"The butcher, Ben-Levi. He must have heard the shot."

A harsh voice, muffled by the thickness of the heavy door, demanded immediate entry. She motioned at Martin with the pistol.

"Tell him you're all right. Get rid of him."

Martin shouted something back in Hebrew. The banging on the door ceased, but the butcher's continuing harangue left no doubt that he was adamant about gaining entry. It took several more heated exchanges between the two before the butcher apparently gave up. They heard his noisy exit moments later as the meat locker door slammed shut.

"He'll be back," observed Martin dryly. "Isser is an obstinate and suspicious fellow. I don't think he ever entirely trusted me. He's sure to call his Arab control and ask for instructions, if he hasn't already."

"The telephone!" Daniella cried. "We can call for help." She grabbed the phone off its hook and held the receiver to her ear. "It's dead!"

Martin didn't appear surprised. "He can disconnect it from the outside. Probably did so some time ago. And you can bet the padlock's back on the meat locker door."

David's eyes traced the outline of the rugged door built into the solid brick wall. "Can they force their way in here?"

Martin shook his head. "Not likely. This room is built like a bank vault. Nothing short of dynamite would do it. They're aware that a blast like that would bring the police down on them."

"So it's a standoff," David summed up. "They can't get in—we can't get out." The closeness of the cordite-tainted atmosphere in the sealed room was starting to get to him, the illusion of walls beginning to crowd in on him like an Edgar Allan Poe scenario. It wasn't a standoff at all. The butcher had the upper hand. They couldn't stay here. They had to get out. He could detect similar claustrophobic symptoms in Daniella. Surely Martin must feel it, also.

But Martin was playing it cool. "That's about the size of it. Looks like we're stuck here indefinitely. Unless, of course, we can strike up some kind of a bargain among the three of us." Too cool, David told himself.

"What kind of bargain?" Daniella asked suspiciously. "What re you driving at, Martin?"

"There's another way out!" David exploded. "That's it, isn't it? That's why he's so damn blasé. I should have guessed. The bastard's too clever to paint himself into a corner."

Singer ignored his outburst, choosing instead to answer the question put to him by Daniella.

"All I ask is that you hold off blowing the whistle on me for another twenty-four hours, both to the Israelis and the American authorities. As far as America goes, it's a CIA matter, anyway. And the government can take up the responsibility for my actions with Israel."

"You're unreal!" David gasped. "You murder a fellow diplomat in cold blood; you stand by and allow other innocent Americans to be slaughtered in a plot against the AWACS that you knew about—probably had a hand in engineering—and then ask us to look the other way! Let you disappear and get off scot free? Forget it, Buster—no deal! There are some people in Washington with a lot of questions to ask you—people with no connection to your precious Company."

"I have no intention of running," Martin replied with icy calm. "I'll gladly surrender myself to the proper authorities. All I'm asking is the normal period of grace extended to any accused citizen to put his affairs in order. And to have counsel present when the arrest is made. 'Counsel,' in my case, being my CIA superiors."

"David, we can't stay here," Daniella interjected. "I must reach my office, report what has happened. I want to see justice done every bit as much as you do. But can't we agree to a day's grace period, if Martin pledges to turn himself in tomorrow?"

"I don't trust the slippery bastard." David's eyes swept the interior walls of the secret room, looking for some sign of an emergency exit. But there was solid brick on all sides; with the exception of the entry from the meat locker, there were no cracks visible between the rows of bricks. The floor was an unbroken expanse of concrete, the ceiling composed entirely of rough-hewn wooden planks.

"You'll never find it." Martin had been watching him, following his eyes. "This vault was designed by an expert. An Israeli," he added for Daniella's benefit. "He copied the plan of the Haganah slik, used in Tel Aviv during the Mandate. The British snoopers never came close to uncovering it. Now—do I get my twenty-four hours, or do we stay bottled up here indefinitely?"

He looked from David's face to Daniella's. David thought i

over. "On one condition. I stick to you like glue during those twenty-four hours. I don't let you out of my sight."

Martin shrugged. "Suit yourself, if you've nothing better to do with your time. It's agreed, then?"

David nodded slowly, his eyes locked to the CIA agent's. "Better let me have that gun, Daniella. This man is my prisoner, until we get him behind bars, where he belongs."

"It's getting stuffy in here." Martin took a deep breath and let it out. "Time to leave."

He reached behind the safe, moving his index finger back and forth until it found the precise spot in the raked mortar joint between two of the bricks. There was a whirring of gears similar to the sound David had heard when the door to the slik had first opened. He watched for a breach in one of the walls, but none materialized. His gaze traveled upward, and then he saw it, a crack in the low ceiling at the other end of the room, as the entire ceiling of rugged planking slid noiselessly overhead, moving slowly away from the far wall.

Fresh air spewed in through the opening, dispersing the acrid fumes from the gunshot. He filled his lungs with the welcome infusion. Martin was already struggling with the desk, sliding it to the opposite end of the room. They would need to stand on it to effect their exit through the gap in the ceiling. The whirring stopped, leaving an opening of scarcely more than a foot in width above the desk, as Martin motioned impatiently to Daniella.

"You'd better go first. You'll need a boost."

She clambered onto the desktop, then hesitated. "Wait a moment. What is up there? How do I get out?"

"There's a narrow ledge," Martin explained hurriedly. "You'll feel it when you reach up there. It runs under the eaves of the roof rafters. We have to crawl along it for about twenty feet. You'll see slits of light at the far end, a ventilator panel. It opens onto the roof of the adjacent building."

Together, they helped her climb through the narrow opening onto the ledge above. On hands and knees, her back toward them, she halted.

"It's so dark. I can't see a thing. Which direction do I crawl?"

"To your left," Martin instructed. "Look for the slits of light."

She began to move. "You next," David ordered, motioning with his gun hand. Martin climbed onto the desk and thrust his head through the hole in the ceiling, hands and forearms on the ledge above. As he strained to haul himself upward, his progress was arrested by a sudden sound from the room below—a man's voice speaking in Arabic.

David whirled around, his gun at the ready. "It's the damn radio!" he reported in relief. "The receiver must still be working."

"Shh!" Martin hissed. "Listen!"

"What is it?" David demanded after a few seconds. "Who's talking?"

"It's the Israeli fliers. They've almost reached Baghdad. The strike on Osirak is about to begin."

Lieutenant Colonel Moshe Eitan peered out through the canopy of his lead F-15, squinting his eyes against the late morning sun. Perched over his right shoulder, an echelon of identical gleaming white jets trailed off into the distance, the nearest a scant hundred feet away. The fat black bomb suspended from each of its wings bore visible chalk marks—insults and epithets scribbled by the ground crew to an enemy who would never read them. The sleek two-thousand-pounders would carry their own message to the Arab world: don't mess with us! If a signature was necessary, the black Star of David prominently displayed by each warplane on either side of its fuselage would provide it.

Eitan stared back into his empty radarscope and scratched his head. The continuing absence of hostile aircraft activity should have been reassuring. But his instinct told him that something was *lo beseder*—not okay.

His squadron of a dozen Strike Eagles, reduced to eleven by Captain Lieb's untimely engine flameout, had negotiated the remaining three hundred miles of Saudi Arabian desert without further incident. Nearing the Iraq border, the first challenge had come from an air controller at a Jordanian air base to the north. In the tight formation they were flying at the time, they had appeared on his radar screen as a single giant aircraft, which had indeed been their intent. Eitan's response, first in English, then Arabic, had identified that "aircraft" as an American C-5A bound for Dhahran and under Saudi control.

Shortly thereafter, a precision turn to the right had placed them on a new heading of 115 degrees, running parallel to the Iraq border but still in Saudi Arabia, apparently bound for Dhahran. Still in close formation, they had lost altitude gradually, until assured that they had dropped below the Jordanian radar pattern, before turning back toward their true objective.

All the while, the air controller had continued his harangue, persisting in his demand for further identification and threatening armed interception. A hollow threat, Eitan felt sure; jets from Jordan were not likely to violate Saudi airspace without permission. The real danger lay in whatever alarm the Jordanian might raise in neighboring Iraq. A check with Saudi authorities, he realized, would ultimately expose their cover story as a hoax, their sudden turn southward from their original course toward Baghdad as nothing more than a feint. Iraqi air control was almost certain to be alerted. Meanwhile, they had bought a little time.

Entering Iraq, Eitan had dispersed his aircraft, returning to the ruse of simulating Jordanian pilots on maneuvers, conversing only in Arabic. Expecting to be jumped by Iraqi fighters at any time after they crossed the border, he had been keenly alert for any sign of enemy aircraft. But none had materialized, not even the single interceptor customarily sent up to do a visual identification on an unidentified aircraft. At first he had been thankful. Not that he had any doubt that his fliers would acquit themselves well in air skirmishes with Iraqi MiGs, if the need arose. But he hoped it wouldn't. It would be a distraction from the all-important primary mission.

In Eitan's view, it had been a gamble to go with a force composed entirely of multipurpose fighters in lieu of the dedicated F-16 strike aircraft used in Operation Babylon, with F-15 fighters for air cover. A traditionalist in these matters, he believed firmly in the separation of roles and missions into air to ground and air to air. As a dyed-in-the-wool ground strike pilot charged with training other pilots for these missions, he was painfully aware of the difficulty of attracting good candidates into this less glamorous end of the business. His strike aircraft were disparagingly referred to as "trucks", the air-to-ground missions as "air to mud." Everyone wanted to be a dogfighter, swooping around the sky and taking potshots at MiGs. The air-to-mud role of dropping bombs on stationary targets seemed dull and lusterless by comparison. Yet he knew it to be the most telling of the air force missions.

Good truck drivers were scarce, hard to train. Once trained, they were worth their weight in gold. Eitan prized his team highly. They would rip hell out of that A-bomb plant if they could just get to it. But if they started hassling with a bunch of MiGs, who could tell? Once they got caught up in the excitement

of aerial combat, he might never get them back to the mundane
chore of dropping their ordnance on target. It could turn into a
michdal—a real fuck-up.

He glanced again at the radarscope set into the left side of his
instrument panel. Two thirds of the way from the border to
Baghdad, and not a single MiG. It was certainly serendipitous. It
was also unbelievable. They had not even sighted any commercial planes. Something was rotten in the state of Iraq.

But there was no time for speculation now. The strike force
were within sight of their IP. From here they would descend to
treetop altitude for their final run into Osirak, minimizing the
reaction time of the SA-6 missiles and whatever additional radar-
actuated local defenses might be implanted there. Depressing the
mike button on his throttle, Eitan gave the order.

Like a formation of giant migratory birds in perfectly
synchronized flight, the string of eleven Strike Eagles swooped
earthward. The right echelon transitioned smoothly into a single
file, as each bird played follow the leader onto the new heading
that would take it over its objective at precisely the desired approach angle. Less than a hundred feet above the parched,
sparsely settled terrain, Eitan watched the occasional dirt road or
dilapidated building flash by below.

Ahead lay the fertile crescent of Mesopotamia, the confluence
of the two great rivers that formed the cradle of mankind. The
land that had spawned the ancestors of Abraham, whose remarkable migration westward over the same arid wastelands so speed-
ily traversed by Eitan's jets had been the start of a new people;
the heritage of the young republic that now carried the name of
that ancient kingdom of ten Israelite tribes.

An overwhelming sense of destiny gripped him as he hurtled
on toward the green banks of the Tigris and Euphrates to keep the
rendezvous for which he had been preparing for a solid year. Or
perhaps, he reflected, much longer than that. Perhaps for his
entire life.

The observation post was the minaret of a dilapidated mosque
no longer used for public worship, though its loudspeaker still
broadcast the call to prayer five times daily. Sergei Brastov, prepared by his daily afternoon constitutionals, had little trouble ne-
gotiating the steep spiral staircase.

Reaching the top ahead of the others, he did his best to suppress his amusement at their discomfiture, most notably the

wheezing and coughing of the corpulent army chief of staff, a heavy smoker. Even the nonsmoking defense minister and the air force chief, both slender men by comparison, were puffing hard. Little al Fawzi, the intelligence director, staggered up the last few steps, out of breath and eyes bulging. But the wraithlike Ali Mustafa, looking too thin and frail for such a climb, took it perfectly in stride, as indeed he seemed to do in all situations.

At the top of the stairs, round Byzantine arches led in four directions to the circular balcony. The first to step out onto it, Brastov was immediately impressed by the selection of the vantage point. It was the highest spot amid its relatively flat surroundings, providing an uninterrupted view of the walled-in expanse of dun-colored buildings known as Tamuz 17. Yet it looked to be a good two kilometers removed from the looming nuclear site, far enough to minimize the danger from a stray bomb or piece of flying debris.

One of the new SA-10 batteries protecting the facility was also visible, its missiles hidden from view by the heavy camouflage net. Tiny figures could be seen scurrying about in preparation for the impending attack. There were no signs of activity around the atomic plant. It was Friday, the Muslim Sabbath. Only a skeleton force would be on duty.

Brastov checked his watch. It was one minute after eleven in the morning. It would be a good half hour before the action began. The alert had come earlier that same morning, confirming that the Israeli strike was going ahead on schedule. The news had reached him as he was concluding a late breakfast of gruel and figs; the Israeli jets were on their way! He had tarried only long enough to ascertain from his own sources that the planned separation of the Iraqi agent, El Aurens, and his F-15 from the rest of the strike force had come off as planned.

Buoyed by the news, he had arrived in excellent spirits to witness one end of the long-awaited doubleheader in person. The outcome of the other deadly game would be reported by radio, on a shortwave set just now being readied by a technician on the balcony where they were standing. It would be tuned to the secret wavelength El Aurens would use to communicate his encounter with the AWACS somewhere across the Saudi Arabian border.

Its portable antenna deployed, the radio sputtered into operation, heavy static followed by garbled snatches of Arabic spewing forth as the operator fiddled with the tuner. For a split second Brastov thought it might be the Iraqi pilot, his pulse quickening.

Then he realized that what he was hearing was only stray pickup, the technician still working the dial to find the correct wavelength. Satisfied at last, the man in fatigues abandoned the tuner and turned up the volume until the static was unbearably loud, then turned it back to normal. There was nothing being transmitted yet. They would have to be patient.

The most difficult part of any such operation was the waiting, when the outcome hung in the balance and there was nothing more one could do to influence it. His final move on the chessboard had been played out. But this stage of the game was more like *kriegspiel*, blindfold chess, where you were not permitted to see your opponent's men and could only deduce what his moves had been by what happened to your own pieces. If you had properly assessed the disposition of his forces, your final move would bring victory—checkmate. But there was always uncertainty—that last agonizing wait—until the blindfold was removed, until the umpire who controlled the board with all the true positions assessed the impact of your move and informed you of the result.

He had gambled his whole future on that result. He couldn't understand the relaxed behavior of the others. Didn't they feel it—the tension, the suspense? Instead of straining their ears for some word of the AWACS encounter, they were chatting together lightheartedly, like schoolboys on a holiday outing. Not quite. The body language of the generals gave them away, an unmistakable undercurrent of anxiety that rippled their surface calm. He detected the same signs in the defense minister, the pupils of his eyes dancing restlessly about.

But the "assistant president" was another story. Ali Mustafa seemed to be actually enjoying the wait. He looked every bit the part of the detached spectator at the start of a sporting event, with nothing wagered on the outcome. Yet Brastov knew he probably had more at stake than any of the others. He had stuck his neck out by recommending the AWACS gambit to the President. Anyone at all familiar with Saddam Hussein was aware of the retribution the dour chief executive was capable of exacting if things went wrong. Mustafa assuredly had as much to lose as Brastov. But you would never know it to look at him.

What was it he was saying? Brastov tuned in on the conversation. President Hussein had wanted to be present at the observation post to witness the engagement firsthand. He had stubbornly resisted all attempts to talk him out of it by informed members of the Revolutionary Command Council, concerned for his safety in such close proximity to the conflict. But the argument that had finally dissuaded him was that his presence here at Osirak at the zero hour might be noted by hostile eyes and tip off the Zionists that the Iraqis were expecting them, giving them time to abort the mission and avoid the elaborate ambush. So the disappointed President had reluctantly agreed to be elsewhere. At the moment, Mustafa confided with a twinkle in his eye, he was appearing at a women's gathering, a fish-fry luncheon along the Tigris benefiting war orphans of the war with Iran.

There was general laughter among the Iraqis, which Brastov did not join in. Their levity at such a moment irritated him. He glanced again at his watch, then broke purposefully into the conversation.

"Why is there no word from your pilot—from El Aurens? He should have made contact with the AWACS by now. Shouldn't we send a query to him?"

"No." The intelligence director, who obviously considered himself in charge of communications, shook his head emphatically. "Too risky. A transmission from here could be picked up by the Zionists and might jeopardize both operations."

"But if a suitable code were employed—," Brastov protested.

"Besides," the petite spy boss added, "our portable transmitter is not powerful enough to reach him." He checked his own watch. "He was instructed to transmit every fifteen minutes on the hour. It is not time yet for the first transmission for another five minutes."

Inwardly, Brastov fumed. How slipshod! No two-way communications. If this were a Soviet operation, under his total control, it would have been done differently. But what could one expect from a second-rate intelligence organization with a man like al Fawzi at the helm? He forced himself to be calm, using a chess problem from one of his ongoing correspondence games to pass the time. He was black, holding a major piece advantage in the end game. Black should mate within a half-dozen moves.

When ten more minutes went by with still no radio contact with El Aurens, Brastov was beside himself. Heightened restiveness was beginning to show in some of the others. "Where can he be?" sputtered al Fawzi. "What can have happened to him?"

"Patience, my friend," the still-unruffled Mustafa counseled. "Under fire, things can't always be performed on schedule. Your man is no doubt very busy at the moment. We are sure to hear from him soon."

Brastov couldn't stand it. "I will return shortly," he announced, and ducked back through the archway to the staircase, taking the steps two at a time as he hurried down. His own sources had invariably proven more reliable and timely than the Iraqis'. While driving to the observation site, he had spotted a public telephone in the doorway of a run-down hotel two blocks back.

His pace left him somewhat out of breath as he dropped a coin into the slot and dialed the accustomed seven digits. It was a dummy number; a special hookup would patch him into a secret line to his source in Tel Aviv, routed through Syria and cleared through Lebanon. The procedure had been worked out by the KGB experts. There was no way the call could be traced from either end.

He had used the arrangement sparingly but often enough to be familiar with the characteristic aural responses of the network in the telephone earpiece; the sequence of delays, clicks, and buzzings that invariably preceded the final ringing and the answering voice at the other end. But this time there was no final ringing or answering voice. Following the initial sequence of familiar sounds, the receiver went dead, subsiding into a state of noiseless suspense.

He cursed aloud into the mouthpiece. It had never happened before; it must be the fault of the antique piece of equipment. When he hung up to try again, the relic spitefully refused to cough up his coin. He dug out another from his trousers pocket and redialed the number, agonizing over the inevitable delay for the circuits to close. The end result was the same. Exasperated, he banged the earpiece back onto the hook and hastened back to the observation post.

What could have gone wrong? His calls had invariably gone through before. The phone at the other end was always attended. There had been no busy signal or any audible ringing. Could the Mossad have discovered it, had it disconnected? Not likely. They would have left it intact, monitored the calls.

This time the hurried climb up the minaret staircase took a good deal more out of him. Somewhat red-faced, he emerged onto the balcony, just in time to catch a final flurry of Arabic from the radio speaker before it went silent again.

"El Aurens?" he gasped. The few words he had heard told him nothing, only that the party was signing off. The downcast looks on the faces of the others said a good deal more.

"He failed?" There was incredulity in his voice. How could his plan have failed? It was airtight; there was no way—"What went wrong?"

He directed the inquiry to the group as a whole. Only Mustafa chose to answer. "Apparently the American missiles were a bit overrated. They missed the mark. The tactics employed by the AWACS pilot may well have contributed to this. Don't blame yourself. It was not the fault of your plan."

Brastov found the condescension in the presidential adviser's words galling, the reinforcing half smile on his face intolerable. What was the man made of? Was this the reaction of a man who had just seen his whole career go down the drain? The defense minister, too, he noted, seemed less than devastated by the unhappy news. Suddenly Brastov had a strong inkling that the two men knew something he didn't.

"El Aurens—where does he go now? What will he do?"

Mustafa looked at Zahadi, their eyes meeting, some tacit understanding passing between them, culminating in a barely perceptible nod by the assistant president. It was the defense minister this time who responded to Brastov's question, the gleam in his eye and the importance in his tone promising something momentous.

"He was given an alternate assignment—a secondary target. At the moment he is navigating to the vicinity of—"

With Brastov and the other officials hanging on his words, the defense minister's voice trailed off in midsentence, his eyes drawn to the eastern horizon by the snarl of powerful jet engines. "They are coming!" he shouted, pointing excitedly. "The Zionist warplanes!"

Brastov followed his eyes. A speck of white was clearly discernible against the green and ecru background of surrounding fields, streaking toward Tamuz 17. It appeared to be on the ground, so low was its trajectory. But its speed was far greater than that of any surface vehicle, the angry whine of its engines already noticeably louder. In seconds it would close the gap, be in position to drop its heavy load of explosives into the heart of the nuclear complex.

From much nearer to the observation post came an answering roar of such a sustained, earsplitting intensity that it set the frail balcony of the decaying minaret to trembling. All eyes were immediately drawn to the source. Above a brilliant orange fireball, a slender silver cone was literally exploding skyward, dragging one tongue of yellow-orange flame behind it. Brastov, who had witnessed the SA-10 tests in Siberia, was struck once again by the incredible launch speed generated by the new Soviet missile.

An elongated streak of silver, the missile arced up and over the nuclear site, then shot back downward at a tremendous velocity, almost faster than the eye in its total concentration could follow. The white blur and the silver streak came together, disappearing abruptly into a blinding circle of white-hot incandescence. Brastov's hand rose involuntarily to shield his eyes from its awesome brilliance. By the time the terrible sound of it reached his ears, the flash had faded, leaving no trace in its wake of silver missile or white jet, or of the man who had been flying it. Nothing at all except an eerie green afterglow, which slowly dissipated itself into the pale blue sky until it, too, had totally vanished.

Eitan could hardly believe his eyes. One second his lead-off F-15 was flashing in toward the target, ready to send its two tons of TNT ripping into the hateful structure. The next second it was gone—disintegrated, vaporized—in one instantaneous, all-consuming burst of light! Ari. His best pilot, his best friend. Lost! Poor Ari!

There had been no advance warning. The first inkling of trouble had been the belated flare-up from a spot near the target, when Ari was already nearing the end of his bombing run. One of their obsolescent SA-6 missiles, Eitan had thought. Too late. Far too late. It could never catch up with Ari. Then the thin line of silver, etching its way up into the sky at such an incredible speed; he thought at first it was a harmless tracer bullet from some ineffectual gun emplacement. And then, suddenly, the sickening airburst, removing all doubt, the premonition that had been nagging at him through most of the flight fulfilled with a vengeance.

The explanation leapt at him, stark and chilling. The Iraqis had been expecting them. They had arranged a welcoming party, with the help of their Russian friends. Some new Soviet superweapon of undreamed-of potency was the guest of honor.

Yudi! Yudi was next in line, following Ari into the target. It would be suicide! He had to be stopped! Eitan depressed the mike button on the throttle with his left hand as his right manipulated the controls to recapture the target area in his field of view. "Yudi!" he shouted. "Abort, Yudi, abort!"

There was no answer in his headphones. The complex of uniformly spaced, earth-colored buildings, arranged in the form of an H, slid back into his windscreen, and he caught sight of the white jet with the black markings rocketing across the ground toward it. "Break off, Yudi!" he shouted. "I order you. Turn back!"

But the streaking jet showed no sign of complying. Eitan watched helplessly, awaiting the telltale burst of flame from the spot on the ground to the south of the target. Seconds passed, with no apparent response from the Iraqis.

"He's going to make it!" he thought. "Yudi's going to do it!" Abruptly, the flash erupted from a different point on the ground, and this time he knew it was too late. Not for the lightning-swift missile, but for his pilot.

Like a man in a dream, he counted off the seconds from launch, witnessing the instant replay of Ari's encounter with the unknown weapon. Before his count reached four, it was all over. He closed his eyes at the blinding brilliance of the explosion. When he reopened them, the uncanny emptiness of the shimmering spot near the horizon where the plane had been only moments before sent chills through every part of his body.

Dear Lord! Yudi gone, too! What were they to do? What could anyone do against such a weapon? The jammers didn't seem to affect it. Was there any conceivable way to outfly it?

His earphones began to buzz with comments from the other pilots, all talking at once, shaken by what they had seen, requesting instructions. He had to pull them back, abort the original plan, regroup. Keep them out of harm's way until a new strategy could be worked out. There was panic in some of the voices. He knew what they were thinking. It was time to abandon the field to the enemy and live to fight another day. A day when the new weapon had been run through the Israeli computers and identified, analyzed by their incomparable team of systems experts, its flaws ferreted out, new tactics devised to deal with it. It was an option he didn't have. His orders were very clear and explicit on that point.

"Commander to squadron. Code Alef Zero. Repeat, Alef Zero. Rendezvous 11:42." They would re-form back at the IP. He had precisely three minutes to come up with an alternate attack plan. He was on his own; radio contact with home base had petered out shortly before they crossed the Iraq border. It wouldn't have changed things anyway. He knew what the instructions from his wing commander would have been. "Find a way to get the job done. Don't return until Tamuz 17 is a smoking ruin."

Was there a way? What options were open to him? The new missile had amply demonstrated its deadliness from short range, against low-flying targets. But the missile's maximum range was unknown, untested. They could try coming in at high altitude, lobbing their bombs in with a lofting maneuver and turning off immediately to stay out of range of the new missile. But the delivery accuracy would deteriorate, the chances of a direct hit on the reactor greatly reduced. And there would still be the presence of the SA-6 missiles to contend with. It was their established lethality at high altitude that had mandated the extreme-low-altitude bombing approach to begin with.

No, there was only one strategy that made any sense. Saturate the enemy defenses, overload them. Come at them from all directions at once. Maximize the number of shots the enemy must get off within the time available; minimize their time to do it. That way, some of the attackers were bound to get through. The others? He wouldn't let himself think about the others.

There was just such a tactic in his squadron's repertoire. It was one of the maneuvers they practiced regularly, even performed at air shows—a spectacular maneuver to watch, requiring close teamwork and precision timing. It was facetiously known as their "Irish Act"—the "Four-Leaf Clover" tactic.

His jets would converge on the target at treetop level from four directions at once. There were nine Strike Eagles left; eight, not counting his own. He would put two at each corner of the cloverleaf, eight warplanes converging on the target simultaneously from four directions. He had observed two separate batteries of the new, superfast missiles below; he prayed that there were no others. Each would have to cope with four Eagles at once, within the few seconds they would be exposed after popping over the horizon on full afterburner. An impossible task for any conceivable weapon system.

The original IP appeared below, a solitary water tower where a dirt road crossed the railroad tracks in the middle of nowhere. Eitan wheeled his F-15 around in a tight one-eighty and started back across it on the original attack heading. As the squadron began to form up once again off his right wing tip, he announced the new attack plan.

"Commander to squadron. We're going back in, code Teth Four. You all know the procedure; you've rehearsed it often enough. We'll set up our four quadrants off this heading, a leader and wingman at each corner. Elli, you'll take Ari's place in quadrant three. Yaacov, you'll be his wingman. As I call off your quadrant, please acknowledge."

He ran through the list to make sure that each pilot knew his assignment. When all had answered affirmatively, he checked his watch.

"I'll contact you again at 11:47. You should all be in place by then. The first contingent will deploy seven seconds from now. Six, five, four, three, two, one, zero."

The two Strike Eagles at the end of the formation separated and sped off toward the eastern horizon. Eitan banked left into a shallow turn, the rest of the squadron following suit. The loiter maneuver would allow the first two jets time to get into position on the opposite side of the target. To do this safely, they would have to navigate around it.

Pulling out of the 360-degree turn, Eitan sent out the next two pairs, one to the left, the other to the right, then initiated another 360. A minute later, the last pair of warplanes were on their way to the fourth leaf of the clover. A slow-climbing turn brought him to an observation point a few thousand feet above the scene, far enough from the target to be out of reach of any of the missiles, and he cut back his throttle to the slowest practical cruise position. The second hand of his watch was coming up on 11:47. It was time.

"All units in position?" He called off their names, one by one, receiving their acknowledgment. "Then I will start the final countdown. Shalom, my friends, and Godspeed! Five, four, three, two, one, go!"

From the four corners of the imaginary shamrock, pairs of sun-glinting specks began to converge toward the target, tiny pencil points of white drawing faint charcoal lines in the sky with the exhaust from their afterburners. Eitan was struck with the beauty of the spectacle, pride swelling within him. They were a precision team—the best—and he had trained them.

It would take them a scant thirty seconds to reach their individual weapon release points, about five hundred meters downrange from the target. The objective was to arrive at these points simultaneously, release their bombs, and break right, avoiding direct overflight of the target. Even allowing for timing errors, all sixteen bombs should be dropped within a few seconds, with the attendant advantage that there would be insuffi-

cient time for smoke buildup to obscure later pilots' view of the
target. His team had performed the maneuver successfully many
times. But never with live bombs. And never under fire.

Like spokes on a wheel, the soft gray lines from the spent fuel
traced the path of the jets toward the common hub. They were
well past the halfway point now. Within the next few seconds
they would pass into the crucial window of vulnerability, reaching a point where the protection of the intervening terrain no
longer shielded them from the view of the radar controlling the
missile batteries. Eitan sucked in a breath and held it, his eyes
darting back and forth between the two points on the ground that
were etched in his memory—the points from which he had seen
sheets of yellow-orange flame erupt, hurling the deadly cone-
shaped payloads skyward. Time seemed suspended, the waiting
interminable. Still nothing happened.

The Strike Eagles were nearing the target, only seconds away
from their bomb release points. Again the surge of euphoria
gripped Eitan, the conviction that his boys had made it through,
had carried it off and were safe. The impression was fleeting; he
should have known by now.

Simultaneously, the two spots he had been scrutinizing exploded into fiery prominence. But this time, further explosions
continued to ripple through each site, as though some unseen
hand had touched off a chain of firecrackers. Accompanying
bursts billowed up from a third spot to the east of the nuclear
plant, and he watched in horror as processions of glistening metallic darts shot into the air above each launch site. In only moments the sky was filled with lethal streaks of silver, converging
like tracer bullets on his hapless pilots with a speed that by comparison made their aircraft seem frozen in space. How many had
been launched? He lost count, the crisscrossings of multiple tra-
jectories too confusing.

"Drop your bombs!" he exhorted, knowing it was already too
late, even if they heard him. "Break off! Get out of there!" An
instant later, the first weapon made contact, a miniature sun
lighting up the sky with an unbearable brightness that quickly
decayed into the chilling green afterglow of nothingness. The
process was repeated again and again, until Eitan, eyes mostly
shielded from the terrible spectacle, had counted eight separate
bursts.

He dropped his hands from his face, praying that his count
had been faulty—that just one F-15, one of his precious pilots,

had made it through. The deserted skyline above a still-intact Tamuz 17 confirmed his worst fears. Not a single bomb had been dropped. Not a single one of his eight Strike Eagles had survived.

"Dear God!" Eitan wailed into the emptiness at the other end of the intercom. "What kind of a God are you to let a thing like this happen?" He was not a deeply religious man; a religious Jew wouldn't think of addressing his God by name, let alone fling blasphemous questions at Him. But the unbearable burden of what he had just witnessed, with its overwhelming sense of loss and guilt, demanded sharing with the One Other Being who might have had a hand in preventing it.

His burden of guilt stemmed not only from the knowledge that his orders had sent the others to their doom, but also from his undeniable and shameful feeling of relief that he hadn't been one of the ones to perish—that he was still alive. That circumstance, he now became painfully aware, was subject to change. In his agony over the fate of his fliers, he had become heedless of his own safety. His course had taken him dangerously close to the target area. At his present altitude of 4,200 feet, he was a sitting duck, high enough above the horizon for even the SA-6 to have a pop at him.

Spontaneously, he kicked in the right rudder pedal, pulling back on the stick. Midway through the wingover, inverted weightlessly over the ground, he was jolted by the sight, through the top of the canopy, of a missile lighting off below. Was it the SA-6, or one of the deadly new ones? Whatever it was, it was after *him* this time. Trimming the rudder, he jerked the control stick into his belly, the g forces building immediately, sucking the blood from his head. He had only one chance. Get down on the deck fast, where the radar would lose him. Break the magic chain between radar track and missile guidance.

He eased the stick back to neutral and pushed the throttle wide open, diving for the ground. If it was another silver streak chasing him, it would be on top of him, with its vaporizing warhead, in a matter of seconds. One eye on the altimeter, he watched the tableau of rich, irrigated farmland move up to meet him, the individual patches on its jade and emerald checkerboard growing slowly at first, then mushrooming in size as the countryside exploded into his windscreen. Five hundred feet, four hundred!

He closed back on the throttle and pulled the stick into his lap, the fighter plane responding with a suddenness that sent the landscape spinning across his vision and left him lightheaded and heavy-limbed as the g forces took hold. Like a punch-drunk fighter, he struggled with the controls, just managing to level off as the altimeter bottomed out at a bare fifty feet. In his preoccupation, he failed to see the gleaming metallic cone, half the size of his own warplane, hurtle down past his left wing tip, and was unaware of the closeness of his brush with death. Unaware until the Strike Eagle was rocked by the concussive force of the warhead's massive ground detonation, and he was bathed in the pale green aftermath of its blinding sunburst.

He had survived! The same God that had permitted the rest of his squadron to perish had preserved his own life. Could there be any more convincing sign that the mission that had brought him to this godforsaken place was part of some preordained plan, some ultimate destiny, his and his people's?

His own role in shaping that destiny was suddenly clear. With the singlemindedness of the reborn whose eyes have been opened to some elemental truth concerning life and the universe, he dedicated himself to it. He slammed the throttle forward, all the way into afterburner. With a vengeful roar, the lone remaining Eagle shot up into the sky. He was already marginal on fuel for the trip back, he knew; the use of the afterburner would deplete it further. But getting home was secondary now. Getting even was all that mattered.

Eitan's next act was to check the weapons slung beneath the wings of his rapidly climbing warplane. A cursory glance over his left shoulder verified that the sleek, black Mark 84 bomb with its ton of high explosive was still firmly anchored to the wing pylon just outboard of the Sparrow station. It no longer figured in his plans; there was no way to get close enough to the target to use it. He twisted his head back to look over his right shoulder. The bomb attached to the right wing pylon, though similar in size, looked quite different. More cylindrical in shape, it sported stubby wings, which were folded back along its body like those of a slumbering bat. And instead of coming to a sharp point, like the Mark 84, the nose of this bomb was rounded and reflective, like a glass mirror.

The weapon was a remotely controlled glide bomb, the first of an experimental batch purchased from the United States, as yet untried in combat by the Israelis. The weapon's advantage over conventional bombs had been convincingly demonstrated by the U.S. Air Force; they could be launched much farther away from the target and guided in with high accuracy. Eitan was the only pilot in his wing to undergo the USAF indoctrination program on the use of the new glide bomb. The training had been minimal, not including the opportunity of actually launching one. But he had been favorably impressed with the weapon, nonetheless.

Some sixth sense had convinced him to apply for permission to have his own F-15 fitted out with one of the new weapons for this secret mission, though he had fully expected to be turned down. To his surprise, he had been asked to brief none other than the chairman of the Joint Chiefs himself, Yigal Tuchler, on the glide bomb's capabilities. Tuchler had asked a number of penetrating questions, not only concerning the glide bomb, but about the Osirak raid also; he was a smart old bird. The general had ended up granting his request, endorsing the use of one of the new weapons in the Osirak venture.

The theory and workings of the glide bomb were totally familiar to him. The "glass" window in its nose was actually heat-resistant quartz. Behind this window was the lens of a special TV camera that recorded the scene out ahead of the bomb—the target area toward which it was launched. A data link sent the TV image back to a scope aboard the launching aircraft, allowing the pilot to adjust the cross hairs over the point he wanted to hit, data link commands to the missile repositioning its control surfaces accordingly. Under visual flight conditions the Americans had achieved phenomenal accuracy with the glide bomb, if you could believe their data. But it had one flaw. Its time in the air was much greater than that of a conventional bomb, its terminal speed much slower. It could thus become an inviting target itself for antiaircraft batteries.

Eitan was fully aware of this shortcoming but was counting on the element of surprise. The Iraqis and their Russian advisers would not be expecting a glide bomb, did not even figure to know what it was. When the altimeter of his F-15 read thirty thousand feet, he leveled off, banking to the left to bring the target back into his field of view. He was now more than twelve miles from Tamuz 17, well out of range of any of its local defenses. But the now-familiar H-shaped complex of squarish buildings was still clearly visible.

He flipped a switch on the newly attached control panel, rigged just below the F-15's main armament panel, activating the glide bomb, sending power to its TV sensor and arming its warhead. On his radar display, a television picture materialized, fuzzy and ill defined. A knob at the bottom of the display brought the image into focus, the farmland ahead at which the bomb's TV camera was presently staring. His right hand began manipulating the small joystick protruding from the makeshift panel, and a recognizable replica of the nuclear facility moved into the lower right-hand corner of the display. Gingerly, he adjusted the joystick until the cluster of buildings was centered under the cross hairs inscribed on the face of the scope.

A ready light flashed on the panel. With his Eagle still under afterburner to give the bomb its strongest possible impetus toward the target, he depressed the launch button. It was gone! His surprise package was on its way! Allowing a few seconds for the bomb to separate, he closed the throttle partway and hit the dive brakes, to slow his own speed and avoid outflying the bomb.

It was like running into a wall. The F-15 shuddered and he was flung toward the instrument panel, the shoulder harness cutting into him as it jerked him to a stop. The image on the scope had disappeared, only the barren lines of the TV raster still visible. But as he trimmed the controls of his aircraft, the replica from the bomb's TV camera returned, and he looked down to see the glide bomb soaring gracefully out ahead of him.

Manipulating the joystick once again, he recaptured the objective under the cross hairs. Now it was no longer necessary to keep the bomb in sight, and he began a wide turn to the right to avoid flying into the lethal zone of the Osirak missiles. His eyes darted back to the image on the scope, verifying that the tracker was still clinging tenaciously to its target. He watched the object of his pent-up wrath slowly grow in size and definition, the blurred cluster of buildings beneath the cross hairs gradually taking the shape of the letter H.

Painstakingly, he adjusted the image beneath the cross hairs until they were tracking the crossbar of the H, continuing to make minute corrections as the glide bomb made its tortuous way to its destination. It would take at least another minute to get there, provided that nothing sprang up from below to intercept it. A suspenseful, agonizing minute that would seem more like an hour.

A prolonged moment of stunned silence gripped the observers on their lofty perch adjacent to the abandoned mosque. Then the reality of the unbelievable spectacle that had just unfolded in front of them sank in, and bedlam ensued. In a display of emotion that Brastov was unaccustomed to seeing, the Iraqis embraced one another, tears of joy and gratitude flowing freely. The Russian was inundated with congratulations and backslapping effusions, even the self-important little intelligence director joining in.

His stomach had not yet recovered from the impact of the gut-wrenching onslaught that had so suddenly engulfed them. Scarcely a minute before they had ducked their heads in terror as two Israeli Strike Eagles came thundering past, almost directly overhead, so low that Brastov could read the numbers emblazoned alongside the Star of David, even catch a glimpse of one of the pilots in the glass bubble protruding above the white fuselage. His ears still rang from the din of their fire-spewing jet engines; at that moment they had seemed supremely formidable—indomitable. The sight of more of their ilk converging on the target from all sides made his heart sink. By the time the answering thunder had finally erupted from the SA-10 site nearest the minaret, Brastov had been almost ready to concede defeat.

But the sight that greeted his eyes had quickly changed his mind. Instead of a single silver cone exploding skyward, there were four at once, rocketing upward with the same incredible acceleration he had witnessed in the earlier encounters. Within the few seconds it had taken them to reach their apex above Tamuz 17 and begin their downward arc, he had discerned sister missiles from other sites streaking up to join them. Then the sky before him had become mass confusion, criss-crossing streaks of silver, flashing flecks of white, and gray-black lines of jet exhaust intersecting in an eye-boggling tableau that was awesome in portent.

Heart in mouth, he had awaited the first of the macabre green flashes that would signal success: success for his newly unveiled family of missiles—failure and sudden death for the intrepid pilots. When it had come, it was followed so quickly by countless other flashes that the sky resembled a scene he had once witnessed in Northern Siberia, when the aurora borealis had transformed the heavens into a panorama of shimmering, iridescent light. But these were man-made lights—man-killing lights—and already beginning to fade from the sky as the terrible sound of the encounter reached his ears. Unbelievably, he had continued to stare into the faintly scintillating patch of sky above the still-intact nuclear plant—a sky that moments before had swarmed with hurtling metal machines, some with human occupants. Now it was totally empty, engendering a corresponding feeling of emptiness in his vitals, a sensation of numbness that even the adulation of his colleagues and his own elation over the brilliant success of his defenses could not totally dispel.

Was it over? Was there another wave to come? His eyes swept the western sky. At least ten warplanes and pilots, by his own count, had already perished at the hands of his new miracle weapon, eight in the last concentrated foray. Surely the surviving Israeli pilots would see the folly of continuing the futile venture, would turn for home if there were any remaining to do so; there were none visible to his eye against the noonday sky.

His fellow spectators had also been watching the skies apprehensively. Now Ali Mustafa and Amahl Zahadi stepped around the others to stand next to him. "It is all over," the defense minister announced. "They have retired. We have won a great victory." He seized Brastov's hand. "Congratulations once again, Comrade General. Your new weapon is truly astounding."

Brastov's pulse began to return to normal. The excitement had certainly done one thing. It had driven the AWACS disappointment totally from his mind, and he had no doubt that the stunning success of the SA-10 would have the same effect on his superiors, helping them to overlook the less-than-satisfactory outcome of his AWACS venture.

The news exploitation of the Osirak clash had already been planned, the headlines composed and texts roughed out, awaiting corroboration and details that he would supply. *Pravda* and *Izvestia* would have a rare scoop on the rest of the world, with the exception, of course, of the local Baghdad news agency, which had scant exposure outside of Iraq. It was a big story—a sensational story. It would make headlines in every corner of the world. All those western news magazines, which specialized in tweaking the Russian bear's nose, would have to report the one-sided outcome. *Time* and *Newsweek* in America he particularly despised, and also *Aviation Week*, which had run an especially irritating editorial on Soviet weapons' inferiority after the destruction of the MiGs and SA-6s in Lebanon. He couldn't wait to see them eat crow.

The truth, the whole truth about the Soviet miracle missiles— and that might not surface for years—would be even more galling to the Americans when they found out: that they had been beaten with their own technology. The SA-10 guidance that enabled multiple missiles to attack separate targets simultaneously was an adaptation of the Phoenix missile guidance in the first-line U.S. Navy fighter, the F-14 Tomcat. And the SA-10 propulsion, the controlled explosion that shot the missile so rapidly into intercept position—the key to the missile's quick reaction—was almost a carbon copy of an abandoned American antiballistic missile technique. In fact, the new Russian missile, with its cone-shaped aerodynamic surface, was a dead ringer for the U.S. Sprint missile, developed as a companion to the bigger, longer range Spartan antiballistic missile, both casualties of the canceled U.S. ABM program.

It was an old Russian trick, the Soviet weapon developers long known as the "copycats" of the trade. Brastov smiled wryly. There would no doubt be more talk of this when the truth about the SA-10's lineage came out. Let them talk. It would not diminish the satisfaction in the least. Employing the U.S. designs was like beating the Americans at their own game. The incorporation of an ABM approach and an air-to-air technique into the design for a new SAM had been a true stroke of genius. And the Soviets had added a secret ingredient of their own that was the final key to success. The warhead. The device that literally pulverized its target, so powerful that the missile did not even have to make contact with its quarry, a near miss sufficient to destroy it. For the warhead was a tactical nuclear device, its lethality equivalent to detonating ten tons of TNT in the target vicinity.

The Russians had solved the problem of controlled nuclear explosions, the de-escalation of the explosive force released from a critical mass of fissionable material with a minimum of fallout. The blast from the SA-10 warhead was only a tiny fraction of the force from the earliest, most primitive atomic bomb that had ravaged Hiroshima. Yet it was totally awesome; it would strike terror into the heart of enemy pilots when word of its vaporizing lethality got around, make them eternally wary of venturing into any airspace controlled by the Soviet Union.

A deterrent. That was the way the Soviets would defend the incorporation of a tactical nuclear device into their newest missile. Like its infinitely bigger, multimegaton brothers, it was not meant to be detonated, only to deter enemies from attacking. In the debate that had raged privately within the closed circle of Soviet military planners over the advisability of being the first nation to employ such a weapon, it was this point of view that had prevailed. If nobody knew about it, your deterrent didn't work. There had to be a first time, when its awesome lethality was demonstrated for all the world to see. What better opportunity, then, than the present one, where the Zionist warplanes were the clear aggressors, a thousand kilometers beyond the borders of their homeland, violating the sovereign airspace of another nation?

It was time to depart. As the Iraqis prepared to take their leave, Ali Mustafa stopped for a final word with the Russian military adviser. "Let me add my compliments to the ones you have already received." President Hussein's right-hand man winked at him, his face wearing a secret smile. "I hope to have some news later in the day that will add additional spice to our great victory."

El Aurens's "alternate mission"! Brastov had completely forgotten, Mustafa's earlier allusion to it driven from his mind by the riveting events that had intruded. What was this mysterious follow-up assignment? From the expression on the Grand Vizier's face, it must be something extraordinary.

"What kind of news?" The question on the tip of Brastov's tongue was never vocalized. His attention was abruptly arrested by the sight of an object no bigger than a speck in the sky that seemed to be suspended in the air above Tamuz 17. As his eye continued to follow it, the speck grew larger, and he could see that it was actually moving, approaching the atomic plant, floating slowly downward toward it. The others, in the process of leaving, had not noticed it, but Mustafa, seeing the sudden alarm in the Russian's chubby face, swung around to have a look, following his eye.

Against the sparkling blue backdrop of the midday sky he saw something resembling an ungainly, heavy-bodied bird gliding slowly down on ridiculous, stubby wings toward the complex of dun-colored buildings. Mustafa rubbed his eyes in disbelief, then alerted the departing defense minister, just starting down the stairs, with a shout of warning. The others in his entourage raced back with him to the balcony railing, all eyes focusing on the strange, soaring object that seemed to be picking up speed, its glide path now clearly intersecting the center of the nuclear facility.

"Don't they see it?" shouted the air force commander. "Are they asleep? Why don't they fire?"

"The radar cannot see it," mumbled Brastov, in a listless monotone intended for no one but himself; he had lapsed into Russian. "It is too small a target. Perhaps also too small to do much damage."

The force of the explosion disabused him of any such notion. The dome of the central building housing the reactor disintegrated before their eyes, reinforced-concrete beams flung up through it like so many toy parts from a child's construction set. The blast shook their makeshift command post so violently that Brastov feared for a moment the balcony might break loose or the entire minaret collapse. As the quaking subsided, he watched the debris settle back to earth. It was like seeing a page from his life fluttering down before him—the page that was to have recorded his crowning achievement, to have illuminated the waning days of his career in military intelligence, perhaps even staved off retirement for a few more years.

That page would have to be discarded now; rewritten. The ending had been changed by a capricious fate. The destruction of the American-made jets by his missiles counted for nothing, after all. He had won the battle, but lost the war. Despite his efforts, the target he had been charged with defending had been destroyed.

He could visualize the condition of the nuclear plant only too well; he had inspected Tamuz 17 shortly after the first Israeli strike had knocked it out. The violence done to its interior had been incredible. The concrete floor of the main building that housed the reactor, several meters thick, had buckled, popping out huge blocks of concrete that were strewn randomly about, imparting to the room's wreckage-strewn surface the grotesque appearance of a disintegrating iceberg. The heart of the nuclear complex, the atomic reactor core with its priceless rods of enriched uranium—the spent fuel that was to become weapons-grade plutonium—had been smashed to bits, crumbling into a lethal mass of hot, radioactive waste. It had taken many months for a team of trained French and Italian technicians in protective suits, using heavy equipment, to clear away the hazardous wreckage before new construction could even begin. And now it had happened again. For the Iraqis, it was like setting the clock back to 1977. Like starting all over again.

He could read the realization of it in their shocked faces—faces that only minutes before had been flushed with victory, had reflected unbound elation. They were subdued now, regarding the smoking ruin in hushed disbelief. The silence was profound; no one wanted to be the first to break it. What was there to say?

It was high noon; the silence was broken for them. Brastov started, along with the others, as the loudspeaker just behind them, suspended above the arched doorway to the balcony, blared forth with the midday call to worship.

"Ah-laa-aa-aa-aa-hu akh-bar!" sang the recorded voice of the muezzin, rising and falling in its tremulous rendition of the drawn-out syllables, then rising again to its triumphant final note. For good measure, the muezzin repeated the message broadcast five times daily to remind all Muslims of their own relative insignificance: "Allah is most great!"

CHAPTER

11

The figures of two men and a woman were crouched behind the low parapet surrounding the flat roof of the bakery. Llewellyn jabbed the small handgun into the other man's side, the index finger of his left hand crossing his lips in the universal signal for silence. Voices were coming from the street below—unfamiliar men's voices commingling with an all-too-recognizable one, singular in its undertone of menace. The butcher had called in reinforcements. They had collected in front of the meat market, only a few paces from the spot where the fire escape descended from the bakery roof to the sidewalk below.

David caught Daniella's eye and motioned toward the far corner of the rooftop. On hands and knees, she set out across it, Singer reluctantly following after another prod from David. The roof was covered with heavy gravel embedded in its black tar base, a difficult surface to negotiate on tender knees. He winced as a sharp point of rock penetrated his trouser leg. But Daniella, with no more protection than her sheer hose could provide, seemed oblivious to it, setting a rapid pace. When they reached the opposite corner of the roof, where they could stand without danger of being discovered, he saw that both of her knees were bleeding, the hosiery torn to shreds.

Martin ruefully surveyed the disheveled knees of his suit trousers. "I hope you know what you're doing," he hissed. "There's no way down from here."

David peered over the roof's low mansard. They were facing a sheer drop of perhaps sixteen feet to a very unyielding surface below, the concrete of a paved alleyway. Broken bones or bad sprains would be almost a certainty. But midway along the rear wall of the bakery stood a trash gondola, loaded with refuse from the adjacent stores; cardboard boxes and wrapping paper, and garbage of a more perishable nature, judging by the swarm of flies it was attracting. Not a very appealing kind of nest to drop into. But at least it would break their fall.

There was no time to deliberate. If the butcher and his henchmen started nosing around, they'd be spotted. He motioned to Daniella and pushed Martin ahead of him until they were standing just above the gondola. Martin stared down at it distastefully.

"You don't expect me to jump into that?"

David handed the gun to Daniella. "I'll go first and chase away the bugs." He threw a long leg over the three-foot-high roof enclosure and swung himself easily astride it, then hesitated. "Will you be able to climb up here?"

She nodded reassuringly. He dropped over the side, clinging to the top of the parapet with both hands, his long body dangling momentarily above the refuse container. Then, pushing out with both feet, he released his grip.

The metallic thud of his landing was largely muffled by the accumulated debris piled into the garbage container. He dug himself out of it and stood up unscathed, waist deep in refuse. It had not been a long drop for him; suspended at arm's length before dropping, he had, after all, about an eight-foot head start. For Daniella it would be more difficult.

"Martin next!" he whispered up toward the rooftop before vaulting out of the gondola. With her miniature persuader, Daniella prodded the CIA agent into compliance. He turned out to be a good student, imitating David's maneuver perfectly.

As Martin came up sputtering, fighting his way out of the foul-smelling garbage, Daniella tossed the small handgun down to David and boosted herself nimbly onto the low wall. Without a moment's hesitation she lowered herself over the side, hung momentarily at arm's length above the trash bin, then pushed off. David sucked in his breath—she was falling over backward, her head dangerously close to striking the metal side of the container. It missed by inches as she came to rest on her back, a safe and comparatively soft landing.

What a gutsy little thing she was! Tenderly, he helped her out of the bin, brushing the debris from her clothing. Moments later the threesome were tiptoeing down the alley toward the end of the block where David, more than an hour earlier, had parked his Simca.

He led them cautiously along the wall of the last building, approaching the street on which the meat market fronted. Motioning for the others to wait, he peeked around the corner. The car was still there, but so were the butcher and his party, continuing their discussion in front of the meat market, halfway up the block but in plain view of where the Simca was parked. One of the men glanced in his direction and he pulled his head back. Should they chance it—make a dash for it—or abandon the car and try to find a taxi? Locating a cab in this neighborhood might take time, and he was frantic to contact the embassy, find out about Richy and the AWACS.

He stole another look around the corner. The butcher and his entourage had disappeared, presumably into the meat market. He motioned to the others. "All clear! Let's go!"

Less than halfway down the southeast runway of Ben Gurion Airport, the sleek twin-engine Cessna was already airborne, its wheels in the process of tucking themselves up into its belly. As it picked up speed and altitude, it began a gradual climbing turn to the left.

Inside, the blond pilot, wearing dark glasses, concluded his final communication with the control tower, signing off. He relinquished the microphone to the man in the copilot seat, already engrossed in changing frequencies on the radio panel. In the seat just behind him, the third passenger leaned forward to shout something into his ear, her right hand clutching the small handgun that still held five unspent cartridges.

"The Mossad may have some word about the AWACS by now. I know their frequency band. I have to contact them anyway."

David Llewellyn nodded, turning his head so that Daniella could hear his words above the din of the wide-open engines. "But first I want to try going direct. There's just a chance—"

The radio was similar to the one in the meat market hideaway, powerful enough, once they were airborne, to reach all the way to Riyadh. It had been one of the inducements in Martin's proposition to them, the proposal that he fly them from Tel Aviv to Jerusalem in the private plane, saving time and providing radio contacts en route that would ease their anxieties. Despite their misgivings over his motives and the danger of putting themselves in his hands to that extent, they had been persuaded. David was obsessed with finding out about his brother; nothing else seemed to matter at the moment. Daniella was seized by a similar sense of urgency to reach the Mossad headquarters and brief her control. And after all, they would still be holding a gun on their prisoner-chauffeur.

"AWACS C-103, this is David Llewellyn in Tel Aviv. Come in, please. Over." He listened for the reply, fearing the worst, not really expecting an answer from the doomed aircraft. But perhaps a sister ship, tuned to the same band, would hear the call letters and respond, with information on the outcome, on possible survivors.

Daniella regarded the face reflected in the windscreen with compassion, straining her ears for some positive response in her own headset. Her expectations were no higher than David's. But she realized that there would be no rest for him, no peace of mind, until he had news of his brother, favorable or otherwise. At the moment he was unable to look beyond the personal tragedy that the demise of the AWACS and its crew would spell for him. In the less chaotic aftermath of the escape from the spy hideout, she could now perceive the other terrible consequences, the blame and censure that would fall on the heads of the principals of the Likud government, its prime minister and his cabinet, including her own beloved proxy father, Shimon Kedar. How could the government ever convince a suspicious world, outraged anew over the repeat attack on Iraq, that the act of a pilot in the Israeli Air Force, flying an Israeli warplane, was not Israel's responsibility? She sent up a silent prayer that the radio headset would pronounce the AWACS and its crew alive and well, that the two men closest to her heart would be spared the anguish of the grim alternative.

But only noise continued to emanate from those headphones. David slowly turned up the volume until the static became unbearable, then turned it back down. He repeated the message. Again there was no reply. He tried a third time.

"Give it up," the callous voice behind the sunglasses advised, breaking in on the intercom. "Face it, the AWACS has bought it. There's no possible way it could have survived."

El Aurens swung his head around for one last look at the bizarre aircraft with the giant saucer suspended above its fuselage—the target that had somehow withstood his sustained onslaught with weapons that he had employed so successfully against much more difficult targets. Why had the Sparrows not worked against AWACS? He was still puzzled by it, confused and angered. The final close encounter with the radar plane had been out of sheer fury and frustration. He had never had any intention of ramming it. He couldn't afford to. He had to save himself for an even more important assignment.

At least it had thrown a scare into them, he thought with some satisfaction. He had caught a quick glimpse of the startled crew in the big plane's cockpit a split second before he flashed beneath them. The simulated ram maneuver had given him an unexpected thrill of excitement. Funny, he still felt a tingling sensation from it, all over his body, somewhat like the aftereffects of the electric shock he had once received when he had accidently touched the hot terminal of a transformer.

But apart from the excitement, the unsuccessful engagement had left a bitter taste in his mouth—a taste he was unaccustomed to—the taste of failure. He was not in a position to assess the impact of that failure on the Arab struggle against the Zionists; the big picture was not his province. What mattered to him was that, for the first time in his undercover career, he had been unable to carry out his orders. But he had work to do; he couldn't let himself brood about it. The Muslims had an expression that covered the situation: *"Insh'allah."* It was pointless to question God's will.

Completing a wide, sweeping one-eighty, he turned his thoughts to his remaining mission. He checked his fuel gauge. It registered somewhat below the half-full mark. Probably just enough, if he stayed off afterburner. The original plan had called for him to land in the Sinai. But the new orders would take him farther north, aggravating the fuel situation. It would be close. He would have to navigate carefully, conserve fuel.

He punched the coordinates of his new destination into the nav panel, coordinates he had committed to memory after receiving the orders for the additional mission. Funny how those orders had come to him. It was the first time a personal contact had not been used, the first time a written message, in the chess code, had specified what the assignment was. And the accompanying injunction not to communicate the nature of the new orders to any of his undercover contacts had further surprised him, made him suspicious at first. But the orders proved to be authentic; his follow-up inquiries had been validated at the highest level of the intelligence headquarters in Baghdad.

Recalling the sequence of events, he relived the excitement of the moment when he had finished deciphering the message, had first discovered the new mission assigned to him. It had blown his mind, had made the AWACS attack pale in comparison. It was something he could throw himself into wholeheartedly, a master stroke on behalf of his great republic, and for all the Arab nations—for all Islam—if he could accomplish it. He was confident that he could; his strategy was clear in his mind. He could hardly wait to go into action. But first, there was the little matter of getting there.

He stared out through the windscreen at the bleak desert wilderness that surrounded him. The terrain below gave him no clue to his position. Praise Allah for the inertial navigation system built into this miraculous machine he was flying. Atop the INS panel set into the right-hand console of the F-15 cockpit, his latitude and longitude were read out continuously on the digital display. It was accurate to within a fraction of a kilometer.

He had spotted one reliable checkpoint near the end of his southward flight, not long before engaging the AWACS: a dirt road intersection that showed on his sectional chart. Punching its coordinates into the computer as he flew over it allowed the computer to determine what effect the wind had had on his flight path. The same effects would be applied automatically by the computer to determine his position on the return trip, on the theory that major wind shifts were unlikely over so short a period of time.

Working in conjunction with the inertial platform, the computer would register the proper heading in the "steer" window of the INS panel to bring him over his selected destination. All he had to do was follow the command heading; it was child's play, no thinking involved.

Fortunate, he thought, settling deeper into his seat, trying to make himself as comfortable as possible for the long trip back. He didn't feel up to any heavy thinking right at the moment. His stomach was killing him. It must have been that heavy Israeli breakfast at the officers' mess that morning.

"Mayday! Mayday! This is Eagle One. This is Eitan. Do you read? Over."

For the tenth time in the last five minutes, the pilot of the solitary jet fighter floating high over the North Arabian Desert hit the receive button and listened in vain for a reply from his home base. Was his transceiver malfunctioning? Surely he should be back within radio range by now. Why didn't they answer? His situation was getting critical.

In the last half hour his eyes had hardly left the fuel gauge in the lower right corner of the F-15 instrument panel. He imagined that he could actually see the motion of the needle as it dropped progressively lower. It was already dangerously close to the red hash marks. Once it reached that point he would have to switch to his reserve tank. Then there would be no more than ten minutes of flight left before facing a dead stick landing in the remote fastnesses of a hostile Arab desert. It was not a happy prospect. The two-engine Eagles were too ruggedly built and heavy to make good gliders. When they lost propulsion they dropped like rocks. He had lost a close friend that way.

"Oh, God!" he implored. "If I'm not to survive this, at least let me reach them first, so I can tell them!" He had to talk to someone, give his accounting of what happened. This burden must be shared; it was too much for one man to take to the grave with him.

The return flight from Osirak had been the loneliest experience of his life. More than once he had found himself glancing back toward his right wing tip, looking for his wingman, the chilling reality of the void around him crashing in on him afresh, bringing with it the sickening realization that Ari was gone, that they were all gone, permanently and irrevocably, his entire squadron. His orders—his judgment, or lack of it—had sentenced them to death.

Their faces kept coming back to him, parading in front of his eyes. Yudi, his next closest friend, the first to go after Ari. Nachum and Yaacov, the inseparables; "Meir the greater" and little Meir, standing only five-foot-four, feisty and irreverent, inch for inch the best pilot he had ever trained. And Elli and Joel and the hardheaded, irascible Emanuel. And Levi, who had been such a "mama's boy" when he had first taken him under his wing. They had all become so close, he like a father figure among them. It was like losing his entire family in one unbelievable catastrophe. No, it was worse. Ten other families would grieve for their loved ones, blame him for their untimely loss.

Their faces, their accusing eyes! He couldn't shut them out, no matter how he tried. And superimposed on their images was the uneradicable vision of them hurtling to their doom, the awesome spectacle of the all-consuming green-white fireballs that had suddenly enveloped and devoured them. The spine-tingling aftermath, the strangely scintillating residue in the emptiness of sky where solid metal planes and flesh and blood men had been only moments before.

What was the explanation of this mysterious phenomenon? How had the Iraqis gotten their hands on such a devastating, diabolical new weapon? It was too much for him to ponder in his present state. He would leave that to the experts, waiting to debrief him on his return to home base. If he made it to home base.

The pointer indicating fuel remaining was beginning to overlap the empty mark. In desperation, he switched the radio to an auxiliary channel and tried the Mayday call again. The immediate response that blasted back into his headset almost deafened him, saturating the receiver so that the words were too distorted to make out. Cursing his own stupidity, he turned down the receiver gain and repeated his call. In his anxiety to contact them, he had turned the volume up to maximum, forgetting that the base had plenty of signal to reach him; it was his own weak signal that had not been getting through until now.

"Eagle One, this is Mother. What kept you? You're way overdue."

Relief flooded into him. It was Ground Control at Tel Nof. Finally!

"It's a long story, Mother. First things first. I need a drink badly. Is there a bartender handy?"

"Affirmative, Eagle One. We have a 'bartender' orbiting at coordinates J-37. Can you get there?"

Eitan referred to his navigational chart, eyeballing the distance from his own location to the tanker's. J-37 was almost a hundred miles beyond his present position. He would never make it.

"Negative, Mother. I'm almost on reserve. Fifteen minutes of fuel remaining at the most."

"Eagle One, we'll split the difference. Bartender will fly out to meet you. Rendezvous at K-38, at twenty-thousand feet. His ETA ten minutes from now. Do you read?"

"Affirmative, Mother." Ten minutes. That would leave less than five minutes to transfer fuel from the tanker to the fighter, sufficient fuel to make it back to base. It was cutting it awfully close. The rendezvous with the big refueling aircraft would have to come off like clockwork.

"Eagle One." The voice of Ground Control came back into his headphones. "Wing Commander Rabin would like to begin the interrogation now, in the event you don't—" There was an awkward pause in Mother's transmission.

"Understand, Mother. Proceed."

"First, the objective. Was the operation successful?"

Eitan hesitated. "If you mean by that, elimination of the target, the answer is affirmative. Destruction appeared to be total. Over."

"Splendid, Eitan, well done! Congratulations!" It was the wing commander's voice, filled with jubilation. A jubilation that would be short-lived. He braced himself for the question that he dreaded, the inevitable question that he knew must follow.

"The others, Eitan—where are the others? None of your squadron has landed yet or reported in. Are they with you?"

"I'm afraid not, general." His clenched teeth could not suppress the sob that escaped into the microphone. "I'm afraid I'm all there is."

By the time he found the tanker on his radar screen, Eitan was already flying on reserve fuel. He switched to range-while-search and read the tanker's range. Still more than sixty miles away—that meant at least another five minutes to hookup! Would he make it; could he remain airborne long enough to execute the complex fuel-transfer maneuver?

It was suddenly of overriding importance that he do so. His lassitude toward his own survival, born of his overwhelming sense of loss and guilt, had dissipated, replaced by a smoldering anger inside of him that burned increasingly hotter. The unburdening process he had just completed in his five minutes of interrogation by the wing commander had turned into a different kind of catharsis than he had anticipated.

While his report on the fate of his flyers had clearly shaken the general, there had been no words of recrimination toward Eitan. Initially, Eitan had felt disappointment; there was something in him that craved his commander's condemnation, that sought punishment as partial atonement for the guilty fact of having survived, of being alive when they were all dead.

But the wing commander's reaction reflected the bigger picture, the broader implications of the new weapons encountered. He had asked for a detailed account of the appearance and behavior of the missiles. It was only after Eitan's description of the unbelievably destructive explosions that had erased his pilots and their jets, with the green phosphorescent afterglow, that the general had broken in. His expostulation was muffled, obviously not intended for broadcast over the airwaves. But Eitan had caught it, nevertheless. "Special warheads!" the general had gasped.

Of course! Why hadn't it occurred to him? Those warheads

must have been tactical nukes. That would explain a lot, why his planes had appeared to disintegrate, vanish into thin air. They had been literally vaporized by the irresistible forces of atomic fission. His poor, unsuspecting pilots had never had a chance. They were set up, ambushed by devilish weapons of which they were totally ignorant, warheads outlawed by general agreement of every civilized nation on earth, the Soviet Union included.

The Soviet Union! That could be the only explanation, the only source of such weapons for a second-rate Arab country still decimated by the effects of a ruinous, drawn-out war with its neighbor. Hatred for the Soviets and their treatment of Jews, their hard cynicism toward the country they referred to as the "Zionist Republic," welled up in him. He had no illusions about the depths to which they would stoop to stir up trouble. But this time they had outdone themselves. Giving MiGs to the Arabs was one thing; giving them nukes was an act the world would brand as criminal and genocidal. He would make them pay! He would testify to their crime in a worldwide forum, eyewitness to the cold-blooded murder of his fellow pilots.

The transference of his guilt feelings and self-condemnation was not restricted to the Soviets. He and his pilots had been totally unprepared for an encounter with the revolutionary new weapons. Why had there been no warning, no mention of such a possibility during any of the briefings and readiness exercises that preceded Operation Fiery Furnace? Surely such a project as the emplacement of a new family of missiles in the suburbs of a city with a population of several million could not have gone totally unobserved. Where was the Mossad when this was happening, the prestigious Central Intelligence Institute, second to none in the world by its own assessment? What about Aman, the giant military intelligence complex?

The parting words of Eitan's wing commander still rang in his ears. "Don't blame yourself. You couldn't have known. And yet, we all should have known." Contradictory words, cryptic words. But now he sensed their meaning. A wave of bitterness swept over him. A dozen years before, on the eve of Yom Kippur, unsuspecting Israeli soldiers on the Syrian and Egyptian frontiers had been surprised and slaughtered by hordes of Arabs who had been preparing for the attack for several weeks. The Mossad had known of the planned attack well in advance, had warned the military intelligence authorities. But Aman, in its campaign to discredit the rival service, had convinced itself otherwise, disregarding the warning and failing to alert the military garrisons. Eitan smelled another such foul-up, his tight little family of pilots the unhappy victims this time.

If Central Intelligence had known of the Russian missiles, if the information had been deliberately withheld, someone was going to pay! He wouldn't rest until he got to the bottom of it, exposed the guilty party. His military career be damned! He would resign his commission, go directly to the press, the other news media. He owed it to his pilots, to their families, to get the truth in front of the people. He owed it to his country, a tiny island surrounded by a sea of enemies, which would ultimately be inundated unless all of its factions and dissident elements mobilized together against the common foe.

"Eagle One, this is Bartender." The radio voice jerked him back to the reality of his own present predicament.

"Go ahead, Bartender."

"Approaching K-38 at twenty thousand feet, heading one-one-zero, speed three-five-zero. Do you have me on radar?"

"Affirmative, Bartender. Your range now nine miles. Maintain present speed. When you reach K-38, begin gradual ninety degree left turn. You'll see me on your tail in approximately one minute."

He reduced the throttle and set the mode selector switch on the nav panel to the pursuit steering position, glancing anxiously at his wrist chronometer. Only five minutes of fuel remaining! He fought off the impending sense of panic. You couldn't afford to let yourself get nervous or impatient during a refueling operation. The hands on the controls required all the sensitivity of a surgeon's touch in a delicate brain operation.

The steering dot popped onto his head-up display, and he instinctively made the pursuit steering corrections that would center it in the circular reticle, bringing him in on the tanker's tail. His eyes swept the windscreen for the first visual contact with the larger jet. It might be a little difficult to spot, its camouflage paint job designed to give the defenseless aircraft some measure of protection from hostile fighters. It should be right there, coaltitude, about ten o'clock.

There it was! He had it. He could fly by visual contact now, the cues on the HUD no longer necessary. His overtake rate was five miles a minute, the intervening distance diminishing rapidly. He began to throttle back.

Now the "fun" part would begin. Watching his overtake meter

out of the corner of his eye, he continued to throttle back carefully, the tail of the big jet looming ever closer. He began counting the overtake rate aloud. Thirty knots. Twenty. Fifteen. Ten. He was almost on top of it! Five! Three! Two!

Like the retractable stinger of some giant winged insect, a slender, rigid shaft thrust out from the abdomen of the refueling aircraft and extended itself slowly toward the smaller jet. He tripped the switch that opened the refueling port just inboard of the left wing root. The refueling boom was making straight for it, two small control surfaces near its tip used by the boom operator in the rear of the tanker to steer it into position.

Easy, now, easy. Careful! He forced the jittery fingers on the stick and throttle to hold painstakingly steady, one eye on the hulking tanker a mere fifteen meters ahead, the other on the overtake meter. The nozzle of the refueling boom was suspended only a few feet in front of his head. One slip now, and the heavy boom could come crashing through his windscreen. Beads of sweat popped out on his forehead; how long could he keep this up? He felt, rather than heard, the clang of metal on metal as the boom made initial contact with the Eagle's fuselage. It inched its way toward the open receptacle. It was almost home.

The F-15 lurched sideways, a sudden gust driving it momentarily from its steady, rock-solid flight path. Instinctively, Eitan ducked his head, jerking back on the throttle. The boom slid away to the left, losing contact with the Eagle's body. He cursed his luck. Precious time wasted! They would have to start over.

Again he edged his fighter into position, the boom operator repeating the delicate process of guiding the tip of the slender shaft into place. Contact! The nozzle slid slowly toward the opening in the F-15's skin. Steady, now. *Mazel tov!*

With a hollow, clanking sound, the nozzle of the refueling boom snapped into place. "We have lockup!" Eitan shouted into the radio mike.

"Roger," came the reply from the tanker. "Opening flow valve. Here comes your drink. Enjoy! I hope it's your brand."

"As long as it's JP-4, it's my brand, all right." Holding the controls steady, Eitan watched the fuel gauge out of the corner of his eye, the upward progress of the needle already discernible. His reserve tank must be very close to empty. He knew that it was somewhat chancy to switch back to the main tank while the refueling was still in progress. But it was even chancier to stay on reserve and risk a flameout when the tank ran dry. He decided not to take that risk. He watched the needle climb steadily upward as the kerosene from the tanker flowed into his thirsty jet. Another thirty seconds and he would switch over.

Like a pair of enormous dragonflies in their mating ritual, the two aircraft clung together, drifting aimlessly across the cloudless sky, casting a bizarre shadow on the deserted wasteland below. Eitan watched the strange double silhouette glide gracefully over the flat desert floor, keeping perfect pace with his coasting Eagle. It provided a note of serenity that was a welcome respite from the steady diet of anxiety wrought by the preceding hours. He was all right, now. He was going to make it.

Without warning, the serenity of the moment was shattered. "Bandits, two o'clock high!" came the shout from the tanker pilot. "Disengaging!"

The refueling boom popped loose, retracting back slowly into the tanker's tail, as the glowing streaks of white-hot tracer bullets splashed across Eitan's windscreen. There was no time to speculate on whether they were meant for him or the tanker. He banked up into a steep evasive maneuver, instinctively turning in the direction of the threat. A MiG-21 flashed across his nose, a second close behind, the landing edge of its wings spitting fire.

Hit the throttle! Climb! Climb! His first impulse was to get away. He had to stay alive to tell his story to the world, avenge his martyred pilots, make the guilty parties pay. Those bullets had had his name on them, no question of it. The tanker was slow, relatively unmaneuverable, and defenseless. The MiGs would have plenty of time, later, to finish it off. It was him they were after.

He considered abandoning the tanker. On afterburner he could outrun the MiGs. But then he would surely run out of fuel again and the tanker would be shot down, any further chance of refueling along with it. He made a rapid decision. Thank God he hadn't jettisoned the two Sparrow missiles to conserve fuel. With no gun aboard, they were his only remaining armament.

He hit the missile arming switch as he rocketed upward, craning his neck to find which direction the MiGs were turning. They were pulling out to their right, coming around for another pass. Get up high, into the sun where they can't see you! That's it. Now break right and let them have it!

He was ten thousand feet above them, coming from the south, out of the sun. The tanker had turned tail for home, skittering off to his left. The MiGs were ignoring it for the moment, looking for the Israeli F-15—a smaller plane but a much bigger prize to bag. They had had their chance and blown it. If their pilots had been more experienced, they'd have begun climbing immediately, have turned left instead of right, not allowing him the double advantage of sun and altitude. It was his turn now.

That they had used guns in their first pass didn't rule out the possibility that they also carried missiles or rockets. Getting off the first shot could be all-important. There wouldn't be time for a conventional Sparrow launch sequence; the range was too short. He pushed his Eagle over into a shallow dive, nose for nose with the oncoming MiGs, his radar locked to boresight. He jockeyed the controls, centering the lead MiG under the HUD cross hairs. Steady now, steady—fire!

He squeezed off the first Sparrow, feeling it go, watching its vapory trail fill up the sky in front of him. He fought off the impulse to launch the second Sparrow and get out of there. It was his last weapon. He had to hold off; he couldn't take the chance of both missiles detonating against the lead target.

The MiGs had spotted him as soon as the telltale Sparrow plume appeared in the sky. They showed no signs of taking evasive action; they kept coming straight for him. He held his breath. Hurry, little Sparrow, hurry! Get there before—

Too late! Flashes erupted from both wing tips of the lead MiG. It had launched something at him. He knew that some MiGs were equipped with heat-seeking missiles; he could only pray that this one wasn't. Moments later, the center of his windscreen lit up as the lead MiG was enveloped by a brilliant orange ball of flame. It plummeted downward like a meteor, trailing fire. But whatever it had launched would still be coming after him.

He centered the second MiG in the HUD and hit the launch button again, the last Sparrow blasting away. If only it had been one of his own heat seekers, a Sidewinder, he could have turned away now, maneuvered to avoid the oncoming legacy from the destroyed MiG. But the Sparrow would falter, lose its target unless he kept his radar trained on the second MiG. If he couldn't turn away, at least he could do some jinking, make his Eagle a more difficult target. He began wobbling the control stick from side to side, relatively small excursions, but enough to cause the fighter to career snakelike through the air, oscillating from side to side.

Then suddenly there they were, and there was no time to react. Wham! With a shockwave that rattled the canopy of the

F-15, which they narrowly missed, a pair of miniature comets came hurtling past his head, tails spouting fire. His pent-up breath exploded from his lungs, his chest heaving with relief as he gulped in fresh lungfuls of air. The MiG's wing-tip weapons must have been unguided rockets, not heat seekers. His jinking had been just enough to save him.

He picked up the snowy trail of the second Sparrow snaking its way toward the remaining MiG and saw the answering flashes from the MiG's wing tips. Then, mindful of his partner's fate, its pilot banked sharply into a tight escape maneuver. It was futile, Eitan knew. The Sparrow was capable of an even tighter turn; it could outmaneuver anything with wings. The MiG was a goner.

The instant he saw the fireball envelop the second MiG, Eitan kicked in the rudder and put his own jet into a high-g turn. He saw the twin rockets flash by harmlessly into his wake, then turned back to watch the wreckage of the second MiG windmilling down toward the bleak landscape below, where a black plume of smoke already marked the charred remains of its hangar mate. There were no parachutes to be seen. Neither pilot had survived the brief encounter.

Who were they; where had they come from? So swift had been the action, so sudden the attack, there had been no chance to identify them, no opportunity to read their insignia. But they surely must have come from Iraq. Other than the Syrians and Egyptians, only the Iraqis flew Russian MiGs. And he was nowhere near Egypt or Syria. He felt no sense of vengeance in the victory over the two Iraqis, no assuaging of the deep anger and hatred inside of him. They had been pilots, like himself, doing their job, on a mission for their country. His quarrel was not with them.

What he did feel was profound relief. Now he could get on with his own mission: to bear eyewitness to the world of the Soviets' criminal cold-blooded "nuking" of his pilots; and to expose the unforgivable lapse of Israeli intelligence that had failed to prepare him and his squadron for such an eventuality.

With an unspoken expression of thanks to his maker, he turned to look for the Israeli tanker. It was long gone, out of sight already. He swung the Eagle around and set his course to overtake it, flipping his radio switch back to transmit.

"Bartender, this is Eagle One. Our uninvited guests have been evicted. The two birds I carried turned out to be just enough."

"You got them both? Nice going, Eitan, nice going!" The

tanker pilot's voice reflected his elation at his unexpected deliverance from the MiGs. "You could probably use another drink about now."

"Affirmative, Bartender. But be careful how you mix this one. That last one really packed a wallop!"

Daniella could no longer bear to look at the face reflected in the Cessna's windscreen, the broad shoulders in the seat in front of her slumped in resignation. The lack of response to the repeated messages transmitted to AWACS number C-103 had confirmed David Llewellyn's worst fears. It was no longer flying, its crew no longer able to reply.

He adjusted the volume control knob until the background noise abated, handing her the microphone. "What's your Mossad frequency? I'll dial it for you."

"Wait, David! Listen!" She had heard something, just before he turned down the volume. A short, sputtering noise that might have been only static again, but was somehow different. His hand flew to the radio panel, turning up the gain again.

Against the persistent background interference, a faint voice was discernible in the earphones. A voice familiar to only one of the Cessna's passengers, its inflection and timbre unmistakable to him, yet sounding too mature for the callow face it conjured in his mind's eye.

"Hello, big brother. Thanks for the warning. It probably saved our lives."

Richy was alive! Tears sprang to his eyes, and companion tears appeared in Daniella's as she witnessed the transformation the few words in the headphone had worked on the man in the copilot seat. But the effect on the man piloting the plane was quite the opposite.

Before David could reply to his brother, the small plane banked sharply and violently to the right. The two unprepared passengers were flung forward in their seats, seat belts straining to contain them. The microphone was hurled out of David's hand as his arms flew up to ward off the instrument panel. Daniella just managed to hang onto her pistol, bracing herself against the back of David's seat with her other hand and clinging fiercely to it as the horizon in the Cessna's windscreen tilted crazily. It stabilized briefly at the precariously steep angle, then slipped slowly back in the other direction as the plane righted itself, pulling out of the abrupt turn.

"What the hell do you think you're doing?" David turned furiously toward the blond pilot. The expression in the eyes was hidden behind the dark glasses. But the mouth was a thin, grim line.

"There's been a slight change in plans—and destinations."

"The hell there has! Get this thing back on course for Jerusalem. Right now!"

"Or what? You'll have 'Little Miss Mossad' here shoot me in the back with her toy gun?" Singer laughed sardonically. "And then what? Which one of you skilled pilots will land the plane?"

David exchanged glances with Daniella. They had discussed the advisability beforehand of taking off in Martin's plane, but had rationalized that his concern for his own safety would be a guarantee of theirs. The possibility of a destination other than Jerusalem had not occurred to either. It was obvious, at least for the present, that he had them over a barrel. The choice of a landing place was his.

"Where are you taking us?" It was Daniella who vocalized the question on both their minds.

"You'll know, soon enough. It's only an hour's flight."

The response was terse, the jaw rigidly set. The news of the AWACS survival had really shaken him up, thought David. It confirmed his suspicions that Martin was implicated up to his baby blue eyeballs in the plot to destroy the AWACS, his stake in the outcome only too apparent. Was the CIA behind it, or had Martin been freelancing again, as in the case of Abernathy? David's relief at the news of his brother's safety had not softened his attitude toward his former diplomatic associate. The mole he had been sent here to ferret out was Martin; it was his duty to turn him in. It would eventually be up to a jury of his peers to decide whether any of his cold-blooded acts were warranted.

Trying to deduce for himself what their destination might be, he scrutinized the terrain up ahead, from which the green lushness of the Mediterranean plain was already retreating in favor of desert beiges and cinnamons. The edge of the Negev Desert, unquestionably. The new compass heading read 185 degrees. An hour's flight would take them well beyond the borders of Israel. Depending on the wind, they could be heading for Southern Jordan, a border town in Saudi Arabia, or more likely some spot in Egypt's Sinai Peninsula. There was at least one air base, he knew, built by the Israelis, now operated by the Egyptians.

It figured. The Sinai would put Martin outside of Israeli jurisdiction. It could even save him from arrest. The Egyptians were not likely to take the word of an Israeli and an American against another American, when the latter carried CIA credentials. Martin might very well succeed in turning the tables, having him and Daniella arrested on some trumped-up charge.

He decided to test his theory. "So—big mystery. We're headed for the Sinai, aren't we? I'd always heard the 'Company' had lots of clout in Egypt."

"Bright boy." Martin's expression was unchanged as he continued to stare straight ahead at the approaching desert. "The CIA, as you mention, is in quite solid in certain Egyptian circles. We have some unfinished business to dispose of at this air base in the Sinai. I thought I might drop in to make sure that it's properly concluded."

Whatever business he was referring to sounded thoroughly unsavory to David. They might still be able to head him off. Israeli military jets could turn his small plane back, force him to land in Israel. He retrieved the radio microphone from the floor where it had fallen when Martin had stood the plane on its ear.

"Let's just complete that call to the Mossad, shall we, Daniella? What was that frequency band?"

He dialed in the number she supplied, then flicked on the transmit button. There was no sound in the headphones, not even the click of the transmitter switch. He flicked it several more times, then stared at the radio panel. The power switch was still turned to ON, but the pilot light was unlit.

Singer's sardonic burst of laughter filtered through the headphones. "I took the precaution of removing the fuse," he explained, "while we were pulling a few g's back there. We won't be needing the radio for a while. I'll replace it when we do."

David cursed his own lack of alertness. There was no telling where Martin had stashed the tiny fuse. There was nothing they could do now but go along for the ride. He stared glumly out the front of the airplane at the increasingly desolate landscape, trying to get his bearings. There were few topographic features to go by. A railroad track visible under the right wing ran roughly parallel to their flight path. Off in the distance to their left was a dark expanse that could have been the Dead Sea. But in the haze that clung to the horizon it was difficult to tell.

Daniella tapped him excitedly on the shoulder. "I know where we are!" she cried. "That's my kibbutz down there. See, where the road and railway intersect? That's Sde Boker. It was Ben Gurion's kibbutz, also."

"Ah, yes, your little sojourn in the Negev." Martin, now that he had the upper hand, was becoming somewhat more loquacious. "Did you ever meet the great man in the flesh?"

"Ben Gurion? Hardly. I was only a little girl when he died. We had a special memorial service for him at the kibbutz every year on his birthday. He was, as you say, a great man. The father of his country."

"He was also the father of something else. His country's nuclear weapons program." Martin swept his hand out toward the expanse of desert to the port side of the Cessna. "Just how familiar are you with this Negev Desert of yours? Do you happen to know what's buried under some of those sand dunes out there?"

She frowned. "You're not going to tell me that old wives' tale about atomic bombs hidden there? That rumor has been circulating for years and has been denied by every prime minister since Ben Gurion. I happen to believe they were telling the truth."

"Of course you do." Martin's bland half smile was back. "And they were telling the truth; it just so happens, not the whole truth. Technically, a bomb is not a bomb until fully assembled and ready to be exploded. There are countless disassembled weapons buried down there whose two parts can be coupled together in only a matter of minutes to create multikiloton bombs and warheads. They're stored in lead-lined tunnels dug into the desert floor underneath all that sand. Clever, don't you think? The lead prevents detection from overlying or passing vehicles, and the drifting sands hide any sign of excavation or activity."

Martin pointed to a spot out to the left of the aircraft, near the horizon. "Know what town that is over there?"

Daniella squinted her eyes in the indicated direction. "Dimona, I think."

"Right on," he confirmed. "The ancient biblical city of Dimona. The site chosen by Ben Gurion for his atomic reactor. It's been turning out plutonium to make bombs for almost two decades. That entire area of desert between here and there is restricted to unauthorized traffic, aircraft overflight strictly prohibited. If I were crazy enough to try flying the Cessna through it, we'd be blasted out of the sky before we knew what hit us. There are camouflaged antiaircraft and missile sites over there on continuous alert."

"Why are you telling us all this?" David interjected impatiently. "What's your point? That this Israeli nuclear stockpile, if it exists—which I doubt—somehow justifies the skulduggery you're engaged in? Justifies murder and attempted murder? Even for your warped mind, that's stretching things a bit far."

Martin made an effort to keep his own voice from rising. "It might explain several things to someone who didn't shut his mind to it. Like why the Arabs are so frantic to get their hands on nuclear weapons of their own; the reason the Saudis are bankrolling the Iraq and Pakistan nuclear programs. And the urgency of defusing the situation before it's too late, of getting rid of the present government so that the resettlement of the West Bank can be stopped and a compromise reached on the Palestinian issue before the whole Middle East disappears in a giant mushroom cloud."

David shook his head in disgust. Martin was playing the same old record, the one about the end justifying the means, the last refuge of scoundrels. The CIA's flagrant attempts to depose duly constituted governments whose motivations and objectives they judged to run counter to their own angered and sickened him. The murder of Abernathy and near murder of his brother and other innocents in the unmitigated attack on AWACS could never be justified. He was determined to see that its perpetrators, including whoever was in on this with Martin, were suitably rewarded. He would use his own direct pipeline to the President, if necessary, to do so.

It was an hour to the very minute since their takeoff from Ben Gurion International when Martin finally produced the fuse from the radio and reinserted it. They must be nearing their destination. David squinted into the haze and saw an oddly shaped configuration of runways in the distance, as though someone had scrawled a skewed capital A in the sand with a big stick.

Martin plucked a small manual from the envelope attached to his door and flipped through it until he found what he was looking for. He set the radio dial to the airport tower's frequency and spoke into the microphone in a halting Arabic. It took another half minute before the tower's reply crackled back into their headphones. David looked around at Daniella to see if she had understood.

"We're cleared to land, I think." She looked back at him apprehensively.

"Better stash the hardware," he whispered into her ear. "Somewhere they're not likely to look."

"Why don't you take it?" she whispered back. "They're likely to search an Israeli quite thoroughly, especially if they suspect I'm an agent. But you have diplomatic immunity."

"If they honor it," he acknowledged. "But who knows, once Martin speaks his piece to his CIA affiliates down there." He accepted the tiny weapon from her and slipped it inside the oversized billfold in his inside coat pocket, glancing sideways at Martin to make sure he hadn't noted the transfer.

But the CIA agent was otherwise occupied. His eyes were glued to the scene up ahead as he peered intently down toward the approaching airfield. He appeared to be looking for something—something he wasn't finding, judging by his deepening frown. David followed his gaze, the features of the air base becoming increasingly discernible from their approaching Cessna. The sleek fighters parked along one of the runways were probably MiGs that predated Egypt's break with the USSR.

Martin was indeed "looking for something." The Egyptian interceptors, so neatly arranged along the apron in front of the Quonset hut that served as operations center, should have been airborne by now. They should have already rendezvoused with the single Israeli F-15 that was to have contacted the tower by radio, pretending to escort the hostile fighter back to the base, instead destroying it en route with missiles and rockets. Its pilot must never be allowed to tell his story. By his own timetable for the operation, his F-15 should already be a burned-out hulk somewhere in the shifting sands below. The orders had been explicit, unmistakable. What had gone wrong?

Had he not been quite so intent on the scene below, Martin Singer might have noticed the wispy gray-white contrails high overhead, emanating from a jet aircraft traveling at high speed in the opposite direction. Twin contrails, made by the two engines of a high-performance warplane. A plane whose identity was impossible to discern at so great an altitude.

The Egyptians gazing upward from the airfield below made no move to intercept it. It would have crossed the border into Israel before their outclassed fighters could have drawn abreast of it for a visual identification. Had they been inclined to do so, they would have discovered a wider-bodied variant of the F-15 bearing Israeli markings, its only visible armament the two massive black bombs slung beneath its wings.

El Aurens felt as if he had swallowed a piece of the sun. The searing heat inside him lashed every nerve ending in his body with flaming tongues of pain, pain that had grown more and more acute with every mile flown.

Within the last few minutes, the urge to vomit had become overpowering. He resisted it as long as he could, swallowing the vile taste of it, choking it back until he could do so no longer. The putrid stream poured out of him, splattering against the instrument panel, staining the front of his flying suit. When the retching stopped, he stared down in horror and disbelief. The color of the splotches was a deep crimson. It was at that moment that he knew he was dying.

The realization hit him like the shockwave from a sonic boom. The notion of his own indestructibility had been a foolish fantasy, the charmed life he had led for so long suddenly over. Allah, his protector in all of his prior brushes with death, had abandoned him. Why? How had he fallen from grace?

The vision of the AWACS at the moment of his near collision returned to him, and he saw again the emblem painted on its gleaming white surface, the crossed red swords beneath a green date palm that identified it as a royal Saudi Arabian aircraft. Could that be it, that he had sinned against Islam by attempting to destroy the kindred souls and property of a brother nation, the very nation entrusted with the keeping of the most sacred of Muslim shrines?

Without knowledge of the mechanism, he sensed that the radar plane had been the source of his undoing, the instrument of his destruction. Its image persisted in his memory, glowing mysteriously with a visible aura, like Muhammad and the archangels in the painting that depicted them assisting him on his ascension to Heaven. It was that aura that had somehow infused him, entered his body to set it on fire, the source of the tingling sensation he had felt sweeping over him as he passed through it. Insh'allah. It must have been God's will.

He must dedicate the remainder of his time on earth to one final act of atonement. Somehow, he must hold himself together, cling tenaciously to the life that was ebbing from him much too swiftly, until his singular mission on behalf of Islam had been carried to completion.

He rallied himself, pulling his body partially erect to scour the empty wastes below for some clue to his whereabouts, some man-made scar on the immutable face of the desert that would be registered on his sectional chart of the region. For mile upon mile there had been nothing recognizable. The same bleak, repetitious landscape continued to swim before him, nothing but an endless vista of dunes stretching as far as the eye could see, with only an occasional rocky ridge thrusting up through them to break the monotony, where the relentless desert winds had swept it clean of sand. His eye could detect no sign whatsoever, in God's vast biblical wilderness below, that another creation of his, called man, had ever trod upon it.

He collapsed back into the depths of his foam-padded pilot seat, depleted, his energy spent. The stench of his blood-soaked vomit was like death in his nostrils. He could feel his life slipping away from him, his mission of atonement beginning to subside into a hopeless dream. How much longer could he hold on? The urge to let go was building irresistibly inside him.

With a supreme effort, he forced his bleary eyes to refocus on the small window in the INS panel labeled ETA, reading the number displayed there. He checked it against the time on his watch. Fifteen minutes to go, according to the F-15 inertial navigator, before he would pass over his target. Fifteen more minutes to stay alive; to his rapidly dissipating faculties it took on the dimensions of an eternity. It was hopeless, anyway. The wind was sure to have blown him off course by some amount. Without a checkpoint to locate his position on the chart that lay across his blood-soaked knees, he would never find that target.

His eyes drifted off toward the distant horizon, focusing on that infinity with which he would soon become one. It was then that he saw it, the faint line etched into the undulating surface of the desert. The straight line that nature abhorred. Calling up his last reserve of energy, he raised himself higher in the cockpit to view the part of that line closest to the aircraft. His vision was too blurred to make it out. He fought to clear his eyes, eradicate the uncontrollable moisture that obscured the image of his retina. For one brief moment his clarity of vision returned and in that instant he recognized it. It was a railroad track.

His eyes followed it back toward the horizon, as they did so, picking up the only other man-made thing in the vicinity. Suddenly he knew where he was. He was looking at an airfield, its three runways crisscrossing one another in the shape of a rude triangle.

A surge of adrenaline shot into his veins, counteracting the lassitude that had taken over his body. He found the air base on the sectional chart, eyeballing, with an instinct born of countless hours of pilotage, the heading and distance from that point to his destination. Twenty-two degrees, seventy miles.

He disengaged the autopilot and swung the stick over, kicking in the right rudder. In less than ten minutes he would be there. Ten minutes to go on living so that he could die properly. For his country. For his people. For the greater glory of Allah.

CHAPTER
12

For Technician Fifth Class Schlomo Zukerman, it had been an uneventful day. Not that it was any more so than most days in this isolated desert observation post on the far edge of civilization. It was his job to monitor air traffic in the vicinity of the Dimona restricted zone. It was seldom that there was any traffic to monitor.

He had seen only one blip on his radar screen all morning. A light commercial plane, judging by its low radar reflectivity. It was many miles to the west and no threat at all to the inviolate airspace he was charged with protecting. He had watched its slow progress southward until it disappeared off the edge of his display, into the farther reaches of the desert where the Negev meets the Sinai.

He stretched his back and yawned deeply, an audible groan escaping with the released breath. This was the most difficult part of his assignment, staying awake after the midday meal. The desert heat was beginning to permeate the small room at the base of the radar platform. The day was promising to be a real scorcher for this time of year. The only semblance of air-conditioning was a large fan that did little more than move the heated air about, its steady droning only adding to the other soporific inducements. It was going to be a real fight to avoid drifting off.

At least she wouldn't be there to catch him today if he did nod off. His immediate superior, the only other person assigned to the radar detail, had the day off for her annual physical. It had been a peaceful morning without her there to pull rank or otherwise indulge in her favorite sport, the teasing and tormenting of her pudgy, red-headed inferior whom she outranked by only one grade. Technician Fourth Class Shoshana Liebfried. The bane of his existence; and also the secret object of his erotic, impossible daydreams.

Her hair was red, also. Not the flaming orange of his own, but a much darker auburn. She was always brushing it; it gleamed and sparkled in the sunlight. The unrelenting desert sun, which turned his skin a bright pink while expanding and darkening the baby freckles covering his face and limbs into ugly brown blotches, was much kinder to hers. She had the type of complexion that tanned to a golden brown, like the skin of a chicken turning on a spit over a slow fire. The long, shapely legs projecting from her army issue khaki shorts were bronzed and smooth, not a blemish to be seen from thigh to ankle. In his fantasies that punctuated the tedium of those endless hours ensconced in the radar console, eyes slaved to its untrafficked screen, his own miserable body underwent a magical transformation when those incomparable legs were wrapped around it.

But this afternoon's fantasy, which had started so promising, was going suddenly awry. He had lost control of it; the trim, golden body that he had stripped only moments before of its starched khaki blouse and neatly creased shorts was beginning to swell grotesquely before his very eyes. As he watched helplessly, it became more and more bloated, its flawless skin invaded with unsightly dark blotches. He was hesitant to continue the disrobing process, appalled at what he might discover beneath the sheer, rapidly inflating underpants. What had gone wrong? The explanation, that he had dozed off, occurred to him just before he was jostled rudely into wakefulness by a pair of rough, unsympathetic hands.

"Zukerman, what am I going to do with you?" She stood over him accusingly, arms akimbo. "The minute I turn my back, you let me down. While you were sawing wood, a horde of Syrian bombers could have wiped out the reactor and gotten away scot free. Well, what have you got to say for yourself?"

He stared uncomprehendingly up at her, surprised to see her fully dressed, relieved that the swollen flesh and blotched skin had returned to normal. His eyes swung guiltily to the radar screen; as usual, it was totally vacant of encroaching blips. He looked back into the accusing eyes of his superior number. She seemed to be expecting some explanation.

"I thought you were taking your physical today," he mumbled, as if this somehow excused his lapse.

"They finished with me early. It's a good thing I came back. You might have spent the entire afternoon in slumberland."

"It went well, then?" he asked solicitously. If he could keep her talking about herself, it might get her off his case.

"Exceptionally well. The doctor pronounced me in perfect shape." She emphasized the word "perfect," her hands sliding down her body suggestively, brushing her breasts en route to her thighs. She watched his eyes follow her hands, saw him swallow. Why did she enjoy teasing him so? Well, there was no harm in it. She was feeling expansive, now that she had properly admonished him for his dereliction of duty.

"The doctor was the young, good-looking one. He made me take off all my clothes."

He swallowed again, his eyes remaining glued to the smooth thighs where her hands still rested. "I hate doctors. And physicals."

"Oh?" She sounded surprised. "I rather enjoyed this one. The doctor had such sensitive hands. Strong hands, but gentle." She had a sudden thought. "I'll bet you wouldn't hate being a doctor, examining women with their clothes off."

She saw him color, and it spurred her on. An impulse seized her. "Let's find out. I'd like you to examine me, please, Dr. Zukerman."

Her hands flew to her neck, undoing the buttons of the khaki blouse. She was braless, as always, the impressions of her nipples clearly visible now beneath the square, military pockets of the bulging shirt. It fell open, revealing a perfectly matched pair of bronzed bosoms, a stripe of white across their centers where her brief bikini top had denied access to the desert sun. She watched his eyes widen in fascination, their pupils following every undulation of her dancing breasts as she advanced slowly toward him with an exaggerated wiggle.

She stepped in front of the radar screen, blocking his view of it. "You're supposed to explore me with your hands, Doctor, looking for lumps in the breasts. They must have taught you how in medical school." She smiled encouragement, but he made no response, seemingly frozen into awestruck immobility. Impulsively, she pressed closer, straddling the short legs projecting from the armless swivel chair, then depositing herself on his lap. She reached for one fat, stubby-fingered hand, watching his expression, as his eyes crossed trying to continue focusing on her quivering chest, now a scant foot in front of his face. His eyes seemed to have grown even wider, and there was a strange look about him as his mouth struggled vainly to get something out.

"B-b-b—!"

"Beautiful? Is that what you're trying to say? Yes, I know they are, Doctor." She brought his right hand up to rest on her left breast.

"B-b-b-bandit!" All in one motion, he pulled his hand away, pointed at the radar screen, and lurched up out of the chair. Technician Fourth Class Shoshana Liebfried was deposited unceremoniously onto the floor, her bottom, encased in the trim khaki shorts, making harsh contact with the bare wooden surface. For one dazed moment she remained there. Then, conscious of her loss of dignity, she folded the unbuttoned blouse across her exposed chest and struggled to her feet, her head swiveling toward the radar screen that had precipitated her rude rejection.

Well in from the extremity of the display, already dangerously close to the restricted zone, a faint but still clearly visible blob of light persisted on the phosphorescent screen. As it continued to fade gradually into the background, a fresh blip bloomed on the surface of the cathode-ray tube, closer to its center, establishing a line of motion for the aircraft being illuminated by the radar. Shoshana Liebfried's practiced eye projected its flight path on the face of the display, and she emitted a shrill cry of alarm. The unknown aircraft was making straight for the site of the Dimona nuclear reactor.

When the alarm went off in the officers' quarters of the Sector 4 alert hangar, Lt. Ephraim Spasser was stark naked and flat on his back, deeply engrossed in a paperback translation of an English spy thriller. The protagonist, a Vietnam veteran recruited by the British and American spy agencies for this particular mission, had been just discovered in the act of stealing a prototype of a highly advanced Soviet fighter plane from its secret hangar, under the Russians' very noses. The shrill cry of the alert siren, coinciding almost perfectly with the alarm reverberating through the imaginary hangar in the Russian heartland, gave him quite a start.

It took a moment to dawn on him that he had precisely two minutes to empty his bladder, jump into his flight suit, slide down the slippery fire pole onto the hangar floor, and climb into the cockpit of his F-15 interceptor, whose engines would already be powered up by the crew chief on duty. This was the real thing, not fiction. The paperback flew into the air and landed in the far corner of the room as he exploded off the cot.

Two minutes and ten seconds later the corrugated aluminum sides of the alert hangar quivered violently under the blast from the twin jet engines as the afterburners cut and the F-15 rocketed directly onto the runway and into its takeoff run under full military power. Seconds later it was airborne. The watchful crew chief removed the protective headgear from his ears and glanced at his watch. Not bad. One of their best times ever. Probably all for nothing, though; just another fire drill or false alarm.

In the cockpit of Lieutenant Spasser's rapidly accelerating F-15, the ground control radio voice was telling him otherwise. "Fox-One, this is Fox-Mother. We have an 'unidentified' in the Dimona restricted zone, forty-two miles south southeast of Dimona. Present altitude two-six thousand, speed five-zero-five, heading three-four-zero. Does not respond to radio contact. Your vector is one-five-zero. Repeat, heading one-five-zero. Your ETA is twelve-fifty."

"Roger." Spasser made a rapid correction and pulled out on the command heading. He turned on his radar, read his watch, and went through a quick mental calculation. Four minutes to reach the intercept point and perform the required eyeball identification. In that amount of time, at its present speed, the bogey would reach a point only twelve miles from the reactor site. That was cutting it very, very close. If it turned out to be a hostile, there would be little time for foreplay. He'd better check his armament, have it ready to go.

He flipped up the Master Arm switch on his armament control panel and verified that the ready light came on for each of the four Sidewinder missiles suspended from the Eagle's wing pylons. Then he turned to the gun position on the armament selection switch and fired a test burst from the powerful electric M-61 Gatling gun, which made the whole airplane shake. He was ready for business.

Less than a minute later his radar found its quarry. "Fox-Mother, I have contact. Range twenty-four miles. Closing rate five-eight-zero. Selecting collision steering for minimum intercept time. Over."

"Roger, Fox-One. 'Unidentified' holding previous course, speed, and altitude. We will monitor and advise of any changes."

He focused his attention on the head-up display, a transparent combining glass at eye level on which the steering cues would be projected. A flourescent green circle appeared against the backdrop of empty sky, a bright spot popping up alongside it—the steering dot. He jockeyed the control stick to bring it inside the circular reticle. Keeping it centered here would steer his aircraft to a cutoff point abeam of the other plane, following which he could convert to pursuit steering to bring him in on the intruder's tail, close enough to discern the type of aircraft and markings—if necessary, even the tail number.

He had been through it a hundred times, in drills and practice runs, but only twice when it was for real. On both of those occasions, the intruders had turned out to be commercial aircraft that had strayed from their assigned air lanes through faulty navigation; one a private plane, the other an El Al jetliner on the main run from Cairo to Tel Aviv. He recalled the stricken look on the face of the airliner's captain at the sight of a fully armed F-15 flying close formation off his port wing tip. One waggle of his wings had been sufficient to send the big plane scurrying back toward its proper air lane. For the captain it had meant a severe reprimand and stiff fine. He was unlikely to make the same mistake again.

Two minutes to intercept. He continued to fly the steering dot to circle center, glancing occasionally at the radar display to measure the remaining distance to be covered. At fourteen miles his eye picked up the first wispy traces of condensation from the jet exhaust. Moments later, he established visual contact with its source. It was still only a dot in the sky, too far away to make any assessment of its identity. His eye clung to the spot as the miles between them clicked steadily down. Thirteen . . . twelve . . . eleven . . . ten. Every few seconds, another mile closer.

Now he could perceive that there were double exhausts; the bogey, like his own plane, was powered by twin jet engines. As the range reduced to eight miles, the angular outline of its distinctive tail surface, with its high vertical stabilizer, became discernible. Or rather, stabilizers. There were two of them, jutting up prominently just above the jet exhaust outlets. An unmistakable signature, even at this range. He was tracking another F-15.

"Fox-Mother, I have first visual contact. Range eight miles. The 'unidentified' is an F-15 Eagle. Markings not yet visible. Continuing approach for close-in visual. Over."

"Roger, Fox-One. Its pilot is still not responding. General Davidov, Sector Four Defense Commandant, has been alerted and is standing by, monitoring your progress. Please stay on the air and call out range continuously from this point in. Over."

"Roger, Fox-Mother. Range now five miles. Converting to offset pursuit steering."

Spasser threw a switch on the instrument panel and watched

the steering dot jump out of the circle. He moved the control stick to the left and depressed the left rudder pedal slightly to bring it back. With a gradual banking turn, his F-15 slid into the other's tail cone, until it was trailing the unidentified Eagle, somewhat below and to the left. Advancing the throttle, he crept slowly up on it.

"Range two miles." Now he could see that its fuselage and wings were mostly white, like his own Eagle, except for the dark markings on its nose and vertical stabilizers, which he could not yet make out. The black bulges beneath its wings must be some kind of air-to-ground ordnance; they didn't resemble any air-to-air weapons with which he was familiar. It could very well be one of the "wolfpack" fighters from Tel Nof.

"Range one mile." He began to have misgivings about his earlier diagnosis. There was something very un-Eagle about the lines of this warplane; it looked less sleek, somehow—broader in the beam. Then something clicked in his memory and a fragment of conversation at the last air force party he had attended fell into place. He had overheard two of the pilots from Tel Nof Air Force Base discussing a new version of the Eagle with conformal fuel tanks that were fitted into the fuselage. What were they called? "Fastpaks," that was it. The plane he was trailing must be one of those.

Closer inspection confirmed his conclusion. The symbol painted in black on the massive tail surface was the largest and therefore earliest recognizable marking. The Star of David was unmistakable. The tail number below it was not yet readable. He would have to get much closer. The number would allow Ground Control to identify both the plane and the pilot assigned to it.

He reported back to Ground Control. "I now have positive identification. The bogey is an F-15 with Israeli markings. It looks like a fighter-bomber out of Tel Nof. Range now one-half mile. Continuing to close for tail number inspection. Over."

"Roger, Fox-One. The Commandant wants to know, what is the aircraft's weapons complement? Over."

"Looks like two large bombs, Fox-Mother, one on each wing pylon. No air-to-air armament visible. I'll update you from closer in."

Spasser adjusted the throttle to reduce the overtake rate, zooming slowly in on the strange-looking Eagle's tail. He would have to get within forty or fifty feet of the plane to read its tail number. This was the tricky part of the "visident" maneuver, akin to close-formation flying, except that the unknown aircraft wasn't in on the maneuver, might suddenly alter course at the critical moment. Gingerly, he jockeyed the stick and throttle, until he was sitting just off the other's tail, his rate of closing reduced to zero.

"Fox-Mother, I have the tail number. It's zero-six-eight-seven. Repeat: zero-six-eight-seven. I'm checking the armament."

He let his F-15 sink lower, until he was staring up the under-belly of the aircraft. Two of the biggest black bombs he had ever seen were suspended there. A dyed-in-the-wool fighter pilot, he was not that familiar with bombing ordnance. But from their size, he deduced that they must be the Mark 84 "blockbusters."

"Fox-Mother, I can confirm that the only armament is the two bombs. They look like Mark 84s—two-thousand-pounders."

"Roger, Fox-One. See if you can raise the pilot, get him to alter course, while we get a rundown on the tail number. He's less than five miles from ground zero. Our time is getting very skinny."

Spasser brought his plane back up until it was slightly higher than the other, then edged up alongside it to the point where he could see into the cockpit. The pilot apparently hadn't detected his presence. His head was bowed, and his eyes appeared to be closed, as though he were sleeping. Spasser waggled his wings, trying to attract the other pilot's attention, to no avail. Had his oxygen given out? He could be in a coma—even dead—the plane proceeding on autopilot.

The notion of a ghost plane flying itself, its pilot expired at the controls, sent a shiver along his spine. The pilot's pallid face certainly had the look of death about it. Wait a minute! There was something familiar about that face!

"Fox-Mother! I know this pilot! It's one of our aces, Zev Lieb. I've met him, heard him speak. He appears to be uncon-scious—or worse. I think his plane's on autopilot."

"Roger, Fox-One. We just received confirmation of his iden-tity from Tel Nof." Ground Control's voice seemed to be losing some of its enforced calmness. "We are running out of time line. If he doesn't alter course within the next ten seconds, you have been ordered by the Air Commandant to destroy him."

Spasser gasped. "Destroy him? I can't do that! He's one of ours—a national hero. Have you contacted his wing com-mander? Does he concur in this order?"

"Now hear this, Lieutenant Spasser!" A different voice came

into his headphones, the professional baritone of the ground controller supplanted by a shriller, yet more authoritative voice. "This is Maier Davidov. We can't permit those bombs to get any closer to our Dimona facility. Your orders are to shoot down the intruder immediately. Do I make myself clear?"

Spasser swallowed. "Yes, sir, General." He was sickened by the order, his mind racing to find some alternative, as he slid slowly back behind the intruder's tail to a point where his gun could be safely used. But at this juncture the matter was taken out of his hands.

Without warning, the Strike Eagle centered in his optical sight performed a sudden wingover. Before he could get the pipper aligned for a burst from the gun, the other F-15 was dropping out of the sky in an inverted dive, making directly for the cluster of buildings far below where a railroad and highway intersected in the middle of nowhere. A cluster in which one building, larger and taller than the rest, stood out like a diamond, the sun glinting off its high-domed, multifaceted, geodesic surface.

"Red Alert! Red Alert!" shouted Spasser into the throat mike, his hands and feet acting on their own to emulate the wingover maneuver. "He's diving for the deck! He must have been playing possum. I'm following him down, but he's already out of gun range. Better alert your Hawk missile batteries."

"Use your heat-seekers, Fox-One!" The general's voice sounded even shriller. "He may drop below the Hawk radar horizon before we can get off a shot. Our best chance is a salvo of Sidewinders."

"Roger, General. I'll try it. But the hot desert background may give Sidewinder a problem."

The feeling of weightlessness induced by negative gravity in the protracted dive gave way to lightheadedness as Spasser began his pullout. He leveled off only a few hundred feet above the desert floor, the other F-15 more than a mile ahead of him, racing toward the Dimona complex at top speed. What did Lieb think he was doing? Had he gone berserk? In any event, he had to be stopped. The Hawk missiles hadn't done it—weren't going to do it. He was hugging the ground, where their guidance radar would be unable to pick him up. It was up to Sidewinder.

On the armament control set he selected the two outboard missiles for immediate launch. There would be time for only one salvo. In only ten seconds the renegade F-15 with its brace of blockbusters would be over Dimona. Dropping as low as possible to give the heat-seeking missile sensors a cold sky background for their initial target acquisition, he flew the pipper in his sight onto the still-accelerating Eagle in the center of his windscreen. The first staccato bursts of sound in his headphones turned into steady tones at two distinctly different pitches, confirming that both missiles were locked on and ready for launch. He hit the pickle.

Sidewinders were only half as big as Sparrows, but you could still feel them go. The F-15 bucked as though buffeted by a sudden headwind, and he started a slow turn to avoid overflying the target, pulling a few hundred feet higher for better visibility. Not too high, he told himself. Don't give those Hawks down there a chance to clobber the wrong target.

The twin orange wakes from the Sidewinder missiles were making straight for Lieb's Eagle. They were up to maximum speed already, their overtake rate more than double his aircraft speed. But he had had a big head start. Could they catch him before he released his bombs? Yes, it looked like they were going to do it!

But dropping his bombs had apparently never been part of the renegade pilot's plans. As the heat-seekers zeroed in on his hot tailpipes, his aircraft pitched suddenly over into a steep-angled final dive toward the jewel-like dome that sparkled below. A kamikaze dive, the startled Spasser realized. Lieb was too low; he would never pull out of it. He watched in horrified fascination as his two missiles tried vainly to follow the abrupt maneuver, their infrared sensors disrupted by the horizon line as their target crossed the cold sky background into the realm of hot thermal radiation from the superheated desert sands. They rocketed past the rapidly descending Strike-Eagle, spending their pent-up forces harmlessly in thunderous self-destruction on the dunes below.

But the violence of their impact was nothing compared to the detonation that rocked his plane a moment later. The entire village below appeared to be exploding up to meet him as he banked his quaking Eagle at a precariously steep angle to avoid the approaching debris. For several seconds his plane was shrouded in a dense cloud of smoke and dust, the cockpit dark as night, his visibility totally obscured in all directions. Then he was free of it, his eyes finding the horizon, his reoriented senses communicating the pullout intelligence to the shaky hands and feet at the controls.

The plane righted itself and he stared back over his right shoulder at the scene of devastation in his wake. Dust and debris continued to rain down, the still-billowing smoke borne away by remnants of the fierce winds created by the blast. Where the majestic, multistoried dome had stood only seconds before, there was nothing but rubble.

The destruction was total. David Ben Gurion's least publicized and most controversial bequest to his young country had been removed—erased—by the same American-made bombs intended for the Iraqi nuclear reactor built near the ruins of Babylon, five hundred miles to the east.

Before the blue and white Cessna rolled to a stop in front of the Sinai air base's administration building, David Llewellyn had a chance to size up the welcoming party waiting on the tarmac. Two armed Egyptian soldiers standing at parade rest flanked a uniformed officer and a man in civilian clothes. He started as he recognized the civilian. As if he could ever forget a face like that. What in blazes was he doing here?

Sir Roger Tewkesbury-Cream was impeccably attired in a wrinkleless light tan gabardine suit, looking cool and fresh beside the perspiring officer and his detail. He advanced toward the plane to meet them, the yellowed teeth in the skull-like head exhibited in the inevitable grin. With only a nod to Martin, he extended a bony hand in David's direction.

"Lewellyn, old chap! Fancy this! A second chance meeting in yet another foreign country."

About as chance a meeting as the first one, David surmised, accepting the handshake gingerly, mindful of the crushing force in the frail-looking skeletal extremity. "Another Muslim country, Sir Roger. They seem to be your specialty. What brings you all the way from Riyadh—business or pleasure?"

A hearty laugh rumbled out of the caved-in chest. "Pleasure? Upon my word. Look around you, my dear Llewellyn. Hardly the Ritz Carlton, would you say? But I do, indeed, take pleasure in making new acquaintances, especially among the fairer sex." Sir Roger dipped his ungainly frame in an exaggerated bow toward Daniella. "I don't believe I've had the honor."

Daniella had been regarding the bizarre Englishman in disbelief, her initial revulsion tinged with amusement at the incongruity of his formal speech and immaculate manners. David did the honors, making a mental note that the British agent had nimbly sidestepped the question regarding his business in Egypt.

"Sir Roger Tewksbury-Cream, may I introduce Miss Daniella Zadik, special agent to the Israeli Foreign Minister. Sir Roger," he hastened to add, "is with the British Secret Service."

"And Miss Zadik is with the Mossad." Martin had detached himself from the others to converse briefly with the Egyptian officer, who now approached at his elbow. At the word "Mossad," the officer's eyes seemed to harden. He stared disapprovingly at Daniella.

"Ah, Colonel Said." Sir Roger seized the officer's arm. "Please allow me to present Miss Daniella Zadik, from the Israeli Foreign Minister's office, and Mr. David Llewellyn, special American envoy to Israel. Colonel Said is commander of the Egyptian security forces in this sector."

The colonel's curt military bow was accompanied by a distinct click of his hard leather shoes. His English was heavily accented but passable.

"This is an Egyptian military base. Foreigners are not permitted here unless they file a special clearance and have their visit approved in advanced, as his Lordship and Mr. Singer have done." His gaze shifted from David to Daniella. "Unauthorized individuals entering from Israel must be detained while their papers are processed. You have passports? Visas?"

"I'm afraid not, Colonel," David answered for both of them. "We hadn't exactly planned on landing here. Our flight plan was filed for Jerusalem." He looked sharply at Singer. "But our pilot had other ideas."

The colonel gave him a quizzical look. "No papers. This is most unfortunate."

Sir Roger undertook to intercede on their behalf. "My dear Colonel, I can personally vouch for Mr. Llewellyn. His credentials are beyond question. And I'm certain that an inquiry to the Israeli Foreign Ministry will verify that Miss Zadik—"

The colonel interrupted him with a wave of his hand. "I'm afraid it is not quite as simple as that. I am bound by certain procedures in all such cases. The unauthorized visitors will have to be detained."

Did Singer have the colonel in his pocket? David decided to test the water. "Now look here, Colonel Said! It wasn't our idea to come here. We were en route to Jerusalem when we were abducted by this man, Martin Singer. We were flown here against our will. Formal charges will be filed against him when we return."

"Mr. Singer states that it was the other way around, that it was you who were abducting him when he flew here for sanctuary." The Egyptian colonel gave a sudden, sharp command. The two soldiers sprang toward Llewellyn, pinning his arms to his sides.

Colonel Said patted David's suit coat expertly, then reached into the inside pocket and extracted the small caliber weapon. "So! You were armed and Mr. Singer was not. I am inclined to believe his account rather than yours. I am placing you under immediate arrest while this matter is investigated."

The colonel motioned to the two soldiers, who quickly fell in on either side of them, unslinging their automatic rifles and standing at attention. David felt Daniella tense up, tightening her grip on his arm. It was a scary moment; it must be much worse for her, a solitary Jew suddenly dropped into this alien and hostile Arab enclave, suspected of being a spy in the bargain.

He stared at the officer in astonishment.

"Aren't you overreacting a bit, Colonel? Miss Zadik and I are in the diplomatic service of our two countries, both of which have close ties with the Egyptian government. We have identification to prove it. We have the right to diplomatic immunity. If you lock us up, you'll be violating that right. You could be in serious trouble."

Colonel Said didn't turn a hair. "On the contrary, it is you who are in trouble. You have broken our laws. Entering our country illegally, entering a military post without a clearance, carrying a concealed weapon. These are serious offenses. They are not covered by 'diplomatic immunity.' And I might add——," he turned his gaze on Daniella, a note of disdain on his face, "if the young lady does turn out to be a spy from north of the border, the charges could be even more serious."

Turning on his heel, the colonel gave a sign to his soldiers. David felt the sharp impact of a rifle muzzle in the small of his back. For the moment, it looked like the deck was stacked against him. Martin Singer had set them up very nicely.

He took Daniella's hand and squeezed it to communicate reassurance he didn't quite feel. She squeezed back, managing a weak smile. He knew her too well to imagine that she was concerned for her own safety. She was frantic, he realized, to talk to her headquarters, pass on the information gleaned from the experiences of this frenetic Friday—information that might be invaluable to her government in responding to the challenge facing it.

"We will be allowed to call our offices, inform them of our whereabouts." There was no question mark at the end of her sentence, an assertion of a right so fundamental as to be undeniable. But Colonel Said's answer turned it back into a question.

"In due time, of course."

"What does that mean?"

"We are permitted to hold you incommunicado for forty-eight hours, while our investigation proceeds."

"Forty-eight hours?" Daniella stared at the colonel in shocked disbelief. Llewellyn was beside himself. Sir Roger's gaunt hand clutched his elbow.

"Don't worry, my dear fellow. I'll get word to your embassy. We'll have you both out of here before you can say 'Jack Robinson.'"

At a sharp glance from Colonel Said, the Englishman detached himself, falling in with his CIA opposite number a few paces behind. What was his game? Why was he making such a show of befriending them? Llewellyn had a pretty good idea why the British agent was here. He was obviously wired into the CIA's nefarious operation, the caper that had brought Singer to this remote air base in the Sinai, that had involved the blatant attack on the Saudi AWACS. Was he playing the same game, or a hand of his own?

The door to the administration building was held open by an orderly, who saluted Colonel Said as the prisoners were marched through. It closed immediately behind them, Singer and Sir Roger remaining outside. They've probably got their heads together already, thought David. He'd have given a lot to be able to eavesdrop.

The door had barely closed when Singer grabbed the towering Englishman by his emaciated shoulder blades.

"The Iraqi pilot—what in hell happened to him?" he hissed. "Why weren't my orders carried out?"

"Easy, old boy, easy." Sir Roger extricated himself from the overzealous grasp, straightening the mussed shoulders of his suit coat. "We had everything prepared for him, the welcoming committee primed and ready." He gestured toward the sleek Egyptian interceptors parked on the apron, missiles and rocket clusters slung from launchers beneath their stiletto-shaped bodies. "He simply stood us up. It appears he had other plans."

"What other plans? Where the hell is he?"

The Englishman blinked back at him. "A few minutes shy of landing at his base in Israel, I should imagine. The Egyptians were still waiting for his radio contact when, suddenly, there he was, about six miles up, heading north, hell bent for leather." His eyes tilted skyward. "I should have thought you'd have spotted him. He went by only minutes before you landed."

Singer's face reflected a mixture of fury and disbelief. "Christ! He must have been tipped off, or smelled a rat. But why would he keep going—return to base? The Israelis are sure to be on him, once the attack on AWACS surfaces. He'll be arrested, hanged as a spy. The whole goddam story will come out—our involvement, yours. God! It's a disaster!"

"Quite." Sir Roger's impassive expression reflected his British stoicism. "Good show he botched the job on AWACS. Attempted murder's a far less serious charge, what? You did get word of that, didn't you? Yes, I can see you did."

"It doesn't make sense," Singer continued to ponder. "Why would he fly back here to a hangman's noose?"

"Perhaps he has some escape plan of his own," offered Sir Roger. "Perhaps—"

His words were interrupted by a thunderous rumble from somewhere in the desert reaches behind him. Sir Roger swung around to follow Singer's eyes in the direction of the sound; there was not a cloud to be seen in the sunlit northern sky. The earth tremor that followed removed any question of natural phenomena. It had been a man-made explosion, a very powerful one. Now it was followed by repeated additional blasts, the earth beneath their feet continuing to shake.

"Dimona!" Singer gasped. A plume of black smoke had materialized in the direction of the nuclear site, thrusting ever higher above the desert horizon. He stared at it, transfixed, half expecting it to turn into a giant mushroom cloud.

The man from MI-6 turned back to look into the face of his CIA cohort. "Are you thinking what I'm thinking?"

"The Iraqi pilot!" Singer exploded. "Those goddam Iraqis! The distrustful bastards must have assigned him another target without clueing me in!"

"I'd hardly refer to it as just another target." The Englishman looked back toward the burgeoning inferno. "If he took out the reactor, it's a national disaster for the Israelis. There'll be hell to pay if they connect us with this one. They won't take this lightly. They'll bloody well want our scalps."

Singer was no longer listening. His restless blue eyes were darting about, as they always did when his mind was racing. "'National disaster,'" he repeated softly. "You're right. This could do it. This could be the incident that we've been waiting for, the cause célèbre to bring on a vote of no confidence in the Knesset, a new election, the downfall of the Likud coalition!" His eyes flashed fire into the dull, sunken sockets from which the Englishman regarded him coolly. "Maybe we didn't need the AWACS incident after all! Maybe we're home free!"

"Perhaps we are," nodded Sir Roger. "Still, I should hold off the celebration for the moment. The pilot may have missed, after all. And we'd better hope that he doesn't survive to tell his story. Otherwise, our celebration may take place in the pokey."

"He's a dead man," Singer observed dryly. "If the fighters don't get him, the missiles will. Dimona is about the most heavily defended piece of real estate in the free world. It's remarkable that he got through to drop his bombs."

Sir Roger was unconvinced. "If he did hit their reactor, the Israelis will try to keep him alive. Question him. Expose the guilty parties behind the plot."

"Forget about the pilot, I tell you. Even if he does survive, he doesn't know our names. He can't implicate us in what happened. But there are others who can." Singer's eyes slid sideways in the direction of the operations building, where personnel were spilling out through the door for a view of the billowing smoke in the northern sky.

"Llewellyn? The girl? They know?"

"Not the whole story. But they know enough to put two and two together, ask some embarrassing questions and make some extremely provocative charges in the wrong places."

Sir Roger's mechanical grin was replaced by a scowl that unmasked the full measure of menace in the death's-head face. "We can't permit that to happen."

"I know. Don't worry. I think I have a way to take care of it. But I'll need your help."

A plan had been forming in Singer's mind since the moment the Cessna touched down on the remote desert runway. If it worked out, Llewellyn and Daniella would not get out of the Sinai alive. And the best part was that there would be no troublesome repercussions. All of the blame would fall on the Egyptians.

It was stifling in the tiny room, the heat lag through the upper level of the military barracks bringing the sleeping quarters to peak temperature just when it was time to retire. Stripped to his shorts, David Llewellyn tossed and turned, unable to sleep, the perspiration rolling off him. He had tried vainly to open the single small window above the army cot that occupied most of the floor space; it was stuck tight. The room was like a jail cell. "Not exactly the Ritz," Sir Roger had commented. Even for an Englishman, that was a masterpiece of understatement.

It had been a long and arduous day, a day filled with tension and action and bodily peril. It had taken its toll on him. Exhaustion finally took over. A delicious drowsiness descended on him; he felt himself drifting off.

Slap! Something had been running down his back. His own reflex action, slapping at it, had awakened him. He sat up and switched on the light. There was nothing but moisture on his hand. He explored his back with his other hand. It had probably been nothing but a drop of his own sweat.

He switched off the light and settled back again on the damp mattress. He had to get some sleep; he was too tired to think straight. Tomorrow promised to be equally challenging. He had to find a way to get himself and Daniella out of this; he would need all of his faculties.

Slowly, the drowsiness returned. He was on the verge of dropping off again when he felt something run down his bare arm. Another drop of perspiration. He tried to ignore it. But he couldn't ignore the bite that followed. Ouch! Slap! He hit the light switch again.

Bedbugs! That was the last straw. The bloody corpse of the one that had bit him was stuck to his arm. Revolted, he brushed it off onto the floor. Where there was one there would be others, a whole family. Now sleep was out of the question.

He got to his feet and began to amble about the room, trying to think. Its dimensions were hardly conducive to pacing. Two full strides brought him from one wall to the other. He could understand how people got claustrophobia in a place like this. Knowing that he was a prisoner here was beginning to get to him. He had been locked up in the cramped cubicle since just after the late evening meal, when he and Daniella had been separated and taken to their assigned sleeping quarters. Poor Daniella. She was locked into a cell of her own, somewhere in this same barracks-jailhouse, probably going through a similar form of torture.

But the situation was potentially much more serious for her than for him, much more threatening than mere bedbugs. She could be held indefinitely as an Israeli spy, perhaps even convicted on some trumped-up charge in an Arab-style kangaroo court. He cursed his own stupidity in failing to anticipate Martin's strategy, his abrupt takeover on the flight to Jerusalem that had landed them here, prisoners in this isolated Egyptian pesthole. He had gotten her into this; it was up to him to get her out. They couldn't count on any help from the outside. No one back in Israel even knew they were here, and he had no illusions about Sir Roger keeping his promise to inform the embassy of his whereabouts. The MI-6 man was obviously in cahoots with his CIA "cousin."

The thought of the macabre Englishman reminded him of their recent nocturnal visit to the home of the Saudi prince, and the pressure that had been put on him to spy in the Saudi's behalf. A thoroughly uncomfortable and potentially compromising experience for which he had blamed Abernathy, certain that the embassy intelligence man had set him up. Now it dawned on him that the murdered Cons Op agent had had nothing to do with it. It had not been the unfortunate Abernathy who was collaborating with the Saudi foreign intelligence boss and the MI-6 agent; it had been Singer all along. The still-undercover CIA man had been trying to manipulate his friend and former diplomatic associate by remote control. To what end? What was the Saudi connection?

Whatever Martin's purpose at the time, it had backfired. A chance sighting at the Tel Aviv airport on the day of his return from Riyadh had led to the CIA agent's unmasking. He would have to run now, or face prosecution; and the internment of his principal accusers, held incommunicado with no American or Israeli authorities any the wiser, gave him the perfect opportunity.

Damn! If only they had been able to contact the Mossad before Martin pocketed the fuse from the radio. But he had selfishly given priority to reaching his brother aboard the AWACS. Well, at least he knew that Richy was alive. Now if he could only figure a way out of their own predicament.

He poured himself a glass of water from the pitcher the orderly had brought before he retired. It was lukewarm, but it tasted all right; well water, probably. He forced his tired mind to attack the problem at hand, to pick up the threads of the idea that had started to take shape as he sat across from Daniella in the deserted mess hall, picking at the unappetizing food. They had been under close supervision, two guards standing over them, and though it was unlikely that either understood English, it wouldn't have been smart to chance it. So they had been forced to speak obliquely, yet had been able to convey to each other that they were thinking along the same lines: escape at the first opportunity. And he had implied to her that he had a plan.

"Plan." That was overstating it. All he had was a mechanism, a modus operandi. To flesh that out into a bona fide plan of escape was going to take a great deal of concentrated thought— the kind of concentration of which he doubted his exhausted brain was capable.

The classic white Mercedes convertible was the key. He had spotted it in the base motor pool as they were being marched into the mess hall. Spotted it? You could hardly miss it. It stood out like a rose among thorns, its highly polished surface beaming out at him from the host of drab companions that surrounded it, an assortment of beat-up trucks and jeeps and staff cars in their dingy attire of dark olive camouflage paint. A quick assessment of the motley collection convinced him that there was nothing in the motor pool that could touch the Mercedes, speedwise—nothing that could catch up to it if it had any kind of head start.

He knew a good bit about classic Mercedes autos; he had owned one back in the States. This one was a real collector's item, a vintage car dating from the late thirties. He recognized it as a "Grosser 770," the type of open touring car used by Nazi bigwigs and generals for parades and troop reviews.

What was a car like that doing in a military motor pool? There was no one to ask, and even if there had been, he wouldn't have inquired for fear of drawing attention to his designs on it. He could only speculate that it was the base commander's own vehicle, used perhaps for VIPs on tours of the base or in military inspections. It didn't matter. The important thing was to figure out how to get his hands on it.

His speculations were given further substance on the return trip from the mess hall. A soldier was busily polishing the already spotless auto; he was very likely the commandant's own chauffeur, judging by the tender, loving care he was giving it. As Daniella and he were marched past by their two guards, he saw the soldier climb into the driver's seat and start the engine. There was a throaty roar from the powerhouse beneath the gleaming hood, and the sleek vehicle glided over to the gas pump in the corner of the compound. The last sight David remembered was that of the chauffeur filling the tank of the Mercedes. A heart-warming sight. It meant that the white beauty was refueled and ready to go—for the commanding general or for anyone else who could get it started and drive it out the wide-open motor-pool gate.

Starting it would be no problem, even if the keys were not in the ignition. He had managed to smuggle a knife out of the mess hall, secreted inside his shirt sleeve. As a weapon it was useless, a dull-bladed table knife. But it would suffice for hot-wiring the Mercedes, jumping the ignition and starter wires to turn over the powerful engine. Getting through the main gate might pose some difficulties. But the barriers used on most military posts were pretty flimsy; the powerful car could probably smash its way through.

Once outside the base, there would be no catching it. From his seat in the Cessna the previous afternoon, he had been able to observe the main highway below him, as well as the military road that branched off it and ran for perhaps a dozen miles to the air base. The condition of both roads appeared to be good; like the highway that ran to the Israeli border, the military road was blacktopped and relatively straight. There had been scarcely any traffic on either road. Most important, he had seen only a few small villages between the base and the Israeli border, no military installations nor any major road junctions at which they could be intercepted. Their severest threat would come from the Egyptian border garrison stationed where the main highway crossed into Israel. He would have to rely on his diplomatic credentials to get them through.

But how to escape from this closed-sized bug trap—that was the immediate question. He had tested the door as soon as the escorting soldiers had departed. It wouldn't budge, locked from the outside. Tapping on its surface had revealed no hollow panels that might be broken through. It appeared to be solid hardwood, too thick to penetrate even if he had possessed a suitable tool. Picking the lock or removing the hinge pins was out of the question. Some care and planning had gone into making the cell-like room escapeproof. The lock and the hinges were both on the outside.

The small window was equally unpromising as an escape route. A wooden chair, the single piece of furniture in the room other than the army cot, might be used to break the glass. But then what? The rugged bars outside it looked impenetrable, solidly anchored in the outer wall. The door was his only possible option. He considered using the metal cot against it as a battering ram. It might work, but it would make an ungodly racket. Still, if there was no guard on the premises— When the orderly had brought the water to him a hour or so earlier, there had been no sign of anyone in the corridor outside.

He decided to try it; when would there be a better opportunity? There was no way he was spending another sweltering night among the bedbugs. He turned the cot on its side and folded the legs inward to make it less cumbersome. Then he picked it up off the floor, both arms around its middle. It certainly seemed heavy enough to do the job; it felt like solid iron. He aimed it at the midsection of the door, near the side where the lock would be, rocking the folded cot slowly back and forth in his arms without touching the door, testing the concept. The object was to make the lock fail, break it or spring it. It might just work, if the lock was badly worn or poorly maintained or none too sturdy to begin with. Gradually, he began to lengthen the strokes, until the heavy bed frame was barely missing the door. He took a deep breath. Now!

He threw all his weight behind the blow, bracing himself against the anticipated force of impact with the solid door. But there was virtually no impact at all, only the sharp clang of metal against wood as the latch released with no apparent resistance, the door swinging open. His momentum carried him through the door, and he sprawled headlong on top of the bed frame as it clattered to the floor. Stunned, he lay there for a moment, listening for the sound of footsteps or any other sign of an alarm being raised by the din of his startlingly sudden exit.

There was only silence, the dimly lighted corridor deserted. He extricated himself from the bed frame and got to his feet, staring incredulously at the lock on the back of the door. It was the old-fashioned type, a metal bolt that slid through a solid metal hasp, both parts heavy and rugged. It had not been forced; it had not even been engaged. Someone had left it unlatched.

The dark outline of the army jeep was barely discernible as it coasted noiselessly through the open gate to the motor pool compound, its headlights off, its engine at low idle. It pulled into the first available parking slot and stopped, the engine dying. Without opening the door, its driver threw a leg over the side of the open vehicle and vaulted nimbly to the ground. He ducked his head and crouched silently next to the jeep, listening, his head swiveling slowly about.

"Hist! Over here!" The hoarse whisper came from the shadows behind the low garage. The figure next to the jeep came out of his crouch and moved slowly toward it, quickening his pace as he passed through a shaft of light emanating from a single night bulb above the garage entrance. His two most distinctive features were briefly illuminated before he melted again into the shadows: electric blue eyes set in a face crowned with flaxen hair.

"Mission accomplished?" Martin Singer nodded silently to the whispered question, crouching down next to the other man. "What about yours?"

"Nothing to it, old boy. I simply undid the bolt. I've only just returned." It was too dark to see much more than the outline of the skull head, but Singer could picture the inimitable yellow-toothed grimace that passed for a smile.

"Anyone see you?"

The skull waggled sideways. "There wasn't a soul around. No guards posted. A lamentable lapse in security, I must say." Sir Roger permitted himself a subdued titter.

"Excellent! So our man came through, managed to have the guards pulled off. He was also instructed to make sure they got a good look at the car. Now, if Llewellyn will just take the bait. Was there any sign of activity inside—was he still awake?"

"His light was off," the Englishman volunteered, "but I could hear sounds from inside. He wasn't asleep, at least not yet."

"Good. They'll try it tonight. They're bound to. Llewellyn's not the waiting type, any more than Daniella."

"The insects should persuade them, if nothing else," Sir Roger chuckled. "There's not a hardier breed anywhere in the world. I have the bites to prove it." He scratched absently at his left shoulder. "I say—won't they have a problem getting out the main gate?"

"Not anymore." It was Singer's turn to chuckle. "On the way back in, I dropped a tablet in the guard's coffee while he was examining my pass. He'll wake up tomorrow morning with a king-sized hangover."

"A bit suspicious, what? No guards on duty, Llewellyn's door unlocked."

"They won't even stop to question it. They'll be too busy running." The blond agent yawned. "This could drag on for a while. I could use some sleep. Come get me in the jeep the minute they rip off the Mercedes." He stood up, handing the keys to the other man.

"But I say, hold on! You haven't told me the rest of the plan, what you were doing out there all evening. How is this trap of yours to be sprung? We'll never catch up to them in the jeep; it's far too slow."

Singer laughed softly. "We'll catch up to them, all right. I don't want to go into it, right now. Just take my word for it. I'll fill in the details when we take out after them." He turned to go.

Disappointment gave a peculiarly melancholy look to the browless eyes above the emaciated cheekbones. But Sir Roger knew the CIA man too well to protest further. He shrugged, thrusting the keys to the jeep into his trousers pocket.

"Night-night, then." The grotesque smile returned. "Don't let the bedbugs bite."

As quietly as possible, Llewellyn scooped up the folded metal cot and deposited it back inside the vacated room. He slipped out again immediately, closing the door and resetting the bolt.

Who had unlatched it? His racing mind leapt toward one possible answer. Daniella! She had somehow escaped from her own room, was somewhere outside in the shadows waiting for him. But even as the thought was occurring to him, he dismissed it. If it had been Daniella, she'd have entered his room immediately, seized the moment to conspire on an escape plan. No, she must still be locked away inside a cubicle of her own somewhere inside this same building. There had to be another explanation.

Perhaps the orderly had neglected to set the latch on his departure after bringing the drinking water. But surely he had tested the door after the orderly left—hadn't he? He was almost certain of it, but couldn't remember specifically doing so. No matter. The problem now was to find Daniella, free her, and get going.

He stared down the darkened corridor in the direction he had heard the guard detail move off with Daniella after locking him in his own quarters. The long hallway ran the full length of the single-story building, a dozen or more rooms opening along either side. She must be located well down the corridor; the sound of footsteps had trailed off into the distance, and there had been no audible aftersounds, such as a door opening or closing. Stealthily, he began to move down the dimly lighted hallway toward the other end of the barracks.

But how was he to find her? He couldn't just go knocking on doors. If he raised the wrong party an alarm might be sounded, their escape opportunity blown. A board creaked beneath his feet, bringing him up short. Decrepit old building! It was impossible to move quietly on its loosened floorboards. He stood stock-still, listening for any sign that ears besides his own had picked up the sound.

Apparently another pair had. A faint knocking commenced, somewhere down the corridor. He advanced slowly, one step at a time, listening intently. Knuckles were rapping out a cautious tattoo on the inside of one of the doors. There was a rhythm to it. A long, two shorts; a pause, two longs, two shorts. Then it repeated. Da-dit-dit. Pause. Da-da-dit-dit. International Morse code. D-Z. Daniella Zadik!

To hell with the creaking boards! He abandoned his cautious pace, running toward the sound, until he reached the door from which the knocking emanated.

"Daniella!" His voice was a hoarse whisper.

"In here, David!" Nothing could have sounded better to him than her voice at that moment. He slid the bolt free of its hasp and flung open the door.

"Oh, thank God!" The girl standing in the doorway was the image of the composed Mossad agent no longer. She looked small and frail and helpless, and she fell into his arms with a sob that said it all.

"Oh, David, David." The whispered words exploded out of her, her mouth close to his ear, her breath coming in hot little bursts against his neck. "I was beginning to imagine all sorts of things. As long as we were together, I was all right. But this isolation—this terrible room." He felt a shudder run through her. "I don't think I could stand solitary confinement. I think I'd go crazy!"

"Shh, it's all right now," he comforted, savoring the way she felt in his arms as she pressed her body tightly against his for warmth and reassurance. He wanted to go on holding her, but knew he couldn't afford to. He let her fall back against his arms and kissed her lips tenderly. "It's all right," he repeated. "We're getting out of here. Right now."

Her eyes searched his. "The car—the one near the mess hall? I saw you looking at it. How will you get it started?"

He produced the table knife from his left sleeve. "By jumping the ignition wire with this. In America it's called 'hot-wiring.' It's a trick every streetwise kid picks up."

She looked perplexed. "You were once a car thief?"

"No," he laughed. "But I had high school friends who were. One of them 'borrowed' my car once without the keys. Afterward, he showed me how he did it. It's really quite simple." He took her hand. "Come on. We've got to move!"

They availed themselves of the exit at Daniella's end of the building, avoiding the retracing of steps down the long, creaking hallway. Emerging onto a lighted stoop, they bounded down the few steps and into the shadows behind the barracks. They remained there for a moment, taking stock, their eyes adjusting to the almost total darkness. Nothing seemed to be moving in the vicinity; except for the ubiquitous crickets, there was no sound to break the stillness of the desert night.

David led the way along the back of the barracks, moving in a low crouch, staying in the shadows. They reached the end of the building and paused. A streetlight on the corner illuminated the space between the barracks and the next building along the street leading to the motor pool. The coast appeared to be clear. He turned and whispered in her ear.

"How are you at the fifty-yard dash?"

"Better than I am at the marathon," she whispered back.

"Take a few deep breaths then, and follow me." He sprinted toward the corner of the next building, Daniella following. On his high school track team he had run the distance in less than six seconds; tonight it seemed more like minutes. He reached the cover of the building and threw himself against it, turning to catch her in his arms as she arrived moments later. They knelt down in the shadows, catching their breath, watching for any sign that they'd been seen.

"This is unreal!" he whispered. "No sentries posted at any of the buildings; no one on the streets. It's not like any military base I've ever been on."

"Our guards," she murmured, still panting from the exertion. "I heard them talking at the mess hall, complaining about all the extra duty they'd been assigned lately. It seems there's a shortage of enlisted personnel on the base, something to do with a big war games operation near Suez. Perhaps that explains it."

"Maybe." He sounded unconvinced. His watch read ten minutes after twelve. Lights-out would have been more than two hours ago. But officers and certain other personnel would be exempt, still free to move about. Yet they hadn't seen a soul on the streets so far. It was downright eerie.

The building they were hiding behind was taller than the barracks and not as long. He could see steam pouring from a vent at the opposite end; it was probably the base laundry. There were lights on inside indicating activity, perhaps a night shift. They would have to move carefully.

They crept stealthily along the darkened side of the building away from the street, ducking their heads when they came to one of the lighted windows. The droning of light machinery and sounds of sloshing water reached their ears; it was the laundry, all right. As they neared the end of the building, they were suddenly frozen in their tracks. A door had opened just in front of them. Two men dressed in fatigues came out.

David shrank down into the shadows, pulling Daniella with him. They flattened themselves against the ground. A scant fifty feet ahead, the two men from the laundry detail hadn't seen them. They stood on the steps of the low porch, wiping the sweat off their faces, breathing in the cool night air. They were evidently on a smoking break. One pulled a battered pack out of his breast pocket and offered it to the other. They lit up on a single match.

David held his breath. He and Daniella were not exactly invisible. As soon as the soldiers' eyes adapted to the diminished light, they would be spotted. It was only a matter of seconds before their night vision would take over. Desperately, his eyes swept the immediate vicinity for cover, someplace to crawl into and hide. There was none. They were hung out to dry!

Correction. There was one place to hide; right under the soldiers' noses. Signaling Daniella to follow him, he began to crawl toward the porch on which the men were standing. Careful, now, no sudden movements, stay low. On knees and elbows, he edged forward, commando style, Daniella close behind, emulating his waddling, snakelike motion, her eyes, like his, riveted on the two soldiers.

Fortunately, the pair seemed preoccupied. One had launched into a story of some sort, holding the other's attention. The tempo of his Arabic discourse increased as the two fugitives reached the cover of the porch and pressed themselves against the side of it.

They were still not home free. If either soldier happened to poke his head over the porch railing, they would be discovered.

The story reached its climax, both parties dissolving in laughter. The narrator started a new one. David squeezed Daniella's hand; the waiting seemed interminable. How long did it take one little cigarette to burn down?

His answer came in the form of a glowing cigarette butt that flew by his ear, narrowly missing it. Praises be, the smoking break was over. But the rustling of cellophane from above announced otherwise. Oh no! They were about to light up another!

Before a second match could be struck, the door to the laundry burst open, emitting a bright shaft of light and a torrent of Arabic invective delivered by an authoritative-voiced third party. The door remained open, the illumination spilling forth an almost palpable reminder of their vulnerability. If the newcomer chanced to glance over the porch rail— They pressed their bodies closer to the ground, trying to melt into it.

There was a scuffle of feet, and a second cigarette butt came over the side as the two men on the break scrambled back up the steps and into the building. The door slammed behind them, the vicinity of the porch again plunged into almost total darkness. Lovely, all-concealing darkness.

They were free to move again. Stepping quickly, they skirted the projecting porch and moved immediately back into the protection of the laundry-building wall. They hurried on to the corner of the building, peering cautiously around it.

A beautiful sight greeted their eyes. The motor pool compound was clearly visible, a hundred yards or so farther on. It was dimly illuminated by the light from a solitary fixture above the garage door of the adjacent auto-repair structure. Basking in that light was the white Mercedes, looking powerful and ready and inviting, its gleaming surface beckoning to them. There was not a single sentry to be seen, nor any sign of other base personnel stirring about.

David studied the intervening terrain. With the exception of several small sheds, the space between themselves and the motor pool was wide open. They would be dangerously exposed, but they would have to chance it, using what cover there was to the best advantage. He grasped Daniella's shoulder.

"Let's go!"

They ran to the first shed and dropped down behind it, protected by its shadow as they crawled rapidly to its other end. The second shed was close by. They reached it quickly and disappeared into its shadow, positioning themselves for the next sally. The last shed, the only remaining cover between themselves and their objective, was a good deal farther off. They sprinted to it and fell, panting, into its sheltering darkness.

They took a moment to catch their breath and plan their next move. Their vantage point permitted them to survey the entire breadth of the motor compound from closer up. The gate through the wire mesh fence surrounding it remained open. The whole area still appeared deserted.

It seemed too good to be true. "There could be a sentry posted in the garage," he whispered. "We'll just have to take that chance, work fast, and hope we can get going before he discovers us."

"How can I help?" she asked.

"By staying out of sight. I want you inside the car, lying down, while I get it started. Are you ready?"

"Ready!"

They dashed for the gate and rushed through it to the topless white luxury sedan. He flung open the rear door on the driver's seat and she plunged in, throwing herself prone onto the back seat. Closing the door carefully to muffle the sound, he climbed over the front door without opening it and dropped quickly to the floor. Opening the door would have activated the courtesy light; there was no point in flashing a warning signal that could catch someone's eye.

On his hands and knees he looked for the ignition keyhole on the steering column. The driver's side of the car interior was in shadow from what little light there was issuing from the front of the garage. He couldn't see a thing; he would have to go by feel. His fingers searched for the ignition insert on the right side, just below the steering wheel. He couldn't find it. It had to be there! Or did it? This was a vintage model Mercedes, a model not available in the States. Could the ignition key housing be in the dash?

He ran his fingers over the instrument panel, discovering all manner of indicator windows and switches and dials, but no ignition key block. It had to be one place or the other! His hands flew back to the steering column, continuing their urgent groping. What he wouldn't give for a flashlight! He felt something. Eureka! It was the ignition housing, farther down the cylindrical column, much lower than he had expected.

Pulling the knife from his sleeve, he inserted the edge of its dull blade between the ignition lock bushing and its rotating collar. A deft twist of the knife should pop it loose, exposing the wires that could be jumpered together with the knife to activate the starter. It had worked like a charm on his old Ford, using nothing but a screwdriver.

But the Mercedes proved to be a tougher nut than his Ford, the table knife less effective than a screwdriver. He couldn't seem to get any leverage with it. No matter how he twisted and pried, the collar of the lock failed to budge, the knife blade invariably slipping out of the shallow groove before sufficient force could be applied. Beads of sweat popped out of his forehead. He tried using the rounded end of the knife in a twisting motion, with no better results.

It wasn't going to work! The only alternative was to find the ignition wires where they entered the steering column, scrape off the insulation, and short them together.

He plunged to the floor of the Mercedes, twisting onto his back, his head below the steering wheel. It was a cramped, awkward position, the drive-shaft bulge in the center of the floor thrusting uncomfortably into his spine. His fingers quickly found the point where the wire bundle penetrated the engine compartment bulkhead, and followed the thick strand back to a terminal board mounted on the rear of the instrument panel. Which wires went to the steering column? His further exploration was impeded by a plastic housing beneath the dash panel. Using the knife as a prying tool, he ripped it away.

He followed the wires leading from the terminal board with his fingers, searching for those that entered the base of the plastic channel running up the back of the steering column. There were eight in all. Too many! He was looking for just two, the ignition wires. The others must activate things like lights and turn indicators and windshield wipers. If he connected the wrong ones together, he could short out the entire electrical system. He knew they must be color coded, but it was too dark to read the codes. God! This was maddening! It was like being blind!

The risk be damned; he had to have some light. He reached for the door handle, depressing it silently, until the door unlatched. He opened it a crack. Nothing happened; no courtesy light came on. Damn! Turning the headlights on dim would give him lights on the instrument panel. But it would also advertise their presence to the whole world. Still, he might be forced to do it; he considered it for a moment. No! There was something else he could try first. The glove compartment—a deluxe model like this would surely have a courtesy light there.

He felt for the release catch. With his luck, it would be locked and he would have to force it. It wasn't; it fell open immediately when he depressed the catch. But there was no light inside. His groan of frustration brought Daniella up from the back seat.

"What is it, David?" The note of anxiety in her whisper reflected the strain of having to sit and wait. "What's taking so long?"

"It's this infernal darkness," he muttered. "I'm like a blind man trying to read braille for the first time. I thought there'd be a light in the glove compartment, but there isn't. I'm going to have to risk turning the headlights on dim. You'd better duck your head again."

Not knowing exactly why she did it, Daniella reached across the front seat to the open glove compartment. Her hand explored its dark interior and came out again with something clutched inside it.

"Will these help?" She dropped the jingling contents onto the front seat.

"The keys! They were there all the time! What an idiot I was not to look!"

The first key he tried slid smoothly into the ignition slot. The motor roared into action, its raucous voice startlingly loud in its violation of the silence to which their ears had grown accustomed. Disdaining the headlights, he swung the sleek auto through the car-pool gateway and gunned the powerful engine, heading for the main gate.

From behind the garage a figure stepped out of the shadows. He stared after the plummeting Mercedes for a moment in silence, his hairless head gleaming as it waggled slowly from side to side in the light above the garage.

"By Jove," he intoned, "they're finally off. For a moment there, I was afraid they wouldn't make it."

Sir Roger Tewkesbury-Cream walked briskly to the nearby jeep, climbed in, and roared off to pick up his passenger.

CHAPTER
13

The jeep slowed as it approached the main gate, its motor whining in strident protest as its driver shifted down. Then, perceiving the gate to be ajar and unattended, the driver gunned it again. The stubby vehicle shot through the opening and picked up speed, Sir Roger, behind the wheel, glancing sideways at his companion.

"They've a good five miles head start," he warned.

"At least that much, I'd guess," Singer agreed, with a lack of concern made more obvious by the yawn that accompanied his utterance.

"Perverse bloke," the Englishman muttered under his breath. "Keep me guessing right up to the last moment, he will." Damned if he was going to beg the man.

He concentrated on the driving, the headlights still on dim, marginally adequate to discriminate the stripeless ribbon of blacktop stretching ahead from the encroaching darkness of the moonless landscape engulfing it. Fortunately it was a straight road, and relatively flat. They surmounted the crest of a low rise and saw lights from a moving vehicle far ahead.

"By Jove! There they are!" shouted the man from MI-6. His companion's only response was to reach over and flick the jeep headlights onto full bright, high beam.

"But, I say!" protested the Englishman. "They'll spot our lights, see that they're being chased. They'll rev up all the faster."

"I want them to," Singer replied evenly. "It's part of the plan."

"What else is part of the plan, might I ask?" queried Sir Roger, a note of exasperation evident in his tone. This titillation had gone far enough.

The CIA agent laughed. "What else? A wadi, among other things."

"A—what?"

"A wadi," Singer repeated. "You know—a barranca—a ra-

vine with water running through it. I don't know what you call
them in England. In America they're called gullies."

"Of course I know what a wadi is," the Englishman replied
impatiently. "I was questioning its relevance to the mission at
hand."

"That's right," the American reflected. "You haven't been on
this road before, have you? There's a wadi cutting across the road
about ten miles up ahead. You can't see it until you're right on
top of it. The road simply dips down into it, and there it is,
directly in your path: a streambed filled with jagged chunks of
rock and immense boulders. All traffic has to slow to a snail's
pace and ford the stream, following a narrow channel cleared
through the rocks to reach the road on the other side of the wadi."

"My word, what a bloody nuisance," observed Sir Roger.
"How do the locals put up with it?"

"Used to it, I guess, by now. Any civilized country would
build a bridge over it. The Israelis evidently didn't get around to
it before they pulled out. Anyway, the military traffic to and from
the base moves only in the daytime, when they can see where
they're going. At night it could be a lot more treacherous going,
especially when you're doing a hundred clicks or better, and you
don't know in advance that it's there—and the warning sign by
the sign of the road is missing."

The Englishman suddenly got the picture. "So that's what you
were up to earlier this evening! What a lovely scheme you've
concocted." An appreciative titter escaped through the double
rows of exposed yellowed teeth clenched in the inimitable grin,
the sunken eyes brimming with admiration. He could already
picture the commanding general's prized white Mercedes
smashed to pieces on the giant boulders described by Singer, the
wreckage, including its two passengers, strewn across the riverbed. "And patently, undeniably, an accident; that's the loveliest
part of all." He considered for a moment. "But, I say, supposing
it's not a fatal accident?"

"That's why we're here, to make sure. We're the mop-up
crew." Singer produced the tire iron he had removed from the
jeep's spare tire compartment. "It still has to look like an accident—the sort of wounds that those rocks would inflict on bodies
thrown out of an open car traveling at high speed." He rapped the
blunt end of the heavy iron suggestively against the side of the
jeep.

Sir Roger shuddered, hoping that the mopping up would be

unnecessary. He drove on in silence for another mile, mulling over the situation in his mind. Another disquieting thought occurred to him.

"Llewellyn and the girl flew in with you. Could either of them have noticed the wadi crossing the road from above, be conditioned to look out for it?"

"Possibly." The CIA man considered for a second or two. "But I doubt it. The wadi doesn't show up that well from the air. You'd have to be right on top of it to see it, and it was under my side of the plane when we passed over. Anyway," he continued, "it doesn't matter. Even if they should somehow get through those rocks in one piece, they'll never make it to the main highway. They'll find another little surprise waiting for them farther along the road. And this one's escapeproof, a little booby trap I've arranged for them."

"Booby trap?" the Englishman repeated. "Explosives?"

"Land mines, to be more specific. You see, the entrance to the military road, where it branches off from the main highway, is mined." Having kept his companion in suspense for most of the evening, Singer now warmed to his subject.

"The Egyptians did it, soon after taking control back from the Israelis. In the event of another Arab-Israeli war, their purpose was to deny access to an Israeli armored column trying to move up on the air base. In peacetime, the mined section of the road is closed off by a barricade topped with barbed wire, a clearly marked detour forcing traffic to skirt around it. If war threatened, the barricade would be taken down, the detour and warning signs removed, laying a trap for the Israelis."

Once again Singer uttered a short laugh. "On behalf of the Arabs, I declared war last evening."

"My word, you are a devil! You removed the barricade, all by yourself?"

"Board by board. Had to practically dismantle it by hand, using this tire iron as a wrecking bar." The American rubbed the bottom of his spine ruefully. "The old sacroiliac may never be the same."

"Scylla and Charybdis," mused the Englishman appreciatively. "If one doesn't get them, the other will." He reflected for a moment. "Or perhaps that's an unfortunate analogy. Ulysses did manage to get by the both of them, after all, didn't he? Despite the wrath of the gods who favored Troy."

"Those gods of yours should have taken out some additional

insurance," Singer rejoined. "We won't make the same mistake."
Laying aside the tire iron, he reached beneath the seat and withdrew a long, slender object. In the dim glow from the instrument
panel, Sir Roger could make out the silhouette of a heavy-caliber
automatic rifle, the thick black arc of a high-capacity magazine
projecting beneath its firing chamber, some sort of oversized telescopic sight suspended above.

"This is my insurance policy—a sniper rifle complete with
infrared night sight. If you're 'Ulysses' gets really lucky, gets by
both traps, we'll be right on his heels. We'll take him out with
this, make it look like an accident afterwards."

"Jove!" exclaimed Jolly Roger. "And I thought we Whitehall
types were thorough! It seems you've planned for every contingency."

Singer fell silent. "Contingency" was a word not much in
favor in his vocabulary. It smacked of the unpredictable. And the
unpredictable, by definition, could never be planned for.

"It was too easy, wasn't it?" Alongside Llewellyn in the front
seat of the white convertible sedan, Daniella waited for his reaction.

He nodded in silent concurrence, his eyes straining to see as
far down the road as possible. The powerful motor was wide
open, the headlights on full bright now, switched to the high-
beam position. The threat from behind was over; it was what lay
ahead they had to worry about.

Yes, it had been too easy. Someone had wanted them to take
the car, escape from the base. Someone had gone to a lot of pains
to make it happen that way. The initial exposure to the Mercedes,
two trips past the motor pool to plant the idea in his head. The
door in his detention cell in the prisonlike barracks inexplicably
unbolted from the outside, the lack of guards, the keys to the
Mercedes left in the glove compartment. And the final "coincidence," the sentry asleep at his post at the main gate, enabling
them to open the gate and make good their escape.

Who was behind it all? Did they have a secret friend, an
Israeli undercover agent perhaps, operating on the air base? Or
was it an enemy, with other kinds of plans for them—plans un-
suited to the continual jurisdiction of the Egyptian military authority?

If he knew the "why," it wouldn't be hard to figure out the
"who." There was only one person on the base who fit neatly into

the implacable enemy mold. But that didn't make sense. Why would Martin Singer help them to escape? It was he who had arranged for them to be interned, incommunicado, in this remote spot in the Sinai, allowing him time to make good his own escape from American and Israeli prosecution. Singer had them right where he wanted them, was probably long gone by now for some unknown destination. Or was he? The chilling realization swept over him. He and Daniella, as far as he knew, were the only potential witnesses to Martin's crimes and duplicity. With the two of them out of circulation permanently, there would be no case against him, no need to run.

He could be out there right now, lying in wait for them, somewhere along the road. A roadblock arranged, an ambush. David let up on the gas pedal, watching the speedometer needle drop down from the hundred-plus-kilometer-per-hour clip he had been hitting until it leveled off at eighty. They would have to proceed carefully, be extra vigilant. At any sign of danger—another vehicle appearing in his headlights, an obstruction in the road—he would be prepared to stop before reaching it, turn back if the threat of an armed ambush materialized. Better to return to the Egyptian air base again as prisoners than as corpses.

Daniella, who had been watching to the rear for any sign of pursuit, swung around in her seat at the rapid deceleration. "What is it, David? Did you see something up ahead?"

He shook his head. "Just being careful." Why alarm her prematurely? "There's no one chasing us, no point in taking unnecessary chances on a strange road."

She wasn't to be put off so easily. "You're expecting trouble, aren't you? The Egyptians—you're expecting them to try to intercept us?"

"It's not the Egyptians I'm worried about." He kept his gaze straight ahead, far down the roadway, where the collimated beams from the twin headlights merged into one.

"Martin?" There was a note of disbelief in her voice. "You think Martin helped arrange our escape so he could—" She couldn't bring herself to complete the repugnant thought.

"He certainly has the motive. We seem to be the only ones who have his number. With us out of the way, he's got it made."

"No, David. I can't believe Martin would really ever—" She hesitated, second thoughts seeping in.

"You know him better than I do, I'm sure." The words just came out. He hadn't meant them to sound the way they did, putting her on the defensive for something they both knew was over, a closed chapter. But she didn't choose to take it that way.

"Martin seems so—changed, now. A different person from the one I knew—that either of us knew. More detached than ever, more—unfeeling. But he was always a man with a conscience, a deep, underlying morality. I don't think that part of a person changes. How could such a person commit cold-blooded murder?"

"By persuading himself that his 'cause' is sacrosanct, that it exonerates him from any and all crimes committed in its behalf. The old chestnut about the end justifying the means, for the good of humanity, and all that. You heard how he carried on in the plane coming down here. And don't forget, we've both seen his handiwork up close. Abernathy's blood was very, very cold."

Daniella turned silent, lost in a world of her own. Was she thinking of Martin, he wondered, how things had been when they—? Stop it, he told himself. That was eons ago. B.D., before David. The present was what mattered, and the future. And getting her safely on the roadway.

In his preoccupation, he had been focusing so intently on the roadway up ahead that he had neglected to check the rearview mirror. The two blobs of light reflected in it, catching his eye, sent a shot of adrenaline surging through him. They were being followed! If he could distinguish the two separate headlights, the vehicle must already be close to overtaking them! How had it gotten so near without his seeing it?

He checked the speedometer. No wonder! It was down to seventy. He'd allowed himself to become distracted, had slacked off too much on his own speed.

His foot hammered the gas pedal and the Mercedes shot forward. Daniella came out of her reverie, darting a questioning look toward him.

"Look behind us."

She swung around in her seat, and he could hear her breath suck in. "Oh, David! I should have been watching. It's catching up with us! Can we get away?"

"We'll soon find out." He watched the needle climb past the century mark on the illuminated dial in the dash panel. A hundred and ten . . . a hundred and thirty . . . a hundred and sixty kilometers. They were flying now, devouring the straight, flat, blacktop road as fast as the headlights could illuminate. Except for the assorted rattles and a slight vibration in the steering wheel, the vintage auto took it unfalteringly.

He kept his eyes on the roadway, leaving it up to Daniella to monitor the threat behind them. At this speed, he couldn't afford the distraction of the rearview mirror.

"It's falling back, whatever it is. I don't think it can stay with us." She glanced nervously at the speedometer. "We're going awfully fast. How long can we keep this up?"

"As long as we have to." He reached for her hand. "Don't worry, it's a good car. And a good road."

The image of the portion of the road that lay ahead, as he had glimpsed it from the Cessna the previous day, bolstered his confidence. It had been straight as a string, not a single turn in evidence. He had had an even better view of the main highway as the light plane flew parallel to it for several minutes. Two wide lanes, premium blacktop, with a bright yellow centerline to follow. Once on it, there would be no catching them.

"They've dropped way back," Daniella reported. "I can barely see their headlights now." She was still anxious about their speed. "Shouldn't we slow down a little?"

"Not yet. I want to get as far ahead as—" Something about the view in the headlights arrested him. In the extremity of the beam, there seemed to be an anomaly in the appearance of the black stretch of highway far ahead. Instinctively, he removed his foot from the accelerator. Then he saw what was different about the section of road he was fast approaching. There wasn't any! Less than fifty yards ahead it simply disappeared!

Hitting the brakes, he had a momentary sensation of déjà vu. Another night, half a lifetime ago; college students on a lark between semesters. Another road, an unpaved road in Mexico, straight and flat like this one, except for one spot where it suddenly dropped away, vanishing in front of the driver's eye. An arroyo, invisible until the last second, swallowing the roadway; a streambed littered with huge rocks, illuminated by the headlights, directly in his path.

The brakes locked. Swerving hideously, its tires screaming unmercifully, the Mercedes skidded sideways, on the verge of tipping over. He let up on the brakes and jerked the wheel to the right, turning into the direction of the slide to regain control. The lurching auto tottered precariously, then righted itself, pulling out of the skid. But he had overcompensated. The big auto swung to the right and careened across the road, threatening to bury itself in the sheer bank that had materialized in the headlights. He swung the wheel back the other way.

The heavy sedan spun on the shoulder of the road, its right wheels digging into the soft, sandy surface. It was going to roll! If it did, they had bought it; there was no roll bar in the topless vintage auto! He jerked the wheel back to the right.

For another agonizing moment, the Mercedes did a balancing act, its two left wheels completely off the ground. Its low center of gravity eventually prevailed; it recovered itself, its airborne whitewalls slamming back onto the roadbed. But its headlights, once again aligned with the road, carved a nightmarish sculpture out of the blackness just ahead.

The déjà vu continued, the revisitation now complete. At the foot of the sharp incline where the road dropped into the bottom of the wadi, its blacktopped surface was terminated abruptly by a creek that cut across it. Standing out prominently in the stark illumination of the headlights, the jagged tops of heavy boulders protruded from its shallow waters. The Mercedes was hurtling down toward it, intent on smashing itself and its occupants against the giant rocks.

Riding the brakes again with all his might, he was back in Mexico, his startled companions, so rudely awakened from their back-seat catnaps, still pinned to the floor of the sedan where they had been thrown by his first desperate braking. The heavy Mercedes went into another skid, its tires complaining unrelentingly as it swung slowly around, counterclockwise, executing a complete semicircle. Sliding backwards, he lost his sense of direction, could only keep the brake pedal jammed to the floorboard and hold on. He felt totally helpless. The Mercedes was steering itself; he could no longer control it, his frantic manipulation of the wheel having no effect whatsoever.

Inexplicably, the big sedan began to rotate back in the opposite direction. Its headlights found the road again; then the lethal mass of granite loomed immense and impenetrable a scant few paces ahead as the momentum of the heavy auto continued to hurl them toward it. Above the high-pitched screeching of the tires he heard a competing shriek from the seat beside him as his companion threw one arm across her face in anticipation of the approaching impact.

It never came. The prolonged skid terminated itself, the earsplitting tire noise dying out as abruptly as it had begun. The motor, too, had died, and he found the sudden, almost total silence startling and unbelievable. They were sitting stock-still, not in Mexico, but in the middle of the Sinai Desert, the stars above them fiery bright in the moonless sky, the only sound the faint ripple from the waters now lapping at the front tires of the Mercedes. Waters that also lapped at the nearest of the giant boulders, less than an arm's length beyond the point where those tires had come to rest.

The captain of the guard was not unused to being awakened in the middle of the night. The dubious privilege went with the territory, the hours after dark his special domain. While the protection of Shibh Jazirat Air Base was his responsibility twenty-four hours a day, the daylight periods were generally uneventful. If anything untoward happened, it was likely to happen at night.

Usually, it was something trivial. An AWOL soldier trying to sneak back onto the base, a fight in one of the barracks, petty thievery among the enlisted men. Once the PX had been broken into by a private who was high on hashish. The most serious incident in his twelve months on the base had been a near-fatal stabbing of an officer by a non-com, the victim eventually recovering. But something in the voice of the sergeant of the guard told him this time would be different.

Fully dressed except for his boots, he sat up on the bed and groped for them unsuccessfully beneath it, then gave up and switched on the light, blinking his eyes at the sudden brightness.

"Go ahead, Sergeant; I'm awake now."

"It's the two prisoners, sir—the illegals that Colonel Said ordered interned yesterday. They've escaped!"

The captain of the guard prided himself on his ability to remain calm under stress. There was really nothing to get excited about. As far as he knew, the internees had committed no more serious offense than straying onto a military base without proper clearance.

"Start at the beginning, Sergeant," he instructed.

He laced up his boots, listening to the account of the escape without comment. The sergeant of the guard hurried through it, with a minimum of detail, to give his superior the "big picture" the first time through, as he had been taught; the captain's subsequent probing would flesh out the remainder. At the mention of the getaway in the base commandant's pet Mercedes, the captain stopped lacing and looked up sharply. Allah be merciful! The old man was going to have a conniption!

"We've got to get that car back!" he exploded. "When did all this happen? What steps have you taken to recapture them?"

The sergeant decided to answer the last question first. "I have a staff car with a squad of MPs standing by the motor pool, ready to roll. It requires your approval, sir."

The captain of the guard picked up the phone and dialed the motor pool number. "This is Captain Barrani," he barked. "Get going! After them!"

He slammed the receiver back on the hook. "How big a start do they have?"

The non-com looked uncomfortable. "I'm afraid we don't know, sir. We haven't found anyone who heard or saw the Mercedes leave."

"That's incredible! What about the guards at the gate?"

"Out cold, sir. He claims he was drugged."

"Someone must have seen them!" the captain fumed. "Did you question all the guards?"

"I did, sir. The only clue we have is the time the jeep left. The guard at the BOQ heard it roar by at 13:12, headed for the main gate."

"They stole a jeep, too?" Barrani's eyebrows knitted into a puzzled frown. "Why would they do that?" He checked his watch. "A twenty-minute head start. That staff car will never catch them."

"No, sir, it won't," the sergeant agreed.

"The chopper! We could send the chopper after them!" the captain exclaimed.

"Afraid not, sir. It's still at Cairo, with the general."

There was an awkward silence. The non-com avoided Barrani's eyes, waiting respectfully for his superior to decide what to do.

The momentary indecision in the captain's face was quickly resolved. He swept up his flight jacket and headed for the door. "There's nothing for it. Come along. We'll have to wake up the colonel."

Colonel Said was not nearly as philosophical as the captain of the guard about having his night's repose interrupted. He answered the door wearing silk pajamas and a look that told Barrani his captain's bars were in jeopardy unless there was an awfully good reason for the predawn visitation. Reasoning that the bearer of the bad news would receive the brunt of his superior's displeasure, Barrani ordered the sergeant of the guard to deliver his report firsthand.

As the sergeant hurried through a rerun of his terse summary, the colonel's scowl deepened, his eyes widening in disbelief. At the point where his commanding general's pride and joy vanished through the main gate along with his prisoners, Said's wrath could no longer be contained, the storm breaking indiscriminately over both of his unfortunate inferiors.

The tirade threatened to go on forever, the sergeant and the captain both standing at attention, eyes straight ahead, waiting for the colonel to run out of breath. An unforgivable lapse of security, Said declared hotly. Those responsible would be dealt with summarily; the sentry at the gate would be shot for dereliction of duty. He wound down abruptly, the realization dawning that he, himself, was in big trouble unless the prisoners were apprehended and their precious escape vehicle returned in one piece. The general was due to arrive back from Cairo that very day!

"What are you doing about this?" he demanded, his eyes jumping accusingly from one man to the other. "Why aren't you out there chasing them?"

This was the opening the captain had been waiting for. He quickly explained that the escapees had too big a head start on the soldiers in the staff car already dispatched in pursuit.

"Our only hope of stopping them is the army garrison at the border. An interception party could bottle them up at the other end of the air base access road, before they reach the main highway. It will take a call from you, personally, sir, to the colonel in charge of the border station. I have the number here."

Colonel Said snatched the scrap of paper with the telephone number from the captain's hand and squinted at it, unable to make it out without his reading glasses. The captain, having committed it to memory, recited it for him. "Shall I dial it for you, sir?" With a withering look, the colonel turned on his heel, striding across the darkened room. Signaling to the sergeant to stay put, Captain Barrani followed Said into the bedroom.

It took several minutes to raise anyone at the Egyptian army's border station near Al Qusayman, an interval punctuated by Said's acerbic references to the brother's service's abysmal inefficiency. Barrani said nothing, dividing his time between staring at the ceiling and watching the time flit by on the sweep second hand of his government-issue wristwatch. At last a voice at the other end of the line identified itself as the night duty officer.

"About time!" fumed the colonel. "This is Colonel Said, head of security at Shibh Jazirat Air Base. We have an emergency here. Two important prisoners have just escaped in the base commander's personal limousine and are heading your way. I must speak to your commanding officer immediately."

There was a momentary silence at the other end of the line. "Lieutenant!" shouted the colonel into the receiver. "Are you still there?" He clicked the disconnect bar furiously up and down.

"Yes, sir," the voice came back, "still here, sir. It's just that I hate to awaken Colonel Mitla at this hour. Perhaps it's not necessary. If you'll give me a description of the escaped prisoners and their vehicle, I can alert the border guard to be on the lookout for them."

"I'm afraid that won't do, Lieutenant. There's no guarantee that they'll cross the border at your checkpoint on the main highway." A note of condescension crept into the colonel's voice; the necessity of explaining to an inferior officer was obviously taxing his patience.

"They have also stolen a jeep. They can go cross-country. There are a hundred other places to cross into Israel. You must dispatch a squad of soldiers immediately to intercept them before they can fan out."

"Impossible, sir." There was no hesitation this time. "I couldn't possibly do that without my colonel's concurrence, and I doubt if he would agree anyway."

"Then get your colonel on this line immediately!" Said thundered. "That's an order! There's no time to lose!"

Cursing the delay, Said paced the small bedroom impatiently, the telephone receiver affixed to his ear. The captain of the guard watched the seconds tick by, the white Mercedes and the jeep in his mind's eye racing unimpeded for the Israeli border. They should be just about to the wadi by now; they would have to slow down to ford the stream. But then it would be off to the races again. The wait seemed interminable. But it was actually just under two minutes, he was surprised to note, before the deep voice of the border garrison's commanding officer came on the line.

"This is Mitla. Whom do I have the pleasure of addressing?" His tone clearly conveyed that he found the unaccustomed nocturnal rousting anything but pleasurable.

Colonel Said introduced himself, begrudgingly offering a perfunctory apology before repeating his demand that an interception party be dispatched immediately. Colonel Mitla would not be rushed. To Said's further exasperation he insisted on a full recapitulation of the nature of the emergency, then began asking additional questions.

"There isn't time!" shouted the frustrated security officer. "They're getting away!"

"My dear colonel," the garrison commander replied blandly, "I can't set up a roadblock on the public highway without higher authority. I would need my commanding general's authorization, in writing."

Said's knuckles tightened around the telephone receiver. "My commanding general outranks yours," he remonstrated, "and he has a violent temper. If you disregard this request for assistance, I wouldn't want to be in your shoes. Now hear me carefully. If you act at once, there's no need for a roadblock on the main highway. Send out a squad of men immediately in a lorry, and you can head them off before they reach the highway. I have full jurisdiction over the military road that leads from the main highway to the air base. If it's paper you want, I'll cut an authorization for a roadblock on our road and send it to you first thing tomorrow. But you must act now, while there's still time!"

There was no immediate response, and Said could hear the subdued intermingling of voices in the background. Then Colonel Mitla came back on the line.

"We'll do as you suggest, Colonel Said, but if anything goes wrong it will be on your head. I have taped our full conversation. Now, as regards the action you've requested, I have just ordered a troop carrier dispatched with a detachment of six soldiers. We will be in touch with them by radio. I must have a full description, at once, of the two escape vehicles, the former prisoners, and their identities."

A little pocket of cool, moist air had settled into the hollow of the desert floor, adding its bite to the increasing chill of the desert night. Whether the shiver he felt run through her was attributable to the drop in temperature or a delayed reaction to their near catastrophe, he couldn't tell. His arms tightened around her, and the tremor subsided.

"We're all right, now. It's all right."

"David—how can you say that?" She pulled away from him, squirming around in her seat to look back toward the road above.

"Whoever was chasing us is sure to catch us now. We're trapped here!" She turned back to stare at the hopeless maze of heavy rocks and boulders in the streambed that blocked their further progress.

"Maybe not. There has to be a way to get through. This is the only road to the base. I saw traffic moving on it yesterday."

He pointed off toward the right to an area in the extremity of the headlight beam. "See how the rocks are smaller and scarcer there? It must be the entrance to a channel that's been bulldozed through."

Dubiously, she followed his gaze. "Yes, I think I see where you mean. But it still looks terribly rough. And suppose it doesn't go straight; how will you see to steer in the darkness? If we get stuck in there, we won't have a chance." She looked nervously over her shoulder again, but the crest of the hill where the road descended into the wadi was still free of headlights.

"That's where you come in. You'll be my lookout." He jumped out of his side of the car and came around to open her door.

"I want you up on the hood. Quickly!" He gave her a boost. "Now, sit on the front of the hood, with your feet on the bumper. That's it."

He turned the headlight switch to low beam. "Now, can you see down into the water from there?"

"Yes, but how will you—"

"You'll give me hand signals. It's the way we did it in Mexico."

Her puzzled response was lost in the guttural roar of the classic auto's engine as the starter kicked it over. One of these days, when this was all over, he would have to tell her about that Mexican jaunt, that half-forgotten joyride of many years before that had almost ended in tragedy. An experience that had come back to him so vividly tonight to guide his hand as he relived some of its more harrowing moments on another desert eight thousand miles away.

The Mercedes crept forward, its tires almost immediately inundated up to their hubcaps as he made a gradual turn to the right toward the hoped-for opening in the rock-strewn stream. The heavy auto rocked up and down and sideways as its wheels began to negotiate the jagged surface of the riverbed.

From her perch atop the hood, Daniella stared intently into the murky water. Her lips were moving, the engine noise drowning out the words. But he had no trouble reading her hands. "Keep coming," said her right hand. "A little more to the right," said her left. "Now back toward the left, again. Slow down!"

Encountering a particularly rough stretch, the Mercedes bounced violently, bottoming out on its vintage shocks. Daniella was forced to hold on tightly to the hood ornament to avoid being thrown off.

He braked and almost came to a standstill. She motioned him forward again. They were nearly to the middle of the wash; the water was getting deeper, almost up to the top of the front bumper now. It was becoming increasingly difficult for her to see the bottom. A large boulder, its crest just beneath the water's surface, loomed almost directly ahead, and she waved frantically for him to stop until she could decide which side of it to steer toward.

He slowed to a snail's pace, reluctant to come to a complete stop for fear of stalling, aware that the water had risen dangerously close to the auto's low-slung engine. At the last second she saw that the channel veered back to the right again and signaled a sharp turn in that direction. The left fender scraped against the giant rock with a nerve-rasping noise that could be heard above the sound of the engine. Then they had cleared it and Daniella was motioning him back in the opposite direction, where the tortuous channel snaked back to the left again.

He noted with relief that the water was getting shallower; they were beginning to climb out the other side of the wash. The bottom seemed smoother now, and Daniella signaled full ahead. He eased down on the gas pedal, and the big auto picked up its pace a notch or two. They were making straight for the point on the opposite shore where the blacktop surface emerged from the water. Another thirty feet. Another twenty.

Without warning, the front wheel dropped away, followed instantly by a hideous jarring of metal striking rock. Daniella had failed to see the deep hole and was taken by surprise. She was almost flung from her perch, but somehow managed to cling to it. The Mercedes shuddered and threatened to come to a dead stop. But the momentum of the heavy car carried its front wheel out of the hole, and he goosed the accelerator to help get the rear wheel through. There was another violent lurch to the right and a second jarring impact as the right rear dropped into the same recess.

This time Daniella was not so fortunate. She was flung unceremoniously from her seat on the hood, somersaulting over the right front fender of the struggling auto. In a pure reflex action, he hit the brakes. They had no effect at all, totally washed out by the sloshing waters. The ponderous auto barged ahead another few feet before halting dead in the water.

"Daniella!" he shouted, preparing to go to her rescue. But a sputtering Daniella resurfaced immediately, struggling to her feet in water that reached just above her knees.

"I'm all right," she called reassuringly, shaking the water out of her ears. "Keep going!"

She stepped onto the bumper, preparing to resume her vigil on the front of the hood. As she started to climb back on top, something caught her eye.

"David! Lights! I can see headlights! They're coming!"

She scrambled onto the hood, and he got the big car moving again. It crawled forward, buffeted by the rough stream bottom, its progress agonizingly slow. She waved him straight ahead, signaling for more speed. Warily, he complied. The terrain beneath the wheels seemed to be smoothing out now, the bouncing no longer as violent. He edged the accelerator down a bit more.

Suddenly, the front wheels of the Mercedes were on dry land. They had done it! They were through the wash and out the other side.

Daniella was just in the act of stepping down from the front bumper when the twin shafts of light exploded over the horizon on the opposite side of the wadi. He held the door open for her, revving the engine as she vaulted into the front seat. Seconds later, they were impaled in the blinding beam of the other vehicle's headlights as the Mercedes headed up the embankment, gathering speed.

He heard the loud report almost simultaneously with a sharp clang of a bullet striking the body of the vintage car. "Down!" he shouted, his right hand grasping her shoulder and thrusting her forward. A thunderous burst of shots followed in rapid succession, beating out a metallic tattoo on the backside of the accelerating Grosser 770. But the half-century-old armor plate forged to its sides for the protection of some high Nazi official or Wehrmacht general proved as impregnable as ever. And then they shot over the crest of the rise and into the protective darkness of the moonless desert night.

● ● ●

"I couldn't have missed! I had the gas tank dead in the sights!" Martin Singer stared in disbelief toward the far bank of the wadi, where a hoary cloud of exhaust gases still hung in the jeep's spotlight, the only remaining trace of the white Mercedes.

"You didn't miss, old boy." A twinkle escaped from the deep eye sockets above the gaunt cheekbones to augment Sir Roger's painted-on grimace. His CIA associate's preparation had evidently not been quite as thorough as advertised. "You simply aimed at the wrong spot."

"What's that supposed to mean?" Singer lowered the smoking AK-47 and glared through the fumes at the Englishman. "Where should I have aimed?"

The MI-6 man wrinkled his nose at the acrid odor and waved away the smoke. "At their tires, I should have thought. Or perhaps at their heads."

The American agent still didn't get the drift, and was in no mood to be toyed with. These damned Brits certainly liked to beat around the bush. "What are you getting at?" he snapped.

"Not much of a vintage auto buff, are we?" Sir Roger couldn't resist a restrained chuckle. "The purloined Mercedes happens to be a 'Grosser 770,' one of only a handful that survived its former masters when the roof fell in on the Nazis. Be interesting to know how one got all the way down here to Egypt," he digressed.

The Englishman was clearly enjoying himself at the other's expense. Singer's patience was wearing thin. Sir Roger caught the dangerous glint in his eye and got quickly to the point.

"These special cars were built in the Stuttgart factory to Wehrmacht specifications. They were used by field marshals, SS generals, high party officials. Hitler, himself, had several at his disposal."

"Armor!" exclaimed Singer.

"Armor," echoed his companion. "Half-inch-thick steel plate, all the way around. Windup windows of bulletproof glass. The Mercedes has probably saved a few Nazi necks in its time."

"And a couple of others, just now," Singer observed dryly. "But not for long." He vaulted from the jeep and came around to the driver's side.

"Slide over. I'll drive us across. I know where the channel is. You can operate the spotlight."

Sir Roger hastily complied, gazing unappetizingly at the murky waters from which the menacing rocks projected. He was relieved; he hadn't relished trying to steer a course through its

unmarked reaches. He lowered the jeep's spotlight to the point
where it just grazed the front of the short hood, its beam penetrating the surface of the water.

The four-wheel-drive vehicle lurched forward, plunging into
the wash. It bounced around like a toy on the rough bottom, the
Englishman forced to hold on with both hands to avoid becoming
airborne. Singer drove like a madman, head down, eyes peering
intently into the water, swinging the wheel first one way, then the
other.

"I still don't believe it," he muttered. "How did they get
through this in the dark without the channel markers? How did
they avoid piling up on the rocks to begin with? They had to be
doing well over a hundred, running away from us!"

A sudden severe bump lifted his companion completely off the
seat; he fell back into it with a jolt. Singer seemed not to notice,
maintaining his breakneck speed.

"I say—what's the bloody hurry?" protested the Englishman.
"They may have escaped Scylla, but Charybdis is still waiting for
them. And from what you've told me, they jolly well won't be
able to drive away from that one, much less walk."

"I want to be there," the American responded through
clenched teeth, as the jeep reached smoother terrain and began its
climb out of the other side of the wash. "Close enough to see it
happen—to make sure. When they set off that mine field, it'll go
up like the Fourth of July, the biggest fireworks show this side of
Disneyland. I don't intend to miss it."

As they emerged from the shallow water, the jeep jerked to a
halt. "You drive," directed the CIA man, vaulting over the
driver's door and sprinting around to the other side. His companion slid over.

"Floor it!" prompted the American, jumping aboard. The
stubby vehicle seemed to shake itself for a moment like a wet dog
before it sprang forward, racing up the embankment. As they
reached the crest, they were greeted by a strange half light. The
moon had finally risen; the macadam road trailed off toward the
horizon, an ebony thread stretched taut across the moon-drenched
dunes of the Sinai Desert.

"You won't be needing these," Singer observed, reaching toward the dash panel. "From here on the road is straight and flat."
He switched off the headlights, and the twin shafts of yellow
dissolved into the soft silver of the moonlit background.

Singer lapsed into silence, staring straight ahead toward th dimly perceivable line that separated sky from desert. No sign of their headlights, yet. They must be traveling very fast. That was good; they would hit the mine field going full tilt. They had been lucky to survive the wadi. That kind of dumb luck didn't figure to happen twice. But just in case—

The high-pitched whine of the jeep's motor straining toward its maximum speed all but drowned out the sound of a fresh cartridge clip snapping into place on the automatic rifle in the CIA man's hands.

Llewellyn fumbled with the heater switch, clicking it repeatedly off and on. The wide-open engine of the powerful Mercedes must be generating plenty of heat. But none of it was coming through the air vents below the dash. The heater was probably as old as the car itself. It had apparently not received the same tender, loving care.

He was worried about his passenger. Her unscheduled early morning dip in the stream had left her chilled to the bone. He had wrapped her in his suit jacket after persuading her to remove the drenched top to her own suit and the blouse beneath. There hadn't been much else he could do. Her bare feet, freed from her wet shoes and hose, were tucked beneath her. His pocket handkerchief encased her damp, disheveled coiffure.

A sneezing spell engulfed her, and he slowed the big, open car to reduce the buffeting from the cold night air. He had already wound up the side windows as high as they could go, but the chill air continued to pour in from above.

"No, David," she protested, "you don't have to slow down. I'll be all right. I'm warmer now."

She clung tightly to him, her chilled body pressing against his, needing its reassuring firmness as much as its warmth. The episode at the wadi, culminating in a hail of bullets from the chase vehicle that had suddenly materialized to capture them in its blinding spotlight, had taken its toll on her. She had never been shot at before; her first experience to automatic weapon fire at close range had been terrifying.

Worst of all was the suspicion, gnawing away at her stomach, that had now become a certainty. Their invisible assailant, the unknown enemy lurking in their wake, the operator of the fearsome automatic weapon intended to snuff out their lives was none other than her former lover. She felt this, rather than knew it; she had felt it back there, staring into the blinding light that prevented her from identifying the man behind the weapon, when his face had flashed into her head.

She opened her eyes and looked up into the face of the man she now loved, his features only dimly perceived in the wan light of the newly risen half moon. It was like a caricature by a skilled and perceptive artist that captures the essence of a face with a few simple lines. They were strong lines, intelligence conveyed by the brush strokes that defined the eyes and long, straight nose and high forehead, the prominent chin and set of the jaw reflecting an inner vigor and determination. She marveled at the resourcefulness he had shown, the coolness he had displayed under fire. He would get them through this, out of this nightmare—if anybody could.

Llewellyn sensed her need for reassurance. He squeezed her hand tightly. "There's no sign of them back there, no headlights. I think we've left them behind."

Her hand escaped from beneath his, moving up his forearm, sliding inside his unbuttoned shirtsleeve to explore his biceps, her fingertips caressing his sturdy musculature.

"David," she murmured, savoring the name as she pronounced it. "Thank you for my life, David."

"You helped," he reminded her. "Or we'd never have made it across the wadi. Anyway, we should probably both be thanking those Bavarians for building this car like a tank. Those bullets back there definitely had our names on them."

In his own mind, it was the Mercedes that was the real hero. The performance of the magnificent relic was the only thing that had saved them so far, their only chance of continuing to outstrip the forces bent on their destruction. Its reassuring voice—the smoothly purring engine beneath its elongated hood—gave him supreme confidence. He suddenly realized that he had begun to think of it no longer as a thing but as a person, an individual with its own character traits and personality. It had style, it had verve, it had tenacity and dogged determination. It was more than a match for whoever or whatever was chasing them.

"We're safe now," he said. "They can't catch us now. We're only minutes from the highway to Be'er Sheva."

Her eyes said how desperately she wanted to believe him, but a shadow of doubt still clouded her face.

"You'll see," he continued. "In another half hour you'll be back in your own country."

Far across the sandy expanse to their right, a faint light caught his eye, flaring suddenly, then just as abruptly extinguished. It came back again, disappeared, and returned once again, playing hide and seek with him like some kind of desert will-o'-the-wisp.

Another light began winking at him from a different spot, and he felt some of his pent-up tension begin to drain away as it dawned on him what he was seeing. The mysterious lights were the headlights of traffic on the Be'er Sheva-Ismailia highway bearing in from the right, the blinking due to their periodic eclipsing by intervening sand dunes. They must be very close to joining up with it!

Drawing ever nearer, the scattering of headlights to his right grew stronger and steadier. There was not an abundance of vehicles on the highway, only a few isolated travelers at this hour. But the signs of life outside the Egyptian military compound gave him a warm feeling. It was like coming back to earth from a hostile, alien world on another planet. He squeezed Daniella's hand and motioned with his head.

"Look over there, off to the right."

She lifted her head from his shoulder and turned to look. "David! It's the highway, isn't it? Oh, it looks—so good!"

"We'll soon be on it. The junction has to be just ahead." He began to ease off on the accelerator in preparation for the transition, his eyes straining for some sign of the intersection in the wanly lit landscape beyond the range of his headlights.

That section of landscape was abruptly flooded with illumination. Twin shafts of light swept across their path as a southbound vehicle swung off the main highway and onto the military road.

"Oh, oh. Trouble!" David warned, immediately killing his lights and reducing his speed still further. But he wasn't quick enough. The driver had apparently seen their lights. The other vehicle swung across the road into his lane, blinking its headlights on and off in an unmistakable warning. It was a big mother, whatever it was; it had running lights on both sides and on top, like a land cruiser or semitrailer.

He felt Daniella's body go rigid. "Oh, David! What is it?"

"I'm not sure. Let's find out." It had already spotted them; there was nothing to lose. He flicked the headlights back on, continuing to slow down.

As the high beams flashed on, the steep sides and sharp corners of an armored troop transport stood out in stark silhouette. "Soldiers!" he gasped, his worst fears realized. The Egyptian air base must have discovered their absence and alerted the border guard. An armed patrol had been sent to intercept them.

His first reaction was to turn and run. As he hit the brakes, the army truck slowed and began to turn itself broadside in an effort to block the road, its headlights sweeping out a broad arc as they swung across the terrain to the left side of the roadway.

The events of the next few moments occurred so rapidly, there was scarcely time to think. Framed in the other vehicle's headlights, he saw the heavily rutted detour road running alongside the blacktop. He made his decision quickly, swinging the wheel to the left and gunning the big car's engine. The next instant the Mercedes was rocked by a gigantic explosion, its windshield erupting with a blinding flash of light as the army vehicle appeared to lift off the ground momentarily, then settle back again, engulfed in flames.

"Oh, my God!" said a voice that didn't sound like his but must have been. Somehow he held the quaking auto on the dirt road, thankful for the deep grooves that helped keep the wheels from straying. They shot by the furiously burning truck, the heat blast on the right side of the Mercedes so intense that it drove his companion onto the floor. And then they were past it and swerving back onto the blacktop and approaching a stop sign that marked the junction with the highway leading north to Israel.

Daniella pulled herself up slowly from the floor of the Mercedes, looking back in shocked disbelief toward the burning wreck. "Oh, how horrible! The soldiers inside—they must all be dead!" None of the doors appeared to be open; there was no sign of survivors. "What was it, David? What made it explode like that?"

"Land mines. That part of the road must have been mined. Someone forgot to tell them, I guess." The same one who forgot to tell us, he added to himself. Someone who masterminded this night's sequence of events, who had intended that it would be a white Mercedes burning back there, not an Egyptian army truck. Someone who was still following them, probably not far behind; someone with CIA credentials. Someone named Martin Singer.

There were no other vehicles in sight. He rolled through the arterial stop and turned left onto the smooth macadam of the superhighway, lining up with its bright yellow center stripe, pushing the accelerator toward the floor.

Timing. It was all timing. And luck. He looked at his watch. It was almost an hour since they had escaped through the gate of the Egyptian air base. If they had arrived in the Mercedes just one minute earlier, the charred bodies reposing at the terminus of the military road would have been theirs.

"Pity!" Sir Roger eased off on the accelerator as both men continued to stare at the brilliantly burning pyre a mile up ahead that had erupted before their eyes only seconds before. "That Llewellyn seemed a sterling chap, and the girl was a real beauty. Still, we had no choice, had we?"

His companion made no immediate response.

"It's a pity we couldn't have turned him," the Englishman continued, "recruited him to our side, as you had hoped. Prince Turki made a good job of it. I was sure we had Llewellyn leaning in the right direction."

"We'd never have turned him," Singer replied laconically. "I wasn't sure of that until about two hours ago." He reached inside his jacket pocket.

"This came for you. I found it when I returned to the barracks for my nap. I took the liberty of reading it."

He tossed the crumpled envelope to the other man. Sir Roger smoothed it out as best he could with his nondriving hand, extracting the message from the envelope. He squinted his eyes. It was a cablegram, in code. There was insufficient light to make it out. He looked back at his passenger questioningly.

"Llewellyn was a trained counterintelligence agent. He was sent here to find the source of the top secret leaks at the embassy."

"Good Lord!" The Englishman's mouth fell open. "He was after you all the time, then!"

"Yes. So, as you say, we had no choice." The CIA man remained staring at the eerie spectacle directly ahead, like a man in a trance, flickering pinpoints of fire reflected in the glazed eyes. Then he turned his head away. "It's finished," he commented in a flat voice, devoid of emotion. "Now we can get back to work."

"Quite. But I say—won't there be repercussions? When the bodies are found, they may suspect—"

"Not if we put back the barrier the way it was," his partner cut in, "and replace the detour signs. It will look like they strayed off the dirt road in the dark, somehow got back onto the paved road, and triggered one of the mines. The Egyptians will be blamed for mining an accessible road in peacetime without taking proper precautions."

"If you say so." The Englishman still sounded doubtful. "It's Colonel Said I'm worried about. If he finds out that we—"

A restraining hand on his arm arrested him in midsentence. Singer was staring down the road, beyond the burning vehicle, where headlights were visible moving away from them toward the junction with the main highway.

"It's them!" the CIA man gasped. "They're getting away! After them!"

The Englishman's face was a picture of confusion. "How can it be?" he protested, his eyes traveling back and forth from the headlights to the flaming wreckage. "They're trapped in the burning Mercedes. They're dead!"

"That's not the Mercedes, you fool! It's some kind of army jeep that stumbled in here, can't you see?" Singer was rummaging about on the jeep floor for his weapon. "Get moving! We can still catch them!"

He came up with the powerful automatic rifle equipped with its telescopic night sight. "I'll go for their tires this time. If we can stop the car, they're as good as dead."

Somewhat uncertainly, Sir Roger pushed down on the gas pedal. "How shall I get around that burning hulk? There may be other mines in the vicinity." They were bearing down rapidly on the still furiously involved remains of the troop transport.

"Don't you see the detour road?" Singer snapped back impatiently. He was preoccupied in drawing a bead on the Mercedes as it slowed to turn onto the main highway, becoming an almost stationary target. "Just get on that dirt road and stay on it!"

"Where?" demanded Sir Roger urgently. "Which side?"

The American's answer never registered. The driver's attention was distracted by a grotesque figure that suddenly loomed in his headlights, desperately waving his arms for assistance. He had stumbled directly into the path of the jeep, his soldier's uniform engulfed in flames, his face a pitifully charred mask.

There wasn't time to stop. The Englishman's reflex was typical of anyone trained to drive on the left side of the road, accustomed to having the open lane to his right. He spun the wheel to the right, narrowly missing the pathetic soldier, the jeep careening onto the right shoulder of the paved road.

"No!" shouted Singer, gesturing frantically. "Left, I told you! Stay left!"

Sir Roger swung the steering wheel back again. But the jeep failed to respond immediately, its right wheels imbedded in the soft sand of the shoulder, starting a skid. The burning truck was now directly in the jeep's path, extending across the entire roadway; the Englishman saw that it was too late to pass it on the left. His only chance of avoiding the impending collision was to turn out of the skid to the right, remaining on the shoulder. He took it.

The jeep pulled out of its skid and shot forward, passing so close to the flaming wreck that he could feel its blistering heat on his face and arms. As he maneuvered the speeding vehicle off the shoulder and back across the macadam surface toward the safety of the unpaved road running alongside it, he felt a sudden buildup of pressure on his eardrums. A split second later, the pressure was so excruciating he felt that his head would burst open. His lungs fought for air. It was the last breath he would breathe.

The jeep leaped into the air as though being driven up an invisible ramp, the roadbed beneath it dissolving into a black cloud of finely pulverized asphalt. Its doors exploded outward; torn from their hinges by the force of the blast, they began a desultory windmilling back toward the ground. As the jeep somersaulted through the air, its wheels detached themselves, one by one, flying off at crazy angles, one with an unblown tire bouncing on down the road another fifty meters, like something still alive, rolling off into the sand.

The bodies of the two occupants didn't carry nearly as far; dead weight doesn't travel well. They fell to earth quite close to the carcass of the Egyptian Air Force jeep, where they were discovered only minutes later by a passing truck driver from the main highway, who had parked his rig and run across the sand to investigate the fire.

It gave him quite a start when he stumbled onto them. One of the bodies had come to rest on its back, the grinning face of the hairless head pointing upward, toward the night sky. In the subdued light thrown by the still-flickering flames from the burnedout truck, it bore an uncanny resemblance to a human skull.

CHAPTER 14

"REBUILT IRAQI A-BOMB SITE OBLITERATED!" screamed the two-inch headlines. The English language newspaper was propped on the nightstand where he couldn't miss it. David Llewellyn sat up in bed and rubbed the sleep from his eyes, blinking at the strange surroundings. Then he remembered. It was Daniella's flat in Jerusalem. They had come directly here to crash in the early morning, just as the city was waking up.

The rattle of dishes from the kitchen told him she must be in there, preparing breakfast, no doubt. Or perhaps dinner; it must be late in the day. Hungrier for news than for food, he snatched up the paper, the electrifying caption of the lead article catching his eye: "OUTLAWED RED WARHEADS NUKE TEN IN FATAL AMBUSH!"

What in the world? His eyes devoured the columns of newsprint, which included an eyewitness account of the Osirak engagement by a Col. Moshe Eitan, the sole survivor of the strike force he had commanded. Sole survivor! It was incredible! The ten other fliers in the attacking squadron had been lost, along with their specially rigged Eagle fighterbombers, destroyed by some fantastic new Soviet missile that defied all attempts to outmaneuver or evade it. A missile which, according to the astonished commander, employed a nuclear warhead that had literally vaporized his squadron's aircraft. Yet that same Colonel Eitan had somehow managed to prevail, to wipe out the Iraqi atomic facility with a single secret weapon of his own, an air-launched missile of some sort that was only sketchily described.

The newsprint blurred as the enormity of the implications dawned on him. The first peacetime use of nuclear weapons! Small tactical warheads, to be sure; nonstrategic warheads. But what could the Russians be thinking, to deploy such weapons to an Arab country? It was an unprecedented escalation of the cold war.

He flipped to the next page. The attack on the Saudi AWACS —would there be any mention of it? Singer had contended that the attack was the handiwork of the Israelis, to prevent the radar plane from detecting their strike force en route to Iraq and spreading the alarm. There was no hint of this in the front page articles. Pages two and three were mostly filled with photos; Eitan at a news conference, Eitan beside his Strike Eagle fighter-bomber, an artist's concept of the new Soviet supermissile as described by Eitan.

On the bottom of page three, all but buried, he found a short item under the caption "SAUDIS REPORT ATTACK ON AWACS." He scanned it quickly; there wasn't that much meat in it. A Reuters dispatch reported that an AWACS aircraft on patrol north of Riyadh had come under fire from a mystery aircraft deep inside Saudi Arabian airspace, which had launched two missiles toward it. Neither missile had found the mark, but the AWACS had been damaged during evasive maneuvers and forced to return to base. There were no serious injuries among the crew members, who reported no prior warning from the aircraft, which they identified as an American-made F-15 fighter with Israeli markings.

Since Saudi Arabia and Israel did not have diplomatic relations, the release noted, no formal protest had been lodged by the Saudi government. But Prince Bandar, the Saudi defense minister, had announced his government's intention of bringing the incident before the United Nations.

The brevity of the article was disappointing, no reference, even, to the fact that there were Americans aboard. Well, at least it had confirmed that the big craft had landed safely and without casualties, that Richy was safe. He flipped to the next page.

Buried even deeper, he discovered another brief item on page four: "REPORT AIR CRASH AT DIMONA; REACTOR DAMAGED." So the fire they had seen in the distance from the Sinai air base actually had been Dimona! It took only a minute to read the article in its entirety.

An unidentified aircraft crashed inside the Dimona restricted zone yesterday afternoon, killing its pilot and causing some damage to the nuclear reactor. The extent of the damage is not known at this time. Authorities at the nuclear site were at a loss to explain how the aircraft was able to penetrate the sophisticated air defenses that surrounded the facility, and refused to speculate on the identity of the plane or its pilot. Asked if the crash could have been the result of a deliberate suicide attack in retaliation for the raid on Iraq, an official government spokesman declined comment.

The brainchild of Israel's first president, Chaim Weizmann, the Dimona reactor was purchased from France in 1957, in a secret undertaking by the Ben Gurion government. It has been consistently characterized by that government and all subsequent administrations as nothing more than an atomic physics research tool. However, the stringent security measures surrounding the Dimona installation have led some observers to speculate that the facility plays a key role in an undisclosed nuclear weapons development program.

Did Israel, indeed, possess a stockpile of atomic weapons, as Singer had charged? He remembered the grim look on the President's face as he spoke of the threat of nuclear war in the Middle East, and his words: "Both sides have it, or are on the verge of getting it." The speculations voiced by the writer of the Dimona news article could be right on. A suicide attack by an Arab fanatic? There was a lot of that going around these days. Or a solo military strike mission by one of the Arab countries dedicated to Israel's downfall? In either case, the plane would have been loaded with explosives.

"How badly was the Dimona reactor damaged?" he wondered aloud.

"Quite badly; there's very little left of it." He hadn't heard her enter the room. She was standing at the foot of the bed, holding a tray with rolls and a steaming cup of coffee. In a figure-flattering blouse tucked into a neatly pressed skirt, she looked none the worse for her ordeal of the previous night, her hair freshly washed and brushed to a burnished ebony sheen. But the set to her mouth suggested that her world was not quite as serene as its surface appearance.

"I was wondering when you'd come out of it. You've slept the day through; it's almost dusk." Her look softened a bit as she set the tray down on the nightstand. "You must be starved."

"How did you know?" he asked, taking a sip of the coffee. "About Dimona—the reactor being totaled?"

"I've been on the phone for more than an hour, talking to my boss. Both bosses, actually—the Foreign Minister and my Mossad control. What's happening to my country is unbelievable."

"I know," he nodded, indicating the newspaper. "I've been reading about it."

"You don't know," she corrected him. "What's in there only scratches the surface. There's much more to come. We have a crisis on our hands. The government—"

"Whoa!" he interrupted. "One thing at a time. Start with Dimona."

She bit her lip. "It was a bomb. A huge bomb, called a 'blockbuster,' or rather two of them, still attached to the aircraft that carried them. The plane dove straight through the dome and crashed into the reactor, detonating the bombs. Several laborers were killed on the spot. And a scientist—one of our top nuclear physicists."

"Then it *was* a suicide thing!" He frowned, still puzzled that such an attack could be carried off against the well-prepared Israelis. "Has anyone claimed responsibility? Was it that Shiite suicide cult, 'Islamic Jihad'?"

She shook her head. "That's the worst part. The bombs were ours. And so were the plane and its pilot."

"What?" he gasped. "You mean an Israeli air force pilot—a traitor?"

"Yes, to the first question, no to the second." Seeing his puzzled look, she hastened on. "He's been identified as Capt. Zev Lieb, one of Israel's top fighter pilots. But the Mossad received a tip from a CIA agent yesterday, and it appears to check out. Lieb was an Iraqi undercover agent. He's been masquerading as an Israeli pilot for more than three years."

"Good Lord! Your Air Force's security must be totally compromised. Those poor bastards on the raid that never made it back—Baghdad must have known they were coming! If the newspapers find that out—"

"They already have. United Press International broke the story an hour ago. It's already on the TV news. The extra editions will hit the streets any minute. They're saying that the government was grossly negligent, that our counterintelligence people had plenty of time to ferret out the mole. The Prime Minister is under heavy pressure. The opposition parties are calling for his resignation, for a new election."

"That's nothing new. They've been doing that, off and on, for years. Shamir isn't taking it seriously, is he?"

"He has to. He's already getting calls from some of his marginal supporters. They're protesting that they weren't consulted or informed beforehand, and disclaiming any responsibility for what the news media are beginning to refer to as the 'ill-considered, ill-fated raid on Osirak.'"

"Not totally ill-fated. They knocked out the reactor, didn't they?"

"And lost our own reactor in the bargain."

"But there's no established connection between—" He saw something in her eyes that made him pause. "Wait a minute! You said the plane that destroyed Dimona was one of yours. Was it by any chance an F-15?"

"Yes," she said, watching the light dawn in his eyes.

"Then we heard him, didn't we? That was his voice on Singer's radio, detaching his plane from the strike force, feigning an engine problem. After which, he headed straight for Saudi Arabia to keep an appointment with their AWACS. Just like Singer told us, except for one small detail. The pilot wasn't an Israeli; your people knew nothing about it."

She nodded, waiting for him to go on.

"Only it didn't come off as planned. The AWACS somehow escaped; maybe the warning I sent helped. So the pilot went after an alternate target; one he probably knew quite well from countless hours of flight in air force jets all over the Negev. And he still had his bombs attached, those 2,000-pounders intended for Osirak."

He shook his head in admiration. "That would explain how the plane got through the Dimona defenses. They'd be reluctant to shoot down one of their own first-line jet fighters."

"Apparently that was the case," she agreed. "Another F-15, sent to intercept the intruder, got close enough to identify it. He recognized the pilot as someone he knew, an Israeli war hero. His hesitation in taking action allowed the mole just time enough to dive his plane into the reactor."

"The media have this part of the story, too?" he asked, and saw her nod her head again. "What a bummer. I'm beginning to see what the prime minister is up against. What's he going to do about it? He's too much of a fighter to give up."

"There isn't a lot he can do. You know how shaky the Likud coalition is in the Knesset. If only a few votes shift, they will lose their majority. There is only one chance of avoiding a new election. Someone will have to pay the price first. The prime minister is quietly preparing his resignation speech. He is asking the cabinet to support the foreign minister as the new head of government."

"Your boss—Shimon Kedar?" David remembered how impressed he had been with the foreign minister in that initial meeting. "He'd make a great prime minister!"

The pride showed in her face. "Yes, I think that also. But he is not that well known. The Knesset is not likely to accept him, even if the cabinet does. A new election may be inevitable."

"The democratic process at work? I guess we shouldn't knock it." He shook his head slowly from side to side. "Ironic, though, isn't it? The AWACS plot fails, but its perpetrators get their way, after all. The change of government they were so fanatical about. Singer's probably laughing his head off right now, somewhere in one of the Arab countries where your government can't get their hands on him."

For a moment her face registered surprise, then comprehension. "That's right—you don't know. Martin's dead, David; killed by a land mine in the Sinai. One of our agents down there just reported it."

He was stunned by the news. "Then it really was Singer chasing us. That second explosion we heard behind us—"

"Yes. That must have been when it happened."

His reaction to the news of Martin's death surprised her. He was shaking his head as if he didn't want to believe it, his face drawn. "It might have been for the best, David," she suggested. "He was spared the public exposure, the disgrace."

"You don't understand. There were things we had to find out, some crucial questions we had to ask him that can't be answered now." I've failed, he was thinking. A presidential commission, and I've blown it.

"I may understand more than you think." She sat down on the bed next to him. "I have a confession to make, David. I know about your 'other job,' your counterintelligence assignment."

She caught the momentary reflex of surprise in his eyes before they glazed over, masking his reaction. "I found out through the Mossad. They were concerned about rumors of security leaks at the embassy that might have compromised some highly sensitive Israeli defense information. When the President sent you here, they learned about your counterespionage background and put two and two together."

"So they assigned you to stick to me like glue, hoping to find out what material was lifted and where it went."

She nodded, her eyes downcast. "That's about it. Please don't look so disgusted. I refused to do it, at first. But in the end I had to."

"You could have saved yourself a lot of trouble, for all the good it did you. You almost got yourself killed, and for what? All we really found out was that Martin was the embassy mole. We don't know what he took or whom he gave it to."

He had a sudden thought. "Why are you telling me this now? Aren't you breaking some kind of blood oath to your precious Mossad?"

"It was my control's idea. He was hoping you'd agree to co-operate, tell us whatever you know about what was taken and who might have received it."

"I told you," he said impatiently. "That secret died with Martin. Abernathy might have known part of it, but he's dead, too. So it looks like we've both struck out."

"Weren't you briefed before you left Washington?" she persisted. "Couldn't that shed some light on what was taken?"

He shook his head. "Sensitive information, potentially detrimental to Israeli security, embarrassing to the U.S. That's all I was told. My job was to find the mole so that he could be interrogated, the damage contained, the leak plugged up."

"I wasn't given much to go on, either," she admitted. "I only know that the main document the Mossad is concerned about has to do with a top secret nuclear weapons program."

"Nuclear weapons program?" he exclaimed. "That doesn't sound like the kind of material your government would share with any country, even the U.S."

"We didn't. At least not intentionally. No one knows exactly how it happened, but somehow copies of these two sensitive documents were made by our Defense Planning Agency and delivered to the embassy, in care of the chief security administrator."

"Abernathy!"

"Yes. The Mossad has had suspicions for some time that he was spying on us. But we had no proof. When the mistake surfaced, we retrieved the copies immediately and launched an investigation. The paperwork at Defense Planning was all in order, down to the approval signatures. We still don't know how Abernathy accomplished it. Of course, he denied any knowledge of the affair. He was only the repository for the documents, he said.

and had not even looked at their contents; they were still sealed in their original wrappings."

"That's when the Mossad heard the rumor about the leak, the files being broken into."

She nodded. "And your arrival on the scene convinced them that the rumors might be true."

So that was it! No wonder the President was so embarrassed. The Mossad had caught a State Department spy red-handed! Why had he been kept in the dark by the President, he wondered heatedly, not told the whole story? But he could answer that one himself. It was typical of the goddam spooks who were probably running the show to disclose as little as possible to their field men.

He took hold of her arm. "You mentioned two documents that were copied. What was the other?"

"I'm not sure," she answered. "Something to do with oil; that was all my control could tell me. Some kind of contingency plan."

"Did you say 'contingency plan'?" Llewellyn smacked his head with one hand, his brain ready to burst at the sudden revelation. It had been there all the time, right in front of his eyes. Prince Turki's manila folder, the Israeli contingency plan to take over the Saudi oil fields! He had just been too blind to see it; blinded by the classification stamped on its pages that had thrown him off, made him see it as an official CIA document, not as something stolen by a mole as yet unmasked.

The moment he had learned of Martin Singer's CIA affiliation, he should have made the connection. Seeing Martin with the outlandish Englishman fresh from his *Arabian Nights* experience should have been the clincher. The meeting with the Saudi prince took on a new light now, everything falling into place. After breaking into Abernathy's safe and making a copy of the sensitive Israeli contingency plan, Singer had prepared his own English translation, assigned it a CIA black document number to give it legitimacy, and imprinted the Hebrew original as well as the translation with the official-looking CIA classification stamp. A copy had gone to the Saudi director of foreign intelligence through Singer's MI-6 crony, one Roger Tewkesbury-Cream.

And the elaborate effort to proselyte him, using a prince of the royal family and the incriminating Israeli plan of conquest as persuaders? Singer had put them up to it. He no longer had access to the embassy; he needed a proxy to get back into Abernathy's safe. The contingency plan might be dynamite, from a propaganda point of view, but it contained no hard information on Israeli nuclear preparedness. But something mentioned in its pages did. A report on a project known as Operation Bright Sun, which the Saudi prince had believed to involve the threat of nuclear blackmail. "An Israeli nuclear weapons program," the words that Daniella had used to describe the other document that Abernathy had lifted. Singer and his confederates must have found out that the Bright Sun document was also in Abernathy's safe.

"What is it? What did you remember?" It was obvious to Daniella that her own revelations had triggered something significant.

"A document that I happened to see recently," he replied. "I think it will turn out to be one of the ones that Abernathy ripped off—and Singer afterwards. The bad news is that he gave it to the Saudis, which probably means that every Arab nation has a copy by now."

He saw the alarm in her eyes. "The good news is that it wasn't the document your people were most concerned about. It was the other, the contingency plan. And there's good reason to believe that Martin never got his hands on the other document, the one you said concerned a top secret nuclear weapons program."

Relief came back into her face, mingled with a lingering doubt. "Have you got something concrete, some specifics I can give them? My control will want factual evidence of what you're saying."

"Not right at the moment. I'll have to make a deposition, with what facts and details there are, get it cleared by State for you people. That will take time. Tell your control what I said. It's the best I can do right now."

It's also what I'll be telling the President, he added to himself. He felt suddenly elated. He hadn't botched the assignment, after all. With Daniella's help, he had run down the mole; there would be no more leaks. And now, again, with clues she had provided, he had been able to identify the single document that appeared to have been compromised and where it had gone. They were turning out to be a pretty good team.

He reached for the coffee she had poured. "It's cold by now," she protested. "Let me get you some fresh." She got up off the bed and picked up the tray.

"No, it's fine." He took a gulp. "Don't leave. I want to drink toast to you—to us—to an undercover team that made out, even though we were under cover to each other."

She managed a wary smile. "You're not angry at me for deceiving you?"

"Damned angry." He pulled a long face. "But you can make it up to me; I'll think of a way."

He frowned, scratching his head for a moment. "I've thought of a way. Come over here."

He kissed her lightly on the lips, then pulled her onto the bed with him. "Let's get this undercover team under the covers."

"David!" She flung her arms around him. "Oh, my darling, it's been such a long time since Saturday!"

The blouse and skirt flew off. She climbed in beside him. Her lips found his, the pressure of her soft upper body against the firmness of his own, urgent, demanding.

The perverse instrument on the nightstand chose this moment to exhibit its shrill, insistent voice. After several rings, a heavily involved hand managed to extricate itself and lift the receiver.

"Hello," he muttered. "Goodbye!" He slammed the phone back into its cradle. Someone's ear at the other end would never be the same.

That someone was not taking it lightly. The ringing resumed almost immediately. With a groan, he lifted the receiver again and dropped it onto the night table.

"Hello!" called a bluff, authoritative voice. "David! David Llewellyn! Are you there?" Even the tinniness of the foreign telephone's audio couldn't disguise that voice. He rolled back over and grabbed for the phone.

"Mr. President?"

"That you, David? I'm not used to being hung up on."

"Sorry, Mr. President. If I'd known it was you, I—"

"Am I interrupting something?" There was an insinuating touch of humor in the voice; he could visualize the twinkle in the President's eye.

"No, sir." Daniella was sitting up in the bed and had drawn the sheet up to shield her exposed breasts, as if the telephone had eyes. His eye caught hers. "That is, nothing that can't be resumed later." The toss of her head said not to take that for granted.

"David, my boy, I tracked you down because I couldn't wait to extend my personal commendation to you. I've just been on the phone with King Fahd, concerning the Saudi AWACS attack.

He reports that it was your timely intervention, your warning to the AWACS crew that helped them escape and avoided what could have been a catastrophic international incident. I have no idea how you managed it, but congratulations. There'll be a presidential citation coming your way."

"Thank you, Mr. President. I'm overwhelmed. To tell you the truth, I was only thinking about my brother—"

"Ah, yes, little Richy," the President resumed. "Apparently, the youngster I used to bounce on my knee has grown up. You'll be pleased to know that Richard has also been singled out by the Saudis for commendation and will be honored by the King in a special ceremony. The plane's pilot gives him the major credit for helping evade those missiles fired by the Israeli fighter."

"I hadn't heard that, Mr. President. I haven't had a chance to talk to Richy. There's been so much happening, so much I need to fill you in on. The Israeli fighter plane you refer to, for one thing. It wasn't an Israeli pilot after all; the pilot was a—"

"I know all about it," the President interrupted. "That was the reason for my talk with King Fahd. I was asked by the Israeli Prime Minister to intercede on his country's behalf. We're getting that little matter straightened out. The Israelis are furnishing irrefutable evidence of the pilot's true identity, which our ambassador will put in front of the King."

David had never heard the President so ebullient; it was puzzling. Surely he must know about Osirak, the debacle of the new Russian missiles. "Mr. President," he broke in, "you've had the news about the Baghdad raid, the Soviets' brazen employment of nuclear warheads?"

"Yes, my boy, I have. It was a stupid blunder on their part, and they're already regretting it; it's going to cost them. The Soviets are taking an unprecedented pasting from the press and news media all around the world, almost universally condemned by public opinion and by virtually every government except the Arab countries and their own satellites. It's the biggest propaganda coup in years, bigger by far than the Korean Airlines incident. It's going to put them right behind the eight ball at the reopening Geneva nuclear arms talks. They'll finally be forced into making some concessions."

"It's good to get the big picture, Mr. President. Things are pretty confused around here, at the moment, what with the loss of Israel's own reactor and the revelations about the man who did it, the Iraqi spy. You know about that also?"

"Affirmative, my boy. And I can understand the reaction in Israel. But in the long term, it may have decreased the chances of nuclear war over there. It's brought this nuclear thing out in the open, where we can deal with it."

"I hope you're right, Mr. President. But in the meantime it's bound to have some repercussions on the government here. I need to talk to you about that, and also about the special assignment you laid on me. To tell you the truth, I thought that's what you were calling about."

"I was, in fact. I need a verbal report from you on that. But we'll need a secure line with a scrambler. Call me from the embassy, why don't you, sometime within the hour. And David—"

"Yes, sir?"

"I think you should come home for a few days, receive your citation personally, and we'll talk about reassigning you to a country more to your liking. There may be a position opening up. In all fairness, you should be considered for it."

David's face fell. "Leave now, Mr. President? But, sir, I don't think you realize how serious the situation is here. There may be a major upheaval, almost certainly a change of government, perhaps a general election. It would be a bad time to be away, even for a few days. Besides—"

The President's hearty laugh boomed into the receiver, cutting him off. The chief executive finished the sentence for him. "Besides, you've had a change of, shall we say, heart? Can I possibly be speaking to the same person who indicated, in this very Oval Office only a few weeks ago, that Israel was about the last place he wanted to be assigned? Very well, my boy, stay on, by all means, and continue doing the job I sent you there to do. A government crisis, you say? I'll need a full report on what you're alluding to as quickly as possible. I spoke with the ambassador there earlier today, and he didn't mention it. Evidently there have been some later developments, or perhaps you are better informed."

"Maybe a little of both, sir. To begin with—"

"Not now, my boy. I'm afraid I have to go. Call me a bit later, on a secure line from the embassy. And David, one more thing."

"What's that, sir?"

"Give my regards to Miss Zadik. She must really be something special."

With a click, the line went dead. "Yes, sir," he said into the defunct receiver, "you can say that again." The President didn't miss much, he reflected, the reference to his "change of heart" remaining in his mind. Was he crazy, passing up a possible promotion?

Daniella had heard only one end of the conversation. "The President's calling you home. You're being reassigned." She had donned a robe and was sitting in front of the vanity, brushing her hair, staring into the mirror. All the music had gone out of her voice, and she couldn't look at him.

"He was just—testing me," he answered.

She spun around, not knowing quite how to interpret his answer, her face suddenly hopeful. "You're staying on, then?"

He nodded. "I guess I kind of like it here."

He watched the color return to her cheeks, the light to her eyes. He stood up from the bed and picked up his trousers from the back of a chair.

"I have to go to the embassy right away. The President wants me to call on a secure line, fill him in on everything."

"Right now? You have to leave right this minute?" She had never looked more beautiful, more appealing, the pale green velour robe dangling loosely from her shoulders, revealing the deep crevice between the twin protrusions that bulged beneath it. The same robe she had worn that first evening when—

He saw himself on the bedroom floor on his hands and knees, helping her retrieve the undergarments dumped from the vanity drawers by the untidy prowler, saw her kneeling in front of him, the irresistible patch of exposed skin on her upper back; felt the deep thrill run through her body at the kiss that had started at the base of her neck and traveled down her spine, stripping the robe away.

He fumbled with his trousers, watching her. "What—what are you doing?"

She had stood up from the vanity and extracted two of its drawers, holding one in each hand, extended toward him. In one deft motion she turned them upside down, their contents sprawling onto the carpet.

"David, before you leave for the embassy—there's one little chore I'd like you to help me with."

Richard Llewellyn took out his handkerchief and wiped the perspiration from his forehead. It was a warm, sticky morning, and they had been standing here under the relentless sun of Arabia for a quarter of an hour or more, waiting for the king to arrive. He stared longingly at the inviting shade inside the tent set up for his majesty and wondered how much longer it would be. Probably a while yet. Kings made up their own rules.

The sun glinting off a photographer's lens caught his eye. The man had stationed himself on the roof of the three-story airport terminal building, from which his camera could capture a commanding view of the spectacle. Richy tried to visualize the finished picture. The panoply of rich Oriental carpets in shades of deep cobalt blue to cranberry red, spread across the tarmac; there must be a half acre of them. The traditional Bedouin tent of the desert nomad, erected atop the carpeting, a striped canopy extending from the tent to the point across the sea of carpet where the king's limousine was already overdue to deposit him. And the contrasting backdrop, the big, shiny, modern aircraft parked parallel to the terminal, U.S. military designation E-3A, tail number C-103. The Saudi Arabian AWACS that had weathered an onslaught from the worst that the world's premier military jet fighter could throw at it, its entire crew arrayed proudly in front of their vehicle, waiting to receive the Saudi monarch's commendation.

Well, almost the entire crew. Only one was missing: one Jules Berger, alias Julius Bergstrom, sometimes informer for the Israelis. "Raunch" had pulled out the day after the big radar plane's ordeal and returned to the States, fearful that his cover had been blown. Richy missed the little guy, whose antics invariably kept the other American crew members amused and loose at times like this. His heavyset sidekick was still present. But "Paunch," standing next to him, wasn't the same person with the other half of the act missing. He was fidgety and uncomfortable and seemed to have nothing to say.

By contrast, the Saudi crew members appeared relaxed and cool, standing at parade rest in their freshly pressed light tan gabardines. They remained respectfully silent, appropriately imbued with the solemnity of the occasion.

"Christ! How fucking much longer we gotta wait?" Even delivered sotto voce, Hauser's outburst caused several disapproving Saudi heads to turn his way. The perspiration was pouring off the big man, who had doffed his habitual fatigues in favor of the only suit he had brought with him to Arabia, an ill-fitting vested affair, its dark fabric soaking up the sun's rays like a sponge. "Standing in the fucking sun like a bunch of fucking morons! I'm drowning in my own fucking sweat!"

His remarks seemed to be directed at the supervisor of *

American group, Hanson, cool and dapper by comparison in a tailored, pale green tropical worsted. "Cool it, Hauser!" he hissed back. "It's all that booze from last night percolating out of you. I'll bet your sweat would test a hundred proof. If you hadn't personally tried to kill every bottle we smuggled in for the party—"

"Quiet, please!" The admonishment came from a prissy Saudi official, the royal advance man who had arrived on the scene an hour before to coordinate the affair. It was at his insistence that the crew had lined themselves up in advance in front of their airplane.

"Fuck you, asshole!" Hauser muttered back under his breath. For once, Richy found himself in agreement with the irascible IBM engineer. They could be waiting comfortably in the air-conditioned interior of the AWACS. It would have taken but a minute, once the royal limousine was sighted, to redeploy themselves alongside the plane.

He stole a glance to his left, where Roxana was standing by herself, ten paces away, in a frilly white frock she had filled out in all the right places. Her isolation from the others was another of the self-important royal coordinator's silly ideas of protocol. Nonplussed at the presence of a woman among the flight test crew, he had glared disapprovingly at her neckline, shaking his head from side to side. It was only after the intercession of the plane's captain that he had grudgingly agreed to let her participate on the condition that she be segregated from the other crew members and her exposed neck and shoulders swathed in a white scarf.

Richy was well aware that she had been trying to catch his eye. She had tried to talk to him twice since that final flight together that had almost ended so tragically. Safely on the ground, immediately afterwards, she had approached him, a new respect showing in her eyes. He had quickly excused himself, citing fatigue. The next morning, she had come to his room, knocked on his door. He hadn't answered; he had nothing to say to her. Her whirlwind affair with Hanson had burned him. But the sting had gone out of it now, and he wanted to keep it that way. He wanted a clean break.

Then this morning, when he thought he had his feelings about ⟨ ⟩ sorted out, the sight of her in the appealing feminine attire of her habitual flight garb of mannish shirt and blue jeans ⟨ ⟩ced some unexpected pangs. Standing there by herself, isolated from the rest of the group, there was something forlorn about her, a hint of vulnerability he hadn't seen before. Hanson was dumping her, of course, headed back to his wife on the next plane out of Riyadh.

The Boeing manager had dropped in on him the previous afternoon, as he was cleaning out his room and completing his packing. The party that night was to be the last hurrah for the Americans. They were officially disbanded, all scheduled to depart within the next few days. Hanson had started partying early; he was a little drunk already. He had stopped by, he said, because he had heard a rumor that Richy wasn't coming to the party and wanted to persuade him to reconsider.

In fact, Richy hadn't been planning to attend, but hadn't mentioned this to anyone. Either Hanson was a mind reader, or there was some other reason for his visit. That reason soon developed; Hanson began thanking him for what he had done aboard the AWACS several days previously to save their collective necks. He became so effusive that it was downright embarrassing; Richy tried vainly to shut him off. While Hanson babbled on, one freeze-frame from the AWACS episode had lingered in his mind's eye: the picture of Hanson and Roxana alone together in the supervisor's compartment, cozy and oblivious, while Richy was racking his brain to find a way out of their predicament.

Then things had really started to get out of hand. Hanson had his arm around his shoulder and was blubbering an apology about Roxana. "I couldn't help myself. Jesus, I didn't mean to hurt you. I didn't realize how you felt about her."

"I didn't either," Richy had answered. "You helped me find out. So don't apologize. You did me a favor." And he had finally managed to bundle the supervisor out the door, with a promise to see him at the party that night. A promise he hadn't kept.

The sight of the Rolls-Royce Silver Cloud limousine beginning its slow crawl across the tarmac brought him back to the present. A ripple of excitement and relief ran through the AWACS contingent; the waiting was over. The elongated Rolls halted near the canopy entrance, its chauffeur jumping out to open the rear door, then snapping to attention.

All eyes strained for the first glimpse of the king, but the man who stepped out wore the dark blue uniform of the Royal Saudi Air Force. Richy recognized Prince Bandar al Faisal's thick head of dark hair and prominent, clean-shaven chin below the small mustache. He had seen the prince once before at the original

AWACS dedication ceremony. A murmur of disappointment
escaped from the waiting throng. Had the king changed his plans,
sent his nephew instead?

The prince paused by the door of the car, waiting respectfully
as another figure emerged, a taller man, considerably heavier in
build. He was simply dressed in a reddish brown, ankle-length
robe, and crowned only by the traditional headdress, a white
kaffiyeh with a black headband. Richy had never seen the king in
person, only in pictures. The neatly trimmed black mustache and
goatee were insufficient identification, favored as they were by
virtually every male member of the royal family. But he was
nonetheless certain that it was Fahd; there was an aura of enormous energy about the man. High-liver, administrative genius,
workaholic. Fahd had actually been running the country since
1974, the beginning of his brother Khālid's reign.

For the medal recipients whose stand-up stint in the sun was
now approaching the half-hour mark, the awards ceremony was
mercifully brief. There were no speeches. The Saudi crew
members received their awards first, each delivered with a con-
gratulatory buss on both cheeks, first by Fahd, then Bandar.
Richy found himself wondering how it would feel to be kissed by
a king, and whether the royal hirsute would feel soft or prickly.
But when the medal bestowers arrived at the Americans, the routine was changed, polite handshakes replacing the royal oscula-
tions.

His turn came and he leaned forward, as a velvet ribbon holding a heavy medallion was dropped over his head by the Saudi
monarch. For a brief moment he was looking directly into a pair
of dark eyes only inches from his own—energetic, restless eyes
that were hard as steel. "Congratulations, good work," Fahd repeated mechanically, with virtually no accent or show of emotion, and began to turn away. The royal handshake had been
disappointingly flaccid. Is that all there is? Richy wondered.
Prince Bandar mumbled something in Arabic and the king turned
back to him, a flicker of interest registering in the peripatetic
eyes.

"So you are the American whom Captain Zamani reported to
us about, the one he credits with saving his ship from destruction.
Please accept my personal commendation and the thanks of every
member of my family."

Bandar, sporting a new general's star, added his own congratulations. "I have just finished reading your report of the engage-

ment with the Israeli Eagle. Your evasive strategy was most ingenious. An amazing escape against all odds."

The royal party moved on. Roxana was the last to receive her
medal. The congratulations were cursory as Fahd hastily hung the
medal around her neck, the handshakes perfunctory. Richy
watched the royal pair turn abruptly on their heels and head for
the refreshment tent. Had there been a gleam of appreciation for
Roxana's apparent charms in the eyes of uncle and nephew, or
had he imagined it?

The crew members followed Fahd and Bandar into the tent to
join them in the ceremonial refreshment taking. Roxana was excluded. Big deal! thought Richy. "Refreshments" turned out to be
tiny cups of the strong, presweetened Arabian coffee. Fahd had a
few more words with the Saudi captain and several of his crew,
ignoring the Americans.

In the brief time that it took to down the small demitasse, the
ceremony, it seemed, was over. Without formal leave-taking, or
fanfare, the Arabian king and prince departed the tent through the
connecting canopy and were whisked away on their modern-day
magic carpet, the Silver Cloud. What he had heard about Fahd
might be true, Richy decided—that he didn't particularly care for
Americans, resented his country's dependence on them for
weapons and military security. The ponderous medallion hanging
around his neck seemed suddenly ridiculous; he removed it and
dropped it into the inside pocket of his jacket.

"That's that," he thought. It was the end of an era for him, his
AWACS saga and its final chapter, the Saudi Arabian campaign.
The inevitable letdown was beginning to set in. He said a quick
good-bye to the Saudi crew, with an embrace and pat on the back
from his personal friend, the radio operator, and left the tent.

One last look. He walked to the ladder and climbed up the
steps to the flight deck of the AWACS. There was no one inside.
Most of the havoc wreaked on the aircraft's interior by its violent
evasive maneuvering appeared to have been repaired. He walked
aft along the darkened corridor lined with controller consoles to
his radar compartment and dropped into the swivel chair facing
the complex bank of displays and controls. But the familiar surroundings only seemed to increase his depression; he felt as
empty as the blank, lifeless displays facing him.

There was a faint, whirring sound from the aft sector of the
aircraft, and the console in front of him sprang to life, light erupt-

ing from its various screens as their iridescent test patterns materialized. Someone had switched on the power.

"Bogey at six o'clock!" He spun the chair around. Roxana was standing in the doorway, only dimly illuminated by the fluorescence emanating from the radar console. "May I come in?"

"Why not? It's your radar now; your station, your chair."

He started to get up, but she stopped him, pushing firmly down on both his shoulders. "I have to talk to you. I missed you at the party."

"Yes. Well, I didn't want to intrude on your good-bye session with the Big Boss."

She reacted to the sarcasm in his voice, her hand caressing the side of his face. "I hurt you, didn't I? I didn't mean to."

He pulled his head away. "Don't flatter yourself."

She took his hand. "Don't be angry with me. How can I make you understand about me? All right, I'm adventurous, I make friends easily, and sometimes I get carried away. The thing with Hanson—it was over almost before it started. That type of casual relationship doesn't mean anything—not to me."

"I know," he said with a bitter laugh. "I found that out."

"No!" she said, her hands back on his shoulders, pressing him into the seat. "You don't know—you don't understand! I didn't mean about you, about us. That's what I came here to tell you. You're very special—I didn't realize how special until a few days ago. You took charge up there, kept your head when everyone else just got scared and didn't know what to do. You saved us all. You deserve a reward, something better than that silly medal."

He couldn't think of anything to say. He watched her unwind the long white scarf from her neck and shoulders. She passed it behind his neck, then knelt in front of him, sawing playfully on it to slide its silken fabric sensually over his skin. The scarf carried her scent to his nostrils; she began to draw it in, pulling his head down toward her bosom.

His lips touched her crevice. He groaned. "What do you want from me?"

Her cool bare arms encircled his head. "Let's have a party, to make up for the one you missed, our own private party, back in your room; say our good-byes properly. We may never see each other again, but I intend to make sure you never forget me. Part of me will fly out of here with you tonight, when you leave for Jerusalem."

He extricated himself and drew back, eyeing her suspiciously. "So you know about that. Do you also know why I'm going there?"

She nodded, realizing belatedly that she had tipped her hand. "Of course. Everyone knows. Your brother's getting married next week; you're the best man. The wedding will be at the American Embassy; there'll be a huge ball. VIPs all over the place."

He watched her in silence, her eyes wide and staring, focused far away, visualizing the gala celebration, no doubt, herself in the middle of it, the center of attention.

"Oh, please, please! Take me with you! You're all leaving, everyone's deserting me. I need to get away from this depressing place, just for a few days. We'll have fun together. I'll make you happy!"

Incredulous, he stared back at her. "Roxana," he said gently, "you know that's not possible. A visa to Israel for a Saudi resident takes an act of God."

"Your brother could arrange it, through diplomatic channels. He did it for you. He knows me; he—"

"Forget it, Roxana. Even if I agreed and he agreed, there wouldn't be time." He saw the disappointment in her eyes, saw her fight for control, regain her composure. He stood up.

"I've got to get moving. I have a wedding gift to buy, and—"

"No, Richard, please!" She struggled to her feet, grasping his arm. "I meant what I said—about our own little party, a proper good-bye. There's time for that, certainly. You can make time; your flight isn't till this evening."

She was panting softly, her ample chest heaving up and down. The pale green glow cast by luminous displays wrought a magical network of light and shadow on her face, highlighting her cheekbones, adding mystique to her sensuous persona. She was a goddess, an enchantress. She had never looked more alluring.

Why not? he asked himself. One for the road. What would be the harm?

She took his hand in both of hers, holding it to her breast, smiling up at him in blatant invitation. "Why not?" she coaxed, echoing the voice inside him.

The only answer he could find was ages old, the response made by countless parents in defense of decisions manifest to themselves but incomprehensible—unexplainable—to their children.

"Just because, Roxana. Just because. . . ."

The clock on the minaret at the Cheik el-Galami Mosque read 4:40. Dusk was rapidly approaching. This was the hour at which the Baghdad traffic was typically at its very worst, and today proved to be no exception.

As his privately hired airport limousine crept through the congested streets, Sergei Brastov leaned back into the plush upholstery and tried to calm his frayed nerves. There was plenty of time, he reminded himself. While aircraft departure times from Baghdad airport were unpredictable, there was one thing you could rely on. They would always leave considerably behind schedule. In any case, no flights would depart until well after dark, to remove the threat of attack by Iranian jet fighters.

The last several days had been something of a nightmare for the Soviet military adviser. Repercussions from the debacle at Osirak had been stormy and bitter. Despite all efforts of the government to keep a lid on it, the story had been broken by the news media in its entirety, including the role of the hitherto secret Soviet missiles. Notwithstanding the brilliant showing of those missiles against the Israeli jets, the Russians were blamed by the local press and citizenry for the loss of the nuclear plant, their fantastic new weapons denigrated because of their inability to counter the single remotely guided glide bomb that had sneaked through the defenses to destroy the Iraqi reactor.

As the senior member of the Soviet delegation, Brastov had been forced to bear the brunt of the criticism. His former friends and associates in the Iraqi defense establishment cut him dead. Defense Minister Zahadi would no longer talk to him or answer his calls.

For the Iraqis, the blow had been softened considerably by the success of their own sneak attack on the Israeli reactor. The news of the Dimona victory had been trumpeted to the populace with headlines in the Baghdad newspapers that were even larger than those that had told, only hours earlier, of the Osirak outcome. Iraq had a new national hero, albeit a posthumously recognized one—Adnan Ibrahim al Amiri, code name El Aurens, the undercover agent who had successfully masqueraded as an Israeli air force officer for three years before delivering the coup de grace to their nuclear facility.

Today's editions continued to chronicle the exploits of the intrepid repatriate, whose martyr's death at Dimona was universally acknowledged by the predominantly Shiite populace to have won him a high place in heaven. There was a continuing series on his life story, gleaned largely from interviews with Iraqis who had participated in his espionage training program, with more fragmentary information on his earlier life in Haifa, liberally embellished by the imagination of the writers. On the editorial page of the same newspaper was another condemnation of the Russians for their inadequate defense of Osirak.

Brastov had crumpled the paper into a ball and cast it angrily onto the hearth of his cleaned-out flat. How could they be so ungrateful, so grossly unfair? If he hadn't interceded with his AWACS plan, they would have had no Dimona triumph to boast about. But he received no credit from the Iraqis for this contribution. While the blame for the failures had fallen on the Russians, the credit for the singular success at Dimona had all gone to Saddam Hussein.

Bitter as it was to experience, the reaction of the Iraqis was mild compared to the judgment that awaited him at the Kremlin. Uncharacteristically, it had taken the Politburo only a few days to arrive at a consensus. He had been summarily suspended from his post in Iraq and summoned back to Moscow to explain what had gone wrong. The precipitous new orders had shocked him, particularly since there had been favorable initial signs from the military contingent of the Politburo, who were openly pleased with the devastating victory of their newly developed weapon over the Israeli jets and couldn't care less about the setback to the Iraqis' upstart nuclear program.

But when world opinion came down so unexpectedly harshly and universally on the heads of the Soviet leaders, the military bloc had quickly caved in and changed their tune. With the benefit of hindsight, the decision to deploy the nuclear-tipped SAMS, they decided, had been a great mistake. The reaction of people everywhere, it seemed, with the exception of the Soviet bloc nations and Arab states, had been shock and alarm over the Russians' blatant disregard of the ban on peacetime use of atomic weapons. Ignoring protestations that the warheads employed were tiny, purely defensive nonstrategic weapons and that it was the Israelis, after all, who had been the aggressors, the news media around the world had gone on a rampage against the Soviet Union.

In the western press, the Israeli fliers were held up as martyrs, slaughtered in a cold-blooded ambush employing the overwhelming force of the atom, against which they had no chance whatsoever. The condemnation of the Soviet actions was not confined to the West; even among the unaligned and Third World nations, the Russians were taking an unprecedented shellacking.

Being called on the carpet for his sponsorship of a policy that the Politburo itself had endorsed was a bitter pill for Brastov to swallow. If only the AWACS part of the plan had succeeded, the focus of public outrage and condemnation would have been on Israeli heads rather than Soviet. He still had no inkling of what had gone wrong, how the fat, helpless, unmissable target had managed to elude its fate. But his informant in Israel had apprised him of signs that the hated Likud government might be tottering anyway, the repercussions from Osirak and Dimona rendering its future at best shaky.

Bringing down that government had once been the most important end of all his machinations. Now it seemed almost incidental; even if it transpired within the next few days, he knew it would not be enough to save him. The Politburo needed a scapegoat. There was no question in his mind that he was earmarked for this role.

He had no intention of accepting it. He hadn't spent a lifetime fighting for his country, pouring heart and soul into his work, to end his career by sulking home in disgrace to accept a fate that could only culminate in some form of banishment. If banishment was inevitable he would pick the locale himself; and it wouldn't be some cold, desolate place like Siberia or the Gulag Archipelago.

His right hand slipped into his trousers pocket, fingering the single key encased in leather. His security, his ace in the hole. The lock that it fit into was on a safe deposit box in the basement of a Zurich bank. Much cleaner than a Swiss bank account, much more impersonal. You presented the key, you opened the box, you took out what you needed.

What was in there was more than adequate for his needs; it would keep him comfortably for the rest of his life. The double agent business could be a very profitable one, but only if you didn't get caught. If you were painstaking and discreet, trusted no one, and didn't get greedy, you had a chance. Provided you knew when it was time to get out. For Sergei Sergeivitch Brastov, the time had come.

Running his stubby fingers fondly over the serrated edge of the key, he pictured the way the box would look when he opened it. Packet upon packet of American currency, crisp bank notes of large denominations, the eyes of long-dead presidents staring up at him. The fodder of capitalism, symbol of everything he had been taught since his earliest school days to shun and abhor. But he had no guilt feelings; his conscience was clear. It was not as though he had betrayed his country for that money. He had done only what he would have done anyway in his country's best interest. And had been clever enough to get paid for it—by the wealthiest spy agency in the world.

The fact of the despised CIA's Israeli policy inexplicably aligning itself with that of the USSR had not troubled him for a minute. He was aware of many instances in the past where CIA machinations had played into Soviet hands; here was simply another case in point. Upon learning that they were willing to pay handsomely for a gambit that would unseat the hard-line Israeli government, he had not troubled himself over the reason why. His CIA contact, an agent known to him only as "Little Brother," had accepted his AWACS plan and his assurance that he could deliver. The courier had arrived promptly in Baghdad with a substantial down payment. The money was as good as gold; that was all he had to know.

The jerky stop and go of the traffic-clogged streets had finally subsided. They were in the outskirts of the city now, the limousine moving smoothly and rapidly. A light rain had begun to fall. In the swiftly descending darkness, the headlights of approaching vehicles turned the wet pavement ahead into a listening pathway of gold. A golden road, leading to Zurich.

Other headlights glared abruptly through the rear window. His head swiveled to look, an involuntary reflex. The auto was dangerously close to his own, little more than a car length behind. With a start, he recognized it as the same vehicle he had seen behind them in city traffic. Relax, said a calm voice from somewhere inside; if it was following you, it wouldn't come so close. It wasn't that unusual for two cars out of the city to end up together on this road. The airport was, after all, a popular destination.

In any case, the deception he had planned should be adequate to throw any pursuers off the scent. He was booked out on the Aeroflot flight to Moscow, scheduled to depart at 7:00 P.M. He would check in at the Aeroflot counter, surrender his ticket, passport, and luggage, then melt into the crowd coursing through the terminal's lounges, shops, and restaurants. Once persuaded that he had shaken off any unwanted shadows, he would make for the other terminal, where a Swissair jet for Zurich was due to leave at 6:30. In his right-hand coat pocket was a coach-class ticket for that flight in the name of Helmut Sorge, a West German businessman; the same pocket contained a FRG passport under that name, with a picture that bore a pronounced likeness to Nikita Khruschchev.

His luggage would of course be loaded on board the Aeroflot jetliner. Before anyone discovered that he had no intention of accompanying it, he would be winging his way westward aboard the Swissair jet under his new identity. The loss of his luggage was a small price to pay. The only luggage he really needed was one small brass key encased in leather.

It was almost pitch dark now. Through the rain-sodden surroundings he could make out the faint blue glow of perimeter lights along one of the runways off in the distance. The limousine swung right, onto the access road that led to the terminal entrance. He peered out the back window; the other car was no longer there; it had never been a threat. Mounting the ramp to the departing passenger level, the driver slackened his speed. The limousine pulled into the unloading zone in front of the Aeroflot sign, the driver alighting to open the door for him.

The chauffeur unloaded his bags, handing them off to one of the swarm of youthful Arab porters who had suddenly materialized to vie for the hoped-for prodigious tip that a private limousine projected. The chauffeur and porter were both in for disappointment; Brastov was not a heavy tipper. The chauffeur stared contemptuously at his single-dinar gratuity as the Russian turned on his heel and followed his luggage into the terminal.

As usual, he noted with satisfaction, the interior was bustling with activity. The proximity of the continuing war with its neighbor notwithstanding, Baghdad over the past several years had become an increasingly thriving business and commercial center, its hotels and the flights in and out of its airport almost invariably booked to capacity. A predominately male horde of incoming and outgoing travelers occupied its large waiting room and the shops and cafes adjoining it, their attire a bizarre admixture of trad tional and western dress. It would not be difficult to lose himself in that crowd.

The line at the Aeroflot counter was not long; he was quite early. A young Iraqi accepted his ticket and passport without comment, then looked up at him with new respect. "Would you prefer a window or aisle seat, General Brastov?" he inquired in passable Russian. As he always did, Brastov opted for the window.

"Enjoy your flight, sir." The attendant handed him his boarding pass, retaining the ticket and passport. "Dinner will be served as soon as you are off the ground."

"And when will that be?" Brastov queried brusquely, playing the part of the overbearing general. "Are you running as late as usual?"

"No, sir," the Iraqi replied defensively. "We're showing an on-time departure."

Brastov snorted. Delays were never shown on Aeroflot announcement boards, even when equipment was known to be down for some needed repair or servicing chore. If you went by the announcement board, all Aeroflot flights arrived and departed on time. Mentally predicting at least a one-hour delay, he headed for the opposite side of the waiting room, where a small bookstall afforded him the ideal vantage point. He could stand inconspicuously behind its glass enclosure and appear to be browsing while sweeping the entire waiting room for suspicious individuals or signs of covert surveillance. The reflection in the window would allow him to keep his eye on the interior of the bookshop, as well.

He selected the thickest paperback from the bookshelf, which turned out to be an Arabic translation of *War and Peace*, and commenced leafing through it, eyes peering over the top of the book beneath lowered lids. There were certain indicators to watch out for: heads ducking behind newspapers, loiterers rooted pointlessly to the same spot or wandering aimlessly back and forth, an attendant sweeping an already-clean floor, the overly prolonged browsing of a window-shopper. After ten minutes of surveillance failed to turn up any questionable activities of that sort, he wedged the Tolstoy classic back into its allotted place and headed for the men's room.

His stay was brief, just long enough to relieve himself. Public facilities in Muslim countries were not as a rule very agreeable spots in which to tarry. Emerging from the men's room, he commenced laying down a trail that would take him helter-skelter through the entire expanse of the south terminal. He walked past several shop fronts, pausing momentarily to peer through one of the display windows while he perused its reflection of the foot traffic behind him. His next stop was a cafe, where he sat down on a stool and consumed a cup of the thick, syrupy Arab coffee. Up again, he walked back toward the waiting room, then rode the escalator to the lower floor, where he changed some dinars into rubles at a money-changing stall. Back up the escalator, he walked into one of the biggest and busiest shops, which was doing a brisk business in souvenirs, and mingled with the other customers, fingering the various kinds of knickknacks that tourists delight in acquiring, which invariably end up on a shelf somewhere, gathering dust.

No hostile signs, so far, at least none that he had been able to spot. He moved through the crowded counters, to all intents and purposes absorbed in the hunt for travel gifts and souvenirs, biding his time. He checked his watch. It was coming up on 6:15. He would have to make his move soon.

A large and noisy party, probably some sort of tour group, began to move out of the waiting room toward the long corridor that led to the north terminal and departure gates in between. There must be at least fifty of them, he guessed, a few women included in the group. As they straggled by the gift shop, he strained his ears to detect the language they were speaking.

German. That was perfect! He slipped out of the shop, using a different door from the one he had entered, and became one of them. "Where are you from?" he inquired in a polished hoch-Deutsch.

"*Aus* Hamburg," came the answer from several.

"*Sie gehen jetzt nach Hause?*" Yes, they replied, with an evident glow of anticipation; they were going home.

He continued along the corridor with them for another hundred paces or so, until they arrived at a small waiting area adjacent to the gate from which their Lufthansa charter would depart. They peeled off as he continued on, feeling suddenly naked and conspicuous. "*Auf wiedersehen,*" they waved to him. "*Wiedersehen,*" he answered perfunctorily, quickening his pace.

He passed the last south terminal departure gate. Now came the critical phase; it would be clear to anyone observing him that he was heading for the north terminal. Time was running short; the Swissair flight would be called at any minute. He wanted to look back over his shoulder one last time but resisted the impulse. He was committed now; there was no more time for playing games.

As he passed the first north terminal departure gate, the corridor began to fill up with people coming the other way. He felt relieved; he could lose himself again, if necessary. The passageway narrowed and was soon glutted with humanity flowing in the opposite direction. He was jostled by someone, a lady with an umbrella. As he sidestepped, a man in native dress bumped directly into him, and something fell from the Russian's pocket onto the floor.

His German passport! After his first panicky reaction, it occurred to him that the man might be a pickpocket who had bungled the job. But no, the man was not running away. He had stopped, murmuring an apology, and was bending down to retrieve the document. As he turned to return the passport, their eyes met briefly, and Brastov realized, suddenly, that he knew this man.

"A thousand pardons, sir!" As Brastov accepted the passport from him, the apology was followed by an urgent whisper. "Look inside!"

"Wait!" Brastov shouted. But the man was gone, swept along by the surging throng. Bracing himself against the onrushing horde, he flipped open the passport. A single slip of paper bore two lines of handprinted lettering. Chess moves; the chess code! He deciphered it in an instant. "Be careful. They know." That was all it said. He stared down the corridor at the sea of retreating backs. There was no sign of the man in the black and white *abaya*. In a flash, he remembered where he had seen that face before. It had been under decidedly more pleasant circumstances. The man was known to him only as Rashid, probably an alias. He was the courier who had delivered the currency from the CIA.

How in the devil had Rashid found him? Why was the courier, or his employer, trying to warn him? He groped for an explanation, wishing the message had been more specific. The "who" he could guess—the KGB. But how much did "they" know?

There was no more time for speculation. He had a plane to catch. The next gate down was the Swissair departure point; he could see his flight number posted there. Most of the passengers had already boarded, a few stragglers still making their way down the narrow flight of steps to the tarmac. He presented his ticket and passport.

"*Wilkommen*, Herr Sorge." The young man in the Swissair uniform handed him a boarding pass stamped with the seat number he had reserved earlier.

"We leave on time?" Brastov asked. "*Jawohl!*" came the reassuring reply.

His window seat was in the back of the plane. There was no one sitting in the aisle seat adjacent. He hoped that this situation would hold up; it would be good to be able to stretch out on the long flight to Zurich. With a sigh, he settled his ample midsection into the narrow seat, his hips squeezed tightly against the foam rubber lining. He fastened the seat belt and looked at his watch again. In two minutes the door should swing shut, the engines begin their whining crescendo. He counted off the seconds, staring apprehensively at the doorway, the pounding of his heart providing a rhythmic accompaniment to the sweep of the second hand on his watch dial.

But the Swissair timetable proved no more reliable than Aeroflot's. After ten minutes of agony, during which Brastov watched and waited for heaven knows what to come after him through the open doorway, the head steward made his little announcement. There would be some further delay in their departure, the passengers were informed in German, due to procedural difficulties beyond the control of the airline. In the meantime, the bar would be opened for their convenience. The announcement was repeated three times more, in French, Italian, and Arabic.

Beads of sweat stood out on Brastov's forehead. If the Moscow flight should leave first, it could be trouble. They would discover he hadn't boarded, come looking for him on other flights. The waiting was unbearable; he unbuckled his seat belt and stood up, uncertain of what to do. As he hesitated, the heavy door at the aircraft's midriff was slammed shut by the steward and locked securely.

He sat back down and ordered two vodkas from the pretty blond flight attendant, beginning to relax a little. It was good to be back in the part of the world where attractive young women could wear short skirts and show off their legs. Sipping at the iced vodka, he picked up where he had left off with the long-range planning that had been preempted by his hurried flight arrangements.

He could afford to live wherever he wanted. It would be somewhere in Western Europe. German and French were his best languages; he had traveled in France and Switzerland and Germany and was reasonably comfortable in all of them. But they were expensive. His money would go farther in Spain or Portugal or Greece. And they had warmer climates, which appealed to his aching old bones. He would travel for a while, try out each country, then decide. He had plenty of time.

It was too bad about Katya and the children, the most recent grandchild that he would never see. But Katya would be all right; the boy and girl would see to that. They had been brought up properly; they would take care of their mother. Both the boy and the girl's husband had good jobs and—

What were they doing? They were opening the door again! His heart sank, and he shrank down into the seat, expecting to see a brace of burly KGB agents step through the open doorway to arrest him. But the only entrant, before the door was immediately slammed shut again, proved to be a solitary Arab in a flowing black abaya, fairly long in the tooth, judging by his bent-over posture and slow walk. Apologizing profusely to the flight attendants for his late arrival, he made his painstaking way down the aisle and took the vacant seat next to Brastov.

With a shrill whine, the first jet engine whirred into action, shortly accompanied by its companions on the opposite wing and tail. Brastov took in a deep breath and held it; in a few moments they would be moving forward, taxiing into position for their takeoff run, his takeoff into a new life. He exhaled slowly, turning his head to regard the passenger in the seat next to him.

From beneath his abaya, the Arab had removed a small, square box. On closer inspection, Brastov could see that its top was a chessboard; there were peg holes in the center of the squares to hold the chessmen in place.

"You play chess, Uncle?" Brastov asked in Arabic.

The Arab turned to him and nodded, with a toothy smile that exhibited a missing bicuspid. "You, also?" he inquired delightedly. "Perhaps we could have a little game?"

Brastov shrugged. Why not? It wouldn't be much of a challenge, but it might help pass the time.

"Good! I shall set up the pieces, then." The old man leaned forward, pressing a catch beneath the box that released a drawer, which popped open. As he bent over the board, the hood to the abaya came loose, slipping down around his neck. That's peculiar, thought Brastov; the collar of a suit coat was visible beneath the loose outer garment. Belatedly, he noted also that the features

of the undraped head were not very Arab-like. They looked more
—Russian!

The hands holding the chessboard moved very quickly for an
old man's. What they extracted from the box bore no resemblance to any kind of chess piece; it was a shiny black Graz-
Burya automatic, the sidearm favored by the KGB.

With a sound like air escaping from a balloon, the starboard
engine cut out, the high-pitched whine of its turbine falling rapidly through several octaves, as the other two engines followed
suit. In the comparative hush that followed, the voice of the man
speaking in the harsh Slavic tongue was particularly loud and
jarring, causing heads to turn toward the back of the plane.

"Sergei Sergeivitch Brastov, you are under arrest for crimes
against the Soviet peoples. You will stand up, please. The plane
to Moscow is waiting. You are coming with me."